The Halfbreed Volumes
-I-
Guardian

Sarah-Jane Allen

For my late uncle, Allan

Prologue

"No matter what happens, I will never let you become a victim."

Huh. To be completely honest, I've always thought that it's always a really weird thing to say. There is no way you can ever prevent a single person from falling victim to anything; no matter how many precautions we set, there are victims in every great tragedy. Even on smaller scales – there are victims in every broken relationship, victims in every little lie and, of course, the people who fall prey to our own selfish whims and desires. We all fall victim to something in our lives so the only way to actually stop *anyone* from becoming a victim would be to wrap them up in cotton wool. But then, wouldn't they be a victim to that?

Trying to constantly keep someone alive is like tempting fate and, at the same time, probably creating a backlog of all the catastrophes that they were supposed to fall prey to. So the person who stopped me from falling off a curb when I was younger is probably responsible for me breaking my leg six months down the line. Or something like that.

So is protecting someone the right thing to do? Sure, it would be good in the short term, I mean, being saved from a crowd of slobbering demons, yeah, I'd take that. But does fate really excuse that little oopsie? Or does it have something else up its sleeve? I can't imagine fate just shrugging its shoulders as some obnoxious ass walks up and attacks its carefully written story with corrector fluid and a pen. It would be like a bad editor with no sense of the dramatic *or* of propriety.

If said editor walks all over my work and takes out all the juicy bits, I would give them the proverbial finger and put in something ten times as exciting. Hence the aforementioned broken leg.

And that's why I think it's silly. Even if you do manage to save this person every time something bad chooses to happen, you're going to have more and more work trying to keep this person alive. In the end, fate will have enough of your evil story-erasing ways and will really hit you where it hurts. Things happen as they should. Period.

However, on some level, I do get it. I do get the feeling of wanting to protect someone from harm or bad experiences. It's entirely natural. Stupid, but natural.

I carried this view for most of my life until, well, up until about a few months ago. I was sitting in a red and white booth at my favourite diner and… I guess that doesn't matter right now because what *really* matters right now is that you just sit there and listen.

My name is Erika Stamford and this is my story; pay attention because I'm only gonna tell you once.

I
Trees and Screams

"You're really stupid, you know that?" Blue was sitting on the edge of the fountain, digging into her ice-cream tub with a plastic spoon that was bending so far forward it looked ready to snap. I lowered my sandwich, flicked my black hair out of my bright green eyes and levelled a calm gaze at her.

"And... I deserved that remark, how?"

"You turned down Joe." Her voice was almost accusatory. I rolled my eyes for the fifth time in an hour and turned back to my sandwich, poking the filling around with my fingertip before taking another large bite.

"How could you do that to him? He's dreamy!"

"Not my type," I shrugged, swallowing my food. "I'm not the type to date someone just because they look good. Come on, he's a complete *dick*."

"A beautiful dick."

"Dicks are dicks, Blue, that's all there is to it," I retorted. She shrugged and looked over at the subject of our conversation. Frowning a little, she methodically sucked the ice-cream still clinging to her spoon. Joe was a guy who attended the same school as my dysfunctional best friends and me. He was the type of guy that seemed to be worshipped by all the other students except my completely sane man-friend, Sam, who hated his guts because he was better at basketball than him, and me.

To everyone's enormous surprise, including mine, Joe had gotten up at the beginning of English class that morning and had asked, in front of everyone, if I'd go on a date with him. I said nothing. I laughed.

His face went white, then pink, then a rather unattractive shade of purple before he called me a "weirdo" and stalked off to his seat. I was still getting glares from some of the girls.

"But still..." Blue winked at me and dug for more ice-cream. Blue had naturally curly chestnut hair that she religiously straightened with every single chance she had but today it was pulled up into a messy ponytail. Not only that, she didn't have her usual health-nut, I-won't-have-anything-that-isn't-completely-organic lunch; she only had a tub of blueberry ice-cream. She had to beg the cafeteria staff to leave it in the freezer during class, and they had relented, with a threat that if she asked again, they'd put it in the oven instead.

"Your mom skip town again?" I bit into my sandwich, but my eyes were carefully on her, waiting for her usual sigh and nod.

Blue sighed and nodded. "Yeah." She started stabbing the ice-cream with her spoon. "She left Mika with me this time too. So I not only had the brat and the brattier and the brattiest but the screeching toddler too! For a whole day! I just *so* love my life."

"And we love it too, aside from the whining." Sam, as usual, appeared out of nowhere and dropped his bag next to where I sat, throwing himself down next to it. "Sorry about the lateness. The demon-witch from hell wanted to know why my report was absent. She didn't like my excuse."

"Inu really should go to the vets if he likes going eating paper so much," Blue raised her perfect eyebrow and dug for more ice-cream now the attention was no longer on her. She hated being in the spotlight.

"But 'my dog ate it' is one of the most common excuses ever," I muttered, "and most of the people who use it haven't even got a dog!"

Blue laughed and slapped me on the arm with the back of her hand. "We've seen it, Erika! We can be witnesses!"

"I am not going to stand in front of a teacher and claim that Sam's dog ate his homework," I laughed before turning to Sam, "did you get in trouble?"

He shook his head. "Nah, I told her that it's all backed up on the computer. All I've gotta do is print another out and bring it in tomorrow."

"It's Saturday tomorrow," I reminded him, examining my sandwich.

He stared at me like I'd just grown another head. "She's expecting me to come in... on a *Saturday*?! What the hell is she even doing in on the weekend?! Is she insane?!"

"Don't forget that we're practice-bound tomorrow," Blue sang and Sam and I looked at each other in dismay.

I thought for a moment. "We meet Sam at the gates and walk to his garage, it's not far."

Blue gave me a disgusted look. "I don't want to *hear* about this place on the weekend, much less *see* it. It's bad enough that I've got so much homework to do without coming here tomorrow... the building... taunting me from behind the bars. I'm never free, not really..." Her eyes glazed over for a moment as if she were seeing something that wasn't quite there, losing us for an instant before she sighed, missing the look Sam and I shared entirely.

"And on that slightly nutty note, that sounds like a plan," grinned Sam. He dug into his bag for his lunch as I watched him.

My oldest friend, Samuel Richards, was a tall, lanky guy with shaggy brown hair, tanned skin and piercing grey eyes and was currently wearing his precious basketball kit. He was a good-looking, funny and kind guy to the point where he probably would have been attractive to me if we hadn't known each other since we both could walk. Our parents had taken us to the same preschool when we were young and we had been all but glued to each other since. It was in high school that we were thrown into a swirling vortex of hormones and rebellion and, so, met Blue.

Blaise Lorenzo, or *Blue,* was the oldest child in a massive brood of half-brothers and sisters, each with a different father and a mother who was never there. Due to this, Blue kinda kept to herself a lot or at least tried to but hadn't expected how much Sam and I could stick to a person. She had been seated in between us in most of our classes, right in the crossfire of our whispered conversations and passing of notes to the point where she became frustrated at our constant giggling and demanded that we either shut up or tell her what the hell we were guffawing at. She had no hope after that.

The afternoon felt much like any other, the weather being dreary and dull with spring yet to make itself known in the wake of a piss-poor winter, with nothing to herald the upcoming changes to our lives. We were seniors, facing our final year of high school, with the prospect of college and employment with a side-order of independence and possible crashing, burning and running back to respective parents with our tails between our legs. Well, most of us had that future... some of us weren't lucky enough to have anyone to run home to.

After school, we slipped into our usual routine, accompanying Blue to the park that separated our homes where she was met, as always, by her much older, my-mother-*will-not*-approve-so-you-*cannot*-tell-a-soul boyfriend Daniel at the gazebo. There, she would always wave to us cheerfully, slipping her arm into his and almost skipping down the path that led to the north side of the park and, eventually, to her street. I liked Daniel, or rather, what I knew of him; he wasn't really one for idle chitchat. We didn't know how they met or when but I could tell that he was completely devoted to her, meeting her every day after school in the same park, rain or shine, and walking her home, listening to her yammer excitedly about her day. While I just wanted her to be happy, Sam seemed to have a massive problem with the age gap between them, no matter how many times Blue had told us that *nothing* had happened and nothing would until she turned eighteen and that it had been *Dan* to add this rule. Blue found his thoughts hilarious but drew the line whenever he started to try and talk Blue out of her relationship with the guy, only telling him that there was nothing Sam could say to convince her to stay away from him.

Sam and I were then left alone to slowly make our way up the path toward our neighbourhood in companionable silence. As we walked, I allowed my mind to drift to more pressing matters as the bare fingers of the trees above us swayed in the light breeze.

What was I going to make myself for dinner? What time should I go to bed, considering we had band practice in the morning? Did I have enough clean clothes left before I had to do the laundry? Wait, how about food? Did I have enough or would I have to do the groceries before meeting them tomorrow?

A scream shattered the still and disrupted my melancholy thoughts. Usually, I would pass this off as a playful couple chasing each other through the park but this time, the sheer terror resonant in each shrill octave sent a chill through my spine. Instantly, I stopped, my friend doing the same only a half a second later, turning to look the way we had come. I reacted before my brain really kicked in then, my feet thudding loudly on the ground as I leapt off the trail and crossed the green, ignoring the *keep off the grass* sign that had been humourlessly edited by the neighbourhood children. I knew that voice.

I squelched loudly over the saturated earth as the wind whipped my hair into my face. We had been parted for a minute, two at most, so she was not far off, especially considering how much she loved to dawdle.

As I turned the corner and past the old dilapidated gazebo, I almost slipped on the soggy ground before my boots once again gained purchase and I leapt forward to where I could just see two huddled people. One of the figures was crouched on the ground and looked vaguely Blue-shaped and in the shade of a willow that seemed to be protecting her.

In my panic-stricken haze, I only just noticed Daniel jump out of my way as I charged toward them, probably considering how much I was probably alike to a juggernaut. I fell to my knees as I realised she was unharmed and wrapped my arms around her shivering body protectively. Without prompting, she automatically reached out and grabbed my hooded sweater, pulling me closer to her as she trembled. "I was so scared," she whispered, her voice scratching more than it should have.

Sam was hot on my heels and mirrored my actions as he slipped his arms around us as if he were protecting myself as well as Blue, as I turned my head to Daniel, who was staring into the distance with his fists clenched hard. I opened my mouth to demand that Dan tell me what had happened, but my words were lost when another, unfamiliar, voice cut across me.

"Dan! What the *hell* is going on?!" An unknown figure joined our worried huddle and I found that I was staring despite myself.

It was rare enough seeing asian men around this neighbourhood in the first place but seeing a man just like the one that was now standing next to Daniel, scowling at Blue, Sam and me, was unheard of. He was tall for a start, which pushed all the stereotypes out of my head as soon as I saw him, and was dressed in a smart blazer, a white t-shirt and blue faded jeans. Tearing his eyes from us, he pushed the mop of blond hair out of his dark eyes and turned his head to glower into the trees.

Daniel ignored him and, now that I had reached my destination and he was out of danger of being knocked off his feet, squatted close to Blue and cupped her face in his hands. I tried to move away, but Blue's shaking grip didn't allow me to shuffle any further than a few centimetres from his face though Sam leapt back like he had just had the pointy end of a snake thrown at him.

"Are you okay?" he asked her softly. She nodded but the grasp she had on me said otherwise. Somehow satisfied with that, Daniel stood up and turned to the newcomer who was staring at Daniel like he still expected an answer.

"A mugger." The eventual response came horribly flat.

"What!?" the voice was mine this time, just the way nature intended it, shocked and angry at whoever thought they could hurt Blue. "How is that... which way did he go?"

Daniel narrowed his eyes at me, probably deciding whether it was a good idea to tell me exactly which way the mugger had gone. After a moment, he either decided that he didn't think I had the bottle or that Blue's vice like grip had no chance of letting me go to stalk the bastard because he shrugged and nodded down the path. "Blue was ahead of me, skipping along like the complete ass she can be upon occasion... and the mugger just jumped out of the trees. She saw the knife in his hand, screamed, he saw me coming and bolted." I could understand why the sight of Daniel could make a mugger pause for thought. He was a tall, muscular man with short brown hair and eyes that seemed to have you pegged within seconds. If I wanted to mug someone, I'd make sure to do it anywhere that was not within a three-mile radius of this man.

"You're not hurt?" I asked the shaking Blue. She shook her head and buried it in my shoulder.

Daniel moved closer to his friend. "Well?" He muttered.

The newcomer muttered something in a language I didn't recognise before he gave a quick nod and said, "it'll be dealt with, don't worry."

Sam was not going to let that exchange pass him by. "I hope you plan more than just goin' to the police? Someone just tried to mug your girlfriend! Hunt the bastard down!"

"A bit of vigilante rebellion in that blood of yours, pint-size?" the newcomer sneered, turning the full effect of his glare upon my friend. "Thirsting for a bit of justice? Go home to your mom's basement, read your comic books and grow the hell up."

Wow. Hostility much? Sam bristled at the insult, probably because he wasn't that much shorter than the man himself, but didn't say a thing, only moving a little closer to where Blue and I were still huddled.

"Shion. Not necessary." Daniel pulled his phone out of his pocket.

"He asked a stupid question, he gets a stupid answer."

"There's giving a stupid answer and then there's being an ass for no reason." Yeah, I knew I liked Daniel, and I was pretty sure he went up in Sam's estimation at that moment too. "Instead of giving us a firsthand experience of your sterling people skills, can you do something useful and take Bee home for me? I've gotta head to work and I don't want to leave her alone."

"NO!" For the first time since I arrived, Blue relinquished her grip on my coat and leapt to her unsteady legs to reach her boyfriend who had jumped a little at her voice. He lurched forward to catch her as she slipped and pulled her into the protective circle of his arms.

He all but cradled her as she latched onto him, shaking. "You can't."

"I need to work, Bee."

She shook her head. "No, don't... don't leave me."

Daniel looked over at Shion, who was staring into the darkening trees with a frown on his face now that the opportunity to verbally abuse Sam had fizzled and died. "Shion." He motioned to his phone. "I'm gonna call Dylan, can you make sure these guys get home?" He nodded toward Sam and me.

"Hey, we don't need babysitting!" Sam snapped, but his objections fell on deaf ears as Daniel began dialling, ignoring him completely. His left arm was still around Blue's shoulders and she had not let go of his jacket, her knuckles white where she gripped him.

Shion glared at Daniel. "Yeah, whatever..." His eyes flicked back to the trees once more before turning to us. "Come on, you guys... my car's round the corner."

"It's not far..." I murmured, looking back the way we had come. "We can walk."

"Then I'll walk with you. Your friend just nearly got mugged. It's not safe." His voice was flat and attitude stoic and I could tell he would probably rather be anywhere but with us at that precise moment but, despite that, he was willing to accompany us home so we'd be safe. Only a good person would be prepared to do so, despite his less than friendly attitude.

While Sam was practically spitting feathers at being treated like a child, I felt grateful toward this stranger rather than the distrust that probably should have been appropriate and I didn't really understand why. I motioned quickly down the path that would lead us home and Shion began to make his way past me, shoving his hands into the pockets of his faded blue jeans. Before I turned to follow him, I glanced back over at my friend but Daniel was already leading her away, his arm around her shoulders as they continued on the journey that had been interrupted not so long ago.

Shion, as it turned out, didn't particularly like talking. He accompanied us through the park in heavy silence, leaving me to stare at the undecorated back of his black blazer jacket while Sam grumbled to himself behind us. With a frown, I tucked my hair behind my ear and jogged forward a little to catch up with our silent guide.

"So, how do you know Dan?" I tried to sound perky, especially considering I could still hear my best friend's muttering and I was attempting to mask it, in case Shion decided to start verbally abusing him again.

Shion's dark eyes sliced into mine as I came abreast with him and he sighed in annoyance. "We work together. Look, do we really have to do the talking thing? Why don't you just do what your annoying friend is doing and talk to yourself? I don't wanna socialise with kids."

"You're not very friendly."

"Hey! I'm escorting you home; that's pretty friendly."

If not for the situation, his tone would have made me laugh. "There's a difference between being kind and being friendly. Escorting us is kind, yes, but marching on like a spoilt kid that's just been told off just makes you look like an ass. Your name's Shion, right?"

He sighed and glared at me for a minute, probably deciding whether he wanted to reply and then visibly gave up. "Yeah, and you?"

"Erika," I replied with a satisfied grin, "and the grumpy dick behind us is Sam."

"You guys probably should stop walking through this park on your way home," Shion sniffed and glanced into the massive wealth of trees that were pressing in on the man-made path on our right-hand side. Our former favourite hangout, the gazebo in the centre of this wooded area that humanity tried to tame, had been built long before I could remember, slap bang in the middle of a nature walk that was hardly used for that purpose. However, about a year ago, it had half collapsed and no one had had the care to either repair it or replace it so it just stood there, some sort of termite-infested testament to how little the world cared. Despite Shion saying we should not walk through the park anymore, I felt my rebellious nature raise its head hopefully and I swallowed, trying to force it down with physical action because I knew he was right. I wouldn't risk Blue again and I could tell Daniel definitely wouldn't, probably right at this moment having the same conversation with her.

"You gonna to call the cops?"

"He's probably long gone, but I will let the authorities know." His eyes sliced into mine. "I'm surprised there aren't more reports of attacks here, it's goddamn creepy."

I smiled. "You don't like it here?"

"Too many places for creeps to hide." He said nothing more for the rest of journey and I didn't really press him. Sam's house came before mine and I saw him hesitate at his front door as he watched me walk away with Shion, but he didn't object. He probably knew that Shion was going to keep me safe and also doubted his own ability to protect me though he would never actually say that out loud.

Shion walked me to my door, nodded his goodbye and left, turning back to retrace our steps to wherever he had parked his car. I watched him go before slotting my key in the lock and pushing the thick wooden door open and closing it behind me.

There was no need for a greeting as I stepped inside and threw my coat lazily at the hanger, not caring if I missed. There was no need for me to go looking for any other soul in this empty house as I made my way to the kitchen and pulled a half loaf of bread off the shelf to make myself a sandwich. There was no need for me to be considerate about anyone else as I threw my iPod on the dock and pressed play, clicking the volume to its highest setting and letting the blast of drums mask the fact that I was all on my own.

The pictures on the walls told another story, however. I remembered the week after my sixteenth birthday I had gone on an impromptu cleaning spree, deleting any evidence that there had ever been anyone else living in the house with me. Picture frames, ornaments, personalised mugs and clothes, everything went into black bags that I threw by the front door in my silly adolescent rage only to be retrieved the day after by a sobbing sixteen-year-old me. I lovingly placed the now shattered picture frames in the different coloured squares in the colour-bleached walls, laid down the chipped and broken ornaments in exactly the right spots where they had been the day before. I gently placed all my mom's dresses in the wardrobe as they belonged, my dad's socks going back in the drawers too. I never touched them again and for the last two years, they had steadily gathered a thick layer of dust that I dared not touch.

Mom could take care of that when she came home.

The spider-webbed pictures on the walls showed a family: a woman, a man and a young girl with bright green eyes and a curtain of black hair that always fell across her eye in a way that drove her mom to distraction and always rebelled against the clips that were there to prevent such activity. A photograph of a young girl opening a doll the same size as her on Christmas morning. A wedding photo of the same man and woman as before but more youthful, smiling at the thought of where their lives would take them.

I didn't look at the photos anymore. Many a night was spent in the hallway, on the stairs, looking at those photographs and wondering if my mom and dad were still alive. Why they left with nothing but a note and a lump sum every week to keep food in the cupboards. Nearly two years and not a peep.

Why?

Sometimes I felt guilty about not telling Sam and Blue about my parents leaving, I mean they noticed when they *had* left because my attitude kinda changed, I stopped talking, came to school crying but I never explained and eventually they stopped asking me what was the matter. After a while, they helped me find my smile again though it always felt a little worn around the edges, I never told them. I didn't really ever understand why; maybe I just didn't want their pity...

As was usual, I didn't sleep much that night, and only lay awake staring at the patterns on the ceiling that were created from the old oak tree in the yard, the same tree that had made it so much easier to creep out at night. However, Dad eventually cut the thick limb that almost touched my window to keep me indoors but it didn't really help as I found other ways to escape. Insomnia wasn't quite so bad when you had friends who liked exploring the wooded area nearby your house in the dark.

Now that there was no one to stop me from escaping the house, it had kind of lost its thrill and instead, we talked online until one of us would fall asleep, usually Sam.

But, for some reason, that night, I didn't stretch to retrieve my laptop from where I left it that morning and just lay there, staring listlessly past the ceiling and into nothing.

II
Claws and Blood

Thinking about it, I didn't really expect Blue to turn up to practice that morning. The weather was cold and wet and as I stood at the gates of our school, waiting for Sam to return after handing in his still-warm-from-the-printer report, I just stared at the rippling puddles collected by the crumbling curb. My body was wrapped in layers, warding off the chill in the air despite the way the month was slowly crawling away from winter and I pulled my black hooded sweater closer to my skin, though it did little good.

The day was slow to start, as always for this time of year, and I had crawled out of bed after a measly hour of sleep to knock half-dead on Sam's door with my case in hand and escort him to the school gates like we had planned, communicating only in grunts and yawns. I hadn't heard anything from Blue at all, even after firing off a quick text that morning to tell her when we'd be meeting at the gates, acting like nothing had happened and apparently, Sam had done the same if I had been interpreting his yawning grunts correctly. It's not like we didn't want to talk about it at all because, in all seriousness, it was all we *did* want to speak about. We knew Blue well enough, however, to understand that all she needed was a distraction and not to be constantly reminded because she, like me, had a tendency to dwell and worry herself sick. Dan had probably spent most of the night on the phone with her trying to stop her from freaking out and I wasn't about to undo all his hard work just because I wanted to know more. It wasn't important. All that really mattered was that Blue was safe and she was so I was content to leave it at that.

Suffice to say, she hadn't replied and I didn't push.

It was nearly half eight, the time we had organised to meet Blue. I wondered if she were up to it as I tapped lightly on my jeans in time with the drums that pounded incessantly through my headphones, heavy black case resting against the railings behind me.

I almost screamed when I felt someone place a cold hand on my cheek out of nowhere and I found myself twirling to face my attacker, eyes wide and ready to defend myself against the smiling face of my friend. Without question, I pulled my headphones out and grinned at her. "Did you piss the bed?" I asked her.

She backhanded me across the arm and grimaced up at the school.

"How long's he been?"

"Not long. Wanna go in to look for him?" I jerked my chin at the school, trying to mask my grin.

The look she directed at me was beyond unfriendly. "You're an ass."

"I know."

Sam turned up a few minutes later and smiled brightly when he saw Blue but, as I had, he didn't bring up the day before and neither did she. We simply made our way slowly back to Sam's place, but walking around the park instead of through it.

Band practice was the best part of my week, I decided as Sam, Blue and I stepped into the garage that felt like it had just been glued randomly to the side of Sam's house. It held none of the care or devotion that Sam's parents had shown the rest of their home and instead allowed it to be used by Sam whenever he felt like making that infernal racket with those two charming girls he was friends with. I liked being called charming by them as it made me feel like they approved of our friendship and really, Sam and his parents were definitely like an extended family to me, having known them for most of my life.

The first thing I always noticed about the garage was the temperature. I was always surprised upon first entering the cavern-like barely-lit hole at the sight of my own breath fogging white from my lips, even when it was blistering outside. It was like a separate plane of existence, somewhere that sunlight and heat could never touch and, oddly enough, it had turned into our favourite place. Eventually, Sam grew tired of my constant teeth-chattering complaints and *borrowed* his dad's convector heater from the attic and hid it behind Blue's drum kit when it wasn't in use, the same heater he made a beeline for as soon as he closed the door behind him.

The whole room was about ten feet wide and just shy of thirty long, the grey cinder-block walls decorated only with ripped and tatty posters of Sam's idols, his favourite basketball players and the bands we liked to believe we could rival one day. Two light bulbs swung from thin wires that jutted without any of those proper fixings that existing garages should have had, weak and unsupported. The lack of any carpets or rugs on the concrete floor was probably one of the reasons why it always felt so cold in here and I was grateful for my choice to wear two pairs of socks under my royal blue converse.

As I settled into my own favourite chair right next to that heavenly heater, I rested the black case I had hefted from my own home between my legs. Frozen fingers fumbled for the zip, even with the half-gloves I had pressed my hands into when I realised how bitterly cold it had become overnight. The surface my
fingers met once I had convinced the case to open was equally as cold as the air, but I yanked it out anyway. I still remembered the first time I felt their sharp bite on the soft pads of my fingers and the way they became too sore to play after my first lesson. It was like greeting an old friend every time I unzipped the bag to reveal the instrument, the glittery silver-blue varnish, the stickers that Sam and Blue had pressed on it to make it more *unique* even as I argued against it and the natural weight I knew I would never forget.

I felt rather than heard Blue's foot tapping against the pedal for her bass drum, the whisper as she ran her drumstick over the circumference of the hi-hat and the feedback from the two amps nearby as Sam sat beside his with his bass resting between his crossed legs. The hair on my arms stood on end as goose bumps rose and I closed my eyes, remembering the connection I would always have with my best friends, even if my parents weren't around anymore.

Blue slipped off her jacket and flung it in the direction of the hanger, a perfect imitation of my own actions in my own home that I grinned and almost did the same while Sam leaned forward and slotted the lead from my own amp into my guitar, giving me a smile and a wink.

"Let's go with Winter," Blue murmured.

"How apt," I felt myself grumbling as I spat the pick I had pressed between my lips into my hand. The set up was simple with Blue on drums, Sam on bass and myself with lead guitar and vocals.

I stood up and pulled the microphone toward me, shivering once before I stepped into the full blast of the convector heater and closed my eyes, listening for the tap, tap, tap, tap of Blue's drumsticks to count us in.

Our instruments were battered and old, the amps had seen better days and my voice definitely worse for wear but as we played through Winter, I began to relax, able to smoothly follow the murmured transition as we each picked our favourite song to play.

After a couple of hours, while we were taking a quick five-minute break, the sound of Blue's phone ringing came as an extremely welcome interruption. My throat was hurting from singing and the tips of my fingers were starting to feel a little delicate despite the hardened skin and I could tell from the way Sam was rolling his neck that he felt the same. Blue leapt from the kit and fished in her bag that she had left upon Sam's broken dryer. With a beep, she answered the call and stepped discreetly from the poorly-lit area and I slid down the wall, closing my eyes.

"She seems okay, doesn't she?" Sam's voice was hesitant and quiet, telling me that he didn't really believe the words he was speaking, obviously just as much attempting to convince himself of the normality in our friend's attitude. Yesterday was still bothering her, but neither of us really wanted to bring it up. There was no use worrying as it wouldn't change a thing.

After a few minutes, Blue came back into the room, gently ending her call with a tap of her thumb. "I think it's lunchtime," she told us with a faint smile. The word *lunch* reminded me of my stomach's existence and it gave a slight grumble in response at my sudden realisation that I was absolutely famished.

Sam laughed, a little strained, at my talkative organ and stretched, lowering his bass lovingly to its stand. "Wanna see what I got?"

"I wanna go out."

Sam and I exchanged a look but didn't actually respond, only reaching out to grab our coats and get ready to leave the cold garage.

The weather had warmed up a little in the time we had spent with our instruments, the sun peeping through the clouds as if playing hide and seek with the rain and warming the damp path that we now took to the bottom of Sam's yard. He and I lived close to one another on the same depressingly quiet suburban landscape that abutted our favourite park-turned-nature-reserve-turned-dump which had been developed as a desperate attempt to add a little greenery to the area before I was born. Other than that, there was nothing that really advertised our small town to the rest of the country. A few chain fast food places were jotted haphazardly through the more urban areas that fought for business with the food court inside the one mall we boasted, which, to be frank, wasn't really worth much boasting as it was depressingly small. In this day and age, though, most things I purchased were ordered online so it didn't bother me any. What did I care if the industry was dying?

Now that we were out, the change in our friend had become more evident. On a day such as this, Blue would usually be practically skipping, delighting at how the sun reminded her that summer was on its way and she could hide her hideous grey parka that her mother bought her in the closet for another six months. Today, however, she was walking meekly beside us, looking everywhere but not seeing any of it. It was odd enough that Blue wanted to eat out in the first place as the nearest fast food place didn't really serve much in the 'healthy options' department which rubbed our favourite health-nut up the wrong way and then some, causing her to moan all the way there on an average day. I think she felt that as long as she moaned about it enough leading up to consumption, it took away from the impact it inflicted on her usual dietary needs, kind of like making it all better by saying sorry. She spoke to us as usual, however, but with a little too much enthusiasm like she was putting on a show and I couldn't help but worry about her.

It was completely understandable though as she had nearly been mugged the day before.

Sam was yammering on about something to do with basketball again as we walked, probably trying to distract Blue and going the complete wrong way about it, and I turned to her, her faraway eyes and downcast mouth. At least in Sam's garage, she seemed at least a little okay.

She looked, for lack of a better word, sick.

"Did Daniel walk you to the school this morning?" Sam stuttered to a stop as I spoke, his eyes darting to glare at me as we walked, but I ignored him, instead looking over at Blue, who now looked kind of uncomfortable.

"He didn't really want me to come," she murmured. Sam's eyes narrowed at me, clearly saying *now look what you've done*, "but relented when I told him I was going whether he liked it or not. He had to work, but Shion walked me up to the end of the street..."

"Shion walked you?" I was surprised. Before yesterday, I didn't know that Shion even existed; now he seemed to be an integral part of Blue's life with Daniel.

She nodded. "Daniel asked him to."

After she had explained, I had to admit that on some level, I expected that. Part of me wanted to wrap her up in cotton wool and never let her go anyway again, so, of course, Daniel would ask someone to look after her. "Surely, he knows you're safe with us right?" I ventured. Something about her expression then seemed off, but Sam cut across us before I could ask.

"Damn straight! We'll kick any mugger to the ground with our powers of absolute awesomeness!" He crowed, slinging his arms over mine and Blue's shoulders. Now it was my turn to glare at him but I couldn't stay too angry at him as it was Sam all over; once he realised something was accepted, he took it to a whole new level.

Blue's lips twitched a little as she tried not to smile and the flood of relief I felt at that little action surprised me.

"We're just worried about you, Blue," I told her. "You haven't really been yourself today, which is totally understandable... but we want you to know that we'd never, ever let anything like that happen to you again, okay? I want my friends safe."

"Me too." There was something in her tone that made me wonder if there was another meaning there but I shook my head, knowing that there were probably a lot of thoughts in her head at that moment, none of them particularly cheery but it was our job to turn them around and make her happier.

The diner was grimy and, as usual, absolutely packed. The stink of burgers and overused vegetable oil permeated the place and stuck to the splitting leather seats, yellowing the foam stuffing that had lost any ability to be comfortable about a week after the diner opened. The once-white linoleum was chipped and peeling, splodges of shiny grey where almost fossilised chewing gum had been trodden down over and over practically added to the decoration where in some places, squares were missing altogether, showing the cold concrete underneath. It was fortunate that the windows were probably the only well-maintained thing in the place as the flickering lights never failed to give me a headache, tacky, overly bright and never working properly, I wondered why they even bothered trying to use artificial lighting. The workers, moping around with both matching uniforms and expressions of discontent, hair shoved hastily into loose hairnets which were in turn tucked under unflattering black caps, didn't really offer much of an improvement.

We crossed to the only empty part of the diner and slipped into a recently vacated red and white booth. Used plates and half-empty soda glasses had been shoved toward the window and Blue wrinkled her nose, pushing them to the other side of the table so one of the waitresses could take them away. Sam, on the other hand, was in his element, filling his lungs with the thick, greasy air holding his arms wide. "I *love* the smell of this place."

"We'll bottle it for you and get it for your birthday. Then you can smell of shit as well as eating it." Now that she was feeling a little more like herself, Blue seemed to want to concentrate her whole, I-don't-want-to-eat-this grumpiness quota into the remaining time she had until she bought her food. I laughed and dug into my jeans pocket where I remembered I had a few crumpled bills, my eyes casting around the surrounding clientele almost absently.

He was standing against a wall, rolling a cigarette between long fingers with his smooth forehead creased in concentration and my eyes focused on the strange man before me that I could not remember seeing before in my life but somehow, sent a wave of recognition through me so strong it left me breathless. He was tall and dark-haired, one side of his head was shaved quite close to his scalp while I could see his bangs curling, twisting toward his long eyelashes. He was clad in an expensive looking black leather jacket, but I could still see the dark edges of a tattoo peeking from over his collar and one from under his sleeve. Navy jeans were shoved into unlaced boots, completing the look of someone who apparently couldn't care less about what anyone thought of him and, on some level, I envied that.

As if he could sense me watching him, his eyes flicked from his cigarette and sliced into mine. Immediately, I looked down, not wanting to be caught staring and spent the next few seconds desperately examining the linoleum until I could bear it no longer.

Unnaturally bright blue eyes bored into me, fingers paused in the rolling of his cigarette though the scowl of concentration on his face had made the slight adjustment into *why the hell is that girl staring at me*? My cheeks began to burn, but I couldn't tear my eyes from his. He had me captivated with the gaze that added fuel to the feeling inside me that screamed louder than all my other stunted thoughts that something felt… *strange*.

"So you came." The shadow that fell across us made me jump but that was before the tone of voice completely registered in my mind and I turned my head up, finally pulling my eyes from the cigarette-rolling stranger and fixing them on the towering figure of an extremely unhappy Daniel with a vaguely interested Shion peering around his shoulder. Sam's eyes went wide as he glanced at Daniel and the now sheepish Blue, who was suddenly fascinated by the floor like I had been a moment ago. "I told you to stay at Sam's place until I came to get you." Daniel's voice was low and angry and for some reason, it annoyed me, snapping me from my daze.

"Hey! We're not completely useless! We can look after Blue!" I argued.

"Stay out of this, Erika, you don't have a clue." I blinked as he practically pushed my objections aside and turned back to my friend. "Why the hell did you ask for permission to go out if you were just going to go against what you knew was going to be the answer?"

Blue scowled. "That was more of an FYI call, Dan. I didn't think I needed your permission to go out with my friends."

"After yesterday!? You bet your ass you need my permission!" His fists clenched. "It's not *safe* out there, Bee!"

"Daniel." Shion's tone was a warning but Blue shot over him, her voice rising do a dangerous level.

"Yesterday just served as proof that nowhere is safe anymore or do you forget what the hell happened out there?!" Sam and I glanced at each other, eyes wide, as Blue's temper rose, something that was rare enough, even without noting that the man she was squaring up to was half again the size of her. The guys in the booth next to ours were beginning to turn around, hoping for a chance to catch a punch-up. "How the HELL are you supposed to protect me from *that*?!"

He was silent for a minute while Blue panted like a wounded animal before he hesitantly opened his mouth, voice pitched low and desperate. "Have I ever let you down?" He peered down at her, sincerity in his eyes and I saw my friend's resolve waver.

I almost didn't spot the shake of Blue's head, but Daniel nodded with a tired smile and pulled her up and in for a quick hug. I tried to hide my grin as I turned away to glance around the diner again which was still far too full and bustling by my stomach's standards while I automatically felt my eyes flick to where the cigarette-rolling stranger had been standing before. I couldn't decide if I were relieved or disappointed that he had disappeared.

I was just beginning to relax, hearing Daniel and Blue exchange apologies and Sam mutter under his breath, when the usual, now peaceful moment was shattered by a crash that sent a spray of glass shards over patrons and staff alike.

Dan reacted first, seizing mine and Blue's wrists and pulling us to duck under our table while Sam and Shion followed behind.

And that's when the screams started.

For the first few moments, I couldn't grasp what was happening, not after being faced with the sight of a man almost being trampled by a stampede of patrons that were rushing toward the exit, after slipping on an upended drink. The screaming, the constant screaming that set the hairs on the back of my neck on end made it impossible to think so I just remained under the table, shaking as Blue trembled beside me, both of us protected by Daniel's strong arms.

When I noticed why the windows had been smashed in, why the customers around me were still screaming, my own voice joined in the harmony, rising to such a pitch that it scorched my throat and tears burned my eyes.

Crouching on four spindly limbs, the creature that skittered into view was vaguely humanoid, thin, grey in colour and for the time being lifting its flat, black-eyed face up to scent the air. Squatting on its two hind legs in front of us, the creature's back was hunched, misshapen by the curved spine that stretched the skin and even split it to reveal white bone which had been sharpened unnaturally into points. Quickly, Daniel wrapped his hand around my mouth and hissed in my ear. "Shut. The. Hell. UP!" he whispered, urgently. My scream faded into a whimper but I couldn't take my eyes off the creature that was still sniffing as if searching for something, eyes as black as oil wide as it crept toward our table.

A woman slipped on a spilled drink a yard or so from us while making a desperate bid for freedom, her knee cracking so loud on the floor that I almost reached out to her. Quick as a flash a second creature, as thin and spindly as the first, leapt over our table from behind the partition and landed on the shrieking woman's back, tearing its sharp, claw-like talons into the fabric of her grey brocade coat. The first creature, now distracted, slipped forward ape-like to where its fellow was still shredding the woman's clothing, now staining red with blood, her cries becoming louder and stricken with pain.

"We have to help her!" I heard Blue snap to Daniel.

"Are you insane?!" Sam was crouched behind Shion, pressed up against the bench-chair that leaned against the partition. "We should just get the hell out of here!"

"So much for your vigilante justice," the blond Japanese man grumbled.

I couldn't take it. I shrugged off Daniel's arm and darted forward, seizing a chrome chair leg that had been broken in the confusion and dashed toward the creatures that were now both clawing into the woman.

"Erika, what the hell are you doing, you moron!?" I heard Shion's cry but ignored him as the nearest creature paused, sniffed the air and turned its head toward me, just in time for me to swing my makeshift weapon and deliver one swift strike to the side of its face. Shrieking, the thing fell off the woman and the second one leapt at me, giving me a perfect view of rows upon rows of sharp black fangs dripping with thick clear fluid and flat flaring nostrils, just before it knocked me to the ground, my precious weapon falling out of my reach.

I rolled twice before I felt the creature pounce on my back, sharp claws biting into the skin on my arm. *"Yooooooou,"* the voice rumbled close to my ear, lisping slightly as the foul stench of putrefaction and fresh blood washed over me and I gagged, reaching my hand up to my discarded weapon, only a few inches away from my searching, desperate fingers.

"Smells taaaasty," the voice gurgled.

This thing was going to kill me.

I bucked my body up in one quick movement, attempting to dislodge the creature enough for me to make a last ditch attempt to escape, but I felt its claws bite further into my arm. The warm trickle of blood ran down my skin at the same time as a scream ripped itself from my throat, filled with terror and pain in equal measure.

"Tasty, tasty little thing." The heat from its mouth burned my ear as it leaned forward and I felt its rough tongue taste the sweat beading at the back of my neck. My struggling did nothing as my scream morphed into terrified sobs, fingers of my left hand still searching in vain.

"Oh, no you don't." I didn't know the voice, but it was nothing like the terrifying hiss of the creature that was covering my body with its skeletal form so relief flooded through me. Instantly, the pressure was gone and I scrambled away, converse squeaking upon the ground as I turned to take a look at my rescuer.

It was him. He was standing where I had been lying a few scant seconds before, holding up the hissing creature by the too-long throat, unbelievably bright eyes glaring into its face. "Are you really that stupid?" he growled at the thing. "Are you and your entire race really, *really* that idiotic?"

"Guaaaaaaaaardian?!" it cried.

The man grinned and I was struck by the wolfishness of it, like he was a predator, finally about to seize the kill he had been stalking for days. The smile didn't fade as he pushed his face closer to the creature. "Surprise." With unbelievable speed, the man dropped the creature and swung his gloved fist down to cave into the side of its head. With an explosion of black gunk, the thing fell twitching to the floor and, almost nonchalant, he stepped over it, making his way slowly to where I sat, frozen in fear.

"Up." His hand grasped my forearm and jerked me unceremoniously to my feet. He whistled once at Daniel, who was now standing by the table Blue and Sam were still huddled under, holding a penknife covered in black blood. A slim grey body was lying, motionless at his feet while the rest of the diner was in an uproar. "You. Go get help." The remaining staff and customers alike were either hiding under tables, attempting to get to the exit or creating makeshift weapons as I had in an effort to push the creatures back as they overran the place, feasting on bodies I would rather not look at too closely. The shrieks and screams were unbearable and I fought the urge to clamp my hands over my ears and shut down like I wanted to, but my protector still had his hand on my arm. This had to be just a nightmare.

"Don't you *dare* summon me like a dog!" Daniel snarled. He slammed his fist into a shrieking monster, forcing it into inactivity with a crunch. "Can't you tell I'm a little busy here?!"

The man's temper spiked. "Does it look like we can handle these ourselves?! *Go get help!*" Daniel rolled his eyes and nodded once, before darting to the shattered window, giving a creature that leapt at him a swift kick as he leapt through the frame.

"What the hell is going on?!" I screamed at my rescuer. "Who the hell are you?! What the hell are these things?! What... WHAT... *What the hell is going on*?!"

"One, don't ask. Two, not important. Three... You don't wanna know." He still hadn't let go of my arm and he jerked me forward.

"Are you going to give me any straight answers?!"

He hissed in annoyance as he glared down at me. "Not really. Now shut up and hi-ARGHHH!" Distracted by my almost panic, he didn't notice the creature creeping up behind him until it was already too late and it launched itself at his back, opening its wide jaws and clamping them over the soft skin and muscle where his neck met his shoulder.

I heard the tearing of fabric under his scream and saw the leather of his jacket run with a dark liquid that seeped from where the monster's jaws sheared into his shoulder. He twisted, impressively, seizing the thing and flipping it with a grunt to face him before letting go and snapping its neck with a quick and practised motion. The thing dropped, black eyes staring at me as my rescuer pulled his jacket off to reveal a ripped white t-shirt, covered in red blood that was now seeping from his skin. "Asshole! This was my favourite jacket!" he spat before turning his blue eyes on me. "You. Hide. Now. I don't have time to be screwing around with a kid like you." I felt that was kind of unfair considering my own age and the fact that he didn't look too much older than me, but I did as I was told, slipping under the same table Blue and Sam were still huddled under. Shion was nowhere to be seen.

Before I could open my mouth, Blue slapped me swiftly across the cheek. "Moron," she hissed. Her arms suddenly came about me and she pulled me close to her, whispering in my ear. "You're a total moron, but I love you, you beautiful, caring, idiotic, heroic, stupid example of humanity."

"Don't do anything like that again," Sam grumbled close by, also wrapping his arms around us.

I nodded and clung to them.

"Haaaaaaaalfbreeeeeeeeed." The cold snarl reverberated through the table above us and we all froze. "Wheereeeaaaaareyooooou, little haaaaaalfbreeeeeed?"

Sam, Blue and I stared at each other for a moment, Blue's face turning ashen while her grip on my arm increased so much it hurt. I stared at her face, the terror there as her eyes rested, unseeing, on the floor in front of us, the chipped linoleum now, in places, stained red with blood.

Not daring to speak, I twisted my arm to touch my fingers to her skin and she jerked from her reverie, eyes finding mine, wide with panic. Before I could mouth a thing to her the table sheltering us shook and a skinny arm protruded from the edge, seeking, clawing for purchase upon something. When the sharpened, stained claw caught hold of Sam's jacket, Blue and I screamed, both of us reaching forward to grab him but it was too late and the creature above us gripped the fabric in its whole hand, jerking him out and up.

Without a choice, I scuttled from under the table, this time followed by Blue. We stood and stared at the creature as it pinned Sam on the surface of the table, its face hovering an inch over his body, scenting him. All the while, the creature was humming and it made my skin crawl.

"Get off Sam," I told it. Now, I didn't really expect it to agree, but at this point, anything was better than nothing. The thing looked at me and sniffed the air, the flat nostrils flaring.

"Move." I recognised that voice and instantly, I stepped to the side, allowing my rescuer to take my place. I had enough time to watch the thing's eyes widen in terror as he grasped its head, pulling it off the table and my friend and throwing it on the ground with a thud. He did not finish there as he turned to meet the creature where it landed, but I did not stick around to watch, darting, like Blue, back to the table.

"Are you okay?!" I demanded of him as he sat up.

"*No!*" he cried. "I am not okay! I am *so* not okay!" He rolled off the table and yanked Blue and me down with him. "What the hell is going on?!"

"How the hell are we supposed to know?!" My voice was louder, shriller than I had expected, controlled by the panic that was thrumming through my veins. "What are these things?"

"Monsters, demons..." Blue's voice was quiet as she glared out at the carnage that had, a few minutes ago, been our favourite diner. Her shaking fingers snarled in her hair as her eyes bugged in her head, staring at the blood smeared linoleum and the *things* that littered the floor in ruined heaps. Her fingertips were digging into her scalp and I reached out to her, pulling her arms down and bringing her closer to me so they could grasp me instead.

I had to admit, as I stared at the corpse of one of the creatures that had been dispatched by either Dan or my saviour, that she had a point. The stubby horns, the grotesque figure... all of it pointed to the disturbing images my over-zealous religion studies teacher had thrown at us in our freshman year of high school. This was what we would be tormented with if we were to succumb to sin.

I shuddered and buried my face into Blue's shoulder.

"We need to get out of here." Sam's voice was a few shades off complete panic.

Blue shook her head desperately as I straightened up. "No, we have to wait for Dan. Dan will know what to do. He'll come back for us."

"*Hello*?!" Sam's eyes went wide. "Were you even watching? Daniel is gone! He high-tailed it as soon as he had a chance!"

She turned on him, eyes flashing. "You take that back! Dan is not a coward!"

"I have to side with Blue on this one. I wouldn't want to go against that dude in a fight, even if I were a demon." I saw Sam roll his eyes and scowled.

"If we stay here we're screwed!"

"Then I guess we're screwed!" I pointed at the guy that had only just recently saved his life. "We're not alone here. We can hurt them! We can do damage to them! We're not helpless! We need to-"

"Err... Erika?" Blue's hand touched my shoulder and I turned to her, not really appreciating the interruption of my rant but what she was pointing at stole my words and made a mockery of any argument I was about to spew in the favour of those fighting against these *demons*.

The corpse nearby, the one with the broken neck was moving. At first it was a small movement, just the fingertips that were twitching, once, twice, a flick of the wrist, the creaking and cracking as the thing tried to lift its head. The thing was dead, so why the hell was it moving?

I opened my mouth, but no sound came out, terror freezing my tongue.

"We *need* to get out of here," Sam repeated, breathlessly. He gently pushed my back, urging me to shift. "Erika, move. You need to move."

Blue's hand wrapped around my arm. "No, we stay."

"Blue!" Sam's voice was a hiss. A loud snap interrupted their disagreement and we all turned to see the creature shifting on all fours, rolling its shoulders, its head lolling in a way that made my blood freeze, creaking, grinding and crunching. It jerked and its head snapped up, eyes focusing on us and letting loose a low snarl though dripping fangs.

"Move," I whispered. Blue and Sam gaped at me. "Guys, run now! Move, move, move, *move!*" I pushed my friends out from under the table as the demon roared, pulling itself forward on the grimy floor, slipping a little as it tried to take us at speed. I rolled out from under the table at the moment the creature collided with the single support leg underneath, the whole thing splintering with a loud crunch, surface collapsing on the beast.

It gave us a few seconds.

I saw Blue and Sam dash toward the shattered window and I

moved to follow, only to be stopped by a demon sliding into my path, hissing like an angry cat. A loud thud from behind me told me that the dead creature that wasn't dead had thrown off the table surface and would resume its interrupted hunt toward me and I was, in essence, trapped.

I glanced up and noticed Blue hesitate at the window, staring at me even as other civilians leapt out while the demons gorged themselves on those who had not been quite so lucky. Nearby the window stood Shion, helping people leap out into the open air while keeping his eyes on the squabbling creatures.

The demon in front of me sniffed the air.

"Tasty, tasties," It whispered to its fellow. "Tasties for us?"

"Tasties for us," the second one agreed.

An exasperated sigh shattered the tense moment and I snapped my head to the right. My saviour was sitting on the edge of one of the tables still standing, massaging one of his gloved hands. The cigarette he had been rolling before was now in-between his lips, lit and smoking gently even as he began to speak. "You know, I really hate it when you demon drones talk. You all think you're so smart but really, you all sound like a bunch of stupid morons." He took a long drag and pointed the cigarette at the demon he had previously killed. "Especially you, did I say you could get up again? No. So what the hell do you think you are doing?"

"Isn't allowed to touch us." The snarling voices of the demons terrified me more than I cared to admit but with my rescuer sitting so close and keeping the monsters' attention on him, I was beginning to feel a lot safer.

He breathed in another plume of poisonous smoke, apparently not caring about the screaming and the carnage that was still happening around us. "Didn't you get the memo? The rules have changed." He slipped off the table and rolled his shoulders, expelling the toxic air that had been circling his lungs. With an easy movement, he flicked the cigarette behind him. "So, I'll give you a choice. You can get the hell out of here before the Agency gets here, and trust me, they have been notified, or you can wait and see exactly what I plan to do to you for attacking this innocent establishment."

His grin was almost boyish.

"The killer bluffs." For the first time, the creature sounded unsure and it glanced at its fellow.

"The killer? Oh, I like that."

"You would." Again I snapped my head to the side as another unfamiliar voice joined our social gathering. Two women stood about a yard from us, one a redhead while the other sported a messy bun of blonde hair, her bangs hiding a pretty made-up face. "Why are you playing with drones?" It had been the redhead that had spoken, her arms crossed over her chest as she glared at the creatures, finally pausing in their constant circling of me, looking between the collected strangers with pure unadulterated fear on their faces. For the first time, I seemed to have been forgotten.

"They started it." My rescuer sounded almost sulky. "Why'd you bring a Ghost?" He jerked his chin to the blonde.

"It's wonderful to see you too," The blonde said sardonically. "I was in the neighbourhood and Isla thought you could use a hand. Besides, the Agency will want to know what happens here."

At the word *Agency*, the two hesitating demons finally took their opportunity to bolt, claws skittering on the ground as they crossed the linoleum at shocking speed, heading straight for the shattered window. From what I could see, the rest of the demons were already following suit as the emptying diner was unexpectedly dotted with figures I did not remember seeing before. Though each person was different, as varied as could be expected from the diner's average customers, the one thing that connected them was the steely look in their eyes, the determination and unnerving confidence that struck me to the quick.

My rescuer watched the creatures flee with a neutral look on his face and leaned again on the table, reaching into his back pocket, from which he pulled a pouch of tobacco.

I don't know whether it was the shock of what happened, the pain that was spiking through my arm or the relief that, by the looks of it, it was over but it became apparent that all my bravado was for naught as my legs gave way. With a thunk that I knew would hurt when I woke, I passed out entirely.

I felt like I was underwater, limbs heavy, eyes glued shut and all sounds indistinct, loud, echoed and fuzzy around the edges. I couldn't move, covered from head to toe with a wet blanket that sucked every ounce of strength and left me with absolutely nothing to give.

Voices, deep and reverberating through the thick air matting around my head, passed through my hazy veil of unconsciousness and vaguely tickled my interest.

"She saw too much."

"Oh come on, do you really think that matters? Look at her! You know what is happening here, what I have to do."

"Yeah but didn't Ben say-?"

"It doesn't matter what Ben said; Ben is dead."

"You don't have to say it like that; he cared about what happened to her."

"It was his job to."

"And what about what they want?"

Silence.

"You can't just-"

"It's too late for that. We'll just have to wait and see what happens now."

I woke up in a room that smelled faintly of tobacco. To begin with, I didn't know where I was or why but after a few seconds of blinking blurredly up at the plastic encased, colour-leeching light bulb above me, the monochromatic dream-state morphed into the fast-paced recollection of what I had just lived through.

A dry sob escaped my lips and I shot up from my prone position, looking around what I realised was a hospital ward. Without waiting for a doctor or a nurse or *anybody*, I threw off the thin blanket and tip-toed over to the door, opening it slowly and sneakily poking my head out to see what the hell was going on.

Out in the corridor, it seemed to be quite busy. People I recognised from the diner were sitting on thick cushioned seats, heads in hands, supporting injured limbs or applying pressure to wounds that were still seeping with horrific red. Nurses and doctors shuffled through the patients, holding clipboards and talking in hushed tones to one another and the patients that needed support from someone kind.

My eyes were flicking through the faces of those congregated, searching, desperate for someone I knew, a face that was familiar in the midst of these nobodies. Where was Blue? What about Sam? Did they get out okay?

In my search for familiarity, I noticed a figure leaning against one of the walls next to the waiting area. At first, the only thing that sparked off any recognition in the figure was the way he was leaning, but then I noticed his fingers, rolling a cigarette exactly like he had been doing the first time I saw him.

Without hesitation, I moved forward and dodged expertly past the muddled civilians and doctors alike, though trying to keep my head down in case one of the doctors noticed that I wasn't in bed like I had been a second ago.

I didn't say anything, but his eyes snapped up when I neared and a heartbeat later, he smirked. "One of the paramedics decided I needed medical attention," he told me without prompting.

"Well... one of them *did* bite you."

He looked down at his shirt which had soaked up the blood from his shoulder as if never really noticing it before. "I managed to convince one of her colleagues that it wasn't my blood..." he pulled the collar of his t-shirt down to reveal his tattooed neck and shoulder, maimed only by the pink puckered flesh of an old wound. I stared at it, at the size and shape of the scar, a perfect match to the monster's jaws. He grinned at my expression. "I heal quickly."

I remembered the creature miraculously straightening its neck after my rescuer had snapped it like a twig and I remembered the speed and confidence with which the man in front of me went against the creatures. It should have terrified me: the strength he used to all but crush the enemy, only didn't. Not really.

"You're one of them..." I whispered, but then I shook my head. "No... Not exactly... but almost... as if you... share something. Same ancestry?"

"You're quick," he complimented me.

Again I merely looked at him. "I notice things." I looked around at the crowd of tired people around me and shook my head to clear the tiredness that had been creeping into each corner of my own mind. "If you don't need medical attention, why are you here?"

He pushed himself off the wall and rolled his shoulders, wincing once or twice. "There's someone I need to protect."

"That's why you were there."

"Yeah."

"You looked out of place to me."

He grimaced. "You don't hold back do you?" He went to walk away and I suddenly remembered my manners.

"Thank you!" I called at his retreating back.

He stopped and turned back to face me. "What for?"

"For saving my friends. Sam and Blue... they would have died if you weren't there."

A strange expression passed his features, but I

III
Truth and Proof

The world carried on. It continued to turn '
had seen what we weren't supposed to had to
now knew.

Sam and Blue had met me at the hospital and they both flew ....
me with about as much force as a freight train, which caused the
doctor that had bullied me back into my bed to turn pale and demand
that they give me a break. Physically, I was fine but the shock of the
gang-related incident that had occurred at the diner had left me in…
well, shock and I had passed out so the hospital wanted to keep an
eye on me to make sure there weren't any underlying issues.

Yeah, the authorities were passing off as whatever happened at
the diner as a gang-related incident. Some sort of stick-up and a few
people had been hurt in the confusion.

However, I knew that that was not what had actually happened.
Blue knew that that was not what had actually happened. Sam knew
that that was not had actually happened. Demons had crashed into
our favourite diner and, without explanation, began to maul and
attack innocent people.

The world, on the other hand, went along with the lie.

I couldn't possibly convince myself that what I saw wasn't true. I
know what I felt, what I saw and what I heard. I knew the truth of
what I saw simply because I knew how much it terrified me. I *knew*
that while a *gang-related incident* would scare me, it wouldn't
warrant the absolute terror that chilled my skin and froze my gut.

Demons were real. They hurt people. They killed people, feasted
on them.

My world would never be the same again.

Sam, Blue and I sat on the edge of the fountain like we did every
lunch time, me with my sandwich, Sam with his sub roll and Blue
with her noodle salad watching the students pass us by.

It was Monday. I had been released from hospital Saturday
afternoon after they realised that it was the shock of what I'd gone
through that had caused me to lose consciousness. I had spent
Sunday with Blue at her house, catching up on the homework we
had missed over Saturday and trying to avoid the topic of the diner
even though it had turned into a massive, obnoxious, destructive

in the room. Sam had called us and we lay around Blue's
om, talking to him hands-free and giving him all the answers to
number problems he always sucked at.

All the while, despite the company and the giggles, my mind
drifted to black hair, blue eyes and a boyish grin.

I'd never noticed anyone before, not really, not in the sense that
someone could be so beautiful and yet so thoroughly alarming all at
the same time so that they occupied my thoughts quite so much.
Yeah, there had been people that I thought were attractive but that
was as far as it went. The guy at the diner... he was something else.
Beautiful and terrifying.

I bit into my sandwich again and leaned back staring at the sky
with my arm bracing myself so I didn't fall in backward.

"It feels a bit surreal," Sam said throwing the rubbish from his
sub in the trash can nearby. He narrowed his eyes at the surrounding
students, thoughtfully. "How everything is going on as normal..."

"We're doing the same thing," Blue pointed out, lowering her
fork. Her hair was back to its immaculately straightened perfection,
eyebrows freshly shaped and clothes looking quite pristine and
altogether well-scrubbed so I assumed her mother was back from her
hiatus. Blue never had the time to take care of her appearance when
she had her younger siblings to care for. "I don't think sitting around
and eating lunch exactly qualifies as being pro-active about what
happened, do you?"

"Alright, I get it but..." He grimaced. "No one's even talking
about it. They're just going on and on about their ordinary everyday
lives... Nothing about demons cropping up and attacking the local
diner."

"It was reported as a gang incident," my tone was bored as I
prodded my sandwich filling around.

"*How*?!" gaped Sam. "And what gangs? We don't get gangs
around here! We have that group of old men that play chess in the
park and that's as close as it gets!"

Blue snorted, picking up her fork again. "Well *someone's* doing
the hushing."

"Looking for a conspiracy there Blue?" Sam grinned. "Maybe
they actually think it was a gang thing... Maybe it *was*... some
whacked-out cult dressing up as freaks and-"

"Killing innocent people?" Blue's eyebrow arched. "You think
that's preferable to what we saw?"

"Do you know how it sounds when we say we saw monsters?" This time, it was Sam's turn to snort. "I know what I'd rather believe."

I sighed. This is why we had avoided talking about it for so long, I realised as I listened to Blue and Sam bicker amongst themselves. We weren't ready to deal with what we saw; no rational human being ever would be, so we took it out on each other.

I wanted answers from someone who knew more. Blue seemed to have her head screwed on the right way at least, but she knew as much as we did and so had no new information I could squeeze out of her. There was only one person I could think of and I had no idea who he was and where I could find him. The diner was the first place I ever saw him and I could hardly look for him there.

Wait. Why couldn't I look for him there?

"We should go back to the diner." It took me a moment to realise I actually voiced my thoughts when I noticed Blue and Sam staring at me, mouths open wide with the argument completely forgotten.

Sam flung his arms up in overacted exasperation. "Okay! So! Erika has totally fruit looped so that leaves you and me as the sane ones, Blue. What do you think wc should do? Because I'm all for locking up little miss nutcase here in a padded room and going home to close all the doors and pretend everything is all sunshine and buttercups."

I glared at him. "Look, I just think there might be something more there. It was chaos so we don't know what we missed."

Blue closed her plastic pot with a snap and stared straight at me. "Anything that had been left would have been picked up by the police; besides... it's not really any of our business, is it? It's totally beyond us."

"Yeah, but aren't you curious?"

She rolled her eyes and grabbed her bag, standing up while shoving the container inside. "Not in the slightest and to be honest, I don't want to talk about it anymore either. I haven't been able to get a wink of sleep since and whenever I do, I wake up screaming. I'm going to class." Without another word, she stomped off.

Sam turned his head to look at me. "Now you've done it."

Music echoed through the lonely house from where I had plugged in my iPod dock right in the hallway next to the stairs, volume high enough to reach me wherever I happened to be in the house. It was eight-fifteen and I was in my pyjamas, soft woolly pink things that my mother had bought me for Christmas one year to chase off the chill and while the bottoms exposed my ankles a little too much to strictly fit, I couldn't bring myself to throw them out. I padded across the hallway with my hands wrapped around a steaming mug of hot chocolate, my hair still wet from my bath and almost ready for bed and the aimless staring at the ceiling I knew was waiting for me.

I had redressed my wound like the hospital had instructed after I had dried off my skin but stood in the reflection of the mirror for a time, examining the five almost black half-crescent shapes marring my skin from where the creature's claws pierced my skin. With a sigh, I wrapped the bandage around, turning away from my haggard reflection.

After placing my drink on my bedside table, I jogged downstairs, turned off my music, checked both doors were locked and returned to my bedroom, pulling down my fresh sheets to snuggle and make myself comfortable before, once again, reaching out to bring my hot chocolate closer to me. I breathed in the intoxicating aroma of chocolate and orange before taking a quick sip, leaning back into my pillows slightly in an attempt to relax myself.

It did work but once I remembered the pallid grey skin, splitting skin and protruding bone with ghastly black dripping grins and oily eyes, all my chill escaped faster than air being let out of a balloon.

The smallest breeze that touched my curtains sent a wave of fear through me and I dug deeper into my bedding.

Crunch.

I jumped. Probably just a fox outside...

Crack.

I lowered my drink and sat up, squinting at my window. A few seconds passed and I heard nothing so, a little hesitantly, I flung off my sheets and slowly made my way out to peer out into the yard.

Darkness loomed back at me, punctuated only by the glittering star-drops of street-lamps past the park and into more urban areas of town but they were too far away to make any difference from where I stood. The glow of the nearby lamps only threw warped and elongated shadows across the lawn, which I mowed once every two weeks to keep it looking presentable, from the haphazardly placed trees that had been growing since before I was born. I used to love the yard at night but since the episode at the diner, I couldn't forget the notion that even now there were creatures that I never knew existed before, creatures that didn't seem to have any issue with attacking large human establishments.

As I stared down into the odd colour-tinged gloom before me, it was a while before what I saw actually registered in my mind.

A shadow moved.

Panic struck and I felt myself give a little, worried mumble, looking around my room in search of some sort of weapon. There was nothing in my room that would do much damage against what I feared were lurking outside in the yard.

My rational mind kicked in then. If there were those demons out there, wouldn't they have just stormed my house by now? They had no problem with leaping into a packed diner so what was there to fear in a house only inhabited by a human girl?

"If you're out there, my dad's got a shotgun and he's not afraid to use it!" I called, pretending to be braver than I felt. Yes, I remembered my dad's gun and yes, I remembered that he wasn't afraid of threatening would-be burglars with it but they didn't need to know that neither my dad or his shotgun were anywhere close to the house at present. "So leave or you'll be sorry." My voice wavered a little and I slammed my window closed, shutting my curtains and backing off into my room so quickly my back hit my wall with a thud.

I brought my hand up to my mouth and whimpered.

It was too much in such a small space of time and I just could not deal with it. I fled.

My parents' room was at the back of the house and it was, not surprisingly, the largest room in the house by far, taking up the same amount of space of the two rooms below with an en suite and walk-in wardrobe. Once inside, I closed the door softly as if scared of disturbing anything and tip-toed inside. When I was younger, I was rarely allowed inside my parents' room, only when I was sick or my mother and I were playing with her makeup. She always looked like some sort of tropical bird when I'd finished and not in a good way.

I paused next to the cupboard that housed my dad's precious vinyl records and the record player that I had always been forbidden to touch. I missed them and it all wound down to the fact that there was a hole in my life that could never be filled without my parents to scold me, encourage me and infuriate me.

I turned to the door and gently I took hold of a sleeve, one of those blues records that I always begged my dad to play whenever we were alone in the house, and gently pulled the record out, blowing the dust off with a shaky breath.

Despite my initial hesitation, I immediately pulled the record player from the cupboard on the wheeled stand my dad had purchased just for this purpose apparently just before I was born.

As the needle gently moved through the grooves of the record, I clambered into my parent's bed, pulling the duvet up around me and ignoring the cloying smell of dust that filled the air with the movement. I stretched out and stared at the ceiling, allowing the deep, rhythmic tones to relax me from my toes to my scalp, sending me back to a time where life was easier.

Sometimes I wondered if I resented my parents for leaving me, yet sometimes I was sure I did, when others, I just wanted them back home with me. I never really settled on one particular feeling long enough to define my views on the matter and I was left feeling lost and confused, without guidance, which made Blue and Sam even more important to me.

I'm not sure when I fell asleep, only that it was a lot sooner than usual, and I woke up the next morning feeling refreshed, three minutes before my alarm was due to go off, which was kind of lucky as I had left the stupid thing in my own room. The record had played itself out and I slipped out of bed, padding to the cupboard so I could push the thing guiltily back into its home as if it had never been touched by my grubby little fingers. I didn't remove the record, though; I thought I might need it over the next couple of days.

School was harder than usual that day. I sat alone in the class, chewing on the end of my pencil, staring at the blank sheet of the pop quiz the hung-over teacher had thrown at us to keep us quiet for the duration of the period. For the most part, it worked, but I was in the unfortunate position of being sat at the front of the class in the perfect location for the target practice of Joe's fan club. Rolled up shreds of paper, torn off chunks of eraser, pens, pencils; it all bounced off my bent head as I struggled to come up with the answers to the barely legible questions my teacher had scrawled. That was the first thing.

The second thing was that Blue hadn't turned in.

Blue had this problem where, when her mother skipped town on one of her little *I'm-fed-up-of-these-stupid-kids* escapist kicks, she had her younger siblings to look after. Even though most of the time her mother took the youngest with her, she sometimes had no choice but to get a babysitter as well as getting the other three up for school and out the door. Now Alex, or the *brattiest* as Blue liked to call him, was the second eldest of the family and he didn't really like Blue's automatic step-up in the chain of authority and wanted to act out, ignoring her attempts to get him out of bed until she resorted to violence. All in all, it meant that she had to get the kids out of bed, call the babysitter and then spend the next half an hour fighting with her brother so he would actually leave, dragging his backpack and laughing at Blue's expense. Sometimes the sitter arrived and Blue was able to make it into school before afternoon classes started but when she didn't, she had no choice but take care of her little brother by herself.

Unfortunately, that meant that I had to deal with the backlash from my probably tactless rejection of Joe with only Sam to jump to my aid. Sam didn't jump. He squeaked and lowered his head so far that his shaggy hair hid his grey eyes and prayed they didn't start on him, only they didn't and never had. They didn't simply because they didn't know how much he hated Joe and, honestly, most of them thought he was cute. Not that he would ever notice that.

School finished without a single word from Blue, but that wasn't really that peculiar given her responsibilities to her younger siblings and Sam and I made our way home, this time giving the park a wide berth. We had stood at the gates for a moment, staring into the gloom that separated the cheerful trees and had, almost simultaneously decided against venturing inside and risking ourselves being mugged, especially considering that we didn't have Daniel's huge intimidating figure to ward off any would-be attackers.

I didn't know what I was thinking until I reached my doorstep alone and stood, quietly, at my front door with my hand resting on the handle, my other half-turning the key in the lock without making a move to enter. I didn't know why I refused to let it go.

The blood, the screams, the sound of shattering glass and breaking bone: The whole scene reverberated through my head pointlessly, over and over, until it became impossible for me to push on and live like normal until I had gotten a few things straightened out in my head.

These things were as follows:

One, the *things* that attacked the diner that day were *not* anything to do with a *rival drug gang*. Or whatever lie the authorities decided to fling at us and hope for the best. They were something else entirely; monstrous, demonic, evil creatures that still haunted my dreams from a distance. You cannot tell me that creatures like that were merely drug-crazed lunatics.

Secondly, there was *him*. The guy that saved my life knew something about those things and they, somehow, knew him. They *feared* him.

Then there were his *friends*. The two women that had turned up out of nowhere were also confusing me more than I liked to admit, especially considering that their arrival and the mention of this *Agency* had sparked off such a fear in the terrifying, blood-splattered creatures that they bolted without looking back.

Apparently, this guy and his friends knew more than anyone else and this annoyed me.

I wanted to know.

I pulled my key out from the lock and let go of the handle, taking a deep breath and turning on my heel and hopping down the stone steps to the path that led back out onto the street.

The diner looked much like I had expected it to.

Usually quite cheerful, the whole place looked like death. Its dark windows and boarded up entryway told everyone who approached of its closure, even without them turning the corner and seeing the smashed window covered from frame to frame with police tape and discovering the extent of damage done to the establishment.

I slowly made my way over to the shattered window and, carefully, peering around to make sure the camera wouldn't catch me, I pulled down on the slip of police tape nearest to me so that I created a hole large enough for me to slip inside.

I didn't really know what I was doing back here, I thought as I stepped gingerly through the scattered glass, squinting in the growing gloom as the clouds skidded over the sun above me, taking away my natural light. I silently cursed myself for not bringing a flashlight as I lifted my cell out of my pocket and used the screen to illuminate the surrounding area.

It was much as I remembered: the broken furnishings, the blood-stained floor and the sparkles from where the light from my phone reflected off the shards of glass. Nothing had really changed, which I thought was kind of odd... as soon as these kinda things had been investigated, didn't they set upon the restoration of the building, fixing the damage to get things back to normal? So everyone would forget?

It was like it had been abandoned.

I made my way slowly to where I had ended up when I had attempted to help the woman beset by two of the things, avoiding the blood smears and discarded drink containers until I was staring down at a smear of blood that I guessed belonged to me. Absently, I pressed my hand against my wound as I knelt down to touch it. It had dried, now a ghastly sort of brown in the half-light that was permeating the building and I felt, once again the disbelief rising up to the forefront of my mind. I sat back on my heels as I surveyed the carnage around me.

How the hell were they succeeding in covering this up?! I remembered everything from that day, down to the smell of blood on that disgusting creature's breath and I just couldn't get my head around the fact that no one, no one other than my two friends and me, seemed to argue with what the media was telling the rest of the town.

I pushed a hiss of annoyance between my teeth before standing up.

Crunch.

My heart jumped into my throat as I span, once more facing the window, wielding my cell as a weapon as I glared into the gloom, attempting to make whatever was lurking believe that I was less frightened than I felt. Something told me that I was not succeeding, perhaps the way I was shaking uncontrollably.

My grip on my cell phone increased as I stepped forward. "Hello?" My voice shook and I cleared my throat. "Is anyone there?" Good, stronger.

When no answer came, the last of my bravery left me and I bolted. I dashed through the window and down the street without stopping to replace the police tape or look back.

The next day at school, Blue was waiting for us at our fountain, ready with a weak smile. She looked rough but cheerful enough so I guessed that her brother had forgone being a total dick today and the babysitter had actually arrived to take care of the little one. "Sorry about yesterday," she said as we approached, tucking a lock of curly chestnut hair behind her ear. "Mom had a date and didn't come home until last night."

Sam punched her lightly in the arm and grinned. Apologies not needed.

School was easier now that Blue had reappeared. Once the 'let's throw things at Erika Stamford's head' game started again around the second period, Blue was immediately sent out of the classroom for standing up and screaming "how do you like it?!" while throwing permanent markers with the lids off in their general direction with startling precision.

The girls then spent the rest of the lesson either trying to wipe off the black dots on their foreheads or attempting to hide them with concealer instead of tormenting me. It amused me how ineffective their efforts were.

At lunch, Blue tucked into a blueberry crumble she had apparently made last night as Sam and I looked dejectedly down at our own sandwiches. It's difficult to find the effort to make yourself a proper lunch, but Blue regularly put our meals to shame and did she offer to make us some too? No, she did not, so we suffered and hoped that, one day, she would take pity on us and our inability to cook.

As she scraped the inside of her tub out with her spoon after finishing her divine smelling gloop, the slight buzz of a cell phone made all three of us jump and, after realising that neither of our butts vibrated, Sam and I peered curiously at Blue. After rolling her eyes and standing up, she dug in her back pocket for her cell phone that we had never, ever known to actually go off in school.

She raised her eyebrow at the text she had just received and made a disgusted sound in the back of her throat. "Absolute *ass*!" She snapped it closed and shoved it back in her pocket before grinning at Sam and me. "Do you two losers want to come round to mine for dinner tonight? Your pitiful lunches deserve some sort of consolation prize." She buffed her nails on her t-shirt with an almost giggle and examined them.

"Hey!" My curiosity at whoever text her was temporarily thrown aside at her snide comment toward my lunch. Only I was allowed to do that and maybe Sam if his lunch was more pitiful than mine.

We were united in the Cannot Cook Club.

"I'm sorry, was I wrong?"

I lowered my eyes and grumbled to myself as I threw the wrapper to my sandwich in the trash can next to us. Through our exchange, Sam had been bouncing excitedly on the spot and as we finally finished, a huge childlike grin split his face, he asked, "are we making Tex-Mex?!"

Blue and I glanced at each other and laughed.

It turned out that I actually needed that downtime with my best friends and as we lay around in Blue's bedroom watching bad kung-fu movies and eating Tex-Mex that we had prepared as soon as we had gotten to her place, I began to relax. My thoughts softened around the edges and the knots in my stomach eased.

I hadn't admitted the fact that I had returned to the diner to either Blue or Sam, mostly because I knew they wouldn't exactly approve of my curiosity. Well, maybe they wouldn't mind my curiosity as such; more that they would be dead set against my new apparent vocation as Private Eye. Snoop, perhaps, would be better.

I still didn't know exactly what drove me to the diner, I thought as I leaned on my windowsill later that night, staring down my yard without even seeing it. I inhaled deeply, held it for a second and then slowly allowed the warm breath fog in a billow of white from my parted lips, watching it fade into nothing almost as soon as I gave it life. I should have been too scared to even think about going there but the way that the media was trying to cover up what had actually happened had gotten me kind of frustrated. Maybe I wanted to make peace with my memories or find some solid proof that what happened was actually the truth.

Come to think of it, what kind of panic would spread if the world knew that those creatures existed? Maybe what the media was actually doing was trying to keep everything calm? But that thought only raised more questions. If that was the case, then how many times had things like this happened before and had been covered up? How many people had died and their family and friends given only a convenient cover-up to give them false closure? Pile-up on the freeway... Gang-related violence... terrorism. How far did it go? How deep did the lies go? How many people knew the truth? How could the witnesses, the victims, keep quiet? Why weren't they screaming the truth from the rooftops?

I pushed myself from the windowsill and turned to my alarm clock, the glowing red digits not only giving the whole room an eerie atmosphere but also telling me that it was now past midnight, and inching toward the first hour. I had time. I chewed my lip. I *definitely* had time.

My coat was barely on by the time I was thudding down the path, laces undone and hair pulled up in a hasty ponytail, shoving a flashlight into my satchel as I ran to where it all began.

The diner had still not changed. Even the police tape that I had left unattached when I had come snooping before was still loose and flapping uselessly in the cold breeze, almost inviting any passerby to pull it open further and step through. Even if that weren't what I had intended to do from the moment I left my house, I would have been sorely tempted.

What was I doing here again? I stepped over the glass carefully and headed to the centre of the main room while fishing in my satchel for the flashlight I had had the good sense to pick up before I bolted.

The sudden blast of music made me jump about a foot in the air, letting out a brief screech of curses as I spun in a tight circle, my eyes scanning the gloom around me for the source of the noise. Through my panic, a single thought came to light that made me feel more than a little stupid: I knew that song.

My heart still racing a mile a minute, I scrambled in my bag for my cell, which was flashing happily at the bottom and illuminating everything with a cheerful blue glow. Cursing my friend who was attached to that ringtone, I pulled it out and glared at the screen.

Blue's name was flashing up unapologetically as her tone echoed through the empty building. Feeling vaguely guilty about it (but not entirely as I was still attempting to recover from my fright), I tapped to ignore the call and shook my head, firing off a quick text to head her off. *-Busy. Will call you later. Xxxxx*

Believing that this would be enough to keep her at bay, I pushed my phone in my back pocket and moved through the gloom once more, taking care not to stare at the dark patches on the linoleum for too long in case I remembered what they were.

Bzzt! The yelp that followed the low buzz sounded, in all honesty, more like a five-year-old girl who had just found a spider in her bed, especially because the pressure in my back pocket caused my whole left leg to jerk at the unexpected sensation.

Cursing, I dug into my pocket and pulled out my cell, glaring sullenly at the screen and the cheerfully flashing envelope announcing I had one unread text.

-Whr r u? Blue. She just would not give up.

I sighed and tucked my flashlight under my arm, tapping a quick reply. *-At home. Xxxxx*

My phone went straight back into my pocket as I sighed and I moved forward again though I didn't get far when the infernal thing buzzed again, making me jump for the third time that night, though I was glad to say I did not scream.

I dug the contraption out of my pocket with an intention to playfully scold her for bothering me when I'd already said I'd call her and froze, holding my phone in shaking hands as I stared at the half-words my friend had sent me. -*No, ur not.*

-*What?* My fingers were shaking so I had to retype the simple word several times before getting it right.

Not two seconds after my cell sent the text message, the whole thing buzzed in my hand, Blue's ringtone filling the dead air around me for the second time that evening. This time, however, to not incur her wrath, I accepted the call and lifted the phone to my ear.

"*You're not at home so where the* hell *are you*?!" It was rare to hear Blue so angry and I blinked. I could hear murmurs on the other end of the call though I couldn't decipher what was being said though I recognised Shion's emotionless drone.

"How do you know I'm not at home?" I tried to keep my voice steady, but it was hard when I could clearly hear my friend panting like a wounded rhino on the other end.

"*Because I'm right here, you moron! I am outside your house and I've been ringing the freaking doorbell for the last fifteen minutes! I've almost got Dan to break a window and go looking for you!*" She dragged in a deep breath. "*So tell me where you are and I swear if you lie to me and say you're at Sam's I am going to hit you over the head with a two-by-four, do we understand one another?*"

"Look, Blue, I'm all right." I tried to placate her.

"*Tell me where you are.*"

I didn't have a chance to tell her anything. As soon as I opened my mouth to speak, I stopped, my eyes focusing on the crouching figure that was crawling with dreadful jerking slowness around the corner of the small counter in front of me. The thing lifted its face as I focused the beam of my flashlight upon it and scented the air, flat nostrils flaring once, twice before it snarled.

"*Erika?*" My tongue was frozen, the hand holding the flashlight trembling as my eyes zeroed in on the black fangs that dripped with oozing clear fluid.

I was right. This was what I was looking for.

"Taaasties..."

Only, suddenly, it didn't seem like such a good idea anymore. "Shit."

ERIKA!?"

With a roar, the demon threw its arms out and pulled itself forward, instantly jerking into a flat-out high-speed stumbling gait straight toward me. I dropped my phone and flashlight both, turning so quickly my converse squeaked and I bolted for the broken window but stopped in my tracks when there were three more demons already there, crouched low and snarling.

I turned again, hair whipping my face, to the creature that had begun to bear down on me, now crouched low behind me, stationary and, for lack of a better word, *grinning*.

For the first time, as I stood there in that broken-down diner, staring at the four creatures that were now creeping toward me with alarming sluggishness, I realised that these bestial things were *intelligent*. They had taken advantage of my distraction and instead of charging toward me mindlessly like I expected they would do, they had blocked off my immediate escape and boxed me in. With the creature near the kitchen, the three now in front of me and the knowledge that every door in and out of this place was locked, I was trapped.

I inched backwards, the tinkle of glass shifting around my shoes sounding far too loud in the uncomfortable silence that was broken only by my shaking breath and the creatures' snarls. Watching me tremble, they began to speak and hiss from between cracked lips, spitting their thick saliva into globs that shone on the linoleum under the beam of my dropped flashlight.

"Tasty girlie... fallen into our net."

"Our spider's web."

"Sticky, sticky, sticky."

"Can we play grab and catch?"

"I want to taste her... tasty, tasty..."

"Bitter sweat... makes it better. Let her run... run and grab. Grab and catch."

The wind was knocked out of me as one of the grotesque creatures leapt on my back and knocked me to the floor, bringing with it the memory of only a few days before when I was pretty much in exactly this position.

"Grab and catch take too long," The thing hissed in my ear. "Tasty, tasty little thing... All for me."

The wound on my arm throbbed uncomfortably at the memory.

Was I really going to die like this? I was lucky enough to be rescued last time but now, here, I was on my own. A situation I had foolishly put myself in. I shook in terror as the demon sniffed the back of my neck to hissed complaints from its fellows and my nails bit hard into the soft skin of my palms.

No! I was *not* going to die like this!

I scrunched my eyes shut and screamed, throwing my whole weight desperately upwards, shocking the creature on my back enough that it fell from me with a squeal. I leapt to my feet just in time to avoid a second demon that leapt at me when it realised that I had bucked its fellow. When the third one leapt at me at the same time as the first one tried again, I was ready for it and sent my fist flying into its flat face, stepping quickly to the left to avoid the thing that flew toward me from behind. The demon screeched in what I believed more to be frustration but I didn't stick around to find out and I dashed over to the counter and slid over the top of it, racing quickly to the kitchen door that was hanging weakly off its hinges. I wasn't sure if it had always been like that or if it was done by the hands, or rather claws, of the demons that had been squatting in the building and I definitely didn't have time to speculate as I bolted inside and slammed my body against the wood. Bracing myself with all my strength, I could feel the surprisingly heavy thuds of thin, elongated bodies being thrown against the heavy wooden door and the hinges crunched weakly under the strain.

I closed my eyes and swore under my breath, feeling the sweat from fear and exertion dripping from my brow in ticklish, distracting beads. "Help," I murmured to myself as the thudding continued. "Someone... help..."

No one was coming to help me.

I was utterly alone.

My eyes snapped open and for the first time, I took in my surroundings.

The whole room was shrouded in thick gloom with only a couple of small, grimy windows that were pressed into the walls close to the ceiling to provide any natural lighting and as the power was obviously out; I found it was a miracle that I could see anything at all. The gleaming chrome surfaces glinted eerily in the low light that drifted from above me and illuminated the fixtures and utensils dotted around the room. For one thing, nothing was where it was supposed to be; ladles and chopping boards were strewn haphazardly over the black and white chequered floor, sometimes broken while others completely shattered altogether. Knives had been thrown into the walls and against refrigerators, denting the doors and even sticking out when thrown with enough strength. Pans and suchlike were pulled out of cupboards, faucets pulled from fixtures and light bulbs yanked from their snug homes, smashed uncaringly upon the ground.

The white walls were smeared with dark substances that I didn't want to look too closely at and gushes of cold water bubbled from the snapped pipes at the massive sinks, filling the whole room with an empty gurgle with a steady background of *drip, drip, drip*, like some bad manufactured music. Two more doors sat at the far end of the kitchen, one that I assumed led upstairs to the staff room and the second was a fire exit that led to the staff car park out back. The chances of it being unlocked were abysmally small and I didn't have the guts to go dashing over to check it if it meant I was stuck in this kind of creepy room with them.

I took a deep breath. So I was in the kitchen right? Surely, some of the objects in here that had been flung around could be used to defend myself; a knife, a skillet or even a rolling pin. Just something, anything, I could use to buy myself enough time to get out of there and maybe after I had armed myself, I could try that fire exit.

Leaving the door was out of the question, I thought as another thing crashed into it, bringing with it the repeated crunching of wood giving way, so I began to scan the ground near to my feet. A snapped ladle, a corner of a glass surface-saver which might do in a pinch and a stained orange Tupperware container without its lid were the only things that were remotely close to me and if I attempted to move any further from the door, I risked letting them in. I could possibly afford to make a mad dash to one of the knives sticking out the wall but who's to say I'd make it in time and even if I did, there was no way of knowing if it would easily come free of the plasterboard.

Either way, I had to make a decision soon because I felt the door beginning to give way and, if I didn't move, there was a significant chance I would be crushed by it falling on top of me.

I had no choice.

I closed my eyes and flattened my back against the door, bracing against the continuing *thud, thud, thud, thud* as the creatures doubled their efforts to get to me. I'd noticed a pattern.

One, two, three, four and a few seconds of silence. One, two, three, four... like they were taking a run-up, preparing themselves.

One. Two. Three. Four. *Go.*

I did not hesitate.

The shard of thick glass of the surface saver cut my fingers as I grabbed it, but I pushed myself up and forward, around the counters and towards the wall that had been some sort of target for the creatures' knife-throwing game. Just before I reached the counter with the wall behind, however, I heard the crunch of splintering wood and a crash as the whole thing finally fell off its hinges and as it hit the ground, the demon that had hit it rolled off in a cloud of dust. It scrambled to its clawed hands and feet quickly and scented the air around it, half closing its eyes to better sense its quarry.

Shaking, I turned and wrapped my fingers around the handle of one of the larger knives and gave it a sharp tug, swearing and whimpering a little when it failed to yield to my strength. I yanked again as I felt rather than heard the scratching of the thing's claws upon the floor, over and over again I pulled. I let go of the knife desperately and tugged on another, reaching for a third when that one, too, did not budge.

"Taaaasties." A blast of hot air touched the already overheated fabric of my jeans and I jerked around, flinging the bloodied hand clutching the shard of surface saver around to meet its shoulder.

The glass shattered upon its skin, slicing my right hand open as the thin slivers of glass stuck into my soft palm and fell between my shaking fingers. The thing looked down at its unmarked leathery hide and then raised its eyes back up to mine, all but screeching in anger, all words forgotten. Part of me felt that I should have been too terror-stricken to feel the sharp pain of jaws being clamped around my left thigh or the burning searing agony as dozens of razor sharp, serrated fangs sliced into my skin, but I wasn't. I felt like my leg was on fire.

I screamed in pain and desperation while, with a final, desperate jerk, I reached back and pulled the first knife loose with a shower of fine plaster dust. I twisted quickly as the demon bit down harder on my skin, still screaming and brought the knife down, hard, onto its shiny, hairless pate. I felt the crunch of the splitting skull, followed by the gush of warm blood that covered my trembling hand as I yanked the blade free and stumbled back against the chrome counter, watching the spindly grey form collapse at my feet. The other creatures had been peering around the shattered doorframe in glee but when they saw their fellow slump, lifeless to the ground with my weakened body hunched over it, they hissed angrily as one.

Whimpering and pressing my injured hand to my heavily bleeding wound, I glanced up at the demons that were crawling toward me with terrible purpose. One had leapt atop the counter in front of me and had braced itself flat, glaring with its oily black eyes as it spat through bared fangs. On either side of the table, the two others slunk forward, cutting me off once again. If it weren't for the fact that I was scared beyond my wits, I probably would have been incredibly pissed off.

"No..." I moaned through gritted teeth.

I felt my blood soaking into my jeans and running over my fingers as I stared at the approaching creatures. The one on the counter reached the edge of the island and hissed at me and I watched the nostrils flare, watched the thick wrinkled skin around its eyes crinkle dreadfully as it grinned and felt with dreadful certainty that I was going to die.

Not. This. Time.

I took a deep breath and pushed myself forward, wincing as my leg almost crumbled under my weight as I put pressure on it. As soon as began to move, the demons hissed and leapt at me, exposing their rows upon rows of black fangs. I felt the breeze on their swings as I bolted, slower than I would have liked and I heard them crash into the counters behind me.

The demon on the left that blocked my escape was less lucky as the other two, screeching as I slashed the knife upwards at it, causing it to squeal and roll out of the way, blood dripping from its chin and lip.

My way was clear and I hobbled toward the fire exit, pushing down hard on the bar, almost praying under my breath. With an empty clunk, the door did not shift and I moaned, pushing down once, twice more in my desperation before turning and moving toward the second door, just in time to hear the two demons that were left following me crash into the fire escape. It still failed to yield to their unintentional efforts and I pushed the notion of getting out of the diner via that door out of my head as I pulled the handle of the door leading upstairs.

Relief followed quickly by disappointment hit me as soon as I pulled open the door and was rewarded with the sight of the narrow, dirty, and uncarpeted staircase leading up to the first floor of the building. My brain was fogging with pain, blood loss and terror, so whether or not I was going to be able to actually make it up there was something I seriously doubted. I shook it clear and pulled the door closed behind me in time to cut off the once-again three demons that had bolted toward it. I held it closed as I eyed the stairs, took a deep breath and began to move, taking them two at a time where my leg would let me.

As I was about halfway up, I heard the door crunch open and I tried to speed up. My leg was growing stiff and sweat drenched my body, sticking my hair to my temples and neck as I exerted myself in my escape. My whole body trembled as I used my hands to pull myself up faster to no avail as I felt one of the creatures seize my ankle.

I kicked out blindly with my uninjured leg, catching the thing off guard and connecting with its flat face. I heard it screech and let go long enough for me to scramble back up the few stairs it had started dragging me down. I could hear the demons scrambling over one another behind me but as I scrambled up the remaining few steps, I felt strangely thankful to how narrow the staircase was. They could only come at me one at a time and, by what I understood, they weren't keen on sharing.

At the top of the stairs, I limped forward and grabbed hold of the door handle that I guessed led to the staffroom as the other three doors had signs for men's, women's and CLEANING CLOSET on spotted brass plaques.

Inside, I scanned the area that was lit only by the glaring streetlamp from outside, my heart falling fast upon the realisation that, from in the staff room, there were no possible means of escape. There were windows, sure, but from this high up and with my already injured leg, I didn't know if I would survive the drop onto direct asphalt. The only door that led from the staffroom was the one I was currently holding closed and the only other things that existed inside were a couple of tablecloth-covered tables and rejected chairs that were apparently taken from downstairs when they began to get too worn down for customers to sit on. The walls of the staff room had once been painted white – paint that had long since faded into a sickly sort of grey – but now it was peeling, revealing the shoddy plasterwork underneath even though someone had made a valiant attempt to hide this with an out-of-date poster. It was quite eerie how quiet the room actually was; my heavy breathing sounding loudly in the silence, and it gave me the feeling of entering into a different world entirely, cut off from the horror I had experienced downstairs.

"Taaasties." The voices were getting closer, serving as an unwelcome reminder of my situation and I closed my eyes, resting my head against the wood.

Considering my options were hide or stay leaning against the door, I sort of knew it wasn't much of a choice at all. With a breathed swear, I staggered forward, heading straight at the tables that were pressed against the wall while my brain fogged over again, vertigo hitting like a battering ram to send me stumbling, falling to my knees only a few feet away from my destination.

My whole leg was saturated with my blood, I was unable to put my right-hand flat on the ground thanks to the glass still sticking into my wound and my left hand was still curled around the knife from downstairs, but I was still somehow able to pull myself under the table. There, after making sure the tablecloth was low enough to hide me, I sat in dead silence and waited.

I couldn't say how long I sat in the dim orange half-light waiting for the demons to find me. I couldn't even say what I thought about as I sat there, staring into space, resting my head against the grimy wall. Time ceased to mean anything while I sat there under the table in the diner's staff room alone, waiting for death to come find me.

I was brought back to reality by the door opening slowly and I froze in fear, eyes widening and breathing stopping altogether. My hand reflexively tightened on my stolen knife.

"Anyone in here?!" It took me a moment to realise that the voice that I heard then definitely did not belong to one of the creatures that had been hunting me. Hesitating slightly, fearing a trap, I pulled up the corner of the tablecloth and peered out, almost sobbing in utter relief when I saw the man that was standing in the doorway.

He looked a little different from what I remembered, face maybe a little less boyish and hair probably a little shorter but one thing that my mind had retained perfectly was the brightness of his blue eyes. They found mine and his face darkened. "You. *Seriously*?" His voice was deep and echoed strangely in the cold, unmoving room but at the same time making me feel so secure as it was so different from the hissing high-pitched screams of the monsters.

A small blackened knife was held expertly in his left hand while he held a small hook-tipped silver baton in his right, which he tucked under his arm as he approached me, quickly. With one swift movement, he lifted the tablecloth fully and ducked down to peer into my face. His eyes caught my bloodstained leg and frowned. Almost nonchalantly, he pulled the tablecloth completely off the table. He tore a strip off the fabric and then reached forward to wind it around my thigh, tightly. A tourniquet for the bleeding. "How many times is this now?" he asked as he worked.

Now he was sure I wasn't going to bleed to death in front of him, he reached out and pulled me out by my left wrist, maybe with little more force than was strictly necessary.

"H-how many times, what?" I tried to focus on him but my vision went wobbly and I was compelled to grab onto his arm as I attempted to steady myself.

"That I've saved your life, idiot." He pulled my chin up, roughly, with a gloved hand and looked at my face, a deep frown creasing his forehead. Despite his darkened gaze, I almost got lost in the brightness of his eyes again. "Are you okay?" He let go of my face long enough to bend and take a closer look at the wound on my thigh, pulling in a quick breath between his teeth as he gingerly touched my skin.

"Where are the... things?" The pain of his touch brought me back to focus on what was happening now.

His smile was a brief flash of humour upon his countenance as he straightened. "For now, they're gone. Saw what you did to the one downstairs. Good work."

"Why are you here?"

His face shifted again into an unhappy scowl. "I was passing through and I saw someone had been messing with police tape. I should be asking you the same thing, you know. You were here the first time they attacked; you saw what happened. Why the hell would you come here again when you *know* that they exist and what they're capable of?"

I blinked. "They're all covering it up. I wanted to know why. I want to know more." My vision was spotting and I blinked once or twice to clear it to keep a handle on consciousness.

He sighed heavily. "We need to get you out of here and get those wounds cleaned and sorted. We can talk about *what's happening* later."

With a promise of information, I nodded and let him wrap his arm around me, supporting me as we left the room.

As he helped me out of the building, I heard him sigh. "Why is it always *you*?!"

IV
Stitches and Tattoos

The cold air hit me like a slap in the face as my once-again saviour dragged me from the diner, one arm wrapped under my arm to grab my waist while the other held open the flap of police tape as he practically pulled me out.

Without question, the man beside me half-carried me across the night time street to a slick, shiny car that had been parked at an odd angle right under a street lamp. As we neared the vehicle, I stopped, wobbling slightly, before bending over and violently throwing up. The man next to me stepped back, swearing, but did not let go of me.

After he was sure I had finished emptying my gut, he stepped closer again and rubbed my back with a sigh of "pain in the ass" that I tried my hardest to ignore. I shivered as I coughed out the final chunks of nacho, listening to him sigh again, a sound that was already grating on my nerves, and I wrapped my arms around myself, trying to ward off the chill air. My injured hand didn't make this an easy task.

My rescuer must have noticed my shivering as suddenly he let go of me long enough to remove and sling his warm leather jacket over my shoulders. While I looked up at him in surprise, he was once again supporting me while he fished in the pocket of his black jeans for his car keys as if he hadn't done anything worth mentioning. After he had found them, he held them by the small silver keyring shaped like a sword between his thumb and forefinger, which he then pointed at me, another frown crinkling his smooth forehead. "You are holding my jacket for me, *looking after it*, until we get to my place. You need those wounds looking at and you need to stay awake." I blinked up at him owlishly. "Do you understand me? Stay conscious because you have a jacket to look after. Got it? It's old and was not cheap."

I nodded.

"I can't hear you."

"'Kay."

Seemingly satisfied with that, he turned around and pulled the backseat door open, helping me inside with surprising care. I immediately lay down on the soft leather, cuddling into his jacket tightly as I heard him slide into the driver's side and start the engine.

He pulled off quickly, slamming his foot down on the gas as we rocketed forwards.

"You're gonna have to talk to me," he said after a moment, the silence between us being broken only by the car's deep rumble, kind of like the voice of its owner.

"I don't want to." I pushed my nose into the jacket, clamping my eyes shut.

"Erika, I mean it. Don't you *dare* pass out on me." I heard his voice over the roar of the engine, identified the smell of cigarette smoke that all but poured from his heavy jacket but the rumble beneath me seemed all too far away like my body was somehow not my own, so I wasn't sure how far I was from actual consciousness. The pain was beginning to ebb and I was all too willing to follow the growing numbness to the oblivion that beckoned through the haze of blood loss and shock. Instead of succumbing to my weakness, I clung onto the smell of my rescuers jacket. Expensive leather, smoke and sweat all mingled together to create a scent that was not wholly unpleasant, yet not quite enough to comfort me either and it set me on edge enough to grasp consciousness like a life raft. "Do you hear me?!"

"Your jacket smells funny," I mumbled into the leather.

"Shit," he cursed and the car swung hard to the left, the blaring of horns that followed teaching me that he wasn't exactly obeying traffic signs. "I'm gonna bill you for that if you hurl on it."

"I'm not going to hurl."

"True, I doubt you've got anything else left in your stomach." The car swung again. "Seriously, what the hell did you eat? I've never seen puke that colourful." He was trying to keep me talking and, well, at this point, his goading had pulled the stubborn creature from me and *really* I hated to disappoint.

"I... I don't... Tex-Mex, I think. Since knowing that demons are real, I kinda stopped caring about my diet. So stop asking stupid questions." I wanted to be friendly, I really did, but once again, priorities shift and I found myself wanting to punish him for my lack of knowledge and the situation I now found myself in, not like either was directly his fault.

I heard him chuckle. "Yeah, you're not gonna pass out. Your attitude stinks."

"Almost as much as your jacket."

Again he laughed and I felt the pull of the vehicle lessen as he finally decelerated. "How are you feeling?"

"Foggy."

"Stay with me, okay?"

"'Kay."

"Can't hear you."

As I hadn't managed to summon the strength to open my eyes, I resolved to imagine myself glowering at the back of his head. "You have pissed me off too much to pass out and if I can't do it now, I doubt I will anytime soon."

He didn't reply, but I could almost feel the satisfaction radiating from his position in the driver's seat. After what seemed like hours but was probably only a couple of minutes, he pulled his car to park in front of a dreary grey apartment block and almost leaped out of the car, opening the door by my legs and leaning into the car to lift me and try to set my feet on the asphalt. As I squinted up at the black sky and the tacky glow of streetlights, the world twisted and I felt my already weak legs give up altogether and I fell into his arms but it was obviously a move he had anticipated as he was already waiting for me. He looked down at me, at the almost black fabric of my jeans, where before they had been light blue and the vast puckered jaw-shaped wound my blood was spilling from. The rational part of my mind knew it wasn't anything important that had been sliced, simply because if it had been I'd be so very beyond screwed and not to mention a bled-out corpse. Then again, I wasn't doing so hot at that moment, so keeping in tune with that particular thought, the less rational side of my mind felt like it was finally a good time to make a desperate bid for unconsciousness.

"Oh, no you don't. Come on you. You're stronger than this." His words were comforting and I grasped his shirt with the shaking fingers of my uninjured left hand, burying my face in his hard chest, taking comfort in the warmth that I felt there. "Hey now, you'll be okay, we'll get you sorted." He sounded awkward, but I couldn't bring myself to let go of him, preferring to pretend that his warmth was the only thing that existed and that demons meant nothing in this private world I created.

With a resigned sigh, he swept me up into his arms quickly and kicked the car door closed. He smelled of cigarettes, washing powder, sweat and deodorant which once again confused me to a few steps off panic but for some reason, never past the line. I could trust this man... He'd protected me again.

The apartment building was just as damp and dreary on the inside; the cold concrete floors were uncarpeted and shiny with trodden-down gum while a large pile of rotting refuse had been pushed idly into an unobtrusive corner. The metal elevator in front of us was sporting a large, smudged Out-Of-Order sign that had been obviously edited by the collective residents of the building. Doodles, mainly of male genitalia of varying sizes, were scrawled on the paper, a trend someone had taken to a whole new level on the surface of the elevator doors with a spray-can. The smell of old garbage and stale urine caused me to gag and I turned my head into his chest as he made his way slowly right past the lift and to a large wooden door to the right which housed a cracked, dirty window displaying a set of crumbling concrete stairs behind it.

It was a mark to my rescuer's favour how he managed to carry an almost eighteen-year-old girl in his arms while taking the steps two at a time. On the first floor, he turned back to another door and kicked it open, strolling easily down the corridor and not even stepping to the side to avoid a haggard old woman who swore and stepped back to let him past. I heard her screeches of expletives even as we turned a corner and for the first time, he lowered me and attempted to set me on my feet. My legs gave one singular wobble and then failed me completely, my backside hitting the cold concrete hard.

He sighed as he looked at me but then rolled his bright blue eyes and leaned over me. Instantly, I tensed, unsure as to what he was doing but as soon as I realised he was reaching into his jacket pocket for his door keys, I felt more than a little silly.

I was an injured, seventeen-year-old girl covered in her own blood and I was actually expecting him to try something on with me? Sure, I was alone with a grown man but I had allowed this to happen. I had let *him*, this stranger that I knew next to nothing about, to take me back to his apartment where he could easily kill me or rape me or... anything. I even didn't ask him to take me to the hospital, but I guessed that, for some reason, it wasn't an option. The media had been covering up the news of what happened at the diner so for me to come with an injury that looked nothing like an animal bite from anything short of a freaking shark would raise more questions.

Though oddly, going back to my concerns about my rescuer, I didn't think he would do that, not *really*. For one, he had saved my life more than twice and he would not have made the effort to do that if he was just going to kill me later down the line. So what if he was rude and had a bit of a bad attitude? Some girls found that bad-boy persona attractive. Not me. So not me.

While he rooted around in his pockets, I found myself gazing over his head to my surroundings. The walls were a faded sort of dull green, the paint chipped and peeling in some places, and dotted, here and there, with bits of graffiti spouting that *Roz was here lovin' Chad* or some derogatory statement about the local cops. The ceiling had once been white but as it had faded into an off sort of yellow, I assumed a lot of people, the man in front of me not excluded, ignored the no smoking laws completely. My backside had already told me that the floor here, too, wasn't carpeted and the lights above us flickered unhappily, their square containers filled with little black dots of dead flies that had been caught reaching for the light.

Having found his keys, he stood up once more and unlocked the door quickly. He kicked it open and wedged it open with the side of his boot as he twisted and hauled me to my feet. His arm went back around me as he all but carried me into his apartment.

The whole place stank of smoke and I could already smell the distinct scents I had already identified on his jacket even before he had reached for the light to bathe the whole place in a warm, dark glow. The lights were shielded with black upturned lampshades and gave the large soft yellow hallway we stood in a nice homey feel. This, coupled with the thick dark rug at my feet and cream carpet that led all the way through to four black-varnished doors at the end of the hall, it was hard to imagine him living here. A dark sideboard rested next to an old coat stand which only sported another black leather jacket almost identical to the one still draped over my shoulders but with a large chunk ripped out of the shoulder. Upon the sideboard stood a vase filled with wilted flowers and a picture frame depicting three smiling faces that he hid with his body as he pulled me forward out of the doorway. As he neared the picture, he lowered it carefully on its front so I could not peer at the faces and I immediately blushed, shameful of my curiosity.

This was his home and I was obviously intruding, despite him bringing me here.

"Come on." He pulled me forward with only a moment of hesitation and pushed open the black door on the right, flicking on the light switch as soon as he entered.

It was unbelievable that this place was where he lived.

The lounge was large and furnished well with a black and silver leather corner sofa, a shining black, almost glass, coffee table and three bookcases filled to spilling with books. A large TV was pressed in the corner upon an impressive TV unit complete with a games console and the two shelves either side filled with games while the windows behind it were covered by thick black curtains. Although my eyes were instantly drawn to a beautiful dark red guitar behind the unit alongside what looked like an amp under a white sheet, I forced them to continue their exploration of his home, though I made a minor note to ask him about the guitar later. A large fluffy black rug was stretched over a white carpet in front of a faux log fireplace while the mantelpiece above was covered with little knickknacks. Small pewter dragons with shining teeth, netted wings and ruby eyes and a metal mesh skull made with evident care. Three of the four walls were cream, setting off the furnishings nicely, yet the wall housing the useless chimney breast was covered in an intricate red pattern of vines and leaves on a deep black background. Red vines weaved in and out, looping and curling through the dark and around a large frameless mirror that had been hung above the mantelpiece. I glanced at it and noticed him watching me as if waiting for my response.

I didn't feel like giving one and eventually, he gave up and softly lowered me to the sofa. I slung off my satchel and dropped it to the side.

"I'm going to go put the heating on and get my kit. Take off your shoes and jeans." I stared at him as he turned to leave the room.

"What?" I gasped. "You want me to take off my... *what*? *Why*?"

He turned back to me, face unfriendly. "Is that what you think? Really?" He pointed to my leg. "How am I going to clean your wound with your jeans sticking to it, moron? Demon's saliva slows the healing process so if I don't get you stitched up, you could bleed until there's no blood left."

"Oh."

Of course.

He nodded at my shameful face and left the room, leaving me to attempt to pull off my jeans. The shoes were no problem as they were so old that all I had to do was kick them off with the other foot, but my pants were a whole other story.

The pain of pulling the fabric over my wound was unbearable, so much so that, despite myself, I found myself sobbing uncontrollably, my head in my hands with the band of my jeans just over my hips and no further. I slumped back into the soft leather, with my head in my hands as I cried, bitterly.

I was crying from the pain, from the sickness in my stomach and the dizziness in my head, from frustration and confusion at what had happened over the last few days to land me in a situation like this. I never cried, not since my parents left but I just couldn't stop myself and that is precisely how my saviour found me when he returned; a pathetic creature with red, swollen eyes, blotchy cheeks and an unattractive nose with her pants not even halfway down her thighs.

He stopped when he saw me and his eyes travelled to my shaking still-clad legs. He sighed, but his face showed that he understood when he approached me, putting down a towel, bowl of steaming water and some kind of first-aid kit on the coffee table.

"Does it hurt?"

I nodded, not trusting myself to speak.

"That's the lovely thing about demon bites, they're agony even hours after." He rolled his shoulder as he perched at the end of the coffee table in front of me and my eyes were instantly drawn to it, searching for the wound that had been inflicted at the diner only a few days ago. I was expecting to see the scar he had shown me at the hospital, something, anything, but the skin was smooth as if he had never had an injury there at all. He smirked when he saw me looking.

"The scar lasted about a day and then healed over."

"You sound awfully smug about that."

"Well, whaddya know... I *am* awfully smug about it." He leaned forward and hooked his figures under the waistband of my jeans. "I'm not gonna be kind," he told me with that matter of fact attitude that was already starting to bug me. Yet, somehow, I didn't think he was gonna try to be nice about it; in fact, I sort of knew that he would make it hurt more as I had a feeling he wasn't the type of guy that was about to cut me any kind of slack. It was my own fault for venturing back into the diner despite knowing what was lurking there.

Strangely, though, it didn't hurt as much as I expected. He didn't hesitate at all when he yanked the fabric off me and the damaged skin only pulled a little when he worked it free. Still, I heard myself screaming.

Once my jeans were removed, I could see the blood-smeared mess the creature had made of my leg and I instantly looked away, cursing my own stupid curiosity while I attempted to keep my bile where it should be. In the moment that I had looked, I could easily see the two half crescent moon shapes where the demon had latched its jaws onto me and I had expected that but what I didn't want to see was the flesh that the thing's rows of serrated hook-pointed teeth had almost shredded. Muscle, sinew and skin were yanked and cut into fine straggly strips and all that was left was a confused, bloody mess. Blood was still flowing freely from the wound, though slower than it had been before, and my whole leg was shiny with it, down to my black and white socks, saturating them thoroughly.

Not missing a beat, he turned around and lifted up the large bowl of water into his lap, while tucking the fluffy white towel under his arm, inching a little closer forward to me so he could focus on my wound a bit better. He rested the bowl of hot water on his knees and dipped the end of the towel into it, leaving it to soak a second before bringing it back out and surveying my blood-stained limb.

He was surprisingly gentle as he worked the wet fluffy fabric across my skin and it didn't hurt as much as I'd feared... or I thought that up until he pressed it against the actual wound and I dug the fingers of my uninjured hand into my bicep in an effort not to cry out again. Still, I let him continue, watching the top of his head through teary vision and the bangs that were flopping cutely into his eyes. He was *absurdly* attractive, I realised through the pain. It was just a shame about his stupid attitude.

As I watched him work, it suddenly occurred to me that I had no idea who this man was; he had saved me from demons more than twice and had even brought me to his home to look at my wounds. Despite his attitude, he seemed like an okay sort of guy and that was kind of necessary in this situation. I wanted to know more about him, especially considering he was going to such lengths to help me out.

"What's your name?"

He grinned at my question, still wiping away blood from my thigh.

"My name?"

I scowled. "Yes, I want to know your name. I don't think it's that much to ask considering that you've seen me half naked and you inexplicably know mine."

He pointed at my satchel by the sofa. "It's on your tag." I looked. Damn. The lovely purple keychain Blue bought for me with my name on it was hanging off the zip, introducing the owner of the satchel to anyone who cared to glance that way.

"I'd still like to know yours," I told him.

"It doesn't matter."

"It does."

He stopped cleaning my wound and focused his gaze on my face. "Why?"

I gave him an incredulous look. "Because you saved my life twice. Because it's polite to introduce yourself. Because if I wanted to send you a thank you card I'd know who to address it to! Because instead of yelling 'Oi you!" if I see you in the street, I could shout your name like a sane person. The list is pretty endless."

He smirked, amused, and went back to wiping away the last traces of blood from my skin. I had given up on hearing him talk again before he next opened his mouth.

"My name is Skye." I stared.

"Isn't that a girl's name?"

He grimaced. "And you wonder why I didn't want to tell you when you give me a reaction like that?"

"I don't hold back."

He smiled. "Yeah, I noticed." He was able to look at my wound now my leg wasn't completely covered in my blood though it was obvious I was still bleeding badly so, frowning in concern, he took a bandage and pressed it hard against my leg. "You're definitely gonna need stitches."

I shook my head suddenly. "I'm sure I'll be okay without them."

He glared at me. "Fine, no stitches. May I just say you would look fantastic as a bled-out corpse?"

"Will it hurt?"

He gaped at me. "Are you seriously considering a death over stitches? I thought girls cared about stuff like, you know, staying alive."

"I meant the stitches. Will it hurt?"

Skye sighed and took my hand in his, moving it so it was lying on the bandage he had left there and applied a little pressure, a silent instruction to keep the bandage pressed on my wound. I complied as he stood up and rooted in the kit he had left on the mantelpiece. "It will hurt," he told me, directly. He knelt back down next to me, placed a small set on the floor, ripped open an antiseptic wipe pack with his teeth and nudged my hand out the way so he could, once again, clean my wound. A clean canvas for the stitching. It hurt when he was just cleaning it so I dreaded to think how it would feel with a needle and thread. What would he use anyway? I remembered mother repairing one of dad's shirts with some navy cotton thread and a sewing needle and for some reason I couldn't think beyond that and I couldn't bring myself to look.

I clamped my eyes shut and tucked the collar of my t-shirt into my mouth, turning my face away as I heard the telltale snap of surgical gloves and felt Skye reposition himself over me. I felt his breath on my skin, a regular flash of warmth as I gripped onto the sofa with shaking fingers.

He hesitated. "Erika?"

"Mmmm?"

"It won't take long. I promise." He almost made me believe him.

I had felt the pinch and the pull before I had really braced myself and I bit down on the collar of my shirt harder, letting out a quick squeak as I did so. The whisper of latex gloves upon my skin as he worked to close my wound, the way I felt his breathing, the sound of the clicking of his needle-holding forceps; none of that was able to draw me from the sensation of Skye slowly stitching my broken skin back together. I wanted him to stop; I wanted to scream at him, but all I could do was just sit there, sobbing into my saliva-soaked collar with my eyes clamped tightly shut.

He worked for longer than I would have liked, especially considering that I wanted to punch him every single time he stitched. When he finally snipped off the excess suture, I spat my T-shirt from my mouth, breathing heavily in relief, before slowly and cautiously peering down at my stitched-up leg in morbid curiosity.

He had done a remarkably good job, especially in light of how mangled my skin looked previously, but I felt my worry twinge a little as I noticed beads of blood leaking from between the black stitches. With a sigh, Skye turned and pulled a roll of white bandage from the first-aid kit and leaned forward again, his thin fingers brushing against the soft skin of my inner thigh as he wound the gauze around my leg, not even glancing up at me as he worked. It was if he didn't even care about how awkward this was for *me*.

Once I was bandaged up and he was satisfied that I wasn't going to die of blood loss at some point during the night, he stretched and reached for another pair of blue latex gloves.

"I need to look at that hand now," He told me.

"It's okay," I told him, wincing as I hid the injured thing behind my back.

"Erika, I saw, it's covered in glass. If I don't get the glass out and, again, stitch you up..."

I sighed heavily. "I get it. Ugh, I'm going to look like Sally when you're finished."

"Sally?"

I shrugged. "She's a ragdoll in a movie."

He chuckled again. "Just bear with it."

His fingers gently tucked the two loose ends of gauze under the main body of bandage before gently lowering my hand down to rest on my thigh. I raised my left hand quickly and brushed my tears away as he began clearing up the mess, throwing my ruined jeans and the blood-stained towel he had initially used to clean me up in the corner, then moving to pick up his first aid kit and the now deep red water. The chunks of glass he had pulled from my palm were now drifting at the bottom of the bowl, dark and indistinct in the muddled water.

Without a word, he left the room and I was left to sit on the sofa and gently prod my injuries until the pain told me to stop. I glanced at the black and silver clock on the wall and blanched when I saw that it was four hours past midnight. About two minutes later, Skye returned with a bundle of blankets and two mismatched fluffy pillows that he dumped on the sofa before turning to me.

"Come on." He leaned forward and scooped me up in his arms without waiting for a response, not that I had the strength to give one and he carried me over to the lounge door that he had left open. He marched straight through the corridor, pausing only once to point to two other black doors that we passed, telling me that the one closest to the lounge door was the kitchen and the one next to it, the bathroom, and then he was off again. He carefully opened the fourth and final door and was confronted with the view of his bedroom.

Much like the living room, a lot of it was simple. A simple black leather divan bed took up most of the room, covered in crumpled red sheets that were struck through with two lines of differing thickness of shiny black. The pillows, the direct opposite in colour scheme, were strewn along the side of the bed as if he hadn't been able to sleep with them properly. Two black varnished side tables were also tucked into the room, supporting two silver lamps with plain black lampshades while the whole of one cream wall was taken up by two large wardrobes with mirrors for doors. The walls were painted cream, all except one, which looked like it had been attacked with a paintbrush long ago with black paint, uneven and haphazard.

I lowered my gaze, not wishing to pry, but the sudden movement of Skye lowering me carefully on the bed and straightening up removed any curiosities from my already crowded head.

The fuzziness that had beset me in the car was beginning to creep back and, now that my wounds were stitched and bound, I felt more relaxed and my body was letting me know that it was definitely time to sleep.

"Sleep here tonight," Skye told me.

"But-"

"No buts, you're sleeping here. If you fall off the sofa in your sleep, you could pop a stitch and there would be no way of me knowing until I found your corpse in the morning." His tone brooked no argument and I shut my mouth, but he continued lecturing me anyway. "You've gotten yourself involved in demons, Erika and that comes at a price. You need to learn how dangerous they are. You're lucky that I found you because if I hadn't, they would have made short work of you... or you would have died of blood loss under that table."

I nodded and his expression softened.

"It's a lot to take in, I get that, but you've done it to yourself. It's not safe to sniff around on your own. All you should know and accept right now is that demons are dangerous... and you really shouldn't go looking for them again."

I nodded again. I wanted to tell him that I wasn't exactly looking for them, just more information but I couldn't bring myself to do it. All I wanted was to sleep.

He sighed, perhaps sensing my unwillingness to speak. "Right, get some sleep. If you need me, I'll be on the sofa. Help yourself to the shower in the morning and I'll find something else for you to wear before I get you home, okay?" Without waiting for a response, he went to leave.

"Wait, Skye!" Calling him by his name felt more than a little odd.

He stopped and gazed at me, curious.

"Thank you. You know, for saving my life. Ah, again."

He smirked. "All part of the service. Goodnight, Erika."

It took me a long time to figure out where I was when I awoke. Sunlight was streaming through the large double-glazed window I hadn't had the time or energy to pay attention to the night before and I swung myself out of the bed I was in to go close the thick blackout curtains, forgetting the reason why I was even in this apartment. The moment I put weight on my leg, it fell from beneath me.

I winced as my knees hit the carpeted floor, which turned into a yelp when my right hand shot out to catch my fall. My hand instantly buckled to take the pressure off and I fell on my elbow, hard, leaving me nothing but a crumpled mess on the floor. Of course, that would be the moment when, upon hearing the noise and worrying I had managed to injure myself further, a dishevelled Skye came dashing into the bedroom, wearing nothing but the same pair of black jeans he had been wearing yesterday.

There was two seconds of silence where we looked at each other, neither of us sure of what to do when, suddenly, he burst into gales of cruel laughter. I understood the amusement; from his point of view I had fallen out of bed, onto my face and I was now stuck on the floor with my butt in the air wearing nothing but a dirty T-shirt and yesterday's underwear. I guessed I was not a pretty sight, but I still levelled a disgruntled look at him until he raised his hands in a mock surrender.

"Okay, okay..." he murmured, still chuckling, "up you get." He slowly made his way to me and bent down to gently lift me to my feet. Once I was sure I was upright again, I rested my weight on my right leg while keeping my hands on Skye's biceps as he leaned over slightly to check my bandages.

I was feeling nervous under his gaze and I shifted self-consciously as his fingers brushed my skin, even though I knew he was only making sure I hadn't popped a stitch in my sleep. The bandage had soaked up the little blood that was still leaking from the wound, turning the gauze a dark unpleasant red, but he seemed confident that it had stopped bleeding because he straightened up with a satisfied look. He then took my hand that was still gripping onto him and turned it over. The blood spotting the gauze on my hand was not nearly as bad, despite the demon's venom in my system and he nodded.

"Come on. Grab a shower, there're clean towels in there, I'll make breakfast and redress your wounds. Then I'll take you home."

The bathroom was a fairly modern affair but had no bath, only a large contemporary shower with far too many dials and shelves full of shampoo and other products for me to keep track of. The products over spilled onto the windowsill but upon further inspection I realised that they were more of the medicinal sort. Several bottles of iodine, packs of stitching needles that I tried not to look at too closely, tubes of burn cream, cream to help wounds heal and even some bottles that were left unlabelled full of stuff that looked viscous and not too pleasant. I turned back to the shower and viewed the collection of shampoos and shower gels – realising that a lot of them were empty. He didn't even throw away his empty bottles, surprisingly lazy considering the immaculate state and style of the rest of his apartment.

Making sure the door was locked and that I had a towel, I began to unwind my bandages. As feared, the cut on my leg looked grotesque, covered in almost brown gunk of late-clotting blood, the skin around it red, raised and puckered, in stark contrast to the rest of my pale cast. The wound on my hand was much the same, but I tried not to look too closely as I shook my head in annoyance at my own idiocy, stripped off my clothes and turned to the shower.

Before I could even figure out the dials, there was a knock on the door and I quickly grabbed one of the fluffy white towels and threw it around my body before moving to answer it. Skye was standing in the doorway, holding a pile of clothes and not caring a whit that I was standing there in just a towel. Once again, I knew that I was just a child but come on, a reaction would have been nice, was I not attractive in the slightest? I took the clothes wordlessly and closed the door again.

Once I had figured out the shower, which took me longer than I would have liked to admit (I would rather die than call for Skye to help me) and had cleaned myself as best I could with what was available to me, I began taking stock of what had happened.

Demons existed, Skye's words and my own memories were proof enough of that and they were common enough for the media to try to cover them up. Unfortunately, the realisation that they were real raised more questions than it answered. Why is it only now that I had seen them if they were so commonplace? Who the hell was Skye and how did he know so much? How come the media was making such an effort to cover them up if people *knew* about them? Who else knew about them? Why did it all *fascinate* me so much?

That was the worst thing: The way I wanted to know more. Last night showed me how dangerous they were and I just wanted to keep learning more about them; where they came from, what they wanted, what they were exactly. So many questions were battling for dominance in my head and it was starting to give me a headache. Would Skye tell me more? The information he gave me last night was enough to tell me that I was right all along, but I was still without a single clue as to what was really going on.

Once I was dry and dressed in the loose-fitting t-shirt and pair of shorts Skye had let me wear, I carried my dirty clothes and the faded grey jeans I was to wear after he redressed my wounds into the hallway. I stopped and sniffed the air as the divine smell of bacon hit me like a battering ram, reminding me that I was absolutely starving. I followed my nose to the only room I hadn't actually been inside yet and entered, maybe a little hesitantly.

At the sound of the door opening, Skye looked at me. "Bacon and egg sound good to you?" He asked. "Wait, you're not vegetarian are you?" He still hadn't put on a shirt and was padding around the stylish black and chrome kitchen barefoot. It was a small kitchen, but he had obviously done what he could with it and I could see how much he cared about it considering how *clean* it was.

"Bacon and egg sounds great," I told him, still moving around in awe. "It's impossible to beat bacon."

He nodded in satisfaction and sidestepped to one of the counters where he had laid out four slices of soft white bread, buttering them quickly before turning back to the frying pan where just browning slices of bacon were sizzling cheerfully.

Now that I had time and the care to observe him, I found myself staring at Skye. He was a thin but well-built guy but without the off-putting self-confidence that was common in a lot of guys my age. His skin was pale and decorated here and there with black tattoos that I found myself admiring, almost despite myself. The most prominent of which was a four-headed snake that curved over his shoulder blades to under the left side of his jaw, flat against his neck while one of the heads crept over to rest just on his collarbone. The tail wandered over his shoulders and drifted down to curl around his bicep once but from there, my eyes travelled the length of his right arm to the collection of other dark marks he had inked onto his skin. They collected together from where the tail curled around him down to his knuckles to form a sleeve. Although the general pattern caught my eye, part of me wanted to get in closer to decipher the different marks as if they would give me clues to this actual personality. His left arm was untouched by any ink, but he made up for it on his back where a large and beautiful sword was depicted, blade down and painstakingly etched with words that I couldn't see from my location by the door. His hair was creeping down to the back of his neck, twisting untidily from sleep, yet it was shaved on the left side of his head to reveal an ear that was pierced in several places. Bangs flopped into his eyes, dark from concentration as he continued to make breakfast.

After throwing two fried eggs on top of the bacon and piercing them deftly, he covered the gooey yolky goodness with another slice of bread each and cut the whole lot in half, passing one to me on a small plate.

"You got any ketchup?" He grinned at my question and grabbed the bottle, squeezing a little under the top slices of bread before tossing it to me. I copied his movements and we carried our food into the living room.

The pillows he had brought in the night before were now strewn about on the floor and the blankets kicked right to the bottom end of the sofa though I decided that he had done that when hearing me fall earlier.

He sat down without question and I lowered myself meekly to the tip of the cornered end, trying not to feel awkward as I sat down, conscious that once again, I was in the shorts he had loaned me. I didn't want to stain his jeans with blood – that's a pretty big no-no when borrowing clothes from someone you've only just met – so I thought I would wait until he'd redressed my wounds. It was probably why he had given them to me. Still felt like an idiot, though.

The sandwich he had made was great, made better by my genius use of ketchup, but it didn't stop me from raising my eyes and gazing at Skye as he made a complete mess of his hands eating his own. Yolk poured between his fingers, mixed in with drizzles of ketchup that fell in large wet splodges on his plate that he had knowingly hovered just beneath the sandwich. His chin was flecked with yolk but the childlike happiness around his eyes was so hard to judge and I found myself smiling in turn, taking a huge bite and not caring when my own yolk dripped onto my own plate on my knees.

It was hard to be self-conscious about eating when the guy you're eating with was doing so like a pig.

After finishing our sandwiches, thankfully finishing without any mess on my part, Skye disappeared, returning a few minutes later with bandages and a tube of cream, yolk free and wearing a light blue t-shirt.

Wordlessly, he sat across from me, once again perching on the coffee table and took the tube of cream in his hand. He showed it to me. "This will help the healing process. It won't do anything special but especially with the venom still going nuts with your blood, you kinda need some additional help." He unscrewed the cap and gently squeezed, a slight squirt of white cream landing cold and wet upon my stitches, which he then began to massage into my skin. Once he was confident that it was all rubbed in, he redressed my wound with gauze, doing exactly the same with my hand. Relieved, I was finally allowed to put the jeans on to find that they fit though were rather loose and I was too shy to ask for a belt.

It was time to go. I realised that I felt a little sorry that I was leaving this place as it meant going back to my usual mundane world. However, I didn't complain, only picked up my clothes, shoved them in my discarded satchel and stood up as Skye peered out of his rain-splattered window and then shot a considering look at me.

"One sec." He left the room again and I peered out too, squinting down through the downpour to where I could see what I remembered being Skye's car. I didn't really notice last night but from what I could see I realised that he had kind of good taste when it came to cars too. It looked like a Buick Electra, a car my dad used to constantly admire before he left.

I jumped back guiltily when Skye returned as if I was looking at something he shouldn't, an action that rewarded me with a raised eyebrow and an unsure "okaaaay..." He had donned his leather jacket but was holding the one with the messed-up shoulder in his hand as he sorted out his collar so it sat right.

"Wear this. It's pissing it down and you'll get soaked... the shoulder is a little mangled but blame the demons, not me." He passed it to me as well as the tube of cream he had applied to my wounds. "You should be okay to keep the bandages off tonight but keep putting the cream on and you should heal nicely."

"What about the stitches?"

He shrugged. Of course, he didn't care about that; he'd saved my life, but I'd have to figure out what to do from here.

I took the jacket and the cream. "Thank you."

As we stepped into the hallway together, Skye paused, frowning and cocked his head to one side as if he were listening out for something. I had my arm caught in the hole in the shoulder in the search for the sleeve and didn't really notice until he grabbed my arm and yanked me back a little. I stopped, staring at him with wide eyes.

"Do you hear that?" He whispered. After I had found the right sleeve, I focused on the total lack of noise from the hallway, wondering if he was actually insane when I heard it. A faint clicking from where the front door sat was echoing through the empty hall and after a moment of confusion, Skye's face became suddenly disapproving and he marched straight toward the door. He flicked the lock and pulled it open, glaring at the figure that was crouching in the doorway holding a lock pick, a hairpin and a sheepish expression on his strangely familiar face.

"*Shion*?!"

My gasp caused both men to turn and look at me, but I was too stunned at the image of the blond Japanese man on his knees attempting to break into my rescuers home to pay attention to the looks either of them were sending me.

"Morning Erika," Shion sighed and pulled himself to his feet before turning to Skye, "you're home then?"

"Obviously." Skye's voice was acidic and I almost stepped away from him in case he decided to start throwing punches and I was caught in the crossfire.

"Next time, call. We were worried." Shion still sounded bored, but there was something else in his tone, something that surprised me. Shion was *angry*.

"It's fine," with those two short words, Skye pulled me out of his hall, reached back and slammed his apartment door shut, giving Shion no choice but to take a few steps further into the corridor behind him.

"Yeah? Fine? Not with your track record."

Skye pushed an angry breath through his teeth. "Is that all you've got to say? Because I'm really busy. Some of us have actual work to do."

Without waiting for another word, he pushed past Shion and I hesitantly limped after him, looking back over my shoulder to where Shion stood, his fists clenched and an annoyed scowl on his normally uncaring face.

"Fall off the wagon again and there's only one person who's going to suffer for it! We're not going to pick up the pieces forever, remember that!"

Skye replied with only a hand gesture over his left shoulder, not looking back as he walked.

Shion wasn't quite finished. "Be careful with him, Erika! He could get you killed!"

Well, that was a bit of a shock, I thought as my rescuer muttered to himself, storming down the long corridor to the stairwell. As most of it consisted of expletives directed toward Shion, I allowed him to carry on without questioning, though my internal monologue wasn't as respectful of his privacy and threw speculation on top of far-fetched speculation about what I had just witnessed.

Skye and Shion knew each other, that much was clear, but what wasn't as clear was the relationship the two had. It was obvious that they weren't friendly but by how they spoke, it was evident that on some level Shion cared about whatever Skye was doing, mentioning being *worried* and even him *falling off the wagon*, whatever that wagon turned out to be. So in layman's terms, they knew each other well enough to fight *and* for Shion to be worried about him; maybe friends turned sour but with some lingering attachment? Maybe some sort of romantic attachment? I stared at Skye's back as he jogged down the stairs before rapidly shaking my head. Definitely not.

He seemed to forget that I was injured or maybe that I even existed because he kicked open the door to the bottom and left me limping down the stairs holding onto the handrail like an idiot. With a shrug, I continued on, looking up in alarm a few seconds later when the door at the bottom opened and Skye poked his head through to look at me.

"Hurry up!" was all he said before slipping back into the foul-smelling foyer again.

Two minutes later, I was hobbling out of the building a few feet behind a still-grumbling Skye, who was now rattling his keys as he moved, head tucked in against the rain, toward the car that I was now certain was an electric blue, well looked-after nineteen-sixty Buick Electra two-two-five. Skye unlocked the driver's side, slipped in and reached over to open the passenger side, still with a face like thunder. I settled into the seat as Skye sat there for a minute, staring at the steering wheel before he swore once.

"That guy *pisses* me off!" He seethed, all but slamming the key in the ignition and turning it angrily. He turned to me. "You know him too, right? Do you get that urge to punch him square in his stupid face or is it just me?!"

I stared wide-eyed at him, surprised by this sudden display of emotion. "I... don't really know him all that well."

"He's just so... monotone and when he *finally* gets an opinion he's all..." his words failed him and he turned back to the steering wheel. "*God*!"

Still muttering, Skye threw the car into gear and slammed his foot on the gas and I barely had time to yelp before we were rocketing forward at shocking speed. He continued ranting even as he drove, about Shion and his indifferent attitude that really seemed to get Skye wound up.

"H... How do you know Shion?" I asked in a small voice.

He ignored me or maybe it was possible to say he didn't hear me as I was so hesitant to ask the question in the first place and I definitely wasn't going to try again in case he *had* heard me and the repetition of my question only pissed him off further. To be honest, I was shocked, listening to him rant, not only because it was the first time I had heard him talk so much about any one thing but also because it was about *Shion*. It was about a guy that everyone seemed to suddenly *know* without myself having any prior knowledge about him. I would normally say what a small world it was, but somehow that seemed like a weak excuse, even in my own head. Shion was an integral part of Blue's life by the looks of things and Shion knew Skye well enough to get that pissed at him so maybe Blue was aware of Skye's existence and I could potentially get some answers from *her*. On the other hand, she didn't really seem to recognise him at the diner so it was possible that Skye wasn't in the same social circle as Daniel and knew Shion some other way.

Skye was driving like a crazy man and he seemed to be excellent at doing so. However, that didn't stop me from clinging to the leather passenger seat like my life depended on it, too scared to let go to actually put on the seatbelt that Skye hadn't given me time to reach for initially. On second thoughts, I felt like I did have time but Skye's raging had distracted me enough to miss the tiny window of opportunity he had given me.

I was more than a little bit relieved when he pulled up in front of my home and finally relinquished his grip on the steering wheel, peering past me and to the large house I lived in all by myself. I started to remove the jacket he had loaned me, but he put his hand up shaking his head.

"Keep it... it's ruined anyway and I think you'd rather not get absolutely soaked, right? Your parents have gotta be pissed enough that you were out all night without adding water all over the place." His tone was uncaring, but I was kinda touched by the thought.

"I really doubt that they noticed," I told him, once again not really lying. "Thanks for the jacket."

He jerked his chin in acceptance of my thanks and I reached over to the handle, stepping out the car and slamming the door. I watched him raise a hand in goodbye before racing off once more, continuing to gaze after him until his car was out of sight, despite how wet my hair was getting.

With a small smile, I made my slow way up my path, wincing as I felt the loose grey jeans stick to my skin as the rain soaked into them but thanks to the jacket, I remained mostly dry if you discounted my steadily dampening shoulder and jeans. It was slow work, but as soon as I made it under the cover of my porch I felt myself sighing with relief. Leaning against the doorframe and closing my eyes, I memorised the feel of the solid wood as if attempting to convince myself it was all just a bad dream and I had just come home from Blue's house after an accidental sleepover.

I was alive, I was safe and I was home. Almost smiling, I rummaged in my satchel for my house keys.

Wait. I stopped breathing for a second, my hand poised over my satchel with a keyring balancing on my index finger as my brain finally clued in on something that should have been obvious, something that should have scared the hell out of me, only didn't.

I didn't tell him where to go. At no point in the evening or the morning after did I tell him anything about myself and that included the location of my home, which left only one explanation.

Skye knew where I lived.

V
Memories and Lies

Blue, to no surprise, was absolutely furious with me. I had arrived back home, changed into my own clothes and had started to make something to eat when my doorbell rang and did not stop ringing. Over and over it chimed until I was forced to lay down my butter knife (just as well as I was making a mess of buttering bread with my left hand) and find out who was attacking my front door.

She glared at me when I opened the door and, wordlessly, shoved my cell phone and flashlight into my hands before marching into my house, dumping her bag and coat in the dining room while I shut the front door, dreading the reprisal I was about to receive.

So instead of following her like I knew I was supposed to, I retreated to the kitchen, knowing it would make her angrier but also knowing that if I did this, it would at least take her a few seconds to find me; a few seconds of preparation I so desperately needed.

Eating was a nervous habit of mine and after the night/morning I had I desperately needed some sugar in my system so I wasn't particularly conservative with the amount of syrup I drizzled over my chunky chopped banana sandwich. Blue stepped into the kitchen just as I placed the second piece of buttered bread upon my creation and I glanced up at her, my face worried.

She was staring at my hand. Without missing a beat, she strolled straight up to me and grabbed my wrist, pulling my bandaged wound toward her face, proceeding to scowl at as if it had just called her mother something unsavoury. Although, thinking about it, maybe that was the wrong analogy as she didn't really have much fondness for her mom.

"How'd you hurt your hand?" Her voice was curt, but I could sense the worry there. I gently pulled my hand free and pulled it close to my chest.

"Glass," I told her softly. There was no point in lying to her because her appearance with my flashlight and phone proved that she knew exactly where I had been last night. "Don't try to hit one of those *things* with a glass shard. It doesn't work and did you know glass shatters?"

Her eyes flashed dangerously and she crossed her arms over her chest. In hindsight, I probably shouldn't have done it but, really, her anger sort of goaded me and by the time I realised what I was doing, it was far too late to take it back. "If you think *that*'s bad, you should see my leg!"

Blue instantly glowered at me before her eyes dropped to my leggings that I had put on underneath my favourite pair of burgundy chequered shorts. It was obvious that my leg was padded with gauze beneath the fabric and I saw a flash of worry on her face, masked only a little with the fierce anger that still simmered close to the surface.

She took a deep breath and leaned back on the doorjamb, her forehead wrinkled and eyes dark. "What happened to you?"

Haltingly, I recounted exactly what had happened the night before, explaining to her *and* myself why I had even gone back there. Suffice to say, I didn't tell her it was my second time back there since the initial attack. Through my story, I saw Blue's expression change from deep anger, to abject fear and then back again, her fists never relaxing from their clenched state even when I mentioned the timely arrival of my rescuer though her face did twitch a little at his name. Only when I explained how he cleaned my wounds and stitched me up did she relax, reaching forward to gently take my hand again, running her fingers along where she guessed the shards had cut me.

"You could have died," she murmured.

"I nearly did."

Blue's flipping emotions finally hit their point and she, for lack of a better word, exploded. "*Of course you nearly did, you complete moron!*" she screamed, letting my hand go and stepping back as if she were likely to punch me if she remained close. "You go back to the place where we saw *demons* and you're surprised to find that they're still there?! What if *Skye* hadn't turned up? What then? You were stuck under a table, waiting for them to come and find you!"

"Do you think I don't realise that?"

"Well, obviously it's taken a bite and a near-death experience for you to actually *wake up* and smell your own damn mortality because you sure as hell didn't figure it out before!" she snapped.

I hung my head in shame, not really knowing what else to do. For a second, panting like a wounded animal, she didn't either and we both just sort of stood there in our own individual bubbles of embarrassment waiting for the other to reach over and make the move to pop them.

What *did* burst our bubbles was not either of us, however, but Blue's cell phone which choked out an old metal track that Sam loved, telling both of us that the call belonged to him. She pulled the phone out of her pocket and glanced at me once before she answered it. "Yo, loser," she greeted him.

"Why the hell aren't you at school?!*"* Both of us jumped as we heard Sam's angry voice. *"Where the hell is Erika*?!*I swear if you two are together I am going to hunt both of you down the moment school is over and shove your homework up your-"* Blue desperately tapped the volume on her phone until I could no longer hear my seething best friend.

I glanced at the clock on the wall above the doors to the conservatory. 10:05.

Aw, crap.

"Erika... did something kinda stupid and I've been picking up the pieces." Blue's unhappy glare made me duck my head again so I was intensely examining the kitchen tiles as I strained to hear Sam's reply. I heard his fuzzy voice on the other end but couldn't decipher the words.

"Yeah... she went back to the diner." I winced and glanced back up at Blue, meeting her brown eyes as she spoke. "Yeah, yeah... Don't worry, I told her what an idiot she was."

There was a moment of silence when, for the first time, a look of confusion crossed her features and she looked down at the floor. "Wait... what?"

"What is it?" I moved forward, but she raised a hand, turning her body half away from me as if that would help her hear Sam's words better.

"No, I heard you but what do you mean... yeah... okay but-! That's not..." Opening and closing her mouth like a goldfish, but after several moments of silence she managed, "aren't you supposed to be in class?" while rubbing her forehead with her other hand.

There were a couple of seconds of silence on our end until she nodded and said, "Okay, go back and meet us after school. We'll be at mine." She gently tapped the end call button on her cell and then turned back to me, her face worried.

"Something's going on with Sam," she told me, slipping it into her back pocket again.

"What?"

She frowned at the kitchen tiles as if it were their fault. "I don't know if he's pulling my leg as he likes to do but...He, um, seems to have totally forgotten the truth of what happened at the diner the other day." She raised her eyes to mine, unhappily setting her features into a worried grimace. "By what he said, he is utterly convinced it wasn't demons that attacked the place."

"Gang-related incident?" Part of me wasn't really surprised while the other part of me was screaming something along the lines of *'he was pinned down by one of the bastards! He should know better than anyone!'* though I left this on the inside, knowing that Blue probably felt exactly the same.

"Got it in one."

Just after lunchtime, Blue and I had gone back to her place to find her mother returned from a date, passed out on the couch in the living room, stinking of alcohol. Without missing a beat, Blue grabbed a comforter from the leather armchair near the large window and threw it over her snoozing mother, pausing to pull the ridiculously high stilettos from her rubbed raw feet and throw them into the hall we retreated back into.

For the next couple of hours, we both pretended to study though something told me that neither of us was actually reading through what we were supposed to. I didn't know what Blue was thinking about but me? I was thinking about Skye.

There was so much that was said and left unsaid during my evening with him. He said he'd explain but with the cleaning of my injuries it didn't really seem important anymore. Now that I was away from him and thinking about it, I realised just how skilful he had been at dodging the subject, only giving me just enough information to satisfy me in that moment, not in the long run. I was just wondering if he had done that on purpose, eyes skimming over an overdue algebra book from the library when Sam arrived at around five in the afternoon.

He looked healthy I thought as I clambered down the stairs, a little bit behind Blue, who had darted out of the room as soon as she heard the doorbell chime. She had already had the front door open by the time I reached halfway down the stairs and I could hear the giggling of Blue's thirteen-year-old twin sisters that were peering down the stairs from the upstairs landing. I noticed they had a slight obsession with Sam around a year ago because they would run squealing from the room whenever he looked at them. Their giggles hounded us wherever we went and apparently today was no exception.

He saw me limping down the stairs and his face shadowed with disapproval.

"Don't start," I muttered, coming to a stop around three steps from the bottom. "I've had all this from Blue." And then some.

He didn't seem to care. "You entered a crime scene, Erika. You know what that tape is for? To keep people out."

"It didn't do a good job then, did it?"

Oops.

"What would have happened if those guys were still lurking around? What if the authorities had caught you snooping on private property? It would have been more than a slap on the wrist, especially given what happened there." He was one hundred percent convinced that what he remembered from that day was the truth, I noticed as he rambled and the way that Blue met my eyes and raised her eyebrows showed me that she had noticed the exact same thing. "We're not kids anymore – we won't get away with curiosity for the sake of curiosity. You can't go back there."

"Yeah. I know." At least he got that part right. I definitely would not get away with going back to the diner again, not that I even wanted to anymore.

He nodded once in satisfaction and then turned to Blue. "Are we in your room?"

She nodded and stepped back to allow him to pass us and he began to climb the stairs. "I'll get drinks. Come on Erika, I'll need a hand and as you only have one working one left, you're perfect."

We didn't say anything until Blue had pulled three glasses from the cupboard and lowered them to the side. She stayed still for a moment, thinking until she looked at me. "He doesn't even act like anything's out of the ordinary," she told me quietly as if he could be listening, "and I can't think of anything that could just... change his mind like that without any... warning?"

"Maybe it's a defence mechanism?" I frowned and pulled the bottle of orange juice out of the fridge, looking down at the colourful label as if that could give us all the answers.

"What do you mean?"

I turned and offered the orange juice to her. "Well... certain creatures do things to help protect themselves from predators, don't they? Venomous bites, changing colour to hide in the area around them... maybe what he's done is like that? His brain might be trying to rationalise what he saw that day?"

She stared at me for a minute and then grabbed the orange juice. "Theoretically, I suppose it's possible. People are known to suffer delusions because they don't want to remember the truth but would it be that much of a clean transition? We would have noticed some sort of change, surely?" While she spoke, she was pouring out our drinks, still frowning heavily.

"We have noticed a change! He's completely forgotten everything!"

"But that quickly? It's not natural..." She pushed a glass of orange juice into my hand and nodded her head toward the door. "Come on. We'd better get back up there; he'll get antsy if we don't hurry."

Sam had already started unpacking his bag when we arrived, throwing dog-eared books and pens onto the floor as he yanked over one of Blue's bean bags over so he could lean on it as was his norm.

Blue's room was tiny but as she didn't have to share with any of her siblings, she was kind of alright about that. She had squeezed in a double bed, a pine wardrobe stuck with so many photos of the three of us that I couldn't see any of the original wood, a tiny dressing table and three large bean bags. These were shoved in the corner leaving only a few square feet of space on the laminated floor covered with a white and blue rug. The pale blue walls had begun taking some of the overspill of pictures from the wardrobe, which were dotted around haphazardly like Blue had no idea where else to put them. Above us, a white mini chandelier dangled around a dozen light-reflecting glass crystals on dainty little silver chains that always managed to send me to sleep when I stayed here, as long as the window was open and it allowed the gentle breeze to brush them side to side like a mobile.

Studying didn't go well. We started strong, each of us quizzing one another on the subjects we were probably going to be tested on when it came to finals with little cards we had prepared for this purpose weeks ago, but that didn't last too long. Eventually, we somehow managed to get ourselves distracted and I ended up lying on my back, head lolling off the edge of Blue's bed as she lay on her front alongside me, peering over to what Sam was jotting down in his notebook as he sat against the bed on the floor beside us.

"What's that?" She asked suddenly, shifting to free her arm so she could point at a little doodle in the corner.

He cocked his head to the side as if it was the first time he noticed it and I rolled over to view it the right way up and I felt my stomach drop.

It was a doodle of a demon.

"I dunno," He muttered. "Some sort of doodle. You know when Demon-witch from hell goes on and on and you just sort of... fade? Found myself drawing this cheerful fella... I think."

"Have you ever seen one of them before?" I glanced at Blue as she spoke and fought the urge to hit her upside the head.

He glanced at her. "It's a doodle, Blue."

She laughed though it sounded incredibly fake to my ears. "Yeah, I know that doofus but have you ever seen one?"

His eyes never moved from her face. "It's a demon, Blue... Demons don't actually..." He blinked twice as if he had something in his eye. "They don't exist."

"How do you know?" Her teasing tone was sobered by the fact that her face was completely straight. I looked over at Sam, suddenly worried that his face had drained of all colour. I nudged Blue's arm in a warning and she looked at me briefly before turning back to our friend.

"I just do... now can we..." He touched his forehead with his shaking fingers. "Can we just carry on studying?"

I looked down at him in concern. "Go have a drink Sam, you look like crap."

"Yeah... I don't feel too good." He glanced back down at his notebook and then slammed it shut, pushing it from his lap as if it were caustic. "In fact... I think I'm going to go home."

"Home? But it's only eight o'clock!"

He crawled forwards and started shoving books and pens haphazardly into his rucksack. "Yeah... I gotta go home. School. I'm tired. Sick. I gotta go. I'll see you later." Without picking up half his books, Sam suddenly leapt to his feet and bolted out the door, Blue scrambling from her bed and dashing to follow him with me in tow.

I arrived at the upstairs landing just in time to see him leap down the last four steps and throw the front door open, fleeing into the darkness of early spring without looking back or closing the door behind him. Blue, who had only made it halfway down before he had fled, continued her way with a sigh and shut the front door, locking it and then turning to face me.

"So that was interesting," I told her with a raised eyebrow.

"You're telling me."

Back in her room, Blue stacked all of Sam's forgotten books and pushed them to the side, bunching his highlighters and biros together and dumping them next to them. I sat and watched her from her bed, sipping my orange juice while she worked to organise the chaos he had left.

After a moment of silence, she sat back on her ankles and looked at me. "Is there anything we can do?"

"We can't make him remember if he bolts whenever he hears anything about them." I chewed my lip thoughtfully as Blue stood up and pulled two sets of pyjamas from the drawers inside her wardrobe. She threw a pink nightshirt at me.

"May as well change, you're staying here tonight so I can keep a damn eye on you."

"I'm not going to go back to the diner..." I said, but I pulled the fabric onto my lap anyway.

"Hmmmm..." Her eyes told me that she didn't believe me, but she didn't say anything else about it, pulling her top over her head instead.

I ignored her lack of trust. "But what about Sam?"

She threw her blouse into the small wicker basket by the door before saying, "Maybe we should just... let him remember what he thinks he remembers?"

I had to think about that for a second as my brain worked its way around her words, pulling my t-shirt off as it buzzed behind my eyes. "Wait," I sat there, staring at her when I finally had it figured, "you want to leave it as it is?"

She yanked on her teddy-bear spotted pyjama tank top. "Maybe? Ugh! I don't know!" She pulled her hair up into a ponytail, her movements quick and jerky with frustration and grabbed her cell phone off the bed, tapping off what seemed like a quick text to, I assumed, Daniel.

"Maybe it's best this way... He doesn't have to remember that demons exist."

She looked at me then, frowning. "Do *you* want to forget?"

"I don't know... I mean, part of me wishes that I didn't know. Ignorance being bliss and all that," I said as I pulled the nightshirt over my head and started to shimmy my shorts off, "but I couldn't risk getting myself and the people I care about killed because I didn't know enough."

She scoffed. "Oh, I think you do that well enough while being in possession of all the facts."

"Oh ha ha." I rolled my eyes. "I don't *have* possession of all the facts though Blue. I still have so many questions."

Her phone buzzed in her hand and she tapped another text in response before glancing out the window, frowning. "You ever hear of the phrase *curiosity killed the cat*?"

I almost groaned. I'd been telling myself that over the last few days almost constantly but it didn't make any difference in how I felt about the situation. "It's less curiosity and more... that I need to know. Why is this happening? Who is covering it up? And now, what made Sam forget it all? There's so much going on and I can't just sit back and let it all happen."

Blue's frown was worried. "But you're going to get yourself killed."

"I've decided that I'm not going to the diner anymore... that ship has so totally sailed." I stripped my leggings off and touched my fingers to my bandage, wincing slightly at the tenderness of my skin. "I just... need to find out what's going on. My whole world has changed and I can't just move on from that... saying that, I believe that I know too much to ever forget it. If something happened to me the way it happened to Sam, there would be plenty of evidence to suggest to me that I'd been tampered with. How would I explain my injury on my leg? Nothing but their jaws could inflict that kinda wound..."

The look she sent me was considering as she stood up again and quickly changed out of her jeans, pulling on a pair of shorts in the same style as her tank top. "So what are you going to do about it?"

"I'm going to look for Skye again."

Her reaction was much as I expected; she puffed up like a bullfrog with disapproval.

After a moment, she opened her mouth and her voice was pitched low, obviously trying to control her emotions as she said "once again with the purposefully looking for things. Can't you ever just leave it alone?"

"How are you okay with knowing *nothing*?"

"I would rather know nothing and live than know everything and *die*! This is totally beyond us, Erika! We need to leave it alone and let the people who actually know what they're doing deal with it!"

"And what if what happened at the diner happens again?"

"There will be people there to protect us!"

"How can you be so sure?! People *died* in that diner Blue! I am sure as hell *not* going to end up like one of them!"

"You will if you continue doing what you're doing! Just *trust* in the people who are there to protect you and keep your nose out! That is the *only* way you're going to stay alive!"

I stayed sat on her bed, glaring up at her, trying not to let my anger get the best of me. She and Sam were my only friends in the world and I was on the verge of pushing them both away, but this was something I just couldn't let go of. "So who are these people you've said will protect me?"

For the first time, I saw the flash of fear in Blue's eyes though to begin with I simply thought she was unsure. It was her knuckles that gave her away; the way they went white as she clenched her fists that told me that it was more than a simple uncomfortable response. Something about my question scared her. "Blue? What do you know?"

The fear flashed over her face again. "I don't know anything!" I liked to think that I knew Blue well enough to know when she was lying to me and the way she was all but twitching every time she spoke *and* flat out denied any knowledge seemed a little suspect after trying her best to convince me that there were people out there who were keeping us safe.

"Then why are you freaking out?"

"Because you're treating me like I know more than I do!"

"You're acting like you do!"

"Well, I *don't*!"

I sat there and looked at my floundering friend. Something wasn't right about her reaction, but I sort of felt that I couldn't continue on with this kind of questioning without doing some irrevocable damage to our friendship. I tried to push it out of my head, turning away a little to stare past her and out of her window. I didn't really know how we were going to move past this without one of us conceding and I wasn't going to let it be me – not this time – but it didn't mean I was prepared to ruin our friendship. I could hold my tongue for now.

After a few minutes of strained silence, she sighed heavily and threw herself back on the bed next to me. "I'd hoped we would have a pyjama party and watch bad chick flicks while eating crappy food." She pulled the fabric of the nightshirt that rested on my shoulder. "It feels like forever since we haven't been arguing about something."

I nodded. "There's a lot going on." I turned my face to her, smiling wanly. "But watching a film with my favourite girl does sound good..."

A flicker of an emotion I could not name crossed her face and she embraced me, quickly. "Only mad at you because I love you, idiot," she grumbled into my ear. "I don't want you to get hurt."

I poked her in the ribs and she squealed, letting me go. "Yeah I know, so let's watch this film and forget about all this unhappy shit! Smiles, sunshine and buttercups from now on!"

"Sunshine and buttercups," she agreed with a giggle and then dashed out of her room probably with the intent to check if her mom had moved her carcass from the sofa yet. I stood up slowly and made my way to the window, pushing away the netting to peer out into her back yard. I could see the skeleton of the old trampoline that Sam broke last year, the slide set that he broke the year before that and the swing set that I broke the year before that, all belonging to Blue's younger siblings. No wonder they didn't particularly like me. Sam, however, could do no wrong in the twins' eyes.

I rested my head against the cool glass, watching the silver-lined clouds drift over a beautiful moon-lit sky. It was hard to imagine that the things I had seen were an everyday part of life for some people and even more unbelievable was the fact that this world didn't even know about it.

I thought that the view would have at least changed since I discovered the existence of monsters; the way the sun shone or maybe a darkening of the sky, but there was nothing. Everything just looked the same.

I saw my breath mist on the window and I reached up to touch the fogged glass, sketching a simple smiley face with horns before I wiped it away with a frown.

Blue was probably right; I was going to get myself killed.

The next day, Blue and I woke early to get ready for school. We were worried enough over Sam's behaviour last night and not going to school would be adding insult to injury and only cause us *more* worry so, despite us staying awake until five watching bad rom-coms, we pulled ourselves out of bed to tackle the morning at Blue's home.

Three of the children were already up; the twins running around the lounge like lunatics while the youngest, Mika, stared at them with wide blue eyes in the bouncer that was set up in the doorway, and Blue's mother was also awake. She was a tall, pretty woman with wavy brown hair and a heavily made-up face that always gave me the impression that she was trying too hard and she completed the look with a slightly rumpled business suit. She was drinking a coffee while busying herself with the kettle, apparently pouring herself a second coffee into a travel mug and she frowned when she saw us.

"Unplanned sleepover again, Blaise?" She asked with disapproval prominent in her tone as she added sugar to her mug.

"You sound all pissy but you were dead, mom, so it obviously didn't bother you any," snapped Blue as she made her way to the refrigerator and the selection of cereals that were placed on top. The family kitchen was a mess, but I guessed that was kind of how it went when you had five children and an adult that was never there living under the same roof. Dirty plates were piled in the sink and the stuff that didn't fit stretched the length of the counter, mugs piled inside of other mugs, resting on plates that were balanced on top of bowls. I had a frightening urge to clean and I saw Blue's eye twitch as she seized her cereal and turned to the empty cupboard where the bowls were usually kept. "Are you actually going to work today? Colour me shocked."

"Washing up needs doing." Blue's mom, ignoring her completely, finished making her coffee and slung her handbag over her shoulder before turning to the mirror in the hall. "The babysitter will be here in a few minutes. Make sure Alex has his jacket and the twins have their kits. I will be home late."

"Another date?"

"Meeting with the boss." The way her mom applied her lipstick in the mirror told me that it was not a regular meeting she was attending, but I kept my mouth shut, instead moving to the sink so I could run the faucet while moving all the dirty crockery out of the way. Blue's mom looked at me but didn't say anything and left the room. A few seconds later, we heard the front door slam.

"Don't Erika, I'll do it." Blue tried to shoo me out of the way, but I stood my ground.

"Nope." I quickly washed two bowls and gave them to her. "Just dry them up and make me breakfast. Do my homework too and maybe order me some Chinese food... then we'll be almost even."

She grinned.

About five minutes later, Alex came stomping into the kitchen, took one look at me and then scowled, heavily. As he didn't share Blue's father, the fifteen-year-old looked nothing like his sister. His blonde hair was shaved quite close to his scalp on the sides and back but flopped slightly over his left eye and was shot with black. He had been suspended from school once for dying the streaks blue and was forced to change it to a natural colour, so black it went. As far as I knew, the school still didn't like his style but couldn't do much about it. He was wearing a black band t-shirt, snug-fitting black jeans, and black converse that were flecked with luminous green paint.

He seemed like a cool kid... until he opened his mouth.

"You know mom doesn't like it when *she* stays over," he said, reaching for the cereal. He pushed past me and grabbed a bowl from the drying rack.

"Yeah well, I don't like it when she brings random guys back to the house so I think we're both gonna be disappointed." Blue had not poured milk into my cereal yet as she knew I hated it when it went soggy, but she stood against the other counter that was built on the neighbouring wall eating hers happily. "Mom said 'wear your jacket'."

"I don't wanna wear my jacket."

"Oh well, I tried." She turned to me, "you nearly done?"

I washed up the last spoon and almost threw it in the little drainage cup with gusto. "Now I am." I reached for the milk and poured a generous helping on my cereal. There were still a few crusted pans and dishes in the bowl, but they weren't gonna get clean; no matter how much I scrubbed, so I left them to soak and Blue could tackle them later. My friend then dumped her empty bowl in the cluttered sink and reached for a glass to fill with the juice she was already picking up with her other hand.

I was just tucking into my cereal when the doorbell went. Blue glanced at the grimy clock on the wall, rolled her eyes and kicked her little brother in the shin in what was slightly more forceful than a playful way. "Go get that, it's the sitter," she muttered, "and get gone; you need to walk the twins but make sure you grab their kits on your way out. They're by the front door; I put them there last night."

"Yes, *boss*." The sarcasm radiating from him as he stomped out of the kitchen, still carrying his cereal bowl which then caused Blue's face to darken and she lifted her fist to his retreating back.

"Brat," she muttered.

Mika's regular babysitter, Emma, was a blonde whirlwind of energy. She breezed into the kitchen with a big beaming smile about five minutes later, carrying little Mika on her hip while slinging her bag on the back of one of the barely used dining tables.

"Morning Blue! Morning Erika!" She sang. "How are we this morning?"

"Fine," Blue smirked. "Kids off?"

"Yep and the twins have their kits." She poked Mika's nose and the child giggled. "Though little Alex looked in an awful mood, didn't he, gorgeous? Yes, he did!"

Blue sighed. "He's an ass." Smiling, I watched the babysitter coo over Mika until she looked back up at us both, her expression a little more serious.

"Hey, Blue... I *am* really sorry about letting you down last week... When your mom didn't call, I just assumed... I have other jobs and I can't just let them down."

Blue laughed and poured herself a second glass of juice. "Don't worry about it Emma, seriously, I got it sorted. Besides, you know how my mom is. She works when she wants to and sleeps with her boss to keep herself from getting fired... so she's impossible to figure out. I feel sorry that you have to work with it."

"Hey, if it weren't for you, Blue, I wouldn't be here. You're the only one who seems to have her head screwed on right in this house." She looked at the clock. "Shouldn't you guys already be gone? You're not gonna make it in time."

The words were barely out of her mouth when a large *honk* from outside sounded, perking Blue up instantly. "Oh! That's Dan. I asked him to give us a lift to school."

I laughed. "Really? It's not far."

"True but if we walk now like Emma said, we won't make it." I checked the kitchen clock again and saw that she was right. She then grinned, wickedly. "Also, having a boyfriend that can drive is so very beyond *awesome!*"

Her giggle was infectious and I found myself chuckling too at her excitement but offering a half-joking, "I wouldn't know," for a mocking sympathy plea.

Again, to this, she laughed. "We'll just have to find you a boyfriend that can drive then!" and she led the way from the kitchen, waving Emma goodbye as she did so.

As long as he didn't drive like Skye... I shuddered.

Blue skipped ahead of me and cheerfully swung into the passenger side while I hesitated a little before shrugging my shoulders and clambering in the backseat of his relatively new modelled family car.

"You do respond to traffic signs, don't you?" I asked him, worriedly, by way of greeting as I slammed the door behind me.

Dan laughed and grinned back at me. "If you're scared, make sure you have your seatbelt on."

Blue scowled and playfully hit him on the shoulder. "Don't listen to him, Erika; he drives like an old man."

He rubbed his arm, pouting like a child. "Only when you're in the car, Bee. When I'm alone... well, it's a miracle I haven't killed anyone."

I sighed in relief as Blue laughed but put my belt on anyway. It seemed like Daniel was in a pretty good mood, bearing in mind that I'd barely heard him talk before the day Blue was almost mugged, and I decided it was time to put my little scheme into action.

After he pulled out of Blue's drive and was making his way down the street at a nice sane pace, I began to speak.

"Daniel?"

"Yeah?"

"Can I have Shion's number?"

"*Huh?*" Blue immediately turned in her seat to stare wide-eyed at me, a reaction I expected and was all too prepared to head off with a lowering of my head as if to conceal a blush. "Erika, what are you playing at?"

"He seems cool... I thought I could get to know him better..."

I heard Daniel snort, "Shion? Cool?!" but I was far too interested in Blue's reaction. She would instantly guess the true reason behind my sudden request. Even if I didn't convince her, I had to be believable in my defence against her inevitable barrage of questions to fool Dan into thinking I was genuinely interested in his friend. If friend was even the right word.

"You like Shion?" As expected, Blue sounded sceptical and I couldn't really blame her. Normally, she would be the first person I'd come to with something like this, not like this had ever happened before in anyway shape or form.

Daniel also noticed her doubt. "Oh come on, Bee, some people might find that asshole-but-lovely Asian persona attractive. What do they call it over in Japan? Tsundere?" he said with a chortle. "Hell, knowing that someone's jonesing for him might give him a bit of vigour! Especially someone like Erika!"

Her eyes hadn't moved from me. "Really, Erika? You've shown *no* interest in *anyone* and now you're saying you like Shion?"

"Isn't it her choice who she's jonesing for?" Daniel at least seemed to like the idea, but Blue wasn't having any of it.

"There is *no* jonesing here!" Her voice was rising as she fought to make herself heard, "Erika only wants Shion's damn number to get closer to Skye!"

"Skye?"

"Is it really so surprising that I like a guy that you have to invent an ulterior motive?"

"I'm not inventing anything!"

"Sounds like you're jumping to conclusions there, Bee," Dan muttered. I nearly whooped. Dan was on my side! Or rather a side where it was a possibility that his friend would get some.

"You, shut up and *you*, you said it yourself that you won't like a guy purely on his looks! You've met Shion *twice*. How do you know if you like him?"

"I said I wanted to get to know him better. Shion might be a nice guy."

"He is," Dan chipped in.

"You, last time, shut up!" Once again she snapped her head toward me. "I don't want to argue with you, but I just don't think you have any intention of getting to know Shion. I believe that you just want to get close to Skye."

"Is someone going to actually fill me in?!"

There was nothing I could really say about that, considering she was right on the money. I thought I was prepared to deny it, but that meant lying to Blue, which I always tried not to do, at least to her face.

"I'll tell you later." Her voice was chipped and firm, not really inviting anyone to argue. Daniel pulled off from the now green lights and I focused my vision on the passing scenery.

The journey to school then passed in silence.

When Dan finally stilled the car in front of the gates, Blue threw open the door, climbed out immediately and slammed the car door behind her.

I moved to follow her, but I felt Dan put his large hand on my shoulder. I felt my hopes rise, but the grim look on his features dashed them almost instantly.

"I'm not gonna give you Shion's number. Bee seems dead set against it," he told me, confirming my fears. "But I will tell you to stick around and wait. Shion's always around so you'll see him again. There're no one in his radar either so don't panic about losing your chance. I'll keep you posted."

I was surprised. "Thank you, Dan."

He grinned. "Don't mention it. Now hop to it. She's waiting for you."

I turned my head to see that he was right and Blue was standing by the gates, frowning at the car.

After I'd thanked Daniel again and joined her, she nodded toward his departing vehicle.

"What did he say?" Her tone was sulky but not as frosty as I'd expected.

"He said he won't give me Shion's number," I told her honestly. I was omitting a large portion of what he'd said, but she didn't need to know that.

She seemed satisfied with my response because she sighed and locked her arm around the crook of mine.

"Do you really like Shion?" she asked me as a couple of faceless guys from the class below us dashed past us to enter the school building proper.

"Don't you think there's something about him?" Atta girl Erika, answer a question with another question, I congratulated myself.

"Asian guys just don't do it for me," she wrinkled her nose as she spoke.

"True. You like the big thirty-something beefcakes."

Despite the fact that she was supposed to be upset with me, Blue suddenly laughed.

"Beefcake! I'll have to use that one!"

It looked like I had managed to sidetrack her from my real purpose, but I'm sure she still doubted that I wanted to get close to Shion because I liked him. With everything that was going on recently, I wasn't even thinking about romance and there was every possibility that, given the chance, I *could* come to like Shion. I could like anyone, given the chance. Thinking like that made it easier to lie to Blue about my intentions because, for all I knew, they could be true.

Sam seemed to have recovered from whatever had happened to him the night before as he was perched on the edge of our fountain with his basketball in his hands, slowly bouncing it over and over again in the same spot between his legs.

"You do know that Einstein classified insanity as doing the exact same thing over and over and expecting different results, right?" I asked him as I lowered my satchel to the lip of the fountain.

He glanced up at us. "Did you stay with Blue again?"

I looked at my clothes. "Is it that obvious?"

"You always look a little more colourful after spending the night. All your clothes are pretty drab." He looked at Blue, who was tying her curly hair up into a messy ponytail. "Get much studying done?"

"We weren't really in the mood to study when you left," Blue said quietly.

"Sorry." He grimaced. "I don't know why...I just felt really sick and I had... I had to get out of there. Clear my head..."

Without a word both of us sat on either side of him and put our heads on his shoulders in a synchronised display of affection for him. Our arms crossed over his back and we squeezed tightly while I made a silent promise to figure out exactly what was happening to our world.

Unfortunately, the weeks that passed did so without any sign of Shion.

This frustrated me, but I had already pushed my friendship with Blue to the edge so I wasn't going to go out of my way looking for him *or* attempt to bring it up with Daniel, who we saw quite often, though always in kind of a bad mood. So, in short, I was stuck without any way of getting more information from the only person who seemed to know what the hell was going on.

During this time, I found I had a problem: my wounds had pretty much healed. Now this would be a good thing if it weren't for the fact that I was stitched together like a bad patchwork doll and had no way of undoing the work that Skye had put into keeping me together. I had picked and snipped at them myself, but the pain and the tugging of the skin of my thigh had put me off trying to do the same to the stitches on my palm. My skin had fused to the sutures as it had healed and after tearful nights of attempting to tweeze them out, I decided to approach someone for outside assistance. Now, I didn't know any doctors and I felt that I couldn't go to the hospital because they would ask far too many questions for my liking. Also, any adults I knew would probably freak out worse than I did so that left only one real viable choice when it came to helping me remove the pesky stitches.

Blue, I remembered, was always kind of squeamish, but she was the only one that I trusted and had the added benefit of being the only person who knew about my injuries.

It was a night of pain, cookies and vomit.

Blue threw up. She threw up a lot.

So our weeks continued, mostly in the way they had done before our encounter in the diner with the added complication of me constantly looking over my shoulders for any sign of demons.

This was soon interrupted, however, by the sudden and, to be honest, quite alarming news that Sam's Uncle was holding some sort of small talent show in his bar downtown and Sam, in his infinite wisdom had entered us… without our consent.

Let's just say I was surprised Blue didn't strangle him then and there.

That is how I found myself sat on a black plastic chair in the back two weeks later, retuning my guitar for the fourth time in twenty minutes as Blue paced nervously in front of me and Sam sat in the corner softly swearing to himself.

It had come as a shock, really, to wake up on the day with the knowledge that we were gonna be playing that night in front of strangers. Blue had called me around two minutes after I had woken up telling me that she wasn't going through with it and Sam and I could burn in hell for ever convincing her that it was a good idea. Suffice to say, Sam and I were forced to go to her home and pry her out of her room.

She had calmed down.

Mostly.

She turned to the back door again, chewing her lip. "Don't even think about it," I muttered and she grudgingly began her pacing once more.

The whole backroom was barely lit, much like Sam's garage and I guessed that's why I felt I still had a semblance of a grip on my sanity. I felt safe in Sam's garage and while this was so far out of my comfort zone it was almost sitting on a cactus, it was close enough that I could close my eyes and go to my happy place. However, with every second that passed, my happy place was fading as if it were water I was trying to keep in my cupped hands. I could feel it trickling away like the sand in an hour glass.

Sam's uncle stepped into the backroom and gave us one big gleaming smile. "How we doing?"

"I think I'm gonna be sick," I heard Sam grumble from his hideaway in the corner and his uncle laughed, uproariously.

"Yeah, a lot of the other acts have said that tonight," Sam's uncle said, jovially. "Don't sweat it big guy; just remember, everyone's in the same boat. Everyone's gonna go up on that stage and perform their hearts out just to be judged and perhaps mocked by my regulars."

"You're not helping, dude."

Sam's uncle left us then, chucking to himself as he shut the door behind him with a click, only to poke his head around the corner a second later, grinning like a fool. "Five minutes and you're up, kids."

As we traipsed onstage five minutes later, I felt the last of my nerve leave as I felt the scorching overhead lights fall onto me. The large function room that took up the majority of Sam's uncle's bar was buzzing with chatter, low and indistinct but enough to set my nerves on edge. Blue walked on alongside me, spinning one of her drumsticks expertly between her fingers and looking like a duck taking to water for the very first time and finding that it was precisely what it was meant for. Sam and I exchanged an equally impressed look at one another before we turned to the patrons that had collected inside.

The bar itself was panelled in a not-very-convincing, knock-off mahogany, carpeted in dark moss-like green and boasted the traditional smells of smoke and stale beer that you would commonly encounter in a bar like this but with the added tacky decoration that seemed to be mandatory for any bar-held talent show.   "Hey," I cleared my voice in front of the microphone and internally shuddered at how awful it was to hear myself being echoed through the hall. "We're Scrawl. I'm Erika, on vocals and guitar, this is Sam on bass and Blue on drums! Thanks for coming and I hope you enjoy our music as much as we do!"

As it was a talent show, we were only allowed to play one, five-minute song and we only had the once chance to do so, so we chose the one we all knew like the backs of our hands. The first song we ever wrote together. *Fire*.

It only took a couple of seconds. At first, I was terrified but with the old familiar bite of fingers on strings I felt myself shift back into what I once knew. I could close my eyes and pretend I was back in Sam's garage. I was able to centre myself and only focus upon the very real guitar in my hands and, if only for a moment, forget everything to do with demons and it worked. For a time, I was able to forget everything that had happened over the last couple of weeks and just be *here* with my friends and the belief that my music was an escape had never been truer despite the fear and the overwhelming heat.

After our set there was due to be a fifteen-minute break where the judges were to deliberate and so I took this opportunity to escape the stifling heat and bolt for the nearest fire exit that all but spilled me into the alley that ran alongside Sam's uncle's bar. I gasped in relief as I felt the cold early-spring night air sting my over-hearted skin and bite my exposed arms and legs but I discovered very quickly that the sensation was more pleasant than painful. I sucked in deep soothing breaths of cold oxygen and closed my eyes, leaning against the brick wall just to the left of the fire exit that had just slammed shut behind me.

I was too relieved that I was able to breathe to care.

I also didn't particularly care when I heard the fire exit open again next to me about a minute later and felt rather than heard someone join me in the cold night air. I guess I didn't particularly mind because I assumed it was one of the guys come to find breathable oxygen like I had but the voice that followed their arrival, while familiar, did not belong to Sam or Blue and my eyes snapped open in alarm.

"I heard you've been looking for me, kid."

"Shion?" I gasped, pushing myself from the wall and turning to face the quarry I had been seeking for the last three weeks. "What the hell are you doing here?"

He hadn't changed – at all – since the last time I saw him outside Skye's apartment. His blonde hair was still sitting messily upon his head, encroaching into his vision but not so far that I could barely see his incredibly dark eyes. He wore the same black blazer over the top of a dark red t-shirt that he had worn the first time I met him and the same uninterested expression though I was starting to believe that he cared more about what was going on than he liked people to see. His exchange with Skye proved that at least.

"Dan dragged me here. He came to support Blue and I just *had* to come with him. Think he's gonna take her home too," he raised his eyebrows in an 'if you know what I mean' fashion as he continued, "I think they're after some *alone time*." It didn't take a genius to figure out what he was getting at.

"*Way* too much information there Shi, thanks." I wrinkled my nose and rested against the wall again, relaxed enough to once again enjoy the cool air. Now that I felt like I was approaching a kind of human temperature, the air was starting to feel a little too cold, especially considering my attire but I definitely did not want to go back inside just yet. Besides, I wasn't going anywhere until I'd wheedled some information from Shion.

His voice was flat when he responded. "*Shi*?"

"What? It's your nickname, right?" I opened one eye to see one of his eyebrows was raised in question. "Don't you like it?"

"Didn't think we knew each other well enough to have nicknames... *Ez*."

I wrinkled my nose again. "Nope, I don't like that; don't call me that."

His eyes twinkled. "Too bad... *Ez*."

Suddenly regretting bringing up the whole nickname thing, I changed the subject. "We can make it home ourselves you know?"

Shion scoffed at that, "are you still saying things like that? Apparently you should know... a bit more about the dangers of wandering around alone nowadays huh?" he asked me in a disbelieving tone.

He knew about the diner.

Which not only meant that either Skye or Blue had told him what had happened there, but also that he understood the significance of that – that demons had a habit of showing up and attacking my friends and me – and for some reason, that irritated the *hell* out of me.

"God *damn* it!" I pushed myself from the wall, throwing my arms down in frustration as I marched to the centre of the alleyway. I turned to glare at Shion. "Why does everyone know everything about... *everything* that is going on around here and all seem to agree that it's the best idea to keep me out of the goddamn loop? Even my best friend is acting like she's keeping things from me and... And all I want is to be on the same damn page! Because I'm missing half the story here! Is that so much to ask?"

A flash of emotion crossed Shion's face and I was relieved to identify it as sympathy.

"I don't know what you want me to say, Erika..."

I looked up at the sky before letting out a deep breath, watching it fog up the air in front of me. "You know what's going on, don't you?"

"Yes."

"But you can't tell me anything." It was not a question; I knew the answers before I had even opened my mouth.

"No." He frowned.

"Then point me in the direction of someone who can." My eyes met his then and I found myself glaring, even though I was pretty sure none of it was directly his fault.

Shion's face darkened and he turned to the side a little, lifting his head to follow my previous line of sight to the black starless sky above us. "Do you know how much trouble I'd get into?"

"I'm just asking for an address." I moved forward to where he stood and reached out hesitantly to lay a hand on his arm. "That's all."

For the first time since I had met him, Shion smiled though it held no humour at all and I was struck by the intense self-depreciation I saw there. "So you *did* want my number to get close to Skye."

Guilt hit me like a battering ram. "I just don't know what else to do! I'm out of options here! I'm sick of being kept in the dark! Just help me find Skye, Shion," I pleaded, holding onto his jacket. "Please. He's the only one who will tell me what the hell is going on."

"I really-" whatever Shion was about to say then was cut off when the fire door next to us burst open and Daniel poked his head around the corner.

"Hey Erika, they're about to- oh!" Dan grinned when he saw us and Shion dropped his head. "Sorry... I didn't realise you guys were out here together. They're about to announce the winners so you should head back inside. Shion, you okay to take Erika and Sam home when it's done?"

Shion gave a lazy two-fingered salute as he stared at the ground. He seemed to be thinking, quickly. "Got it. I'll take them home after."

We didn't win.

That didn't surprise me.

What *did* surprise me was that the act that *did* win was a ventriloquist who just made his dummy tell wood-related puns to an obviously extremely drunk crowd. I also suspected the judges in their sobriety.

Outside, Shion motioned Sam and I toward what I assumed was his car – a large black jeep smeared with mud – but while Sam followed without question, proceeding to help him pack our amps and guitars, I hesitated. I peered back to where Blue was standing by Dan's car, looking over at me with a small smile on her face.

"Dan and I are heading out for a drive first thing tomorrow," Blue told me when I made my way over to her, grabbing my hands and talking almost too fast for me to understand her. She glanced up at her boyfriend who was leaning against the hood of his car, yawning and stretching but then she turned back to me and all but beamed. "A well-done present for playing so well this evening so I'm spending the night at his and then... who knows."

I winked at her. "Have fun," my whisper elicited a cheeky little giggle from her lips and she winked at me in response before then hopping over to Daniel excitedly who then wrapped an arm around her and escorted her, needlessly, to the passenger side of his car.

God, I needed a boyfriend.

Sam offered me a quizzical look upon my return to which I just replied with the exact same wink I had used on Blue. His confusion deepened, but I just laughed and clambered into the passenger side of the car Shion had just unlocked.

Sam passed out pretty soon after Shion had pulled off from the curb and so once again, Shion and I were left alone, but we didn't speak and the silence was kind of uncomfortable. I sort of felt like he was going to refuse to help me when we were interrupted by Daniel back at the bar and so I was too scared to say anything in case it brought it up again. It wasn't exactly a rational way of thinking as in if he wasn't about to refuse me, there was no way he could tell me if we weren't going to talk about it now, but then I guess I wasn't a rational kind of girl. I was more of a do first and think about why I shouldn't have done that later kinda girl. Not much in the way of a thought process.

I found myself looking at Shion though as we made our way toward Sam's place. Through the unruly blonde hair that flopped over them, I could see the concentration in his dark eyes as he drove; completely different from Skye, who looked so free and easy when he was behind the wheel of his Buick Electra but the Shion's attentiveness made me feel so much safer.

"You're staring," Shion muttered. "It's off-putting. Carry on and I might crash, killing us all in a big jeep-sized ball of flame."

Maybe not.

I turned my head to the view the dark scenery.

Sam woke up about thirty seconds before we arrived outside his place and offered us both a sleepy goodbye before almost falling from the door and only just catching himself to stop a potentially painful collision with the floor.

With a chuckle, Shion opened his own door and slipped out, meeting Sam around the back of his jeep to help shift Sam's bass and amp. After making sure that Sam was okay as he ambled sleepily up the path to his home and let himself in, Shion leapt back up to the driver's seat, buckled in and pulled off from the curb to begin the almost pointless car journey to my own home.

Instead of parking at the curb as he had done with Sam, Shion pulled his jeep into the unused drive and engaged the handbrake, leaving the engine going and the high beams glaring before pulling the handle and opening his driver's side, hopping out ahead of me to fetch my own instrument and amp. When I joined him, he handed over my guitar but continued to hold my amp, jerking his head over to my porch in a clear instruction to go ahead.

"Thank you," I muttered.

We carried my things in silence, but it was far more comfortable than the quiet that had beset us in the car on the way home though I couldn't pinpoint why. I lagged behind him a little, my eyes fixed on the back of his shaggy blonde head which, I realised, was kinda high up. Shion was... *kinda tall* and that sort of surprised me. Maybe I was just short because all of a sudden, everyone seemed to tower over me; Shion, Skye... was there anyone who didn't make me feel like a total shortass?

He lowered my amp to the wooden decking of the porch, nodded once to me and then moved to jog straight down the steps again. Ignoring his apparent desperation to get away from me, I reached into my pocket for my keys.

"Erika, wait." I turned to see that his jeep was still idling in my driveway with the driver's side open and my porch illuminated by the glaring headlights. He hadn't managed to get far as he was still on my porch, standing one step down, half-turned toward me with his hands shoved into his jeans pockets and a considering look on his face.

"What is it, Shi?" I flashed him a winning smile. "A girl shouldn't be out after curfew; don't you know?"

He seemed to struggle with his words for a second as he retraced his steps to be closer to where I stood at my door. "Look, you... you're a pretty cool chick, you know, for a kid... and I just..." He looked down at the ground for a second before glancing back up at me. "Well, I wanna do right by you, you know? So..." He pulled a small notebook and a pen from his pocket. With a flourish he jotted down a few lines, ripped the page off and pressed it into my palm.

"What's this?" I glanced at the note to see the name of a place and an address. "The Poisoned Apple?"

"It's a club. Go there this Friday night and you'll find him."

A club? Was this guy actually being serious? "You know I'm underage, right?" I objected with a frown.

A smirk passed onto his features, but I had a feeling he was attempting to hold back laughter. "Don't worry... They never check." He thought for a second while scratching his jaw. "Just promise me you won't get yourself killed looking for that bastard; it would be an awful shame to lose you. Shinanai de, Erika."

I watched him as he turned and jogged down the steps again, offering me a wave once he had reached his car. I continued to watch him even as he reversed from my drive, turned and his taillights disappeared amongst the shrubberies and low-hanging branches of the trees dotted at the edge of my yard.

The Poisoned Apple, huh? Was it just me or was that name kind of fitting?

VI
Fire and Dancers

The Poisoned Apple was a club near the industrial estate that abutted my hometown. I had made a point to avoid that particular location through my years of growing up as it was one of the most disreputable areas and the clubs that had popped up there, even more so.

Frankly, I wasn't surprised that Skye had a habit of lurking there.

In the days leading up to the Friday that Shion had outlined, I pretty much obsessed over my plan. Blue and Sam weren't a part of it, of course, as they would absolutely kill me if they knew I was thinking of even going *near* the industrial estate on my own. So, it turned out I had to figure it all out for myself, which I was starting to get kind of good at doing.

Well, nearly all of it... I didn't completely believe Shion when he told me that the bouncers at the club wouldn't ask me for some sort of identification and so I had decided I would try to dress a little more grown up for the occasion and show a little skin.

Believe me, it was kind of hard to ask for fashion advice from Blue without clueing her in on what I was doing.

I told her I wanted to change my look and apparently, according to what she had thrown at me from her wardrobe following my description of what I wanted, that look was 'Prostitute'.

It was the Thursday before my planned ambush of Skye and I was standing in front of her wearing a small leather miniskirt and a shimmery pink top with no back, but four crossing flimsy threads keeping the thing together. I looked good, sure, but I also looked like I'd give it to anyone who offered me a kind word and a drink and not necessarily in that order.

Not a good look for a proud seventeen-year-old virgin really.

"You look..." Blue was chewing on her nail, her forehead creased in worry as I turned side to side in front of her. Blue herself was wearing light blue pyjamas covered in happy little teddy bears and was sitting on her bed surrounded by piles of not yet tried and rejected clothes.

"I look like a hooker," I finished for her.

"A pretty hooker..."

I started to peel off the top in irritation as I complained, "a hooker is a hooker, Blue, that's all there is to it."

"I don't know why you're worrying about all this anyway." She lay back on her bed a little and flung another top at me, this one black and made of so much more material than the pink shimmery abomination yet was *still* far too skimpy for my liking. "You've never wanted a change of look before..."

I flung the pink thing at her and started to weave my way through a black scrap of fabric Blue had obviously favoured next. "Is it bad if I wanna look good?" I asked her, trying to figure out which of the slits in the sleeves was the actual hole my arm was supposed to rest.

"Normally, a change in look is about a guy."

I snorted. "More like a lack of a guy." Having finally figured out the first sleeve, I moved to the second.

"What about Shion? Dan said you seemed to be getting *chummy* after the gig."

I tried to ignore the insinuation in her tone as I forced my head through what I assumed was the right hole, noting that she seemed to *finally* believe the story that I was *actually* interested in him now. Shion had done me a solid by telling me where Skye was going to be and it wasn't exactly anything that I had any reason to expect from him especially given the fact that he would apparently get in trouble for giving me any information at all.

What begged answering though was *who* would he be in trouble with? He had confirmed that he was involved with this whole *demon* deal but without the information I was going to attempt to wheedle from Skye, that didn't really tell me much. Somehow, though, I knew it had something to do with the *Agency* that was mentioned but again, I was no closer to figuring out exactly what that meant as I was when I had first heard the words.

"Well?" I realised I hadn't answered her question and was standing there with that skimpy black top wrapped around my chest, but I hadn't moved to pull it any further down my body. I guessed I looked rather stupid and to cover my embarrassment and hopefully change the subject, I stuck my tongue out at her and pulled the fabric the rest of the way down before turning to the mirror Blue had liberated from her mother's room.

I still didn't like the skirt, that much I was certain of, but the top I had believed to be questionable and was now wearing was another matter altogether.

Although it was originally designed to cover my whole torso and arms down to the wrists, it had looked like whatever designer had gotten its hands on it had done so with a pair of scissors, glitter and a whole lot of vigour. Wide slashes purposefully split the fabric down the arms, flashing my pale skin in strips of varying sizes and dusted with crystalline gems and glitter so it shimmered in the light. On the torso, more focused lines were cut along the ribs and collarbones, slanted down and vaguely pointed as if literally following the form of my bones. The back was crosshatched with black, clingy, sturdy fabric and met one solid strip in the middle, covering my spine.

"Oh wow." Blue sat up straight on her bed. "Look at you! I could never pull that thing off, but it totally suits you."

I turned slightly in the mirror, viewing the garment from all angles, even turning to view the back while craning my neck over my shoulder. "I like it."

"Good! It would work with a pair of jeans too!" She beamed. "Not too smart and not too casual!"

Well, at least I knew what I was going to wear.

Friday night came quickly after that and although I was a little nervous about being an underage girl sneaking into a club, I could barely contain my excitement at the same time or wait patiently until eleven o'clock when it was time to catch a cab to the industrial estate. Clad in the tricky black top, dark blue denim shorts and knee-high black leather boots that were buckled several times way up to the grey fur trim, I felt like I had managed to assemble some sort of outfit that would not immediately tag me as underage. Coupled with my ink-black hair straightened within an inch of its life and a light dusting of makeup, I felt almost confident. Maybe I was worrying too much.

I just had so much riding on this.

The Poisoned Apple was situated in an old converted factory like many of the other clubs that had popped up over the years and while the outside looked like any of the other large abandoned buildings that dotted the estate, it had one large marking that set it apart from the others. A huge purple apple on a hazy green background had been painstakingly spray-painted onto the red brick wall with the word 'Poison' all but *tattooed* on the apple's shining skin, announcing to anyone of a certain disposition that were looking for a good time that this was definitely the place to find it. The shutter doors had been torn out completely and replaced with a set of double doors that had been sectioned off with tacky red, twisted cord that hung between metal stumps that were trying their hardest to be gold, yet had absolutely no one fooled.

Even though I was still a few yards from the place itself, I could feel the bass of the music practically *ripping* through the ground beneath me, shaking up my legs and reverberating through my insides with a sensation that was not wholly unpleasant. It reminded me of Sam's bass guitar when he pushed his amp up to full whack.

As I reached it, I was relieved to see that the line for the club only consisted of a few people: a guy that looked to be in his mid-twenties smoking by the door and wearing so much white I could barely look at him and a couple that seemed far too focused on trying to suck each other's faces off to notice what was going on around them.

The bouncer at the door barely glanced at me as I arrived and unhooked the red cord in front of him, jerking his chin toward the door so I could pass into the club. Apparently, Shion had been right as he didn't seem to even consider my age and I darted past him and into the gloom before he could change his mind.

For the first few feet, the dim area in front of me was pretty much deserted but I soon found that the further I ventured into the gloom, the more people I seemed to bump into. Soon I found myself all but fighting my way down the suddenly crowded corridor, squeezing in between sweaty bodies, trying not to breathe too much as I felt the stench of stale alcohol, old smoke and urine sticking to my heated skin. From what I could tell, the walls used to be a light, cheerful teal but the combined effects of age, graffiti and the misuse at the hands of the regulars had covered the previous colour with a thick layer of grime. Collected obscenities overlapped in unlovely shades but with the low visibility all this morphed into varying degrees of grey and black, muddled with the dizzying effects of the multicoloured strobe and stage lighting from the next room.

The woman handling money at the entrance to the main room, for lack of a better word, glared at me but said nothing. She pursed her pierced lips, took a crumpled bill I had pulled from my pocket and stamped my hand probably with more force than necessary. The next person shuffled forward and I was shoved into another sweaty crush, this one throbbing and pulsing in time with the heavy music that left little room for anything else, be it conversation or even coherent thought. I battled my way through the violent throng toward the bar. I didn't care that I was underage anymore, because now that I was here, all I cared about was my quarry.

The main room was large and even admitting that; it was almost filled to spilling with people, so it was hard for me to breathe the sweat-saturated air that stuck to my skin. Two black staircases were set in the two south corners of the room, leading to a large balcony that circled the whole room and overlooked the stage and dance floor, once again crammed with dancers. My practical side wondered what the hell all these people would do in a fire emergency. The majority of me didn't really care.

"I'm looking for Skye!" I shouted to the barman when I reached him. I didn't know if he heard me properly because he simply pointed to the stage behind me. I blankly looked at the band that, by the looks of things, had completely won over their enthusiastic audience and, not really understanding what the barman meant, I repeated myself. "I'm looking for Skye. Shion said he'd be here tonight!"

The barman pointed again. "On stage!" he bellowed. I frowned and again looked toward the band. It consisted of a bassist, a drummer and two guitarists, one of which was singing and... was also incredibly familiar. I couldn't help but stare. The man who had saved me from demons, who had practically healed before my eyes, was playing guitar and singing like nothing out of the ordinary had ever happened in his life. His hair was plastered to his neck and temples with sweat and his white t-shirt had been drenched to the point where it stuck to his skin and clung to the contours of his chest leaving very little about his form to the imagination. It took me a moment to realise that I was staring with my mouth open so I turned back to the bar, giving myself a minuscule shake.

I resolved to wait. I had come this far, fought through sweaty, drunken sweethearts to get where I sat and I wasn't about to just give up because he was crooning. I ordered a drink and listened, watching the faceless dancers, drinkers and heartbreakers as the drums pounded relentlessly on and before long I actually found myself enjoying the harsh sounds of the live instruments, the surprising sound of Skye's singing. I felt my nerves untangle and my muscles begin to unclench, feeling anonymity wash over me. No one knew me here. I was just a girl at the bar.

Finally, after what felt like hours, the music drew to a close and Skye's voice announced that the band was taking a quick break and that the DJ would play a few tracks in the meantime. I watched Skye swing off the stage and disappear. I instantly panicked, not being able to see him but after a few breathless minutes, I saw him break out of the crowd and amble to where I sat, resting at the bar right next to me. He gasped for some water and, with bottle in hand, began to take in his surroundings. He glanced at me once and then allowed his eyes to travel back toward the rows of bottles of assorted spirits that lined the back wall behind the bar when he froze and his head snapped back to me. After a moment of stunned silence, he sighed.

"Erika. What the hell are you doing here?" He looked at the drink in my hand. "Aren't you underage?"

I lifted my glass. "Apple juice. Though if you want to talk about under-age drinking, there's a group of sixteen-year-olds over there, sharing a glass of cider between them. If this place gets busted by the cops, I'm going to be the *least* of anyone's worries."

Skye stared. "What are you doing here?" he repeated.

"I came to find you."

"Why?"

I set my drink on the bar. "Demons pop out of nowhere and attack me and my friends... And you appear, always in the nick of time, to drive them off. You once said you're protecting somebody and I guess you won't allow innocent bystanders to get injured so I figure that the safest place to be is wherever you are. Plus, don't forget you still owe me an explanation and this time, I'm not leaving 'til I get one."

He leaned heavily on the bar, still looking at me. "It still amazes me how you are still so hell-bent on learning more; you know? Most people would've wanted to forget."

"What do you mean?"

He opened his mouth to reply but whatever he said was suddenly drowned out by loud, crackling music, now that the inept DJ had finally figured out how to work his shoddy equipment. He glared at the young man at the previously unmanned booth and then shook his head and grasped my arm, yanking me from where I stood and through the crowd that was beginning to flood to the bar to refuel while the band was elsewhere. We had just made it past the stalls and were crossing in front of the stage when a pretty blonde woman in an unbelievably tight-fitting red dress stopped dead in front of us.

"Oh my god, it's *actually* Skye Carter!" She stepped right into Skye's personal space as she spoke, all but pushing me out of the way with her body, but I felt Skye's pressure on my arm increase just in case. "Wherever have you been recently? I've missed you! It's *almost* like you've been avoiding me."

My rescuer cocked his head to one side. "Oh, come on, how could I ever avoid you?" I was surprised at the softness of his voice and the way he formed his words that made him seem like he was automatically placating her before she had even managed to get angry. This guy... was something else.

"I don't know, but it's almost been a week since I saw you... You could never get enough of me before... Have you gotten bored of me already?" I watched her heavily made-up face pout and I decided, right then and there, that I did not like her. Was she his girlfriend? There had been no evidence of another soul at his apartment so I kind of assumed he was single.

"Just been busy, you know how it is." He motioned to the stage with a flippant hand to where his band mates – men I was sure I had never seen before – were checking over their equipment.

She pouted. "It's been a while since you played here either..." For the first time since she had stopped us, the woman seemed to notice me and her eyes narrowed in what looked like annoyance, her voice suddenly turning scathing. "Oh! So, you've been cradle snatching then have you, Skye? I didn't think you went for kids."

I objected before I actually knew what the hell I was objecting against. "Hey! I'm not a kid!" I wasn't even sure what the hell was going on; only that this *woman* had a direct line to a twitch over my right eye and that was really beginning to bug me.

"Now, now... Don't start any fights! The night is still so young." Skye continued to attempt to calm the woman down, despite her growing annoyance. "She's my mom's piano student and I know for a fact she's underage so I'm just taking her somewhere she won't make any trouble. So... just for now why don't you go grab a drink, wait at the bar and I'll catch up with you after the set's done, okay?"

"You promise?" she all but purred at him. I must admit, I was shocked at how quickly her mood changed – Skye wasn't that convincing surely? "You don't have any other dates tonight?"

"Scout's honour." Apparently, he *was* because she seemed satisfied with that and stepped forward suddenly, traced her lips over Skye's once and disappeared into the meandering hubbub of the dancers around us. Skye's forehead was creased as he watched her go but before I could question it, he yanked me forward and toward a small back door that was blocked by a burly bald bouncer. He grinned at Skye and kicked open the door for us, which led into a small sound-proofed room. A practice room, I realised as I watched Skye step over a broken guitar and make his way to one of three orange plastic chairs in the corner of the room.

Sitting down, he motioned for me to join him.

Once I had sat, it suddenly occurred to me that I was alone in a soundproofed room with a grown man. A musician, no less. No wonder that bouncer was grinning like that.

"Right," Skye sighed, "the first thing you need to understand... is that humanity has this one awful habit... which makes it kinda hard for them to notice the existence of demons: Humans... rationalises things. They see things they don't understand, that scare them, and they twist and change it in their heads so it makes more sense. They see a demon eating a corpse and instead of trusting their eyes, they believe it's nothing but some sort of drug-crazed lunatic turned cannibal. Still horrific but just enough of a change to let them believe that their world is still theirs, that science rules and demons, magic and monsters don't exist."

He paused and eyes sliced into mine, but I had no idea what to say to that so I just murmured, "huh."

Sensing my initial confusion, Skye rolled his eyes and continued. "You, however, believe without question that demons exist. You have from the get-go."

"Hey, I know what I saw."

"Exactly. And that's what sets you apart from everyone else. Humans believe that the only demons that are real are the ones in here." He tapped two fingers to his temple. "And that's mostly through religion and only now. Demons used to be more common than they are now, but they were forgotten."

"How could people forget something like that?"

Skye shrugged. "Complacency... Human nature... Ignorance. A sudden rise in intelligence and the demons began to hide, disguising their kills, lurking in shadows, keeping their drones in check... By their ignorance, humanity gave demonkind a chance to disappear and they took it, leading to only halfbreeds and... quick girls... being able to really see them."

"So that's why Sam forgot what he saw."

He winced a little. "He was given a helping hand..."

"You're gonna have to explain that to me."

Skye fiddled with a loose thread on his fingerless gloves. "Sometimes when weaker-minded humans are directly involved with things like demons... it's impossible for them to forget and if nothing is done, it can slowly drive them insane. There are people around who specialize in methods to give the survival instinct in their minds a little push in the right direction... That's what happened to your friend. He was seen to be freaking; steps were taken. He'll be fine."

"Brainwashing then... and I assume that it's all done by the same people spinning these cover-up stories? Gang-related incidents and crap like that?"

He smirked. "Once again, Erika... you're quick. It's why your own mind hasn't been tampered with. Your friend also... there are people who can see what they see and deal with it. It's rare, but it happens."

I thought for a moment. I didn't like it, but it all seemed to make some sort of sense and I couldn't really fault him. I pressed on. "So where do demons hide? You make it sound like they're pretty common but before the diner, I'd never seen them before."

"They rarely attack out in the open like they did in that place... It's why I was so unprepared the first time." He ran his hands through his hair black hair; he looked tired. "But when they do hide, they do so right under our noses. High demons are able to disguise themselves in large crowds, hunting in secret... Any mysterious death in a place like this, it's usually them."

"So places like this?" I found myself looking around the room. "Is that why you play here?"

He smirked. "We play here because we like it here. It's one of the few places where we won't get bottles thrown at us. Not everything I do is connected to demons."

"Just most of it."

His grin grew. "Right." He stood up and I felt myself tense, suddenly hyper-aware of everything he did, but instead of approaching me as I feared, he moved to the door. He paused just as his fingers brushed the handle and his eyes met mine, his smile fading a little around the edges and somehow becoming the saddest expression I had ever seen. "Just stick around, Erika. You're right, you're safest wherever I happen to be but remember that it's still dangerous... Especially in places like this. It could get hairy out there," and he left, closing the door behind him.

I knew that his words were more restricting than they sounded, especially when coupled with his actions. When he was telling me to stick around while leaving me alone in this empty room meant exactly that: Stick around; don't leave this room. I knew that it was my own choice to seek him out, but there were too many questions to just forget everything I had witnessed. He was also the only one who I trusted to give me a proper answer as the other person involved in all this demon nonsense seemed to delight in cryptic riddles and the frustrated expression I had no doubt he incited from me. Not like he did it on purpose, though, I remembered.

As I was alone and it was fairly quiet thanks to the soundproofing, I stayed sat on my orange plastic chair and took stock. It was kind of a relief to know that whatever had happened to Sam had been done to save his mind and wasn't just me going crazy, but I *was* still worried about what this meant for him. If he went all weird whenever anything around him reminded him of demons, then it meant we would have to stop talking about them in front of him. This was a problem, as I had a strong feeling Blue was kind of involved and would find out about my extra-curricular activities here. It was going to be kind of difficult when she pulled me up on it. It was weird, really, that I would be able to talk to Blue more than Sam because it was usually the three of us together without secrets, especially as I'd known Sam a lot longer.

It made me a little sad.

Once again, though, I had another person, someone that *knew* something, that acknowledged that demons were real, fair enough it was the same person as before, but it helped me centre my belief a little. It made me feel safer, being around people who knew what was happening rather than feeling around in the dark on my own though I found myself wondering if that was really smart? Skye wasn't *human*. He had healed right in front of me. So why wasn't I afraid of him? Why did I trust him?

I jumped a little as the ground began to buzz again, along with the bass I could only just hear, so I knew Skye was back on stage.

Again, it had surprised me, watching him play for a crowd that was so *enthusiastic* about the music that they heard. It made my own show with my best friends in that broken-down bar seem kind of pathetic in comparison but even more grounding than that was how *normal* he seemed.

As he had only really turned up when I needed help, Skye had an *otherworldly* feel to him that I felt was just for me. However, seeing so many people respond to him and even the woman kissing him, it just made me realise that he was *more* than just a part of the world I was trying to see. He was *more* than just a man who fought demons and saved me from getting my guts ripped out by them; he had a life and was a person.

It almost made me feel bad for hunting him down relentlessly.

Almost.

I leaned against the chair and looked up at the cracked gray ceiling and the light bulb that hung there, leaving strange burned coloured patterns on my vision when I tried to look anywhere else, listening to the bass that was reverberating through the room in a pattern I realised I could follow.

Hang on, I thought, sitting up suddenly and bracing my hands on my knees, *what the hell was I doing?* Was I seriously going to just *sit* in this tiny room just because Skye told me to? Was I really going to just allow him to shut me away when I did something he didn't wholly approve of? Scoffing to myself, I swung myself to my feet and marched to the door Skye had left by only a few minutes before and yanked it open. The bouncer on the other side looked at me but said nothing and I was allowed to step into the hot, sweating mass of bodies and allow the music to wash over me as I made my way back into the main room.

It was clear that I felt better in here with the crowd and the music and the facelessness that had beset me before. Skye's voice cut through the chatter and the music easily and again, I felt better hearing him and knowing he was close by.

I continued to weave my way through the crowd, thinking that I'd make my way to the bar so that I could ambush him before he went off to meet *her* because, sorry lady, my questions were more important than you getting some. I tried not to feel smug about that as I glanced at the man who had just bumped into me, suddenly.

His eyes were wide and glazed as he stared at, though not really seeing, me, the whites flashing strangely in the multicoloured strobe lighting and his jaw was hanging open, expelling oozing black fluid from between his lips. Wet, hot drops dotted my arm which he had suddenly grabbed a hold of and while I, horrified, tried to yank my arm from him with little success, my slight force instead caused him to stumble and fall straight toward me.

He knocked me completely off my feet and I cried out when I hit the sticky ground, and again when I felt his suddenly limp body fall across me and even though he wasn't huge, I still had no hope of shifting him from me on my own. He continued to dribble the black liquid over my shoulder and neck as he put his whole weight on my squirming body. "Get off!" I screamed out loud, attempting to push his chest with the hands he had trapped under him. "Seriously! Dude, get *off*!"

"Get off her, man, you're scaring her!" One of the party-goers, a tall blonde man, who had seen the guy all but pass out on me reached down and took his shoulder in hand, giving a strong tug. "How much you had to drink anyway?" He was shouting to be heard over the music, but the guy didn't respond and only lay there on top of me. Fortunately, thanks to the aid of the bystander, my arms were free and I was able to help roll him away as I scrambled backwards as far as I could manage without being trampled.

Now that he was on his side and I was able to view him properly, I could see that his eyes were still wide open but unseeing, and the dark red fluid that I wrongly saw as black was still seeping from his mouth. It spilled onto the chequered floor, joining with sickening slowness to the large pool that was all but pouring from the gigantic chunk missing from his abdomen, staining the front of his t-shirt a dark and disturbing red.

Blood.

My scream shot through the room, though getting lost in the music and the chatter that was bubbling up around us nearer the bar on the way, so no one really noticed exactly what had occurred. My would-be helper stood back in shock and his eyes went wide as he realised what I had only a few seconds after me. "HOLY SHIT!" He screamed. "He's *dead*!"

No sooner were the words out of his mouth when a grotesquely familiar grey form leapt from where it had been perching on a shadowed part of the bar behind the blonde rescuer and landed nimbly, on his back. My scream rose in pitch and volume as the creature lowered its horned head to hiss at me before, quicker than my eyes could see, it swung its arm around and savagely ripped its claws into the soft skin of his throat and pulled the flesh from bone, shrieking in what sounded like victory. My voice was gone as I had no choice but to watch, helplessly, as his blood instantly sprayed from the wound and rained upon me and the suddenly screaming bystanders.

Without staying to watch him die, I turned and scuttled back the way I had originally come, slipping and sliding while ignoring the screeching that was beginning to rise throughout the room, all erupting from different directions which led me to believe that we were once again under attack. The music had screeched to a stop and I knew Skye was aware of what was going on.

On my hands and knees, I scrambled through the suddenly dashing legs of the party-goers as they fled for the fire exits and the main corridor they had to come down to enter before I saw my opportunity and leapt to my feet. The strobe lights continued to flash and I couldn't see a single soul on the stage where the band had been only moments before. Instantly my eyes were scanning the panicking crowd for Skye but, to no surprise, I couldn't see him.

Guiltily, I remembered that I was supposed to be in that practice room, laying low.

Oops.

I resolved to make my way over there in the hope I might bump into him on the way and I practically pushed my way through the crowd to avoid the fleeing public, heading toward the back wall where the white door had been, guarded by the burly bouncer.

Only, I didn't get that far. I didn't need to. Just a few meters from the wall, I spotted him standing in the middle of a churning crowd of escaping people, holding a demon off the ground by its throat.

He seemed to be interrogating it. "Where the hell *is she*?" I heard him hiss to the creature. It only rasped as the pressure on its throat increased and dug its claws further into Skye's right arm which was dripping with blood.

"Little giiiiiirl," hissed the creature, still managing to sound smug even in the situation it was in. "Too far away now... Never coming home... Her blood tasted sweet... Sweet and precious." The thing gurgled deep in its throat in what I assumed was a laugh and I saw Skye twitch, his grip, if possible, increasing.

"Do not *lie* to me!" He growled. "I would *know* if you'd killed her so don't try to fool me, you piece of shit. You have *no* idea who you're messing with."

"Skye!" Upon hearing my voice, my constant rescuer's eyes darted to where I stood and then narrowed. With one impossibly swift movement, he pulled a blade from some hidden sheath at his waist and flicked it upwards into the demon's throat without even a second of hesitation. Instantly, the thing dropped its claws from the arm holding its throat but then raised them to weakly attack the gloved hand with the knife, black blood spilling from under Skye's fingers.

I couldn't tear my eyes from him. I'd seen him kill - however temporarily - demons before but nothing like this. His eyes that were now upon me were empty, totally devoid of anything I recognised as human and, for the first time, I realised something that should have been obvious from the get-go.

This man was dangerous.

"Don't you do *anything* anyone tells you to do?" He roared at me, anger flashing into his eyes and removing the vision of emptiness I had seen there. "I tell you to stay in that goddamn room and, oh look! *Here you are*! *Covered in blood*!" He yanked his blade from the demon's neck and it crumpled to the floor in a heap of limbs and bone.

"It's not mine. Besides you didn't *actually* say-" I started to object, but Skye cut across me at the same time as grabbing my wrist and yanking me toward him as he marched toward the bar.

"You know what I meant so just shut up and behave yourself for five minutes!" He shoved me behind the wooden partition and shoved the slippery blade he was holding into my hand, bending to pull another from the inside of his boot. When he looked at me next, it was a full-on glare and I shrank back from his fire. "*Stay. There.* I will be back. I'm going to clear the way out."

I watched him dash off and deliver a swift punch to a demon that was skittering to get away from him, twisting with impossible speed to slash its grey back with the blade he had held in his expert grip.

I ducked down behind the bar like he suggested and surveyed my new surroundings quickly to get my bearings and attempt to identify a quick escape route if one of the demons found me here.

That was when I saw her. At first, I only noticed the flash of red of her dress and I assumed it was just another faceless corpse of one of the unfortunate party goers that had hidden behind the bar when the attack first hit. It only took me a few seconds after that to realise that I recognised her, the knife in my hand clattering to the floor in my suddenly too loose grip. Her eyes were wide and staring, tips of her blonde hair drenched with deep red blood that had spilled from the gaping wound in her throat so I didn't have to venture closer to realise that she was dead.

Despite knowing her fate, I crawled over the wooden floor, made sticky and dangerous by the smashed spirit bottles all around, toward where her body was propped up against the wood, ignoring the shrieking and snarling that was still going on around me as I reached out slowly and closed her eyes with gentle fingers.

I met the girl once if you could even call it that and, no, I didn't particularly like her as the first impression wasn't great, but no one deserved a death like this. She appeared to be only a little older than me, twenty-one perhaps and she had *suffered.*

Besides, the way she was staring was starting to freak me out a little.

I stared at her for a while, the way her blood had darkened the tight material of her dress to a sickly sort of brown and pooled a little in the hollow at her throat, staining the small silver chain she wore. Her hands were limp on the ground and small shards of glass were sticking into her skin as if she had moved to protect herself when the bottles above had initially fallen from the shelves above. Next to her lay another woman, her face shredded beyond any form of recognition though she still seemed to be gripping the smashed neck of a bottle to ward off any attackers. Obviously, it had been ineffective.

Fighting the urge to vomit I turned away from them both, glancing up and around me, to the shattered doors of the cupboards behind the bar, for somewhere to hide and freak on my own.

"Erika?" I jumped and turned, seeing Skye lean over the bar, searching where he had thrown me only a few moments beforehand. Obviously, clearing the way hadn't gone as well as he'd hoped.

"I'm here."

His head snapped to where my hesitant voice originated. "There's too many of them to risk leaving you here..." His eyes rested on the body I was crouched next to and he swallowed hard, yet no emotion crossed his features. "Didn't I tell you not to move?"

I couldn't speak. I stared up at Skye, the man that was, for the moment, keeping me alive and I just couldn't will myself to respond to him so, and to this day I'm not sure why, I turned my head to stare once more at the two dead women. Looking back, I realised I wasn't feeling anything I was supposed to and the whole situation was beginning to feel awfully far away. This wasn't real. It *couldn't* be real. It wasn't happening. I was dreaming. I was going to wake up safe in my bed having dreamt this whole thing up. It was okay, Erika, just wake up. Wake up. Just wake up. Wake up. Wake up. *Wake up, wake up, wakeupwakeupwakeupwakeupwakeup*

WAKEUPWAKEUP!

"*Erika!*"

His voice snapped me out of my internal screaming and I jerked my head up to meet his worried gaze. I noticed then that my whole body was trembling violently and had I gripped my biceps with both hands as if attempting to embrace myself and keep my whole being together. Skye swore and leapt over the bar easily and grabbed the knife I'd dropped before crawling over to where I sat huddled next to the girls. Carefully, he took my face between his hands.

"I will get you out of here, Erika." I stared into his bright blue eyes as I attempted to comprehend what he was saying to me. "I will get you out alive and in one piece, I promise, you just need to trust me! Do you understand?"

I just stared at him.

"*Erika*! Do. You. Understand?!" I blinked and forcibly yanked myself from where I was teetering on the edge of a complete mental breakdown.

"Okay... If you promise you'll get me out... I'll do what you say," I told him and I saw relief pass his features, despite the weakness of my voice. I cleared my throat and tried again. "Though if I die, I am *so* coming back to haunt your ass."

He smirked and passed me the blade I'd dropped. "Deal. Now let's *go!*"

Grabbing my hand, Skye yanked me forward and we both dashed the length of the bar to rush through the shattered counter door. The main room had emptied of people slightly as most of them were still trying to push through the fire and main exits though there were still stragglers that hadn't been so lucky in the original stampede for the doors and were currently being backed off by snarling, grey, disfigured creatures. I felt my hastily headed off panic rise again as I stared out into what had previously been a party in full swing and was now practically a feasting ground for these *beasts*. They crawled along the walls and the ceiling as they surveyed the carnage their fellows had inflicted, slipping in through the open, overlooked skylights even when it felt like the room just could not take any more horror. They crowded onto the stage, feasting upon corpses and attacking the few members of the former crowd that had turned around to retaliate. Some of them had weapons like Skye's; hook pointed batons, knives and, in one case, even a large ceremonial katana, while some of them used broken bottles and shards of glass like I had at the diner the third time around.

As we skirted around the bar, one of the nearer demons noticed our attempted escape and roared, flecking us with clear spittle before leaping toward Skye, maw agape and fangs sharp.

He kicked the demon in its face and I watched it squeal when it hit the ground. Suddenly, Skye swore as he quickly looked around for an escape route. "*Damn it*! I've never seen anything *like* this! What it is about you?! You're making these demons go *nuts*!"

What the *hell*? "ME? What about me?! I haven't done anything!"

"These demons haven't ever done *anything* like this before you turned up! *Damn*, even for a halfbreed, you're a pain in the ass!"

Halfbreed. I'd heard that word before. "Halfbreed?"

"GAH! It doesn't matter!" Skye pushed me forward, ahead of him a little while crouching down low. "You need to run! Now, while they're distracted."

He was planning on staying. "*I'm not going anywhere*!" I screeched, alerting another two demons to our somewhat sheltered location under one of the metal staircases that led to the balcony above. As they moved to flank us, Skye attacked the one from the right and I moved to face the creature approaching from the left, swinging the blade Skye had given me around in an attempted imitation of what I had seen Skye execute, a potential shining arc of death. It sadly failed when the demon caught my hand with what I supposed was a deep rumbling chuckle. Fortunately, it was not a fatal error as Skye had already dispatched his demon and had turned to aid me, using the distraction to his advantage and creeping around behind it before forcing his blackened knife upwards into the demon's armpit and straight into its heart. It stiffened and fell with a gasp.

Skye then turned to me, eyes flashing. "You're going to get us both *killed* if you stay!"

"I'm going to die if I go alone!" I motioned to the demon he had to kill for me as if to fortify my meaning. "What if you weren't here, huh?"

"*You're the one who came looking for me*! *You* shouldn't be *here*!"

"Well I am and it's a little late now for shoulda-woulda-couldas!"

He drew in a deep frustrated breath through his teeth. "*Why the hell are you so stubborn?*"

"Why the *hell* are you so moronic?! Look around! If I go *anywhere* alone, it would be a miracle if I last three seconds! *I am staying with you!*"

"Don't be so *stupid!*"

"STOP INSULTING ME!"

He reached out suddenly and punched the demon that had been creeping up on me from behind and then moved to swing me around so my back was against the wall to protect me from any more sneak attacks. *"I promised I'd keep you alive."*

A screech interrupted us and he spun on his heel, still covering my body with his own as he realised that, during our argument, we had not only attracted the attention of all nearby creatures but had allowed them to completely surround us.

"Shit," he swore bitterly. "Shit, shit, shit, shit, *shit*." He raised his hand, pulled off his glove and looked down at his palm as if considering something really carefully. His eyes then found mine and he scowled.

"What are we going to do?" I asked him in a shaking voice as the demons continued to approach us. There was no way out. There were too many of them.

"You are going to close your eyes and *trust me.*"

His tone brooked no argument and I instantly ducked down, clamping my hands over my eyes as I heard Skye growl, a strange kind of *whoosh* that I couldn't identify and the sudden chorus of hundreds of demonic voices *screaming* in agony. I could smell the sudden disturbing smell of burning skin and hair and even though my hands, a searing bright light reached my eyes. Hesitantly, I lowered them, peering through my eyelids and lashes and at all I could see of Skye, which was just a black silhouette of a man who was protecting me with his own form, arm thrown out in front of him. On the other side of him was a blazing backdrop of white and blue fire, burning, igniting the world around his hand as if being expelled from his palm. A thin line of blue fire trailed up his arm around the tattoos to encircle the tail of the four-headed snake that in turn surrounded his arm.

With a flash, the fire died down instantly and I saw Skye fall to his knees and over his bent head, I could see that every single demon that had been bearing down on us in a fifteen-foot radius only a few seconds ago had been, quite literally, burned to a crisp. Scorched and twisted carcasses lay smoking on the ground, each frozen in the moment that the blaze from Skye's palm had hit them, forever standing in their horrific poses of pain until they would finally crumble to nothing.

Not even a second later, Skye roared in what sounded like anguish and fell full-bodily to the floor, writhing and twitching but still not dropping his knife which he held in his left hand in a white-knuckled grip.

"SKYE!" I fell to my knees beside him as he convulsed in pain but instantly regretting placing my shaking hand on his right arm, feeling the searing pain of a fresh burn all but sizzle the skin on my palm as he screamed.

Skye's eyes suddenly snapped open and he grabbed my sleeve. I could smell the fabric singeing as he pulled me closer so I would hear him spit out one shaking word. "R...*Run!*"

I shook my head dumbly; he couldn't seriously mean leaving him here.

"...Eri...ka... Re...ally. You..." He winced as he pulled me closer. "Go... the... the others... would... have... not...iced that."

"No..." I whispered. "I won't."

"GO!" He suddenly screamed, using his agony to give himself the power to shout and I almost jumped up to activity in alarm.

"*I'm not leaving you here you stupid bastard!*" I choked out. Making sure to avoid his roasting right arm, I grabbed his left shoulder and hauled him up to a sitting position, ignoring the questions and abject disbelief in his eyes. He was heavier than I had expected, considering his thin frame but I wasn't going to let that, or the way he kept hissing in agony and writhing in my arms, get in my way. I was going to get him to safety even if it killed me.

Once I had managed to haul him to his feet, I gently let him rest against the wall, turning to survey our surroundings as I had missed them the first time around. We were in one of the further corners of the main room, behind one of two metal staircases that led up to the balcony that was now crawling with demon activity. While whatever Skye had done had, for the moment, stalled the demons attack, the window of opportunity to escape wasn't going to last long because, as he had said, the others had noticed the big ball of flame and had started to come over to investigate. I could see one of the fire exits had mostly been cleared of people and only a couple of demons stood in our way so if we moved fast enough, we might be able to get past them and out before the other demons had the sense to take us by a massive charge.

We were totally going to die.

I heard Skye hiss behind me as another wave of pain hit him and I reached out to grab a wad of his shirt and pulled. He stayed on his feet, which was good but wobbled a little so I wrapped my right arm around his torso, pulling his left arm around my shoulders. He buckled once with a shout of a pain but then gritted his teeth hard and set his feet strongly on the floor before turning his head to look at me.

"We're going to run," I told him, breathlessly. "You ready?"

"You're... You're gonna... die... if you ... worry about ... me," he told me, haltingly.

I grinned in something that felt like hysteria. "So it's okay if you die?"

Despite his pain, he mirrored my grin though it looked more like a grimace. "I'm tougher than I look."

"Well, so am I. Let's go! We're running!" and I jerked him into a quick, lumbering gait toward the open fire escape. As we crossed the floor, I saw demons look up from their feasts of dancers which I tried to ignore but dotted here and there were people fighting off the creatures with a collection of weapons I couldn't imagine they would bring here by chance. Gone were those fending off the attacks with broken bottles and shards of glass and the few that I had remembered seeing armed well were still alive, injured maybe but fighting without hesitation. It felt like they weren't defending themselves anymore but were actually leading the assault.

Maybe they were the same kind of person Skye was... maybe they, too, were part of this *Agency* I had heard of before. Skye was still gasping in my arms and I quickened my pace until I was practically dragging him to the door.

We were a few feet away when I felt something seize my ankle and I screamed, turning quickly to see a demon, oozing blood from a deep wound in its chest, crawling on its shaking limbs toward me. It had caught my left ankle in a tight hold, hooking one of its claw-like fingers into one of the buckles to make sure I wasn't going to slip away.

"Duck," Skye muttered in my ear.

I complied, quickly, and Skye instantly pushed his full weight down toward the creature, lifting his less-proficient left wrist slightly so the blade of the knife he still held was pointing straight at the creature next to me. He missed me by about an inch but fell across the demon perfectly, forcing the blade right between its black eyes.

As soon as he rolled off the now dead creature, Skye swore in a scream and buckled again, this time spitting red as he hit the floor on his hands and knees. I was instantly at his side, pulling him up to his feet and all but dragging him away now that I was free.

I couldn't believe it when I felt fresh air touch my face and overheated body and I almost felt relief touch me before a flash of grey on the asphalt in front of me as a demon crossed my path at speed stopped it dead. The existence of a demon outside in the fresh, human air told me that the horror that had presented itself was not just limited to inside the club or inside the diner like my mind was foolishly hoping. Outside offered no protection. This could happen... *anywhere.* They were *everywhere.*

Beside me, I felt Skye dig into his jeans pocket desperately even as I whimpered in fear.

He threw a set of keys at me. "Car... Argh! Car... corner to the left. Go. Now."

I caught the car keys in my left hand and stared at him in alarm. He wanted me to drive his car!? His *car*?!

"I can't drive!" I objected suddenly. I'd had lessons, sure, but I realised I had no proficiency in it as soon as I spent most of the time in the local shrubberies than on any form of road.

"JUST GO!" he roared as another demon leapt at us and he kicked his right leg out, catching it off guard and then making a move himself to push us toward where he remembered he had parked his car. I didn't question anymore and followed Skye's movements as the demon rolled off away, clutching its face, black blood pouring from between its fingers. For the first time, I glanced at Skye's feet as we lumbered down the sloping gravel path and I noticed that he had small razors dug into the rubber soles of his boots. I made a silent note to never piss him off enough that he'd kick me out of frustration.

We turned the corner at a faster pace than I believed possible with Skye's incapacitation. I actually found myself sobbing in relief when I saw the beautiful Buick Electra parked just a few yards away, near the back of the Poisoned Apple and next to a few more cars, assumedly belonging to his fellow band mates. I wondered briefly what had actually happened to them as we reached the car and Skye fell against the passenger side of it, panting and wincing.

Not wasting a second, I darted around the vehicle, unlocked the driver's side, threw myself in and reached over to unlock the passenger side without even missing a beat. Skye slipped onto the seat and slammed the door, letting loose a quick scream of pain as if he finally allowed himself to relax.

"*Drive!*" He choked out the word before yelling in distress once again.

Panicking a little, I shoved the key in the ignition and turned it, feeling relieved when the beast roared into life. Quickly, I threw the car into gear and pressed my foot on the gas with a little more force than was necessary and we all but rocketed up the street.

"*Holy shit!*" Skye yelped, suddenly grabbing onto the leather of his seat. "Just... *don't* crash... my ... CAR!"

I repositioned my grip on the wheel and relinquished my force on the gas pedal for a second. I let myself relax a little, breathing deeply and trying my best not to completely welcome back the panic I had fought so hard to keep at bay. This was fine, this was fine... nothing I hadn't done before. I was okay... I turned the car into the waiting warren of streets to find the exit to the industrial estate, calm on the outside but totally freaking out on the inside.

After about ten minutes, Skye's ragged breathing loosened a little and he slowly turned his head to look at me.

"You can... relax..." he panted still, looking over at my tense expression, "you... You're doing... great."

"What's happening to you?" I demanded, finding myself close to tears now that we were safe. Or safe from demons at least, I couldn't promise I wouldn't kill us both in a car accident.

He winced and then closed his eyes. "Just... backlash... from using my powers. Don't worry... I'll be back to normal... AH!... soon."

"Was it really worth it?" I asked him, trying my best not to sound annoyed.

He chuckled but then grimaced as if he regretted it. "If I hadn't had done it... you... me... we'd... we'd both be demon snacks. I had... no choice." He opened his eyes and smiled at me though I could still see the pain behind it. "Thank you... though, Erika...For getting me out... I didn't... expect that..."

"You were gonna die in there?"

"If... I had to."

I didn't ask anything more. Visions of grey bodies, white bone and crimson blood flashed through my mind for an instant, coupled with my own vision of the very same demons closing in on a weakened Skye, who was unable to move after I'd left him alone. I gripped the steering wheel harder and tried not to sob; how could *any* human *do* that to another person? I would have died to keep him safe... he'd already risked his life to help me so what kind of person would I be if I just left him to die on his own? How was that fair?

Despite my best efforts, we didn't die on the way back to my house and Skye's precious car even got through the ordeal unscathed. I stepped out of the car, pulled Skye from his side and once again, helped him up my pathway, up the stairs and once I managed to unlock the door and open it, he spilled straight through and landed in a black and white heap on the ground, wincing but thankfully breathing and alive.

Once I had closed it, I braced my whole body against my front door, sucking in deep mouthfuls of oxygen, attempting, without much success to at last quieten the frantic beating of my terrified heart.

I then found myself glaring at him, despite the fact he looked like he was about to lose consciousness any minute. "You," I gasped. "You have *a lot* of explaining to do."

VII
Halfbreeds and Guardians

We slept on the couch that night. Or rather, *he* slept and I just perched on the arm next to him and silently freaked and panicked to myself.

I had picked him up from the ground after about ten minutes of trying to calm my nerves and had half-carried him into the lounge that my parents had designed and furnished so long before I was born that I barely had right to call it my own and had kind of unceremoniously dumped him on the couch.

Despite not spending much time in here, I did like my parents' lounge. It was a large, brightly painted room, full of creams and whites and blues with none of the dark accents that Skye's own lounge had in abundance. Pictures with shattered glass sat on the mantelpiece, many of myself when I was younger being held by a smiling woman, accompanied by faeries with broken wings and a wooden cat with a chipped tail. The only things that were spared from my adolescent rage were things that didn't remind me of my parents so the harmless watercolour paintings of lakes and innocuous cottages in front of mountainous backgrounds were the only frivolous objects that were still perfect in the whole room. Even the grandfather clock that stood proudly in the corner was scratched from where I tried to shift it and ended up knocking it on its side and smashing the coffee table it fell on. The soft white carpet was kinda shredded too from where I failed at clearing up the glass.

After checking that Skye was well and truly unconscious, I forced myself from where I sat on the floor by the sofa and trudged slowly up the stairs, stopping by my room to unbuckle and remove my boots and grab a towel and my pyjamas before staggering to my bathroom.

Yanking the cord to turn the light on, I leapt a little in fright as I was faced with a familiar, yet oddly alien face, peering at me with the same kind of alarm as I assumed was present on my own face. The girl staring back at me was a pallid, frail creature who was all but shaking as she regarded me with wide, terrified eyes that *burned* with emerald fire in shadowed sockets. Her black hair stuck to the skin on her throat that was crusted with browned dried blood, flaking a little but smeared up her jaw and across her right cheek in a grotesque curve. It was flecked over her face in unlovely speckles too while continuing down her neck to stiffen the fabric of her borrowed top, painting her collarbone and the exposed area of her shoulder. Her hand trembled as she raised it to push her stubborn fringe from her eyes, greasy with sweat and grime and lifeless just like the rest of her.

It took my mind a while to kick into the fact that the girl I was staring at was me.

Disturbed, I lowered my hand and turned away from my shocking reflection. Facing the shower, I focused myself on turning the dials and setting the jet spraying to ignore the fact that my priorities seemed to be focused on how much of a wreck I looked rather than the importance of actually being able to judge my appearance because I was, you know, alive.

I showered quickly, making sure I didn't pay much attention to the blood that was running into the drain after I'd washed my hair and soaked and cleaned my skin. I remembered scrubbing my face with the rough side of my exfoliating mitt until it hurt, feeling the phantom touch of the walking dead man's blood spotting on my face and throat as he died on top of me and it stayed, the memory, no matter how much I scrubbed. I remembered physically using my other hand to pull my arm away from my face and then move to force myself from the shower itself in case I lost it completely and had no choice but to sit and sob like the pathetic child I felt I had become overnight.

Without delay, I dressed in my pyjamas, a soft white and blue short and tank top combo decorated with little talking ice-creams exclaiming that they were 'cooler than you' in little glittery speech bubbles. I tied my hair into a low ponytail before stepping out into the hallway.

What I did *not* expect to see was Skye standing like a lost man in my upstairs corridor, peering around the corner to where my parent's bedroom was located but spinning around in alarm, automatically crouching into a defensive position, when he heard the bathroom door behind him open.

"You're awake then," I muttered, trying to sound unsurprised by this development. I was stunned. He was flat out twenty minutes ago.

"You were gone," he said, standing up straight and finally relaxing. He looked haggard and just as tired as I felt, however, he wasn't on the ground gasping and writhing in agony anymore so I guessed that was a distinct improvement. "I guess I panicked."

Anyone would panic waking up after a night that we'd just had in a place they didn't recognise; I couldn't fault him. "I'm sorry," I apologised, feeling a little more than guilty that his distress was partially my fault, but I had to grab two minutes to myself to take stock... to deal. I noticed again, how tired he seemed and allowed myself to be worried. "Do you want a shower?"

He frowned. "I should probably be getting home..."

Suddenly, all worry was gone as he said that and I felt myself growing annoyed which was a nice change from abject fear. "Oh-ho-ho-ho-NO! You are not going anywhere until you give me a proper explanation, Skye. Like I said, you have a lot of explaining to do." I marched past him and into my parents' room, making a beeline for the chest of drawers where my father used to house his extensive old-man pyjama collection. Skye would look kinda odd in it but there was no way in hell I was letting him walk out of here tonight without telling me a thing and he may as well be comfortable. I grabbed a pair and turned back to where the man had followed me in, offering to them with a no-arguments expression hopefully planted firmly in place.

"Stay here tonight and get some rest. You can go home tomorrow after you've told me what I want to know."

He took the blue and white striped pyjamas from me and looked down at me curiously. "Won't your parents... mind that I'm here?"

I motioned to the empty bedroom. "As you can see, they're not around... A weekend away." I shrugged. "Good timing, eh?"

"As if the word *good* could be used in this situation but then again, I guess you owe me." He raised the pyjamas in thanks. "Where do I get a towel? You got anything other than girl's shampoo?"

I yanked an unmarked fluffy white towel from the airing cupboard back in the corridor and threw it at him, not mentioning the shampoo as if I felt like he had somehow insulted me by suggesting I'd only buy flowery crap. But then, with an apparent guy in the house, maybe he was only joking in ignorance of the actual facts so again, I couldn't fault him as I watched him turn into my bathroom and lock the door.

He was going to be sleeping in my house.

The first guy I ever brought back to my house that wasn't Sam turned out to be some sort of expert demon killer with an arm that could expel fire but somehow burn him from the inside out at the same time, could heal stupidly fast and move at a pace that shocked and alarmed me.

My mom would f-r-e-a-k.

While he showered, I pulled spare blankets and pillows from the same airing cupboard I had taken his towel and dragged them downstairs to make him a little bed on the sofa. It was all well and good for him to let me sleep in his massive queen-sized bed, but a guy like him would not appreciate resting in a teenage girl's double and would probably prefer the couch.

Returning around ten minutes later, Skye had apparently scoffed at the shirt that matched the bottoms because he rejoined me downstairs with a bare chest that was still beaded with moisture from his shower and I turned away from him quickly to hide my sudden blush. I'd seen him without a shirt before so it shouldn't have been such a big deal but coupled with the wet hair that was trailing water over his collarbone, my heart couldn't bear the image of him.

"What was wrong with the shirt?" I took a deep breath to calm myself and raised an eyebrow at him.

"The *shirt* didn't fit," he grumbled. Now that he mentioned it, Skye was *a lot* broader than my dad and *taller*. With that thought, my eyes fell to his unshod feet and the pyjama bottoms that failed to even cover his ankles and I tried my best not to giggle. I failed kind of dramatically when a high-pitched almost hysteric whine escaped from my lips and the glare that he levelled at me then was flat and unfriendly. "Your dad's pyjamas *suck*."

I smirked, his grumpy attitude relaxing my shell-shocked heart, and held out my arms to take his clothes and the damp towel and while he looked at me in confusion, he eventually relented and passed over the bundle of cotton, wool and denim. He then followed me curiously as I bunged the whole lot in the washing machine along with my own clothes that I had brought down with the bedding. Adding detergent and softener, I set the cycle and then grinned up at him to find that his eyebrow was raised, but he didn't say anything, instead turning and padding back into the living room.

"Am I sleeping here then?" he asked me, surveying the makeshift bed as I rejoined him.

"If you want to..."

He gave me a look. "I am *not* sleeping in some teenage girl's bed."

Called it.

I tried not to look too smug as he swung himself onto the sofa and lay back on the pillows as if he was testing the bed I had made for him on his internal comfort meter, only looking up at me after a couple of minutes with a grudging *"not bad."*

I watched him relax and burrow down into his blankets before reluctantly turning away to the white-varnished door that led back out to the entrance landing and the stairs, flicking the light switch off as I went.

"What's up?" I hadn't realised that Skye had been watching me and after I refused to move after placing my hand on the handle, he'd spoken up and I could feel the concern in his voice. "You scared?"

"Terrified," I told him with an honesty that surprised even me. I wasn't used to admitting fear out loud even to Blue and Sam so I wasn't sure why I would be so upfront to Skye of all people. Maybe it was because he wouldn't blame me for being frightened because he understood exactly what I was going through, what it all meant to be scared... It wasn't as if I was frightened of things that went bump in the night and I definitely wasn't because those things, ghosts and ghouls, had no tangible existence, nothing to prove that they were real. Demons, on the other hand, had given me scars as proof.

"I'm really not surprised. I've actually been waiting for you to admit it." His face softened and he patted the couch next to him as if inviting me to sleep there with him and also thinking nothing of it. "Stick with me, kid," he murmured.

I skirted the edge of the couch and settled on the arm, where I had always perched when I was young, though next to his feet rather than my father's as it had been back then. "I'm not a kid." I grumbled and he chuckled in response.

"You gonna be alright there? Won't that make it kinda hard to sleep?"

"I don't sleep much and after..." I sighed. "I probably wouldn't be able to even if I tried."

His bright blue eyes regarded me and, even from where I sat in the gloom, I could see the questions that all but glittered there but he voiced none of them. Eventually, I broke the eye contact, staring instead at the netted curtains that shrouded the large bay window and did little to halt the tacky glow from my parents' solar powered old-style streetlamp lights. The floor boasted the shadows from the patterned lace, elongated and fuzzy, but they stretched toward the couch without stopping, spreading like a disease until the window frame halted any further reach just before they touched where I sat.

I rested my chin on my drawn-up knees, wondering slightly if Skye was still observing me but when I glanced after two minutes of hesitation, his eyes were closed, his long eyelashes dusted his pale skin above his high cheekbones while his chest rose and fell with his deep, even breathing. It didn't take him long to fall asleep so he must have been tired. After what he had gone through, I wasn't surprised.

I sat there for what felt like hours until finally, after revisiting everything that had happened over the last few months, I felt myself beginning to doze, receding into a sort of half-rested state that allowed me to at least give myself enough of a charge to not pass out the next day.

Skye only stirred when the sun began to shine through the window, glaring right into his closed eyes and he twitched, yawned and eventually opened his eyes, his sleepy expression turning straight into a full-on glare at the sun for waking him up so rudely. After a moment, he seemed to remember where he was and he turned his head to regard me, still perched where I had been when he fell asleep and he frowned a little.

"Did... did you sleep?" he asked with another small yawn, pulling himself up into a sitting position.

"I dozed," I told him.

"Sitting up?"

Smirking, I replied in what I felt was the most frustrating way possible, "I have mad skills like that."

He rolled his eyes and threw his blankets off him, swinging from the middle to sit up on the couch in the way it had been intended to be used. I found that my patience had finally run out.

"You ready to talk?"

"Give me a few minutes to wake up, Erika. It's the ass-end of dawn."

He had a point. I shrugged to myself and then slipped off the arm of the couch and entered the kitchen with a mind to check the washing I had completely forgotten about last night. To no surprise, it had finished the cycle so I switched the washer off and pulled the damp clothes from it and into a small plastic clothes basket. Lifting it up on my hip and taking the whole lot over to the conservatory where my parents had kept the dryer, I bunged it in and set it up only to turn and see that Skye had followed me in.

He had a considering look on his features.

"So what is it that you actually wanna know anyway?"

"Everything." Blunt as always Erika, well done.

He sighed. "That's not very specific... I need to start somewhere."

I thought for a minute, trying to find something in the jabbering wreck that was my own head that was screaming a little louder, calling for attention with that little bit more desperation than the rest.

"You said they were after me..." my voice was small, quiet and timid, but I spoke the words without a single thought. I didn't realise what the question I was going to ask was until I'd actually opened my mouth to ask it. "Why?"

This was obviously the question he least wanted to answer because he sighed and ran his hands through his hair. It was a good few minutes until he finally spoke again. "They were after you... because of what you are."

"What I am? But I'm... I'm just a girl. Aren't I?" At his expression, I felt my whole body go cold. "... So...If I'm not...What am I?"

"Do you really... can't I get a drink or something first? I'm gonna need something... If you want me to get into this topic...I need to wake up... I need a bit more than just sleep to give me energy." The look he gave me then was beyond exhausted. "Please?"

I sighed. If this was what it was going to take for me to *finally* get some answers, so be it. "Hot drink?"

"I'd take a coffee if you've got it."

He followed me over to the counters and stood by the island in the middle like a defender of some sort and watched me skip from cupboard to countertop as I busied myself with the coffee granules and hot chocolate power for myself, flicking on the switch for the kettle as I worked.

There was something about me that was making these demons attack. Even when I said it to myself, it made no sense and even less when it was said by Skye, the self-proclaimed not-exactly-human protector that had saved me more times than I cared to think about. He had to be mistaken...

But he'd mentioned a *halfbreed* back at the club. I'd heard that word before; I was sure of it.

While I thought, I offered him milk and sugar, both of which he nodded to, looking quite thoughtful himself as he shifted over to the small pine table on the far side of the room, near the double doors that led out into the conservatory. Once the two drinks were done, I threw the spoon in the sink and joined him, passing him his coffee.

He took it with a murmured "thank you" and wrapped his hands around the mug as if wanting to draw the warmth from it, breathing in the scent heavily through his nose, eyes half closed. I'd never seen him look so contented.

He had his drink and now I wanted answers and I was *not* going to be satisfied until I got them.

I looked up at him. "So...What... What am I? If I'm not normal?"

Skye sighed and sat down. He still looked terrible, even after a shower and rest.

"You..." His tired eyes lifted to look into mine. "Our kind... it's complicated..."

"Our kind?" Wait, I was the same as *him*?

He glowered impressively at me. "Are you going to listen or are you going to keep interrupting like a child?" I glared at him and he continued, sipping his coffee. "Like I said... It's complicated... We're not exactly human. Well, not completely."

I sighed and sat opposite him. I had to be patient; I wasn't going to allow my childishness to be the reason why I had no idea what the hell was going on *or* what I was. Skye was the type of man to withhold information if I pissed him off.

However, patience wasn't one of my strong suits. "You can be vague all you want but you *know* I'm not going to stop asking, so why not tell me? We have time, it's not like we have anywhere to be." When that didn't seem to make any difference, I tried a different tact. "Don't I deserve to know?"

He thought for a moment. "Well, you know about demons right?"

"They're kinda hard to miss."

"The ones you've seen so far are demon drones and are pretty much the underlings. High demons barely get involved in humanity directly anymore and believe me; you want to keep it that way... If you think drones are bad, you never want to meet a high demon. Drones are rats... minions... and can reproduce on their own. High demons are more like us in the sense where they need a mate and sometimes when necessity dictates or the fancy strikes... they dally with the human stock." When his eyes once again sliced into mine, they were hard and for some reason, I knew what was coming. "I'm part demon, you know this... a halfbreed if you will... and so are you." I blinked in surprise.

I sat there, stunned, in the silence that followed, hastily trying to sort my suddenly scattered thoughts. I had wondered how Skye managed, being so different and coping with the evil blood that was pumping through him, only to be told, by him, that I was exactly the same, that I had the same evil ancestry as him. I didn't want to believe him but for some reason, right at the very core of me, I knew that he was telling the truth.

I was a halfbreed.

"You're shitting me."

"'Fraid not."

"That's impossible."

"I assure you, it's not." His eyes flicked up to me. "You have insomnia, don't you?"

My stomach went cold. "How... how did you know?"

He smirked. "It's one of the only symptoms of being a fluctuating halfbreed... the energy is wreaking havoc in your blood and makes it difficult for your body to shut down."

I blinked, trying to clear my head and when that didn't work, I shook it, violently. "But *how* could I be a halfbreed? I don't heal like you do! I can't make fire shoot from my palm or... or move stupidly fast or *anything*! I'm just *me*."

He sighed. "That's because you haven't come into your powers yet. You're still too young."

A heavy silence hit us again as I tried to get my head around what he was telling me while he watched, frowning a little and looking a little worried himself. Eventually, my brain took over. "So I'm half demon...?"

The look he then directed at me was sharp. "You're also human. Never forget that you *are* human too..." He hesitated for a moment, glancing at the smooth surface of his coffee before looking back into my face. "Unless I'm totally mistaken, your human blood is by far the strongest."

"What do you mean?"

He smirked though it held little to no mirth and spread his arms wide. "Look at me... you can tell just by looking at me that something isn't quite right. You, on the other hand... there is nothing out of place about you. You... look human."

I frowned. "You look human to me."

His grin grew and said "but you saw me from across a crowded room. Something piqued your interest." When I didn't answer, he stretched and leaned back in his chair, eyes focused on the ceiling above us as his face sobered. "When people ask how many types of people there are in the world, what would you say?"

"I don't understand..."

Skye relaxed, grinning a little and reached for his coffee as he spoke, "people who watch things happen, people who make things happen and people who wonder what the hell happened." As my confused look deepened, he laughed. "This is truer than you think. There are three types of people in the world and it keeps to the watchers, makers and what-the-hellers idea quite well. Humans, carriers and halfbreeds."

"Are you going to start making sense sometime soon?"

He laughed again. "Humans are the what-the-hellers... They are the ones with no demon blood in their veins at all, or at least not enough to make a difference in their genetics... Like your friend. They spend their time not really understanding the reality in what they are actually seeing to the point of their brains rationalising things to keep their sanity intact."

I nodded. "You've mentioned that before..."

Talking to him was helping me keep my head clear and I reached for my hot chocolate, feeling privately grateful. "Carriers are the watchers... They are regular humans who have a percentage of blood but it fails to awaken any sort of power... though they do have a better grasp of what is going on, able to be involved in our activities. Some carriers are employed as Unearthers and Messengers... and paired carriers produce halfbreed children if the blood is strong enough."

"So my parents..."

"...Are either halfbreeds or carriers." Skye gave a curt nod.

"Would they know... about me?" I was almost too scared to ask the question.

He sighed. "Their permission would have been needed to set you up for the Guardian program so... they would have been told when you started fluctuating..." I couldn't blame the guy for looking as worried as he did. This was obviously not what he had been expecting to tell me when I demanded to know everything, but I was too intent on my search for some sort of information to actually feel bad about the position I was putting him in.

So my parents *knew* I was a halfbreed... They knew I was part demon which actually explained a lot but not why they didn't talk to me or tell me *anything*. They eventually upped and left because of it, I guessed, so that just meant maybe that they were trying to ignore it which made me think, in turn, that they were more likely carriers rather than actual halfbreeds but that just made me more confused.

I let out a small moan and allowed my head to fall into my hands.

"Why wouldn't they *talk* to me?"

"To keep you safe, I guess." I glanced up into his face then, wondering if he actually knew, but his expression was, while not relaxed, calm enough that it told me he was talking about the basest of terms. They literally didn't tell me I was a halfbreed because they were trying to keep me safe. He had no idea my parents had left me, he'd already proved that by asking about them during the time I knew him, and so asking him where they were would be fruitless. I wasn't even sure I wanted him to know that they were gone; Blue and Sam didn't even know.

I took a deep breath, focusing instead on things that I was sure Skye *could* tell me. "So the halfbreeds are the type of people that make things happen? I guess that includes people like you and... and... The ones with active demon blood?"

Skye seemed to understand my hesitation. "Yeah. There are halfbreeds of differing strengths all over, though how strong we are depends on the concentration of demon blood we are cursed with." I noticed his face crease a little as he spoke, bitterness thrumming through every syllable that he uttered. "The more blood, the stronger we are. Each halfbreed is assigned what we call a Guardian to protect them until they come into their powers, usually at the age of seventeen or so." By the time he had finished his uttering, his tone had calmed, the self-depreciation fading into his usual confident attitude I had come to expect from him.

"*Why...?*"

He leaned forward and reached for his coffee. "Remember how we first met?"

I nodded. "At the diner; you saved us when... the demons attacked."

He mirrored my nod. "I was sent there to watch over you, to keep you safe... it was my first day on the job and I was cocky... I didn't think they would attack you in force."

I frowned. "Why did they attack me at all? According to you, I'm half demon!"

A complex expression drifted onto his face then. "Demons are attracted to the... energy halfbreeds give off... When a halfbreed child reaches the age of three, they begin what we call fluctuating... it's how we tell the difference between halfbreeds and carriers and regular humans... Fluctuating is where the halfbreed expels a certain energy that demons and certain halfbreeds can sense... Demons go nuts over the stuff and want to feed on it."

I swallowed. "So they want my energy?"

"They want all of you. Feasting on you would be like the effects of a drug and would make them more powerful for a bit. You don't want to face a demon after they've just tasted the flesh of a halfbreed." His face darkened for a moment before he shook his head and once again sipped at his coffee. "That's why Guardians are assigned until you stop fluctuating and the demons lose interest. Also, by that point, you have your powers and can defend yourself."

"What are your powers? I mean, aside from the epic healing ability and that... blue flame thing."

He winked. "Secret, though the healing doesn't really count... all demons heal quickly, it's what makes them such a pain in the ass to kill."

"How do you kill a demon?" I asked suddenly. His eyebrow arched at my question and I suddenly felt like I needed to explain myself. "One of the drones that you killed at the diner... kind of became not dead again. Why haven't they all done that?"

He shrugged. "It depends on how you kill them and how strong the demon is. The one that woke was the one I broke the neck of, right? It could fuse its bones together again, but it needs a certain amount of power to do that." His nose wrinkled. "It's the blood. It's why it's best to draw blood when you attack the things, brings the likelihood of recovery way down. It's one of the first things we're taught when we come into our powers and join the Agency."

Ah-*ha*! "And the Agency is...?"

His face darkened a little. "The Agency... is...*complicated.* The Agency is responsible for the management of the demon population in the world. We have several different offices in different countries, but the one here is more or less our HQ or the largest working office anyway that hasn't been demolished by arguing halfbreeds. Like I said last night, demons have been around for a long time and the Agency has always been there too, to fight them off and protect innocent civilians, using us to kill the enemy as carriers and normal humans had almost no hope of doing so themselves. It wasn't called the Agency back then, though."

"So they kill demons?"

He winced. "They used to. It's more diplomatic than that now, though. According to the Agency, high demons are kind of intelligent and, as some unnamed bigwig once said in a fit of *feeling*, alive. By some members of our happy organization, it was viewed as *inhumane* to kill high demons unless they give us no choice. Nine times out of ten, the demons are all too quick to gift-wrap a reason to exterminate them but every now and again, they get too clever for their own good and are able to avoid the prying eyes of our Ghosts. Drones are animalistic and we're allowed to slaughter them out of hand but high demons... it's too *unethical* to just go on a big killing spree. It's where the Agency and I do not see eye to eye."

"So the Agency allows them to survive?"

"No. They're just more lenient than I would be. Given the choice, I'd slaughter every single one of the bastards. Anything else?"

"So the Agency is the one covering everything up?" I asked and to his nod I continued, "Wouldn't it be better if everyone knew?"

"Could you imagine what would happen? Think back to the times the drones have attacked the establishments you've been inside... what was the initial reaction?"

"Panic."

"Eeexactly. And that is why you do not want to put out a mass announcement about demons or quit employing damage control. Humanity can't cope with it; it's shown that already and so we do our best to protect them."

I stayed quiet for a while, processing what he had just told me and, instead of meeting his gaze, I stared at his hands and the way his thumb worried against a small chip on the handle of his mug.

"You're taking this really well."

"I'm not sure if I believe you yet," I told him, only half telling the truth. "I mean the demons and the Agency... yeah fine, whatever but telling me that I'm a halfbreed? That I'm the same as you... it's a little bit much to get my head around."

He nodded. "I've had the knowledge ever since I could remember but just finding out when you're seventeen? Maybe this is why they told me not to tell you."

"Who *the hell* told you not to tell me?"

"The Agency."

"*What*? Why?" Well, that was just peachy. It annoyed me that the Agency knew about *my* existence before I knew of theirs... What kinda organization were they to flaunt their downright omnipresence, anyway?

"Who knows? They give me orders and expect me to follow them." He grinned wolfishly. "Too bad they don't really know me that well."

I suddenly felt extremely grateful that Skye was who he was or I probably would have never known what exactly was going on. I watched him drink his coffee as I thought about what he had told me.

I was a halfbreed and it was his job as a Guardian to protect me from the demons that were hunting me down because they could sense my, what was it, fluctuating energy? I must admit that it was farfetched, but all the pieces of information that he gave me all seemed to interconnect with what I already knew or had figured out for myself, even guessed at.

Unbidden to the rest of me, I felt another question make itself known and I snapped my head up as it came to light, my 'Guardian' jumping a little at my sudden activity.

"You said that the diner was your first day." Skye nodded, frowning a little. "So... why haven't I been protected since I was three... like you said normally happens with halfbreeds?"

He winced. "You noticed that, huh?"

I narrowed my eyes at him, hoping that I looked shrewd. "Yes, I did. Start talking."

He obviously didn't want to talk about it and he grimaced a little like there was foul taste in his mouth. "You had a Guardian before me..." he muttered eventually, keeping his eyes low.

"I never saw or knew about anyone protecting me..." He must've caught the scepticism in my tone because he sighed.

"He protected you from a distance... some Guardians do that though it's not really my style." Something about his answer seemed off.

"What happened?" I felt like I was a little curter than I'd meant, but I couldn't bring myself to correct myself and besides, if he gave me more information because of my attitude, thinking that I was pissed, so much the better.

"He was killed." Ice shot through me like an arrow and I felt a small pang of loss despite never even knowing the guy. I guess it was a natural feeling as, according to Skye, he had protected me for the majority of my life and it felt kind of sad that I'd never known him. Skye continued though I didn't really ask for any more details. "His name was Ben... he was killed by a scouting group of demons just before the deal with the diner and I was sent as his replacement. Always thought I was thrown in at the deep end and, after meeting you properly, I'm tempted to agree with my first damn thought."

"Hey! What's that supposed to mean?"

"It means that you're a handful. Never has a Guardian ever had so much trouble with a charge." He grinned at me and drained his mug, lowering it carefully to the surface of the table.

"What about Shion?"

Skye froze for a second and then snapped his head up at me, for the lack of a better word, glaring. His exhaustion only made the expression look frightening and I kind of regretted my question.

"Shion. You want to know about that dick?"

"You know, he said the same thing about you."

"I'm not surprised." He ran his hands through his hair, groaning in what sounded like intense frustration. "Shion is part of the Agency."

"A Guardian?"

"Pfft, he wishes." At my less than impressed face, he rolled his eyes and then leaned forwards again, leaning on his elbows as he pressed his palms and long fingers together and looked at me over the top of them. "Shion is a Hunter, not a bad one but not good enough to match up to *me* and he can't stand it. When I was doing my Guardian training, I used to swing by the Hunter training grounds at the Agency HQ to talk to the guys and he'd be there. We don't get on."

"What's a Hunter?"

"They hunt demons."

"Oh." I blinked. "Of course."

He half-laughed at my expression. "Any halfbreed can kill a drone but when a high demon causes shit and gets into trouble with the Agency, the Hunters are the ones that either apprehend or kill it because it gets far too political to just kill them outright. Also... when there's a hell of a lot of demon drones lurking nearby a collection of known fluctuating halfbreeds, any spare Hunters give the nearby Guardians support and that's what Shion is doing. He's helping keep any young halfbreeds nearby safe."

"There are more halfbreeds nearby?"

"Who knows?" Well, he sounded like he knew so I allowed myself to think of that as a yes.

I lapsed into silence then. Knowing that there was a chance that there were others like me *nearby* was something that gave me a little hope and helped with the feeling that I wasn't drowning in a big mess of *what-the-hell*.

"Curiosity sated?" I looked at him and quickly thought back to my questions that were jabbering at me when we first sat down. All seemed to be fairly quiet, aside from the abject *confusion* at everything so I slowly nodded and finished my own drink quickly.

"For now."

He smiled in relief. "Good. Needless to say, though, you can't talk about this to *anyone*." His look then told me that he was totally serious and that none of this was to leave my kitchen.

I also had an inkling that he knew that I was going to completely ignore him. It wasn't as if I was totally spoilt for choice when it came to people I could actually repeat this to – most people would have me locked in a padded cell quicker than I could say 'what are the men in white coats for?' – leaving me only with one real option.

Blue. To be honest, part of me was still kinda suspicious that my friend *knew* more than she was letting on about what had been happening and, despite the total lack of *any* evidence, my little hunch was *really* starting to bug me. However, after Skye had all but attempted to swear me to secrecy, I was a little surer of my fears though I wasn't totally sure how I felt about it. If Blue did know more than she was letting on, then it was obvious that she had been lying to me about everything since our world had shattered into this *mess* and, despite me already understanding that it was done with only the best intentions, it wasn't really something I was ready to deal with. I knew I could probably ask Skye straight out, right now, about her involvement, but for some reason, that seemed more than a little wrong to me. This was between Blue and myself and I would be betraying my friend by dragging Skye into it. I couldn't do that to her.

Skye sighed then, oblivious to my torn emotions, and almost visibly relaxed, becoming a little less tense around the edges. "It's kinda a relief that you know now... Sneaking around trying to keep you safe wasn't working for me."

I looked at him. "So... what? Have you been lurking where I can't see... keeping an eye on me?"

His expression was a little sullen. "I've *tried*. You don't make it easy! Dashing off to the diner with no warning, barely staying in the right places. You're almost impossible to predict and that's a nightmare for a Guardian."

I felt myself getting defensive again, but I ignored the sudden strange urge to flick his nose and pout. "Don't you think that's a little creepy?"

He rolled his eyes. "It's not like that. You're a kid."

"That just makes it *creepier*."

"No. I'm looking out for you."

"Have you been following me?"

"Well, yes but-"

"See? Creepy."

"Look. I've saved your life far more times than you know." He seemed to finally have enough and his face furrowed in a deep frown as he stood and carried his mug to the sink. Annoyed, I followed him. "Demons go *nuts* around you and even with the help of the nearby Hunters; it's kinda hard to keep you alive. You have no idea how much danger you're in on a day-to-day basis so I would appreciate a little cooperation from you."

That pissed me off. Who the hell was he to talk to me like a naughty child? "What the hell? Isn't it your *job* to keep me safe?"

"Yeah, so *stop* making it harder than it needs to be!"

"I'm just living my life the same as I always have!"

"Like *hell* you are! You never ran off to diners in the middle of the night!"

"*I wouldn't have had to if people just kept me in the loop!*"

"I was told not to tell you!"

"Well, what's so different now?!"

"It's obviously too dangerous to keep you in the dark because as soon as you get the smallest piece of information you go all Sherlock Holmes and have to get to the bottom of it then and there! You can't be stupid around these things, Erika! You're going to get yourself *killed*."

"I'm still alive now aren't I?"

"Thanks to me!"

"Yeah, whatever, I'm reserving judgement on that one."

"What the actual *hell*?! You *know* I've saved your neck more than once! Are you really *that* much of a child that you... you... I don't even *know* what's going through your head! You're being a child and not seeing the big picture here, Erika. You are a fluctuating halfbreed which means you are *constantly* in danger! The demons can sense you from *miles* away and will not hesitate to take you! They've proven that already. When you go running off in the middle of the night or don't tell anyone where you are, it makes my job ten times harder because I either need to watch the demons and risk running late or try to figure out where you'd go! This is not a game and there's always a chance I will be late. Don't tempt fate!"

"Are you actually going to continue telling me what I want to know?"

"If you need to know it..."

"Then I will continue looking for answers myself."

He almost screamed in frustration, instead pushing a sharp breath out between his teeth while his hands gripped his hair. "Why are you such an *immature brat*?!"

Without missing a beat, I stomped over to the dryer, pulled it open and emptied it roughly. Without hesitating, I shoved his still damp clothes into his arms.

"Get out."

"*What!?*"

"Are you deaf as well as stupid?! I said *get out*!"

He seemed to find his voice again. "Me?" he all but spat, "*stupid*?! You're kicking your Guardian out! If I'm stupid, then you're *brain-dead*!"

"Well, I guess I'm brain-dead *and* immature then because here I am, kicking you out. Get out and don't come back."

"I'll leave now, but you've got no choice about seeing me again. I'm stickin' around, princess." He leaned forward so his warm breath hit my face. "So get *used to it*."

Before I could summon the brain-function to react, Skye had turned on his heel and stormed out of my kitchen. Not five seconds later, I heard my front door slam and I was able to slump back against the counter island behind me and let my thoughts finally consume me.

Well... That was... something else entirely.

The rest of the day was spent in my home. It was the weekend now so I had no school. Therefore, I should have been free of all worry up until Sunday night when Monday began to loom threateningly but after Skye had left me, I simply sat in the kitchen and *thought*.

Well at least that explained how he knew where I lived without even telling him *and* it explained why he always seemed to crop up right when I needed him. To suddenly find out that I had this Guardian whose only job was to keep me safe from demons was not really something my mind could take in its stride no matter how much I thought about it

Throughout the day after he left, I ended up in different locations in my room, from sprawled out on my bed to attempting to sit straight-backed at the desk I hardly ever used while attempting to study. By the time it was eight in the evening I was sitting on the floor leaning against the same desk with a cushion between me and the leg, scanning through a book but not really reading anything having studied and messed around aimlessly for the last twelve hours. Really, I was wondering if Skye were outside, yet I was far too stubborn to go check it out. He said he was looking out for me? That thought sort of made me feel a little weird... but kinda comforted...

Bzzt. Almost absently, I reached backward to my desk and pulled off my cell where I had left it before and glanced at the screen to peer at the text I had just received from Blue.

-*Cme stdy. Its 2 hrd 2 do on my own Xxx.* I laughed at the desperation I read in her text and fired a quick one back.

-*Man up. If I came to study, we'd get no work done xxxxx.*

A minute later my phone buzzed again.

-*Pfft. I cn work Xxx.* I lowered my phone without replying and again reached for my book, but I didn't even make it down to the bottom of the page before it buzzed again. *−Cme on. Plzzzzz. Gt lftovr Chinese.xxx*

I didn't hesitate with my reply. *−Give me twenty minutes.*

It didn't take me long to pack an overnight bag and I was just locking up about five minutes after I received the last text message, keys dangling cheerfully when I heard the creak of the decking around my porch and realised that I wasn't quite as alone as I'd hoped.

However, rather than the surprisingly deep voice of my Guardian that I was expecting, a voice that was only vaguely familiar to me cut through the quiet night air to where I stood.

"Wow. He was actually right."

A redhead stepped out of the shadows to the left of me and into the circle of illumination that was created by the old-style lamp above my head. She was wearing tight-fitting black jeans, a white fur jacket, knee-high leather boots and had adopted an uncaring stance I was sure I had seen before. As she neared, my eyes flicked up and focused more on her face.

Her expression was complicated, morphed into something that seemed to be somewhere between attempting to beam while wanting to scowl at the same time and all she was left with was an odd sort of grimace. After a moment, though, her incredibly pretty face figured out how to control itself and a stunningly bright smile flitted there instead.

"Hello, Erika." She nodded to me.

I stared at her for a moment until I realised why I recognised her. Back at the diner, when I thought I was going to die for the first time ever, I remembered a pair of women, a redhead and a blonde. Although I could barely remember any details, I was pretty sure that the woman in front of me was the same woman that had spoken to Skye that time. It was strange how long ago that day seemed to be.

I didn't hesitate. "You're a Hunter, aren't you?"

She blinked in surprise once before she smiled again as if it hadn't even happened. "Skye said you were quick. I'm Isla."

"Nice to meet you. Now, if you'll excuse me." I tried to turn to the steps behind me, but I was kinda foolish to think I'd even get that far.

"Whoa, whoa, whoa!" She took several quick steps to my side, which was, even I had to admit, quite a feat in *those* heels and grabbed my arm. "No can do. I'm here to watch you right now and I'm afraid my orders don't really include escorting you anywhere. As you're now aware of the situation, I'm sure you understand."

"*What?*"

She sighed. "Skye is elsewhere right now. So it's my turn to watch you... not like we *should* be bailing him out like this but we can *hardly* leave you unprotected now can we? So I'd appreciate you hopping back into that charming house you've got there like a good kid... or we'll be forced to spend the evening in each other's company!" The way her voice brightened as she spoke told me she was just as excited about that prospect as I was. This Isla woman, I noticed, was extremely pretty with large hazel eyes, long dark eyelashes and crimson curls that bounced as she moved her head that made her look to me like some sort of model. I shifted a little self-consciously under her steady gaze before realising it was probably natural to offer something to the conversation instead of staring like some creep.

"Skye's out?"

"He has a date and he rang me about an hour ago, calling in a favour." She rolled her eyes and all but pulled me back to my front door again, the white fur of her jacket tickling my arm to an uncomfortable level but as she was freakishly strong, I couldn't break free... Once again with the unfair advantage of halfbreed strength; won't any of them give me a break?

A date, huh?

For some reason, though, that kinda bothered me. Maybe it was because we'd just found the corpse of the woman who seemed to be *close* to him yesterday. Maybe it was because I found it a little unfair that he told me that he was my Guardian, that it was his job to keep me safe and alive, only to forget about this responsibility in favour of some skirt and leave this... this... *woman* in charge of my safety. Maybe it was because I was starting to get a little sick of people treating me like I didn't matter.

Sorry, but I wasn't having it.

"No." I planted my feet as solidly as I could and yanked my arm out of her grip, fixing what I hoped was a resolute scowl on my face. "I think after the day I've had I deserve my friends, don't you?"

She blinked. "I'm sorry?"

I turned to face her. "I've just learned I'm a halfbreed. Half demon. Do you have any idea how it feels to learn that the last nearly eighteen years of your life have been a total lie? I suppose you knew straight from the beginning right? Like Skye did? So you don't understand how much of *shock* this is! I need to see one of the only people who can make this world seem to be the same place it was a month ago and if you try to stop me, I swear to God or *whatever damned thing* exists that I will find a way to escape you."

I threw my keys into my satchel, picked my overnight bag up from where I had left it on the floor and thumped down the steps quickly. I heard her follow me, but she didn't try to stop me so I guess that meant my little rant had won her over.

The night was cool and felt quite fresh against my bare arms, which was kind of nice considering I had spent the eighteen hours either fearing for my life or completely rethinking it and it was starting to soothe my anger a little. It was easy to forget Isla's presence behind me as I easily crossed the yard, concentrating on the cool breeze and the sound of the rustling leaves above me that seemed to give me a strange sense of being protected.

As was our habit since Blue was almost mugged, I avoided the park. Even with the halfbreed Isla behind me, I didn't really feel like testing my luck any more than I already had.

She, for the most part, remained silent and only followed me as I made my way to Blue's place. The only time she spoke was when she, by the sounds of things because I refused to turn around to check, made a phone call to who I assumed was Skye and I couldn't help but strain my ears to overhear as I walked around the park.

"Hey, it's me." There was a moment of silence until she sighed in annoyance. "Yeah, whatever. I know you're... busy but I just wanted to tell you that the kid's on the move... Yeah, she basically had a tantrum at me."

I felt my eyebrow twitch a little and fought the urge to deny the existence of what, in all actuality, had appeared to be quite the tantrum but my denying it would only make me seem like more of a child. So I ignored her. Probably not the best thing to do to prove my maturity but it was the best reaction I could think of. Besides, she had pissed me off.

"She's heading to her friends... maybe we should... yeah, I know that... but... Will you let me get a word in?! *Look,* I can protect one little brat. She's fine; I'll just keep watch over her tonight as long as I'm relieved in the morning. You're abusing our help to be honest."

Yep, definitely Skye. Only he could get someone that pissed off in such a short space of time.

After she had hung up on him, we continued our journey in silence. It was hard to believe that Isla would be able to protect anyone judging by her immaculate hair and pristine clothes. I had the feeling she wouldn't really want to get her hands dirty in the fear of potentially breaking a nail but then again, when I first met Skye and Shion, I didn't really think they'd be trained demon killers. Hell, a month ago, I didn't even believe demons existed.

We reached Blue's place a little after half eight and I pretty much ignored Isla as I jogged up the drive and knocked quickly on the front door.

I'd never been so happy to see a friendly face. Blue opened the front door and I pretty much flung myself into her arms for a hug before my brain could actually figure out what my body was doing. I had a split second view of Blue's shocked face before her mass of frizzy chestnut hair took over my vision as I clamped my arms around her and all but refused to let her go.

"Hey, hey, hey," Blue soothed quietly, stroking my back. "What's up chick?"

"Nothin'…" I murmured as I held onto her tighter and closed my eyes. "Happy to see you."

"You saw me yesterday at school." She had laughter in her tone though I could sense the worry in it. Finally, after a few moments, she detangled herself from my grip and set me back a little. "Come on, let's get that food and get some work done."

I didn't have to turn around to know that Isla was standing just out of view, watching me until the door closed.

I followed Blue through the house to her kitchen where she already had the Chinese food laid out on plates. She bunged the first one on the greasy plate inside the microwave and slammed the door shut before setting the timer and turning around to look worriedly at me. "You sure okay? You look a little… wired?"

I rubbed my eyes and blinked a few times at her before her words actually hit me. She was worried about me. I guess my hug attack at the door had sent alarm bells ringing.

She was really the only one I could actually talk to about what had happened over the last couple of days. She would be the only one who would believe me and not cart me off to some mental institute for the rest of my life. She saw the demons; she knew about them.

But then there was my suspicion that she knew more than she was letting on.

If she didn't tell *me*, why the *hell* should I tell her? I felt my heart harden.

"It's nothing."

She sighed in what sounded like annoyance. "So you're keeping secrets then? That's fine. Cool. Whatever."

My eyebrow twitched. "You can talk."

"What?"

"You know what I mean." I couldn't keep the bitterness out of my voice and I instantly felt guilty about it but at the same time I felt it was justified enough to allow her to sweat a little. Just a little.

"What's that supposed to mean?" She went a little pale at this and my heart sank. That was not an innocent reaction. She was worried I'd found out she had been lying to me. She was feeling *guilty*.

Well, that just made me angrier.

"It means, Blue, that I'm not the only one who has been keeping secrets here," I snapped. The chaotic thoughts that had been battering against my head and chipping away at my self-control finally broke free and the words flung themselves from my tongue before I had thought to stop them. "It really hurts that I had to find out the truth from a complete stranger. A complete stranger who has been honest with me from the first day I actually met him. My *best friend* never told me anything – why we were constantly being attacked by demons, why all this was happening – and I had to find out from *him*! Do you have any idea how that feels?!"

There was a moment of silence in which the only thing that could be heard was the whir of the microwave before Blue finally spoke and to my surprise, her voice felt tiny against the way I had sounded; angry, hurt and disappointed.

"So... you know."

And there it was. I had my suspicions, I really did, but part of me didn't want to believe that Blue had been keeping secrets from me. However, with her words, all doubt flew from my heart and I finally knew that I had been correct. I didn't feel any sense of accomplishment at being dead on the money. I felt nothing. I had gone numb.

It was a few moments before I was able to catch onto one errant thought out of the dozens that were flapping around uselessly in my head. "Wh-*why*... Why didn't you *tell* me?!"

She looked at the floor. "I was told not to."

"You were told not to," I repeated listlessly.

"Daniel said that... He said that if you found out, the people responsible would have to answer to the Agency."

"Daniel? He's a part of this too?" She just blinked at me and I continued. "Is that how you know all of this? Daniel told you?"

She looked uncomfortable. "It's more than that."

I watched her squirm and ground my teeth in annoyance. I couldn't deal with this right now. It was enough to find out I was a halfbreed but to have confirmation that this was all but common knowledge amongst Blue's social circle and I seemed to be the only person who didn't know was beyond what I could handle. This was my *life*. "I can't listen to this anymore," I hissed from between gritted teeth.

Blue gave a start. "Erika, please, you have to just hear me out!"

I stepped back, shaking my head, fighting the tears that were threatening to betray my anger. "Blue, I just... can't. You don't know how this feels."

She reached out, panicked, and grabbed my arm. "But I do! Erika, I know what you're going through!"

I yanked my arm from her as I went to walk away. "No, you really don't." I didn't mean it to come out as such a hateful sneer, but my anger and frustration had reached such a point that it had to come out somehow and it looked like Blue was about to get the brunt of it. "You have *no* idea what I'm going through. So back the *hell* away from me."

She did not relent, instead reaching out and grabbing my arm once more, this time with a grip that refused to let go even when I attempted to walk away again. "Erika, I *know*."

Something about her voice made me stop and I turned my head to her, slowly, heart frozen in my chest as if I could already sense the next four words out of her mouth.

"I'm a halfbreed too."

VIII
Names and Trust

I, for lack of a better word, glared at my best friend. She was rummaging around her kitchen trying to find a clean teaspoon as she attempted to make coffee. She'd never been good at it to be honest and it usually fell to me to make the drinks for the three of us, but there was no way I was in any mental state to make coffee.

Blue was a halfbreed too.

I watched her move to the refrigerator as the microwave dinged again, announcing that Blue's food was now reheated and we could finally eat. I had been picking at mine, but I didn't really seem hungry anymore.

Milk and sugar added as appropriate, she pushed a mug toward me, but I didn't reach to take it, just stared at it and the swirling steam that curled and disappeared into the air.

"It's weird to see you so quiet. I expected more shouting," Blue mumbled into her mug that she had pressed to her lips.

"I'm sure I'll get to it," my response was automatic. I didn't really feel like shouting. I didn't know what I wanted to do at that point.

Amongst the intense feeling of betrayal I felt from being lied to by Blue for, presumably, as long as I had known her, I couldn't deny that there was a lingering flicker of, well, *relief.*

I wasn't alone.

"When did Skye tell you?" Her voice was hesitant.

I sighed. "This morning."

"You were with him this morning?" She managed to sound mildly curious and sheepish at the same time.

"Yeah, he stayed with me last night."

"What?!"

Too late, I realised how that sounded to my friend and turned to face her. Her eyes were wide and bugging out of her face in a way that told me she had totally misinterpreted what I meant.

"No! Nonononononono!" I shook my head and raised my hands as if to ward off her judgements. "We were attacked at the club and I drove us home so I could get information out of him."

She continued to stare at me as if I had grown another head. "One, what? Two, you *drove* from a *club*? Three, *who the hell attacked you*? And four... *WHAT?!"*

"You said what twice."

"*That's not the point!*"

With a wince, I backed down; my previous anger fizzled out in the face of Blue's own fury. Haltingly, I told her the events of last night, how I had gone to the club on Shion's advice to see Skye and how we had been attacked by a literal swarm of demons. We were lucky to have escaped, I realised as I told Blue how Skye had saved both our skins and then how I had to practically drag him out of the club and even drive his car.

By the time I had finished my story, Blue had turned an odd shade of green and was leaning on the counter, staring into nothing as she listened. After a moment, she released a shaky breath and then turned to look at me but said nothing.

"Okay?" I asked her, chewing my lip.

"Um, I'm not really sure if I want to hug you or strangle you right now so just give me a moment," she told me, her voice strained.

Any other day I would have smiled, but it felt like my cheeks had even forgotten how to do that. We stood there for a moment in silence before she sighed deeply and ran both hands through her naturally curly hair.

"I... I don't think I can realistically stay too mad at you," she said. I don't think I remember her ever sounding quite so tired. "There's a lot of stuff going on that even I don't understand so I can't blame you for wanting to find out more..."

"What don't you understand?"

Blue took her plate from the side and took it over to the dining table and slid onto one of the chairs. I followed suit as she began to speak. "I've always known... about being a halfbreed. Aunt Tia would look after me and would tell me about what I was and how safe I needed to be. Because of the level of protection around me, I've never been in any real danger. I mean, before the day in the park, I'd never seen a demon."

"Huh? What do you mean?"

"They... they don't usually come out in force like they did in the diner..." I'd never seen my friend look so small before. Everything about her seemed to fold in on itself until there was only a sad imitation left and even though I was still mad at her for lying to me and hiding my own identity, I still felt the strongest urge to wrap my arms around her and tell her everything was going to be okay. "They normally skulk and pick people off... they never just...." Words seemed to fail her and she sighed, reaching out to pull her food closer to her and grab a fork with the other hand.

"But... what day in the park?"

She raised her deep brown eyes to mine. "The day... the day I was almost mugged. That wasn't actually what happened... I wasn't almost mugged. I... saw a group of demon drones attacking someone." She hesitated. "Your... Your old Guardian."

My whole body went numb as she spoke.

"Ben? You saw him die?"

She nodded and blinked a few times but not before I saw her eyes well up. "Reagan ran over to try to defend him, but it was too late. Shion came back to tell Dan what had happened but with you guys being there, he had to improvise."

I stayed silent, trying my hardest not to cry for a person I had never known. It wasn't as if I was just learning about his death now, I knew he was gone, but learning about the particulars, how he had died, just brought it all back. It was worse that I didn't feel like I had any right to be sad as I hadn't even met the person who had kept me alive for most of my life, but I guessed it was because he *had* kept me alive for most of my life. He had protected me without thanks only to be cut down while doing his job. It stung.

"Daniel said that Ben must've been taken by surprise." Blue's voice sounded far away. "Drones never attack halfbreeds that have come into their powers like that... they only go after fluctuating halfbreeds and never their Guardians. Daniel doesn't have a clue why Ben was even targeted."

I took a deep breath. "...Does... Does Daniel know a lot about Guardians?"

"Of course he does. He's mine."

"He's... your *Guardian*?!" This was just *too* much. "Not your boyfriend?"

"*So* not my boyfriend. I needed an excuse to have him constantly around me and he played the part quite well... I didn't want to deceive, but it was the easiest way to explain why he was constantly with me. I didn't want you guys to worry." Blue chewed on her lip a little sheepishly and I sighed, pinching the bridge of my nose between my thumb and index finger.

"This has been one weird day," was all I managed to say.

We stayed up that night, talking about everything I wasn't supposed to know and it was kinda like a dam had burst because

Blue could just not stop talking. She told me all about her childhood and how it felt growing up with the knowledge I had lived without. She had grown up with a Guardian called Tia, an aged but tough lady who unfortunately retired because she doubted her ability to keep Blue safe and was replaced, quickly, by Daniel. Blue was Daniel's first charge and they got along great, except when she did stupid things that almost got her killed, like go to the diner when he had already given her orders not to. Stubbornness was a trait both of us shared. Her mom knew about her daughter's strange blood and accepted it pretty well, especially when it turned out that Alex had started fluctuating too; the tale of why Alex was such an ass was more understandable than my previous belief of 'because he was'. Alex's Guardian, however, was hardly around and only usually met him when he wasn't at home or at the weekends as Daniel was normally with Blue at her place and took over protective detail. When Blue went out and stuff, that's when Alex's Guardian took over.

We talked in earnest, about stuff that mattered and stuff that didn't. We talked about Sam and that his mind had definitely been tampered with and Blue announced that it was done by a halfbreed called Reagan, who she had mentioned before. It turned out that *she* didn't have any idea that a halfbreed could do that until she asked Daniel after it happened to Sam. Reagan was part of the Shield Corps of the Agency and it was his job to protect civilians and employ damage control measures wherever it was needed. So the whole deal with the attack on the diner being due to rival gangs and drugs had all been created by him and his Corps and he had been altering memories to keep the information quiet. If Skye was to be believed, Sam wasn't dealing well with the truth and had his memory altered to save his sanity and if this were true, I would be forever grateful toward Reagan, whoever the hell he was.

I understood why she had hidden all this from me. The world she had lived in, the world that I now shared with her, was a terrifying one, but that didn't stop me from still being angry at her and I think she understood that. We talked and we shared a lot, but there was an undercurrent of apprehension that I've never known to occur with my friends and it bothered me. It also bothered me that I had no idea how the hell I was going to face Sam with the knowledge I would have to lie to him from here on out. I couldn't tell him any of this. According to Blue, Daniel had told her that if Sam were exposed to any demon activity or saw a picture of a drone or anything, it could undo the work that Reagan had done and Sam could completely lose his sanity. It made me sad that my oldest friend wouldn't be allowed into the world I was now a part of. Even my involvement was against the interests of the Agency and apparently, my parents.

The next morning, we were met by Shion, Dan and Isla, who were all taking it in turns to keep an eye on the house over the night in case there were any more attacks from the neighbourhood's demon drones. Apparently, the sudden rise of drone activity over the last couple of months had everyone on edge and no one was taking any chances over mine or Blue's safety. Blue told me that when we had sleepovers, Dan and Ben would hole up in the shed in the yard and take watching the house in shifts. Since Ben's death though Skye hadn't exactly stepped into his shoes and it was largely left up to the other Guardians and the local detachment of Hunters to make sure I was kept safe while he went AWOL.

It felt weird being protected by so many people.

However, when Blue opened the front door to let the three halfbreeds into her home, it became apparent that not everyone was exactly pleased with this arrangement.

"*You* and I have a problem, brat!" Isla snapped as soon as she saw me, pointing with a perfect fingernail. "The next time you feel like having a hissy fit and marching to your friend's house just because things are not going your way, make sure it is not while I'm taking care of you, you selfish brat. I had to sleep in a *car*. With these morons. Get a clue, girl."

"Wow, I feel insulted." Dan rolled his eyes as he followed Isla in as she stomped past me and into the living room. Thankfully, Blue's mom was out with Mica, the twins were with their dad and Alex would probably not surface from his room until the afternoon so we had the morning to ourselves to bicker. "Don't listen to her, Erika. She's always like this in the morning."

"Actually, she's always just like this. Isla's a bitch," Shion murmured as he, too, stepped over the threshold. "Thanks, Blue, for letting us in. It's cold out there."

"Why didn't you text? You coulda slept in the living room at least."

"Your mom scares me."

"She's not in."

"And you didn't tell me this last night?"

"Didn't Dan tell you?" Blue looked at Dan who had flung himself on the sofa while Isla perched on the armchair as if she didn't want to touch anything. Dan grinned and shrugged.

"Dick," Shion grumbled. He nodded to me with a smirk and then went to go lean on the wall as Blue and I went to make ourselves comfortable. It felt a little intimidating. Now I knew exactly who these people were and what they did, I realised they were kind of scary, though, except Isla, they were obviously doing their best to make the atmosphere easier on me.

"So... Our little Skye spilled the beans," Daniel said after a few minutes of thoughtful silence. He turned his gaze to me and I felt in it the change of his whole attitude as if my knowledge had somehow tipped an internal balance within him and he was able to treat me as he would his comrades or Blue.

"Yeah and he made a right mess while doing so," Isla snapped. "Didn't anyone *tell* him it was supposed to stay secret?"

"Several times," said Shion, "but when has Skye ever listened to anyone?"

"I can think of once," Daniel muttered, "but he's been given no such threat here... just... stay quiet."

I felt this was kinda unfair. "He sort of had no choice," I argued before I realised what I was saying. "I didn't give him another option."

Shion snorted. "The girl has a point. She's been hell bent on finding stuff out since the diner."

"*Why* did you have to know everything?!" Isla snapped in obvious annoyance, "Why couldn't you just leave everything alone?"

I was stunned into silence by the venom in her tone and all I could do was blink stupidly at her. Even Dan and Shion seemed alarmed until the latter slowly spoke.

"Wouldn't you?"

Isla almost growled and threw herself back into the armchair, crossing her arms over her chest. "Skye had best hurry up and take over his *duties* soon. I've things to do." She made the word 'duties' sound disgusting to her.

"Go then. I'll take care of Erika." The words were barely out of Shion's mouth when Isla stood up and practically stormed out of the room. The sound of the door slamming made me jump and I felt Blue do the same in her space next to me on the floor.

"Well, she's... pleasant," Blue commented after a moment.

"She's Isla," Dan shrugged while I relaxed with her exit. "Though she's more pissed off this morning than she usually is. Skye's little exploits do that."

"I don't know why she continues to care so much," Shion mused, mostly to himself I guessed. "It's not like her feelings will ever be returned."

Daniel sighed. "No idea and I don't really care," he focused on me as he spoke. "You okay, Erika?"

I went to nod but for some reason my head wouldn't obey and it took me a moment to realise why.

I was not okay. I was *so* not okay. I was two thousand miles across the line of okay in the wrong direction! I was a halfbreed and suddenly had enemies I didn't even know existed, my best friend had been lying to me, presumably for as long as I'd known her and I was now on the receiving end of animosity I wasn't sure I deserved. Under the same circumstances, *who would actually be okay?!*

"Erika?" Blue touched my arm.

I sighed. "I'm not really okay at the moment, but I'm beginning to get that it's just part of the halfbreed gig." I looked at the people that surrounded me and saw in their faces concern for me and that somehow gave me a little bit of strength. "Skye told me a lot of what he shouldn't have, I get it, but I'm glad he did because if he didn't, I'd probably end up getting myself killed and that would really put a downer on the situation."

No one smiled at my poor joke, but Shion nodded a little bit as if acknowledging the fact that there had been an attempt to somewhat lighten the mood. Dan cleared his voice and then spoke.

"The fact is, Erika, that Skye... he's not a good Guardian," he began, leaning forwards and rubbing his large palms together. "He'll take care of you and protect you when he's not *busy* with his band or going out on dates. The *only* reason we put up with his absence is because if we didn't, you would be dead. Since the attack on Ben, it's been getting harder and harder to keep the drones away from you and we can't trust Skye without putting you in serious danger. It works a little better now you know everything because now we can have your cooperation and no more of this... running off to diners and getting yourself into trouble."

I didn't miss the look he gave me or the way Blue twitched at my side.

In all, though, I felt absolutely awful. Even after Skye had given the same information and the same warnings, I hadn't really accepted how difficult I was making keeping me safe or how many people were struggling to do so. I think it was because I hadn't really accepted that Skye was telling me the truth but with this serious man sitting in front of me and reiterating almost everything Skye had told me to begin with, it started to suddenly hit home. Hard.

Well, shit.

I couldn't deny though that there was a part of me, larger than I wanted to admit, that felt that Dan was being a little unfair where Skye was concerned. I knew that they knew him better than I did, due to the fact I had only met him a couple of times and argued with him each time besides but I felt like there was more to him than someone who would just leave me to die. He would have died at the Poisoned Apple if I didn't get him out of there, all to keep me safe. Those weren't the actions of someone who didn't care. Though the fact that he wasn't there thanks to the 'date' Isla told me he was on last night was a little irritating.

The Hunter coughed. "That's not the whole story."

However, the glare that Dan sent Shion then would have made a braver person than me run in terror but Shion didn't even flinch and met the glare with one of his own. "She doesn't need to know the full story, Shion. That's Skye's business."

Shion snorted. "She should know the danger."

"It won't happen again. That was an isolated incident."

"Isolated?! It was the only-"

"Shion. Enough."

My curiosity, for lack of a better word, was *burning*. Surely, they knew by now about my curious nature? Why were they trying to do this to me? Though, impressively, I kept quiet and simply watched the to and fro between Blue's Guardian and the Hunter.

Shion and Dan stayed for a while after that as Blue and I started on the studies we should probably have gotten through the night before and they lounged around on the sofa and armchair eating chips and drinking soda they had liberated from Blue's kitchen.

Around two in the afternoon, roughly the same time we began to hear signs of movement from Alex's room upstairs, the sound of the doorbell chimed throughout the house and Dan rolled off the sofa for the first time since pouncing on it this morning and lumbered to the doorway. I watched him and realised that I just kept forgetting how *bulky* he was and I half expected his wide shoulders to get stuck in the doorframe.

He didn't though and I heard the front door open a second later. A moment of silence followed until Dan spoke. "You're late."

"And you're big. Let me in." I sat bolt upright when I heard the voice and presumably Dan had stepped aside because a moment later, Skye stepped into Blue's living room.

Almost immediately, Shion stood up. "That's my cue," he murmured, nodding to Blue and me before weaving past Skye and out of the room without even looking at him. Blue watched his exit with wide eyes as Daniel came back after letting Shion out.

"Well, he couldn't get out of here quick enough," commented Blue with raised eyebrows.

Skye only smirked and lowered his eyes to me. He looked better than the last time I had seen him, less tired and with more light in his eyes, but with a jolt I realised that the last time I did see him I had quite unceremoniously ejected him from my home and told him to never come back. His eyes simply said 'told you so' and I tried really hard not to get annoyed by that.

"Are you actually studying?" He asked us, ignoring the fact that Shion had just left like it hadn't even happened.

"Gotta," was all I said.

Skye snorted. "Why have you gotta?" He raised an eyebrow as he nudged my math book with his boot though thankfully he did not appear to be wearing the ones with razor blades pressed into the soles.

"We have finals," I pulled the book away from him as Dan sat back down on the sofa. Blue shifted a little, grabbed her book and then moved over to Dan so he could help her with a problem she had been nagging me to help her on for the last minute, but I had been too distracted by Skye to notice.

"You're a halfbreed, Erika," he said as he sat down next to me though his tone was gentler than I expected. "You don't really need to worry about your GPA now."

"Huh?"

Daniel looked up from Blue's math book. "Skye..." his tone was like a warning.

Skye turned to look at his comrade. "What?"

"Her parents want her to be normal, Skye."

"Well, there's no chance of that now, is there?" He shrugged. "To be perfectly honest, I think she should have been given the choice to begin with. It's not fair to keep her in the dark about the world she's a part of. What about what *she* wants?"

"If that's the reason you told her everything, you're going to be in deep shit with the Agency."

"Oh, shut up. I told her because she literally gave me no other option. Never try to hide anything from this girl, she'll find out eventually." He picked up one of my textbooks and opened a page at random. "She's too quick for that."

Dan sighed. "You're making me go grey, Skye. Stop it."

"What?"

"Oh, just... Just do what you want, I no longer care about the shit you get into."

Now that Daniel had given up trying to stop Skye telling me something I now really wanted to know, I looked over at my Guardian expectantly.

"So," I probed when Skye did not continue and instead sat there, cocking his head in confusion at my math book.

He looked up at my voice and grinned a little sheepishly before putting the book aside. "Yeah, so... Halfbreeds don't really need all this shit to be successful in life. Most of the time, halfbreeds join the Agency when they come into their powers and make a career within one of the different sides of the Agency." His grin grew. "It can be rather fun, you know."

I couldn't deny I was sceptical. "You mean, work for the guys who kept everything from me?"

Dan made a noise from where he sat with Blue. It sounded a lot like the word 'tried' disguised by a cough and I sent him a quick look while Skye laughed.

"They ordered us to stay quiet because it was what your parents wanted. It's not like they did it just because they felt like messing with you."

I wasn't really convinced, but I shrugged and let it go. We'd already touched upon the fact that my parents wanted to keep quiet about my bloodline and to be honest, I did not really feel like dragging it all up again. It sucked.

"So what are the options then?"

Skye had picked up another book – this one an anthology of poetry – and was browsing the stanzas and the black and white photos of long-dead poets and writers. When he spoke, his answer was half distracted. "It depends on what you wanna do." He closed the book, tossed it aside and finally turned his full attention to me. "It doesn't stop at Guardians and Hunters though they are the most popular vocation choice of the whole lot."

"Tell that to the Messengers. Guardians and Hunters are just the most likely to get themselves killed so there's a high turn-over rate," Dan muttered, obviously still listening to the conversation.

"I was pretty sure you were against telling her all this," Skye stated over his shoulder.

Dan appeared a little bit sheepish when he responded with "well, yeah but you can at least get the information right."

Skye chortled and looked back over to me. I noticed, too, that Blue was interested because she had stopped her studying and was watching us with rapt attention, books closed on her lap. "There are five main branches of the Agency which are Guardians, Hunters, Shields, Ghosts and Messengers. There are more, but they more keep to the background like the Unearthers and Carers. Guardians and Hunters, you know but Messengers, Ghost and Shields-"

"Oh! I know about Shields! Blue told me," I yelped suddenly, making the man next to me give a start. "They protect civilians, right?"

Daniel looked over at Blue in an almost accusatory fashion, but Skye seemed pleased. "Yeah, I guess that's the simple way of putting it."

I felt proud and somewhat happy. I was starting to understand stuff. Yay. Skye, however, did not seem to notice my inward celebration and continued.

"Ghosts are information gatherers, mainly trained in infiltration and subterfuge. They are normally gifted with powers that mean they can pass without being noticed and *that*'s how they get their details from demons. A lot of the time, because of Ghosts, we can find out about high demon plots and plans and put a stop to them before they actually happen. The Hunts that are posted for Hunters are dependent on the Intel that has been provided by Ghosts, like which high demons are stirring up drones against us or allowing them to do whatever they want. Ghosts are the reason why our Hunters are so effective."

"What are Hunts?"

"I told you that Hunters are only allowed to kill high demons that have made trouble, right? Well, the Ghosts investigate high demons constantly and when they offer Intel to the Overseers at the Agency, the Overseers judge the information and then choose to post a Hunt for the demon in question. The Hunt is a pretty much permission to maim, kill and slaughter. Hunts are good. Though sometimes Hunts are posted to just bring in a demon for questioning... the permission to rough them up a little in that case is implied, yet not written."

"So the Hunts are like... bounties?"

"Yep."

"Okay..."

Skye smiled. "Next are the messengers. Messengers are probably the lesser of the big five but as Dan said, one of the popular ones due to the safety of the job. No fighting, no real danger... just passing messages between halfbreeds and Overseers. They tell people, parents of new fluctuating halfbreeds, of the situation and offer up the Guardian program to help protect their children. They have to have people skills."

"And now we know why Skye is not, and will never be, a messenger." Dan stood up, stretched and peered at the clock. "Who wants burgers? I'm starving."

The next couple of weeks were pretty much the same. I went to school like normal which was still a nightmare thanks to the exams that were being thrown at us at an alarming rate, but that's where normality ceased. As I now knew what I was, it felt like I was only allowed to go places with either Shion or, when available, Skye as Isla now refused, point-blank, to have anything to do with me. Not like I minded but I was starting to really wonder what I'd done to offend her so much. Whenever I was free, I was always with Blue but we started to make more of an effort to welcome Sam back into our midst when we were not in school. The secrecy was starting to grate on me and we hadn't practiced in *weeks*. Dan said it wasn't safe.

Skye was off on his own a lot but when he was taking care of me when he was supposed to, we got along okay, if you ignored the continuous arguing and bickering and shouting of the words *idiot* and *moron*. It's not like we didn't like one another because when we weren't shouting we were actually quite amiable toward the other, it's just when we did argue, we really went to town.

It was on one of those mornings that we had spent the whole time snapping at each other, due to his lack of sleep on my sofa and my lack of sleep because he was on my sofa, that things began to change.

He had stayed with me because the Hunters had been called back for a meeting the night before and he had to escort me to school. As I still hadn't told him that my parents were no longer living with me, I made up a small lie about my grandmother being sick and my mum going to go visit her in the next city over and my dad going for moral support. I guess he bought it because he didn't ask anything else.

I found, not long after I discovered what I was, that there was a small detachment of Guardians who were without charges that were placed in schools around the world to protect the fluctuating halfbreeds in an environment their own Guardians couldn't enter that were called Carers. However, this meant Skye had to chaperone me to and from the building and that job included getting up early and I soon found out that this was *not* on Skye's list of favourite things to do. He swore under his breath constantly through breakfast until I, annoyed and more sleep deprived than usual, told him that if he didn't shut up I would jam my spoon somewhere he would not appreciate. Arguments ensued.

So when he opened my front door to take me to school that morning, moods were low and I didn't think they could get much worse. Oh, how wrong I was.

Skye stepped out into the morning air, held my front door open for me and paused.

"What the hell are these two jokers doing here?" he grumbled at my side.

I blinked a couple of times in the morning sunlight before I realised exactly what he was talking about and almost groaned.

Standing at the foot of my yard, her arms crossed over her chest as she spoke in low tones to her companion, was Isla. Her friend seemed to be the same pretty blonde woman I saw that first day at the diner. Another Hunter I assumed.

Isla's red hair was up in a stylishly messy bun and she was clad in a leather jacket and a light blue pair of jeans which all but clung to her slender legs. Her fellow's hair was down and straight and she wore a grey hoodie and black sweat pants with pumps that were peeping out of the folds of her baggy bottoms. She did not look particularly impressed at being outside at that time and her face was devoid of makeup and was also creased in worry.

Isla looked up as she heard us approach.

"Finally." I heard her grumble and she turned to us, crossing her arms over her chest. "We need to talk to you."

Skye halted and held onto my arm a little, stopping me in my tracks while his eyes narrowed at the two ladies. "You gotta talk to me?" He snorted. "Well, beat it. I don't wanna."

"Very mature." The blonde rolled her eyes. "Come on, dickhead, it's important."

His eyes stayed narrowed. "That's not very nice, Helena." He turned to Isla. "What the hell is the Ghost doing here?"

Isla rolled her eyes while Helena cut across him. "It's not nice, but it *is* true, now will you just listen? I don't know about you, but I *really* don't wanna be here at the ass-end of dawn."

"Both of you shut up and, Skye, *listen*," Isla snapped. "Skye. It's time for you to actually be a proper Guardian."

I could hear the annoyance in his tone veiled behind his bravado only because I was looking for it when he said, "I *am* a proper Guardian."

"Yeah, right, no. I mean a *proper* Guardian. You need to stay close to your charge, for good. No more running off to dates and calling in favours. This is important."

Skye's expression darkened. "What's changed?" For some reason, no one seemed to want to answer his question.

Helena broke the silence. "Yael's back."

The effect this statement had on Skye was surprising. I felt him tense by my side and his fingers pinched slightly as they dug into my arm as if by reflex and when I looked up at him, his usually pale face had gone white as a sheet, eyes wide and unseeing.

"No." His whisper terrified me.

"So you understand why it's important to keep close to your charge."

"No, no. You must be wrong. Why the hell would he come back?! There's nothing for him here!"

"I heard the news this morning."

"Well, what do you know?!"

"I'm not a damn Ghost for nothing, Carter!"

"So you actually *do* your job? Here was me thinking you just like harassing me!"

"You're confusing me with Isla; I couldn't give a damn about you!"

"Both of you *shut the hell up!*" Isla hissed though I noticed the glare that she shot at Helena. She had her hand on Skye's arm, stroking the skin with her thumb as if trying to placate him in the gentlest way. "Skye, it doesn't matter how Helena got the information. What matters is that the brat is kept safe until she comes into her powers, 'kay?"

He turned his head to look at her and her whole being softened until she was practically a puddle on the floor. I suddenly remembered what Shion had said about Isla's feelings not being returned.

Well, damn. She was in love with Skye. No wonder she did whatever Skye said.

He jerked his arm away from her. "Of course I'll keep her safe. That's my goddamn job." He pulled in a shaky breath and finally released me to thread both of his hands through his hair, pulling it back and looking at the floor, though doubtfully really seeing it. He blinked once, twice before he snapped his head up to Isla and stepped back. "Take care of her for a bit. I gotta... I just..." and he bolted. I watched him with wide, shocked eyes as he turned around, got into his waiting car and sped down my road until I could no longer see him.

"*Dick!*" Isla shouted after him though only succeeding in insulting the fumes his car left behind. She turned to me. "I have to *look after you now*?! So *not* my job."

It didn't take Isla long to get rid of me. Barely twenty minutes after Skye had left us, I was dumped on Blue's doorstep with a totally baffled Blue in the doorway, an even more puzzled Sam behind her and backed up with the looming figure of an irritated Daniel.

I was surprised to see Sam, but in some way, relieved too. It looked like whatever was going on with Blue and myself, the former was not about to let our friendship with that goofball suffer any more than it already had. Despite feeling a little like a flea-ridden stray that no one wanted, I grinned and almost bounded up to them like an over-enthusiastic puppy.

Dan was less impressed and as soon as I was ushered into the house and Blue took Sam to make drinks, he quickly demanded to know where Skye was, why I was here and why the hell I was here alone. When I told him that Isla had dropped me off after Skye had bolted, he instantly tried to call the both of them to little success. His questioning then became more direct.

"Skye was supposed to be on duty all day today," he told me in a low voice.

"I know and he intended to be but..." I chewed my lip. "Someone told him something and he went all... weird."

"Weirder than usual I'm guessing. Who said what?"

I forced my head to recall her name. "Helena? She told him that someone had come back... he went as white as a sheet and bolted."

Dan froze for a second and then peered down at me. "This is really important." He had his hands on my shoulders and was staring into my face for any sign of falseness or if I was unsure of my own answer. "Was the name Yael?"

"Yes!" I pointed at Dan's face. "That was the name. Helena said that Yael was back. Skye freaked and left."

"Shit."

"Is it that bad?" Daniel rubbed his jaw with his palm as he mulled over what I said. I watched his discomfort until he pulled his cell phone from his pocket and grimaced at me with two words.

"Bad enough."

After not being able to get into contact with Skye, Dan took me, Blue and Sam to school. It was an uneventful day in so far that I paid no attention what so ever because I was spending so much time worrying about Skye. His reaction had frightened me and so had Dan's grim acceptance of the, what I assumed was, quite terrible news of this Yael's appearance. I'd never seen Skye spooked and Yael's name had him literally fleeing. It wasn't right by any stretch of the imagination.

Dan picked us up from school and took us back to Blue's, muttering along the way which I was beginning to notice he did whenever he was pissed off. This told me Skye had still not reported back to Dan and my concern spiked. He'd always told people where he'd gone. He'd never just disappeared before.

As Blue's mother had gone for a week-long retreat, we were allowed to use her house as a base of sorts as Mica and the twins had been taken to their aunt's to give Blue time to study on her own for a while. I was surprised her mom had even thought about that but in a way I expected outside assistance. Blue's aunt had always had her head screwed on right.

Shion showed up a couple of hours later while I was studying. Sam had left earlier because he had to walk his dog and he told us, cheerfully, that he'd see us tomorrow which soothed my frayed nerves a little until I opened Blue's front door to see Shion standing quietly on the doorstep. Then I was back on edge and had no choice but to watch Shion cross the living room as I gnawed on my pencil in worry until he reached where Dan was sitting next to Blue, helping her with her homework.

"The Agency hasn't heard anything from Skye and neither has Isla since she saw him this morning," He told him in tones that were just loud enough for me to catch. "I'm gonna head up to his place to see what's going on. Thought I'd keep you posted as you're technically doing two Guardians' jobs. You gonna be okay on your own?"

Dan snorted. "I'll be fine. I'm tougher than Skye anyway."

I'd made the decision before the two men had even stopped talking. I stepped up behind Shion boldly and announced, "I want to come with you."

The Hunter turned around slowly to face me while the Guardian behind him peered around his body to gape at me. "You're kidding right?" Shion didn't sound annoyed, just... amused. I didn't know which was worse.

I shook my head. "No, I mean I actually want to come with you."

"It's too dangerous," he spoke as if he expected me to give up at that point, but I stood my ground.

"Not if I'm with you," I insisted.

"And what if something's happened to him?" he raised an eyebrow as he spoke. "If that place is crawling with demons, there's no way I can protect you and kill drones. I'm not a Guardian."

"It's unlikely for there to be any drones, dude. You know that building's owned by the Agency. It's the safest place for anyone, including her." Dan didn't seem to understand what this would do to my side of the argument and I beamed while Shion glowered at his comrade.

"Yeah but I didn't want *her* to know that!" he hissed.

"Why don't you want me to go?"

"It's best if you stay away from Skye. He's trouble."

"He's my Guardian, I've got little to no choice about staying close to him."

"Right now, you have a choice and I am standing resolutely on the side that means you should stay here while I make sure your Guardian is okay, not like I care." That last bit sounded a little uncalled for to me.

"That was a little uncalled for, Shion," Dan told him. "Look, just take her, she'll be fine. Besides, it should be clear by now that Erika does what the hell she wants. It's best she does it under your watchful eye."

Shion glared at Dan again for a second before turning back to me.

"I don't know why I ever thought I could win against you," he sighed as he made his way to the door again.

IX
Past and Demons

We mostly rode in silence. Shion wasn't really much for conversation at the best of times and I was trying to soothe my frantic nerves.

I wasn't really a hundred percent sure why I had insisted on coming along but now that I had I sort of had the feeling that it was the best thing for me to do, however, the atmosphere in Shion's huge monster of a jeep was definitely trying to tell me otherwise.

Even though I had been to Skye's apartment before, I had been less than in a perfect state of health both there and back so I couldn't trust myself to know the way and, in all reality, I was worried about Skye. It made sense to tag along with Shion and make sure he was okay, if he was even at home.

When Shion pulled up to the same grey building Skye had brought me to when I was sure I was going to die of blood loss, I almost jumped from the car before it had even come to a complete stop. I heard Shion growl in annoyance, switch off the engine and step from his vehicle with a damn sight more calm and composure than I did. I was practically bouncing on my heels in agitation by the time he had circled his car and joined me on the sidewalk so we could both walk up to the path and to the main doors to the apartment building.

Halfway up the pathway, however, Shion stopped and began digging into his jeans pocket to pull out a cell phone that had apparently been buzzing. He motioned for me to stop before answering.

"Nakamura," his tone was quick and business-like but after a moment, his face became concerned and his grip on his phone grew tighter. "Dale?! Dale! Calm down and talk to me, man. What-... what's happening?"

"Shi?" He lifted his hand to silence me and I hesitated, watching him as his expression only grew darker and darker the longer he was on the phone for. Eventually, after what seemed like hours though was probably only a minute, Shion lowered his phone and turned his eyes to me.

He was shaking. "A detachment of Hunters has been ambushed over in the industrial district. They went to go to complete a Hunt," his tone was quiet and numb as he spoke. "They're outnumbered and in hiding... there's a high demon..."

"Then go, Shion! You've gotta help them!"

"I can't! Goddamnit!" roared Shion as he forced his hands backwards through his mop of blonde hair before he turned to stare at me with suddenly panicked black eyes. "What am I supposed to do?! I can't leave you here and I can't take you with me but if I stay here, my guys are gonna get slaughtered!"

There was only one way out of this, I realised as guilt curved its way through my gut.

"Let me go up to see Skye," I said quietly. "The building is owned by the Agency right? So demons won't come close? I'll be safe inside and you can go help your friends."

"And if he's not in his apartment?"

"I'll stay put outside his place until he comes back or until someone comes to get me."

He stared at me for a long moment before he nodded, "give me your cell." I didn't hesitate and several quick taps later, Shion passed my cell back to me. "You now have my number. If *anything* happens, you call me. Understand?! Be safe." He clapped my shoulder with his hand before he ran back to his car, jumped in and was soon tearing up the street toward the industrial district on the other side of town. I breathed a huge sigh as I turned back to the apartment block and stared up at its huge looming structure. I could dimly remember whereabouts Skye's actual apartment was, but there was still something spooktastic about it that gave me pause about entering. The sun was setting and was shooting its lovely flaming rays across the grey stone that made up the body of the building itself. The windows flashed the light back into my eyes and across the shattered slabs of concrete I was standing upon, complete with tiny tufts of grass, evidence of nature's desire to win back the earth. The sky was burning bright orange as I stared and almost seemed warm but the brisk wind that flung my hair into my eyes reminded me of winter's chill, not far away enough to be forgotten completely and it finally made me move to the dubious wind-protection of the lobby.

The entrance and the elevator were much how I remembered, though with perhaps colourful additions to the graffiti, but I quickly moved past it all to slide through the partially open double doors and dash up the stairs two at a time. I recognised Skye's floor thanks to the continuation of graffiti and its insistence that the cops were crap. I'm generalising here. Though the graffiti made less sense now I knew the building itself was owned by the Agency; didn't they wanna clean it up?

I quickly made my way down the corridor until I reached Skye's front door when I stopped. The badly painted black door was slightly ajar and a jolt of fear shot through me like a lightning bolt, something I had not really been used to before all this crap started to change, and I quickly fought the urge to run and scream like a three-year-old. There could be a totally reasonable explanation for why Skye's front door was ajar. It wasn't as if it looked like it had been forced open.

Taking a deep breath, I moved forward and gently pushed the door open further with my fingertips. A soft thud hailed me and a quiet *'ow'* I instantly recognised as Skye jolted my nerves to the point I automatically pushed open the door fully and bolted inside.

A pathetic scene greeted me.

Skye was sitting on the floor, his right side flush against the sideboard that had both doors wide open, exposing what I assumed was Skye's secret liquor stash. The man in question was, at that point, rubbing his head with one hand like he had just tried to get up and had head-butted the door closest to him. Three empty liquor bottles were littering the floor around his legs while in his hand he held a fourth, half-empty bottle of amber liquid.

"Skye? What the hell happened to you?" I heard the pity in my tone before I even thought to disguise it, but I doubted, in his state, he would tell the difference.

He didn't show any surprise at my appearance. "Get out of here, Erika. Don't wanna see anyone." He was completely wasted, that much was clear, but I hadn't really seen him in this state before and the unsteady gaze, the slurring speech, kinda bothered me.

"Everyone's worried about you."

"No, they're not."

"Skye, please... You ran off without a word."

He didn't reply for a long time. I stood there and just watched him finally stop rubbing his forehead, sigh and stare down at the bottle he held in his hands. Finally, he sighed again and looked up at me. "You should really leave, Erika." He lifted his bottle to his lips, the amber liquid sloshing a little on his sleeve with the sloppy movement. "Don't wan' you to see me like this."

I took off my jacket and hung it on the coat hanger where it had been the first time I came here before settling myself down beside him, cross-legged. Without asking, I reached and took the bottle from him, lifting it to my own lips and taking a cautionary sip. I almost gasped at the burn as it slid down my throat, but I managed to keep my expression blank, even as I passed the bottle back to him. I wanted to laugh at the open-mouthed stare he directed at me, but for some reason, his drunkenness made it less hilarious and more depressing, like he was just a sad imitation of what I had come to imagine him as.

After a moment, he sighed, shook his head and moved his eyes to stare down at where the rug ended, continued by the carpet, his eyes tracing the minuscule fibres with his eyes, up and down until it made me sick just watching and I had to turn away. "Seriously," he slurred. "Your parents must be worried about you." He must have forgotten my lie about them being out of town.

I leaned my head back against the wall. "Like your parents are worried about you?"

He snorted. "My parents died a long time ago."

"Is that why you do all this?"

He didn't answer, so I allowed myself to take that as a yes. Judging by the few times I had seen it in person, he fought like he had a vendetta so hearing that his parents were killed by some demon would not surprise me. Someone important to him had died, and he was fighting to either prevent anyone going through the same pain or to inflict as much pain on those responsible as possible. I looked over at him, surprised to see that his position was similar to mine, head against the wall, tipped back, but his eyes were closed and the hand holding the bottle was limp.

"Skye?"

"I was thirteen," He whispered so quietly I could barely hear him, "and I had just walked home from school after having my bag thrown in the pond by Luke Schofield." He snorted again. "It's amazing the details you remember. I had forgotten that spotty dick's name completely until now."

It was hard to imagine Skye ever taking that kind of crap from anyone, but I studied his face intently, anxious for the rest of the story.

"I think they were waiting for me before leaving, because they had their bags packed already, and mine, but I had to fish my bag out the pond and walk the long way in case Luke was waiting for me. So I was late. When I walked in, I thought they had redecorated; painted the whole hallway red. But that's when I saw the pieces." Skye turned to look at me. "My mother and father weren't just *killed*. They were torn apart, because of what they were. Because they devoted their lives to slaying demons, the strongest of their enemies – high demons and drones led by *Yael* – banded together to get them out of the picture. But they forgot about *me*."

I sat there, in complete shock, not knowing what to say. Before he had even started to speak, I knew his story did not have a happy ending, but I did not expect what he had told me. Despite Skye skipping the details, I could almost see it in my mind's eye, no matter how hard I tried not to. A thirteen-year-old boy, walking in on a massacre. A secondary emotion booted up then, in the wake of profound shock, and my whole body began to shake with it, even as I thought how close Skye must have been to being slaughtered too. Rage.

I then knew exactly what drove him to do this every day, forgetting that it was *me* he was supposed to protect. He didn't care if I lived or died, not really, I was a convenience that allowed him to do what he *had* to do. Surprisingly, I did not care. I knew, I understood, *why* he was the way he was and I wanted to help.

He cleared his throat and suddenly lurched to his feet, swaying unsteadily for a moment before righting himself and turning to face me. "Come on. I'll get you home." He burped. "Somehow."

I shook my head. "I don't want to go home."

"Your parents must be worried; it's not safe out at the moment and they'd feel better if you were home with them."

"They don't care."

Silence reigned for a moment until he sighed and tried to smile at me in what he probably thought was a placating way. "I'm sure they do."

Again, I shook my head. "Your parents may have died, Skye, but my folks, no; they left me in a completely different way." At his confused look, I leaned over to where he had left his bottle and took a swig, allowing the burn to wash over my tongue and make me gasp. I cleared my throat and raised eyes to his face. "When I was sixteen, they upped and left. There was no prelude to this, no indication that they were about to flake on me, but when I woke up on my sixteenth birthday, not even two damn years ago, all I found was a note. A freaking note. And you know what it said?"

Skye was staring at me, wide-eyed, like a rabbit caught in

headlights but I didn't care. I took another swig. "It said, 'Erika. Don't come find us. Liz and Andrew.'" I let out a bark of mirthless laughter. "And you know what the real kicker is? I mean, aside from the fact they didn't sign it as 'mom and dad'. I didn't even know *why*. I never did anything wrong, I was never in trouble, always went to bed on time though I didn't always *stay* there and, sure, I was a little weird but what sixteen-year-old girl isn't? What sixteen-year-old girl *deserves* to have her parents walk out on her? *What sixteen-year-old girl   deserves   to   be   alone?*"

A strange thing came over me then. For the two years since I have lived without my parents, forgetting the brief moments where I almost threw out all of their belongings and from utter pain, exhaustion and confusion in Skye's apartment the first time, I had never shed a single tear. However, as I sat there, staring up at Skye's pitying face, I felt my eyes begin to burn. At first, I didn't know what the strange prickling meant, but as I tried to blink the feeling away, I felt it.

"Oh, Erika..." Skye fell to his knees in front of me, his hands reached out to cup my face. I did not flinch away like I thought I would, but accepted his touch, even as his fingers smoothed my hair away from my eyes, a strange shiver crawling up my spine as he did so. "Don't cry."

"I..." I made a move to wipe my cheeks, but Skye's thumb had beat me to it, whisking the tear away as if it didn't even exist. "I don't know... I never cry."

He smiled. "I'm not surprised." When I sighed and tried to look away from him, he laughed a little and pushed my face back towards his. "You're one tough cookie... but crying isn't actually a bad thing you know?"

I shrugged. "I look ugly when I cry."

"Not possible; you're beautiful." It took a moment for my brain to finally catch on to what he had said to me but when it did, I gazed up at him in surprise. He seemed to realise too because he cleared his throat and flung himself back down next to me, taking the bottle from my limp grasp. He moved on while my brain reeled. "I knew your parents had refused Guardianship of you, but I didn't realise that they *left* you physically. Some Carriers just doubt in their strength to protect their child and allow another to do it for them while they carry on with parental duties."

I snorted. "How can you talk like that when you're so drunk?"

He gave me a lopsided grin that was obviously forced. "Practice," he said, simply.

Without really engaging me any further, Skye called me a cab, pressed a few bills into my hands and told me to go back to Blue's place where I'd actually be looked after and kept safe. In his state, he couldn't really promise that, if the drones took it upon themselves to swarm his apartment like they had been doing to every other seemingly safe place in town, I would be kept safe. I had considered going home, but then I thought I'd rather stay alive. Instead, I took his advice and went straight back to Blue's place.

To be honest, I was a whirlwind of emotion when I left. I was kind of smarting at his ejection of me from his apartment and that was mostly considering that it hadn't been easy to convince Shion to take me there in the first place. I was also profoundly confused. The way he had comforted me while I was crying was so *not Skye* that I found myself wondering if I had hit my head and dreamed the whole thing up. However, the way that I could still feel his warm hands gently cradling my face and wiping my tears told me that it had definitely happened and merely had to be chalked up to his drunkenness. No way was my imagination that good. By the time I practically stomped into my best friend's home after Dan opened the door for me and flopped down on one of the sofas, I was in a foul mood and my cheeks were flushed with either anger, embarrassment or, ashamedly, excitement.

By this point, the sun had set properly and the friendly living room was filled with artificial light from the shaded light shade and the muted TV that no one was really watching with a disturbed atmosphere that I supposed would have felt quite cheerful and relaxed before my arrival. Blue had been lying on the floor pouring over her homework with her younger brother sitting calmly next to her while Dan followed me back in, throwing himself next to me on the sofa in his normal spot. Blue watched me warily for a moment but didn't say anything, instead looking to her Guardian to perhaps break through my annoyance while her brother wrinkled his nose at my appearance and took himself upstairs to his room.

"So?" he asked me when it became apparent that I would not be offering any information without prompting.

My response was more acidic than I wanted it to be, "He's alive. Drunk as anything and annoyingly set on being on his own."

Dan nodded grimly as Blue lowered her pencil and sat up, turning around to face us fully. "So... what exactly happened?"

A slow silence had stretched for a couple of seconds before I breathed in, trying to soothe my frayed nerves. "The demon that killed Skye's parents is back in town. Skye's freaking out," I told her with a sigh after Dan peered at me, obviously wondering if Skye had actually told me what the problem really was.

"Poor Skye..." Her face was more worried than I thought was possible for her where Skye was concerned and I was surprised by that. Really, listening to how people talked about him over the last couple of weeks, it felt like everyone *hated* him.

"Is that all he told you?" There was something in Dan's voice that made me pause then and I turned my head to look at his familiar face, seeing nothing but the concern that was etched in the downward pull at the corners of his mouth and creases in his forehead. Daniel *cared*. Not about Skye in particular but in *general*; Dan was a caring guy. With this thought, I instantly sobered with the realisation that Skye was obviously suffering. Why the hell did I think I had a right to be *angry* at him for not wanting me around? Was I *that* self-obsessed?

"Is there more?" I asked him quietly.

Dan heaved a great tired breath and rubbed at his forehead. "Yael is also responsible for the death of Skye's first charge, Matthew Bennett."

I was stunned. Skye had a charge before me? Yael was responsible for his death? Why didn't anyone tell me this? Didn't they think this was important for me to know?! Is this the reason behind Shion's antagonism? Is this what he meant that Skye would get me killed? All of these questions ricocheted through my head all screaming bids to be given voice but the only thing to escape my lips was:

"What?"

Blue's face was white which told me that this was the first she heard of this too. Dan looked at us before he continued.

"I'm going to tell you this Erika, because I think, now that Yael's back, it's important for you to understand why Skye is how he is... and why Shion and I... are a little on guard when it comes to his job." Dan gazed down at his huge paws and fiddled with a silver band he wore on his right ring finger, a little worriedly. "Skye Carter... has always been an anomaly. The usual age for a halfbreed to come into their powers is around seventeen or so but Skye... he did so at the age of thirteen when he walked in on the aftermath of what Yael did to his parents."

Blue made a noise then, one that sounded halfway between a sympathetic sob and a gasp of horror, but I barely reacted.

"He requested to be trained as a Hunter like his parents were before they took over Guardianship duties of him and he dropped out of school, moved into the Agency building with a friend of his parents and instantly went after Yael."

"He went after the demon that killed his parents?!" I wasn't that surprised, but Blue couldn't keep the shock out of her voice. She didn't see what I saw. She didn't know how much Skye both hated and *feared* Yael.

Dan nodded grimly. "He got pretty famous amongst the Hunters to be honest. They called him a demon. Every drone he came across he killed and he didn't do so kindly. I'm pretty sure he had training from his parents or whatever so he was quite proficient. He used Hunts to get information about Yael and his lackeys and then killed the demons that gave him information without remorse. He did all this at thirteen damn years of age."

"So what changed? How did he become a Guardian?"

"It took him two years to track the demon down and in this time, the Agency had figured out what he was doing and intercepted him but not before Skye had left a mark on Yael. After they had taken Skye away, he spent the next seven years training to be a Guardian and then was given Matthew Bennett, a three-year-old halfbreed, to keep safe. Matthew Bennett survived three months before Yael hunted him down and killed him in front of Skye. Yael has always been a vindictive bastard, even for a demon and probably wanted to get Skye back for the scar he left on him."

"Poor, poor Skye." I still didn't have the will to talk so I allowed Blue to speak for me. It was safer that way.

"Just over a year and a half later, he was given another chance: a seventeen-year-old halfbreed who had just lost her Guardian and was close to coming into her powers and was labelled as low-risk," as he spoke, Daniel was staring straight at me.

"Me?" I asked. My voice came from far away.

"You are Skye's last chance to prove himself. I'm not sure what will happen to him if he... fails and I really don't want to know but trust me... Shion and I will never let that happen. You're going to be kept safe, no matter what. I can promise that."

That night as I lay in my best friend's bed with Blue curled up beside me, I thought about what Dan had told me about my Guardian. I understood why Skye didn't tell me everything when I suddenly arrived in his apartment only hours before and I felt guilty for intruding on his misery without a thought as I had. I should have just left Shion to do it himself...

"You're worrying aren't you?" Blue muttered through the darkness.

"How can you tell?"

"Your breathing is all weird." She rolled over and I could see two little bright glints in the gloom where her eyes peered at me, reflecting the light of her glow in the dark alarm clock. "What are you worrying about?"

"Just... it's hard to believe Skye went through all that... I never even thought about it."

She shrugged. "How could you have even known?"

"Everyone has their own stories; I just didn't think."

"Yeah and you have yours. I suppose he's just learning stuff about you too."

I remembered telling him about my parents leaving and sighed. "I guess you're right."

"Don't worry about Skye too much. He won't be with you for long."

"What do you mean?"

"When you come into your powers, you'll lose contact with your Guardian. They get assigned to another halfbreed and it's unlikely you'll ever see each other again." Okay, that bothered me.

"Does that always happen?"

"Yep."

"Really? What about you and Dan? You guys are close, I'm sure you'll keep in touch when you come into your powers, right?"

"A lot of Guardians get close with their charges! I mean, they're usually together for fourteen years so it happens. The only thing is that it tends to mess with the deal of taking care of their new charge when they're still talking to someone who doesn't need their protection anymore. I do like Dan, he's my friend... but that doesn't really mean much when there are halfbreeds like us that need protecting. I'd hate to put someone's life in danger just because I want my friend back." She had a point, but I still didn't like it. I was just learning about all this and *just* getting to know Skye, just beginning to understand him and his plight. How the hell could I just forget about that? I guess it was easier for Blue because she knew all along that it was supposed to be this way, but I didn't just want to forget all about him. I kinda wanted him to be okay.

The next day I went to school with the guys, went through a pretty uneventful day and then headed back to my place with a promise from Daniel that Isla would be on duty as no one had been able to get through to Skye since I ambushed him the day before. My feelings about this were decidedly negative. I didn't want to be on my own really after what Dan had told us about Skye and Yael and knowing that a woman that didn't seem to like me was on my protective detail didn't really fill me with confidence either. Blue's aunt was apparently making an appearance to check up on her so everyone was asked by Blue to stay away for the day so she doesn't get in trouble for having so unauthorised guests though I was pretty sure Alex would say something being the brat he was. Shion, too, was elsewhere, dealing with the backlash from the Hunt that went wrong though according to Dan, he had managed to help his friends.

For the most part, I just made my way around my home and made myself busy with housework and eating, thinking about everything I had learned about myself, my friends and Skye over the last couple of months.

My friend had evolved from a quiet but slightly crazed health-nut to a Half-demon, half-human girl who was stronger and braver than I even thought to imagine of her. She had gained strength and I would ever be in awe of her... despite the fact I was still quite pissed off that she had hidden everything from me in the damn first place.

Everyone, even those people who I had only known recently, had all grown... stronger in my eyes.

Skye, however, was different. He had gone from this other-worldly protector I had begun to believe in, who had killed demons in front of me, who had healed in a few days from a wound that should have taken months, to a very real person with very real problems and fears. Even if those fears were supernatural in nature and more terrifying than things I could dream up in my worst nightmares. It was hard to accept what he had gone through but when I coupled this with how he was, how he acted and how people treated him, I started to feel that my earlier antagonistic attitude to him was poorly founded.

But then, there was the woman that was currently outside apparently protecting me. Isla.

I couldn't deny that the way she had acted with Skye had kinda pissed me off. I couldn't explain how or even why, but there was definitely an unpleasant squirm in my stomach that in turn irritated me more at the inexplicable nature of it. It annoyed me that she was so pretty, it annoyed me that she was so perfect and it annoyed me about her stupid attachment to my Guardian. Stupid Isla.

It wasn't as if she was actually attached to him where *he* was concerned though, I told myself, wrinkling my nose at my reflection in my bathroom mirror and continuing to brush my straight black hair. Where *he* was concerned, he was barely attached to anyone. It felt like the smaller the connection he had with someone, the less pain he believed there would be when that person, in his eyes, was inevitably killed. By Yael.

The name of the high demon made me shudder even though I hadn't had any personal dealings with him before. The fact that he had orchestrated the attack on Skye's parents, killed two powerful Hunters, had absolutely terrified me as the couple would have had more than enough means to protect themselves and their son, but it made no difference. He had then killed Skye's first charge, an innocent three-year-old boy without remorse.

Yael was a monster. A demon.

Smash. I jumped as the sound of breaking glass shattered the silence that usually enveloped my empty home. Instantly, I lowered my hairbrush and slowly moved through the bathroom door to peer down the wooden stairs to the landing and the front door. The small square windows that had been pressed into the wood of the door were now shattered and the glass littered the floor in widespread glittering curves. I could see a dark figure lurking outside, a darker patch of black that drifted slowly against the backdrop of night. A head tilted to one side as if... considering.

Knock... knock... knock. The hair on the back of my neck stood on end as I froze, terrified, at the top of the stairs.

"I'm so sorry little kitten, but I have seemed to have broken your charming door," a gentle voice sang, echoing through the heart-stilling silence that followed the dreadful slow knock. "Please, let me in so I can kill you quickly without any more damage to your delightful house."

My heart stopped and I didn't move a muscle.

A moment later, he began to speak again. "If you don't let me in, kitten, I will have to break in and I so hate committing petty crime. Those fellows at the Agency *hate it* when I do that and *always* have so much to say."

He knew about the Agency and that knowledge coupled with his soft, pleasant way of speaking only left two options as to the identity of the person currently standing on my porch, threatening my life. He was either part of the Agency itself or a high demon.

I had no trouble at all when it came to guessing which was correct and I suddenly knew how much trouble I was in with dreadful certainty.

With a whimper, I turned and bolted for my room and slammed the door behind me just as I heard the loud crunch of splintering wood and a massive thud from downstairs followed by the slight sound of a sigh and a seemingly honest "oh dear."

I carefully flicked the lock on my bedroom door and fought the urge to slip down onto the floor and sob. This wasn't how it went was it? The drones were the ones that charged in without thought, but high demons were *better* than that, weren't they? No, not better but they thought more of the consequences of their actions and they rarely killed a halfbreed in such a way that could be traced back to them. The Agency would put a Hunt notice up and the high demon would be fair game for whichever Hunter found him first. High demons were *smarter* than just killing a teenage girl in her home just because they had a taste for fluctuating energy.

However, I couldn't just wish this all away. I had a high demon in my home and if I wasn't careful and incredibly smart and quick, I was going to die. Too bad I wasn't likely to come into my powers just because I hoped to.

As quick as I dared, I tip-toed over to the window in my room and slid it open. Just underneath the sill was a small ledge that, when I was younger at least, was just large enough for me to wobble precariously on and sidle around the house to my parent's bedroom. My parents were quick to encourage the end of that activity in fear for my life or at least the condition of my bones, but I remembered how easy it turned out to be. The drop from my window could potentially break a leg and I couldn't risk the demon hearing my fall and coming outside to finish me off. I had to be smarter than that. If

I could circle around the outside of the house, get into my parents' room, I could possibly avoid the demon altogether, get out and find my wayward Guardian, who was probably still drunk and maybe incapacitated entirely.

In theory, it was a good plan.

"This hound smells a rabbit. I can hear her tiny heart thump-thump-thumping. Where are you, little rabbit?"

In practice, not so much but I couldn't afford to hang around so I ducked under the window frame, swung my leg over the sill and felt around for the ledge with my bare toes while trying to keep my breathing soft and calm. Having found the ledge, I pulled myself fully out of the window and sidled to the right gripping hard onto the white planks as I moved, feeling the paint crack and flake under my fingers and feet alike. My skin stung with the sudden blast of the cold, evening wind and my muscles groaned at the exertion of keeping myself upright on tiptoes on the ledge.

"Thump-thump-thump..." The wind whipped most of the sound away, but the gentle sing-song voice still found its way out to me and pushed my fear-driven mind to continue my body's panicked sidle around the corner and along the north side of the house. It was slow going, but I was fairly sure that a demon couldn't follow me out or know exactly where I had gone or what I planned. For the moment, I was safe.

I hoped.

Finally, after three near slips and a damn crow that thought it was funny to fly *straight at me*, I reached my parents window and my fingers carefully sought the small gap between the window ledge and the window that existed for as long as I could remember. For some reason, the window in my parent's room never closed properly and my dad was always too lazy to fix it and my mom too scared she'd get it wrong and make it worse to try. As silently as I could, I lifted the window inch by inch and carefully squeezed myself inside to step, bare-footed and quiet, onto the carpeted floor. Thank god for my mom's complaint at always having cold toes to the point my dad decided to get a carpet in the bedroom.

Why was I thinking so much about my parents *now* of all times?

I carefully padded over to the closed door and pressed my ear against it, heart in my throat as I tried to quieten its beating so it didn't give me away. *Thud, thud, thud.* Footsteps heading down the stairs.

"I'm going to find you, little bird." He was still inside and was talking in that same sing-song tone. It sent a shock through me every time he spoke and I bit down on a sob. "I can feel you. I can hear you... I can sense that power pulsing through you. A beam of light... you can't escape me, little kitten..." *Creak*. He paused on the stairs.

My heart stopped.

"Are we playing a game of cat and mouse, little kitten? Or would mousey be more appropriate here?" *Creak*. One step up.

Please, go back down.

Creak. Another one up.

Please, don't come up. My heart was racing, adrenaline turning my fingers to ice as I listened to the high demon slowly creep up my stairs.

"I'm sure you know who I am by now, little one... I doubt your friends at the Agency would have kept it quiet from you for long. How much trouble I've caused your strong, *courageous* Guardian..."

Yael. I let out a terrified sob as my knees threatened to cave from under me. I clamped my hands over my mouth to keep myself from revealing my location.

"I heard that, little mousey. I heard your little squeak... but where did it come from?" I heard him reach the top of the stairs and take a few steps toward my bedroom door. "Are you in here...? No... I smell no energy here..." I couldn't let him find me, I realised breathlessly, because the moment he did, I would be dead, no chance of begging. I had one chance to get the hell out of here.

I took a deep breath as I heard his footsteps come closer, lowering my hands to concentrate on where he was and how long I had to make my move to escape. My right hand slowly wrapped around the door handle.

"How about in this room? Are you hiding in the toilet, little mousey?" He chuckled at his own joke as I quickly pulled open the door and bolted down the hall, past the bathroom doorway where a figure lurked and jerked around in surprise as I passed him and straight toward the stairs. Just before I could grab the banister however, I felt something wrap around my arm and pull me back. Screaming words I no longer remember, I turned and dragged my clawed fingertips across my assailant's face. He yelped in surprise and I took the moment to pull from his grip and practically leap down the stairs, sobbing out of desperation and fear.

"Erika!" Just as I dropped down onto the landing, a second figure came barrelling into my home through the shattered doorway. I looked up as I recognised the voice and almost screamed something intelligible before I pulled myself up and threw myself into my Guardian's waiting arms. He remained strong as I collided with him. Although he still reeked of alcohol, he felt steady, and he pulled me closer but to the side slightly so he could free his right hand while looking up at the demon who was slowly making his way down the stairs.

"*Carter*! I'm so *pleased* you could make it!" To my surprise, Yael looked almost normal. His blond hair that was streaked with grey was mostly slicked back with bangs framing the face of an older gentleman who used to be handsome though his golden eyes sparkled with murderous intent that completely contradicted his human guise. The human guise that was completed by a smart pinstriped black suit and shiny white shoes. There was something else about him, though, something that made him hard to look at directly, that made him fuzzy around the edges.

"It's glamour," Skye murmured into my ear, "certain demons can do it... to make themselves look... human... for a time." Skye's grip on me increased and he raised his voice. "What do you want with her, Yael? She's nothing to do with you."

"Did you know she's shockingly like you, my dear boy?" Yael seemed to ignore him and continued talking like he hadn't even said anything. "The first thing she does is go straight for the face! She is really not a refined young lady at all, is she now?"

"I don't believe in God, Yael, but I'll swear to him... I swear that I will *end* you if you ever come near Erika again."

"My dear boy, you think your Agency will allow that?"

"They won't have a chance to stop me."

"Those are rather big words for a neutered pup."

Skye began to step back, bringing me with him. "Erika, go to the car," he murmured into my ear.

"What?"

"Erika, *move*!" He pushed me harshly through the doorway behind us and followed me as his sudden movement seemed to reignite my desperate desire to be anywhere but there right at that moment. I bolted down the path to his idling vehicle and leapt into the passenger side as he raced to the driver's side and threw himself in. As we pulled away from the sidewalk, I saw Yael demurely walking down the steps that led from my porch, watching Skye's car tear off down the road.

"Give me my cell," Skye demanded after a couple of minutes and both our hearts had relaxed into less terrifying beats.

"What?"

"Get my cell, it's in my pocket." Skye jerked his chin down to the leather jacket he was wearing and I reached over to pull the phone from his right-hand pocket. I offered it to him when I had retrieved it. "Dial Isla."

I did as I was told and I did not expect what had happened when I finally found her number, called her and set it up on speakerphone.

"WHAT DO YOU THINK YOU'RE DOING?!" Skye roared down the phone as soon as she answered with a perky 'Hi Skye!' almost causing me to drop his cell in shock. "ARE YOU ACTUALLY STUPID?!"

"What did I do?!" she gasped in surprise.

"YOU LEFT ERIKA ALONE!"

"I called you to tell you what-"

"Well, thanks to your complete *idiocy,* Erika was nearly killed, so thanks for that." He snatched the phone from me, hung up and threw it in the backseat. It buzzed a couple of times, but we both ignored it and instead concentrated on the roads, or rather he concentrated, hopefully, and I just watched the world fly by.

I didn't ask where we were going because, frankly, as long as we were far away from my house, I didn't really care. We could have been going to have a tea party with Isla and I wouldn't give a damn. I doubted I could ever step foot in my house again. My sanctuary had been invaded. I felt alone and terrified.

I peered to my left at my Guardian, who was still muttering angrily under his breath. No, I wasn't really alone. Skye, despite what everyone else thought and his past all clamouring up to meet him, had saved my life. Sure, he was late but he was there and I was alive.

"Thank you." My voice came quietly and from what seemed like far away. Skye's grip on the steering wheel increased and his brow furrowed.

"Don't thank me, you idiot. It's my job!"

"But–"

"But you're welcome." His grip relaxed and the speed of the vehicle slowed a little so we were no longer breaking the speed limit. "I'm taking you to my place. You'll be safe from Yael... the building's controlled by the Agency so there's no chance in hell he'll go there."

"For how long?"

"For as long as necessary."

X
Swords and Destruction

The rest of our journey continued in silence; it wasn't easy exactly, but it was a silence that didn't feel particularly unnatural between us. I could stop thinking and listen to my heart pounding in my chest to remind myself I was still alive and that my dubious protector had come through right when I had needed him the most. It also helped me understand that his rushing in at the last minute to save my life meant that Isla had not been protecting me like Dan had promised. I doubted it was Dan's fault but more the fact that she did not want to have anything to do with my protective detail and had decided to take the night off... without telling anyone of her absence. I felt strangely detached to that, really, as if it didn't really matter to me. It didn't feel like I had almost died.

Skye opened his car door when we finally arrived at his apartment complex and I followed suit, feeling a twang of *something* when I remembered that the last time I was out here with Skye I was barely conscious. I felt him take my arm at the elbow, gently, and lead me up the broken pathway to his apartment building, walking at a sedated pace and looking at my feet to make sure I didn't trip. He'd had his own run-ins with Yael; he knew what that kind of thing could do to a person.

He kept an eye on me all the way up to his apartment where he set me down carefully on the couch and disappeared for a few minutes, only to return with a steaming cup of hot chocolate which he pressed into my hands.

I took a sip.

Sweet.

"That should make you feel better. Drink the whole lot and I'll take you to get some sleep." His voice was soft and gentle; he was being careful.

"I don't wanna sleep." My words were automatic, but I knew they were true. They were bypassing any sort of conscious censor and I felt I had no more strength to pretend to be strong. I had no more strength to even sit there and carefully drink hot-freaking-chocolate like nothing had happened. Yet somehow, I managed and Skye just sat awkwardly nearby as he watched me stare into nothing and just sip, sip, sip the scalding drink.

I didn't even flinch when it burned my tongue.

"You need to sleep, Erika. You've had a... bad day." I could tell even he knew this sentence was lame so I let it lie. It *had* been a bad day, I couldn't lie, but calling it a *bad day* seemed to bring the day I had suffered into the realm of what was *real*. It made what I had been through a real experience that could be passed off as a *bad day*. Not a weird day, or even a terrifying day or a supernatural day. It was a bad day. Yael had found me and had wanted to kill me.

It had been a *bad day*.

It took me a moment to realise that the strange keening noises that followed my inward rant were coming from me, and even then it was only because Skye had to take my mug from me so I didn't drop it. He placed the mug on the glass coffee table and slowly brought me toward him as I fought to keep myself under some semblance of control. I didn't know if I had started crying or if hysteria had finally hit me after his understatement of the century, but my whole body shook with it as I continued to whine under my trembling breath. My arms came about Skye as he held me and clung to his shirt, ignoring the strong smells of cigarettes and spirits as he comforted me with nothing but his arms and the knowledge that someone was keeping me safe. I could be as weak as I needed to be.

Skye was a better Guardian than the others gave him credit for.

After a nameless amount of time, it could have been days for all I knew, as my whining gently slowed into faint hiccups, Skye gently lifted my powerless body up in his arms and took me across the hall into his room. There, he lay me down on his bed, expecting no arguments when he tried to leave me.

I didn't really have much of an explanation, I still don't, as to why my hand was wrapped around his wrist and refused to relinquish its grip. I could say that I was scared, alone or still in some sort of shock, but I think it was probably a combination of all of these things. I didn't want him to leave me.

He looked down at me with gentle eyes until he eventually sighed heavily and lay down beside me, pulling me closer and stroking my hair wordlessly until all involuntary noises coming from me ceased altogether.

It was there, curled up in his arms, trying to calm my terrified heart while the glowing white numbers from his alarm clock told me it was one o'clock in the morning that I realised I had been eighteen for a whole hour.

Bzzt. Bzzt. Bzzt. Bzzt.

For a moment, the sound confused me as it sliced easily into my consciousness and pulled me out of the realm of sleep. I felt movement next to me as someone who had previously been keeping me warm left my side to cease that infernal buzzing.

"Hello?" croaked Skye sleepily. Skye. Last night's events hit me like a freight train and I buried my face in the pillow as if I could force myself back to sleep to wake up later in my own bed to find it was all just one messed up dream.

"*Where are you*?!" the volume was so loud I could hear the voice on the other end of the line quite clearly, plus Skye hadn't completely left the bed. "*Is Erika with you?! We can't find her anywhere!*" It sounded like a strangely flustered Shion.

"Relax. Erika is here with me. She's safe." Skye sounded tired and I briefly wondered if I had disturbed him much last night before Shion started talking again.

"*Don't you tell me to relax, Carter! What the hell happened last night?! Do you know how worried everyone's been?*"

"What... do you mean?" There was something in Shion's tone that had painted a shadow of concern on Skye's voice.

"*Erika's house had been burned to a goddamn cinder. There's nothing left!*" Shion snapped as my heart dropped into my stomach. "*I swung round to relieve Isla but there was no sign of her, her phones off and there's only a smouldering black ruin where Erika usually sleeps. What. The. Hell. Happened. Last. Night?*"

I sat up and looked over at Skye for a complete loss of anything to say or do. My home was gone?

"There's nothing left?" Looking straight at me, it was like Skye was confirming it for my sake, his eyes soft and expression concerned.

"*Everything's gone.*" Shion seemed to understand Skye's sudden change in demeanour and he lost his fire. "*Can you come?*"

Skye's eyes were still on me. "We'll be there."

An hour later, after eating and showering, Skye took me to my house where Shion was apparently waiting for us. The morning passed strangely for me. At certain moments, it felt like I was stuck in a dream state in which Skye had to almost dress me in borrowed t-shirt and jeans himself while, otherwise, I would be fighting a heavy lump in my chest that threatened to stop my breathing completely. I was sure I was about to wake up screaming.

Skye stopped his car without a word. He hadn't said much since he had gotten off the phone to Shion, only really talking to offer me breakfast and offer me clothing. Thankfully I had 'woken up' just at the right time to dress and saved him the prospect of seeing me naked. Somehow, I was sure he would have called for female backup if that proved to be a necessity.

While Skye kept his silence, I just stared at my lap like I had for the whole journey. I didn't want to see it, not really, but I kinda knew I had to. I had to understand what had happened after Skye and I left, fleeing for our lives.

Eventually, after what felt like hours, he finally spoke.

"You don't have to do this, you know?" he said, quietly. "I could go explain, look for anything..." I almost sobbed at his kindness and the thoughtful nature he had kept hidden so well.

"No," I sighed, "no... I have to go see. I don't want to but..."

I jerked in surprise a little as he took my hand and gave it a reassuring squeeze. It was only for a second but the strength it gave surprised me.

He switched off the engine and then glanced out his drivers' side window. "Incoming."

"Huh?" I jerked my head up but before I could even think about what was happening, the passenger side door was roughly opened and a person-shaped thing practically dived onto my lap. There were no real words, not really, just unintelligible blubbering and sobbing from a body I somehow recognised as my best friend.

"Blue, let her out of the car. I want a go." The voice that chided Blue was so familiar that I almost had to push her off to see through her mess of bushy hair at my oldest friend. Sure enough, as Blue finally relinquished her grip on me and stepped back out of the car, wiping her tears, I could see Sam's worried face. How long had it been since I saw him last? I unbuckled my belt, stepped out of the car and rushed into their waiting arms, leaving Skye to slam his own door and join Shion, who was picking through the ruin that was my home.

"Hey, hey. We've gotchya," Sam muttered into my ear as my grip on him increased. "We've gotchya..."

Blue's arms around me tightened, giving weight to Sam's gentle, comforting words and for that moment as I breathed in the scent of Sam and Blue and tried my best to ignore the smell of burning in the air with my eyes closed, I felt the terror dwelling in me fall away. If I could believe that it was just a bad dream, if only for an instant, I'd be okay.

Finally, I detangled myself from my friends, took a deep breath and turned to look at it.

When Shion said there was nothing left, he wasn't exaggerating. My home, my parents' house, had literally been burned to the ground. The only things that remained were some of the sad, blackened load bearing beams that were still pointlessly reaching up to touch the shameless blue sky as if imploring the heavens to return what had been taken from them in the night. Gone were the friendly white panels that always greeted me when I trudged up the grass or the drive on my walk home from school. Burned and shattered was the brightly painted blue front door with its old and tarnished silver plated knocker. I'd never step through that doorway again and also, now my parents had nowhere to come back to.

All at once as I stood there, staring at the still slightly smoking shell, I felt their loss all over again, the numbness that crept over me as I read that note that sat upon my lonely dining table, the hurt, the abandonment and the sheer confusion at why this was happening to *me*. Why *me*?! This had to be a joke, right?! This was just some sick joke and the punch line was going to be announced shortly to cheering and giggles all around. Maybe I *was* the punch line?

Well, I wasn't laughing.

I had to climb up the brick foundations to stand where my hallway had been now that the fire had eaten the porch. The smell of burning was thick as I carefully stepped over the black rubble; I could see remainders of metal photo frames, shattered glass and the smudged leftovers of my mother's chipped ornaments. I'd tried to throw those out. Well, they were gone for good now.

The stairs and the whole of the second floor were gone. My room, my parents' room, my dad's records and his record player; nothing survived the flames that had eaten my life away. They must have been powerful and burned at a heat that wasn't natural because there was not a damned thing that had been untouched.

Yael had done this.

The same feeling of rage I had felt after Skye had told me what Yael had done to his family curled in my stomach as I stared at the ruin of everything I'd ever known. How much was I supposed to lose for life to be satisfied? I had no more tears to cry after last night, but I was pretty sure that even if I had, I would still be standing there, staring into nothingness and feeling my blood boil as if the flames still roared around me.

I felt Skye approach me from what used to be my living room.

"Shion took care of the police," he told me, "we're somewhat known to them in the sense that they know we're law enforcement agents of a different kind." I wasn't listening.

Everything was *gone*. Eaten. Destroyed by demon fire.

It was my goddamn birthday.

For the second time in as many days, I felt Skye's arms come around me but he was less gentle than he had been last night, pulling me roughly to the familiar breadth of his hard chest and I was able to mask the smell of smoke and destruction with Skye's scent.

"Don't look like that," he told me under his breath. "Please, I don't know what to do."

"It's my birthday, Skye," I told him. "Why is this all happening to me *now*? I've been on my own for two years, my life has been completely turned upside down, I've nearly died three times and now my home is *gone*. Why the *hell* is this happening to me?"

He sighed. He was obviously out of his depth with all this, but I didn't know what else to do. "Come on. I'm taking you back, there's nothing for you to do here."

"What if there's something left?"

"Hellfire burns hotter than you can imagine. There's nothing." He was brutally honest, but I kinda needed that. It brought me back to reality. Okay. I had to be practical.

Where was I going to live?

"Where are we going?" I asked him as he let me go; satisfied I wasn't going to start crying again.

"You're staying with me until I can get Yael out of the way."

'*Out of the way*' sounded awfully final when Skye said it but I was more focused on the other part of what he had just said. "I'm staying with you?"

He shrugged. "You've nowhere else to go. Blue can't have you 'cause of her mom, I'm not letting Shion infect you with his anti-me regime and, believe it or not, I *am* your Guardian."

Despite the situation, despite my hopeless mood and the way I felt like my world was crashing down around my ears, I couldn't help saying, "are you *really*?"

The look he directed at me then was beyond exhausted, but he didn't feel the need to respond. We climbed down from the foundations once more and onto the scorched earth around the house where Blue and Sam came up to meet us. Blue was looking at Skye in a strange way, warily but not quite so hostile as she had used to. Sam just looked curious.

"You two together now?" he asked suddenly. The three of us froze. Sam didn't know about any of this, about Skye being my Guardian, about Blue and me being halfbreeds... to him, my house just burned down and I was fortunate enough to not be inside it when it happened. I tried to think quickly as possible, but Skye was already there.

"Yeah," he slung an arm around my shoulder which didn't help my already frozen state. "I'm Skye."

Sam blinked. "Oh, yeah, hi, I'm Sam! Um... weren't you at the diner?"

Before Skye could hesitantly reply to the question that he knew could have ultimately led to Sam losing his sanity completely, Blue reached out and brushed my arm softly with her knuckles. She looked incredibly tired, even from my eyes. "What are you gonna do?" She asked me as if scared of doing so.

"Skye said I can stay with him..."

She looked like she wanted to object but said nothing and Sam nodded a little by her side.

"With your parents not around, it's probably best you're not alone right now."

I stared at them as they both nodded to themselves, apparently not even noticing what they'd even said.

Quietly, I uttered, "*you knew?*"

Sam glanced at me. "Come on, Erika. We're not stupid."

Well, apparently I wasn't as good as making sure my friends aren't worrying as I thought. It was kind of gratifying, though, to know that even when I was at my worst, my friends were always there for me and never let something even as big as my parents leaving change what existed between us all. I loved them for that.

Blue and Sam said their goodbyes and left, apologising that they had to run errands for parents or had siblings to look after. I didn't mind. I felt better knowing that I always had them with me.

Skye immediately released me as if I had burned him. "Sorry 'bout that. I got the idea from Dan and Blue and I couldn't think of anything else quickly."

I shrugged, but that was mostly to shift the sensation of his arm around me. I felt strangely cold. "It's fine. I get it..."

"You okay?"

I looked up at him as he spoke, a little confused. Under the circumstances, it didn't seem like the right question to ask. I wasn't okay and I was sure he knew that. I mean, who would be after being hunted down by a high demon and having your home burned down by said high demon all on the same night?

"They didn't wish you a happy birthday," he elaborated, slowly as if scared to point it out.

"It's been a weird couple of months..." The smile that graced my face was tired and didn't really feel like it belonged there. "Can't blame them for forgetting, can I?"

Skye ruffled my hair slightly with a worried expression. "Come on, let's go home."

Once we had gotten back into his car and started our journey back to his place, I started to feel a little bit better. I was alive and correct me if I'm wrong but wasn't that the most important thing? So what if I had lost everything I ever had and only had the pyjamas, I wore that night, my bathrobe and my phone left over? I could get other things-

"My guitar!" I gasped, suddenly in a way that it sounded more like a wail. Skye gave a start at my exclamation and tried not to swerve into a white truck we were just passing.

"*What*?" he breathed once he managed to get himself back under control.

Too distressed to pay any mind to him, I was barely able to spit out the words, "my guitar... it was in my room..." I didn't have to say much more. I knew he understood, simply, by the way he gave my hand a reassuring squeeze like he had when I tried to convince myself to look at my sad burned down house. It was strange how much I could come to rely on him in the last twelve hours when apparently, according to the others, I shouldn't even trust him to keep me alive. With Yael back and everything, with his own fear, Skye had come through more than I could have expected.

"Thanks," I muttered, staring out the window. He didn't reply but the atmosphere in the car relaxed and I was able to lean back, close my eyes and drift away to somewhere else, somewhere where this crap wasn't even possible.

I didn't wake up until Skye was gently shaking me awake outside his apartment building. I felt sluggish and tired – more so than usual – and I followed my Guardian a few steps behind as we made our way through the familiar dingy corridor to his apartment. He really did the best that he could with what he had, I thought as he showed me, once again inside and I could see the contrast to his own decor and that of the corridor outside.

I settled down on Skye's couch a little awkwardly as he stepped into the kitchen and started to whip up some drinks and something for lunch. He came back after about ten minutes with two trays, each with a cup of coffee and a plate of pasta with tomato sauce covered with a sprinkling of cheese and we settled down to eat.

It was good. He was constantly surprising me.

I told him so and he chortled. "I don't use dried pasta. It takes too long... I usually only cook for myself so it's not a big issue, but I might have to change my habits with you around."

I almost choked on a steaming pasta parcel as he spoke and looked at him. "I don't want to be a burden to you!" I gasped when I could finally force some oxygen into my lungs.

He patted me on the back, a little late and a little sarcastically.

"It's my job."

"You're my Guardian, not my babysitter."

"There's a difference?"

His laughter was a little strained as I threw one of the throw cushions at him. We lapsed into silence again then as we continued to eat our lunch and he didn't speak again until after he'd finished.

"I'm heading out in a bit," he said.

Boom. With those simple words, my heart crashed into my stomach and the blood rushed from my face faster than you could say 'well shit'. "You're leaving?"

"Just for a little bit, I won't be gone long. I'll ask someone to come take care of you while I'm gone if you want?"

"Is it a date?" Well, it turned out I couldn't forget what Dan, Shion and Isla had been saying about him after all. *He was a bad Guardian. He's always on dates. He'll get you killed.*

His face darkened. "Is that what you think of me? You think I'd be going out on dates while Yael is sniffing around for *your* blood? Do you think I'm that bad of a Guardian?"

I didn't notice what I had said until they were out of my mouth and by that time, it was too late to do anything about them. "The others do..."

He stared at me for a long moment as I sat, frozen in my seat, all evidence of the previous relaxed humour gone as he mulled over my words. "Is that what they've said?"

"Skye..."

He held up a hand to still any more words from me and for a moment, he just sat there with his hand raised, thinking quickly. He stood up without another word, grabbed his keys and stomped off into the hallway. He didn't slam the door which I took as a good sign, but I suddenly felt extremely awkward, sitting in his lounge without him. His exit was abrupt, but I didn't know him well enough to figure out if that was a good or bad thing.

Being left in his apartment alone was not a pleasant experience, especially after what I had gone through the night before and in the morning. I had to continuously remind myself that the building itself was owned and controlled by the Agency and Skye had probably called someone to keep a close eye on his apartment just in case. After what happened with his previous charge, I doubted Skye would just leave me on my own for the demons to come and get me. Even knowing this, I still jumped at every noise I heard that didn't feel like it belonged; distant doors slamming, voices in the corridor, pipes groaning.

It felt like he had been gone for hours but had probably only been about an hour when he returned and the front door banged open with a massive crash, almost giving me a heart attack. Ten seconds after that, I found myself being pounced on by Blue and Sam while Dan and Shion lingered in the doorway to the lounge but squeezing out of the way to allow a sheepish-looking Skye through.

"Sorry," he said to me, sadly.

"So this is where you live, Skye..." Dan sniffed a little, stepping inside while Blue and Sam rolled off me but continued to cling as if they could keep the separate pieces of me together. "I expected... something a bit... crappier?"

"Stinks of smoke," grumbled Shion.

"Shut up," Skye snapped. "The only reason you're here is because I thought Erika might appreciate her friends right now."

Shion was my friend?

Huh. I guess he was.

I watched as he wandered over to me, pressing a slightly battered gift bag into my hands with a wink and a muttered "happy birthday," before he sat down heavily on the sofa next to Blue. Dan shrugged and sat down cross-legged by the coffee table, placing down a large white card box with great care for someone so large.

"This is for me?" I asked Shion, a little surprised.

"Is there anyone else that has a birthday today?"

"How did you know?"

With a slowness that told me that he really didn't want to give Skye any credit what so ever, he pointed at my Guardian. "He told me."

At this point, Blue spoke up. "He also gave Sam and me a lecture about forgetting your birthday. For the record, we didn't forget, we just planned on surprising you. Your presents are in the hallway."

"I bought cake!" Dan sang, motioning to the box on the coffee table.

I couldn't tear my eyes from Skye. He was standing, leaning against the wall, apparently not really paying much attention to what was going on, but I could see his ears had turned a slight shade of pink. He did all of this for me? He fetched my friends and brought them here to celebrate my eighteenth birthday because he knew how much I needed them. Was this purely the job of a Guardian? I thought they only protected people but he was also saving my sanity. I was so grateful and overwhelmed by the display of support and friendship around me that I felt my eyes begin to burn as tears threatened to make an appearance.

"Thank you, guys," I almost wept. His eyes met mine and he smiled briefly before stepping into the hallway and the kitchen beyond to pick up plates and a knife for the cake.

The afternoon went quickly after that, fuelled by cake and the opening of gifts that my friends had thrown together. Blue and Sam had pretty much provided me with all new necessities after I had lost everything I owned in the fire. After purchasing me new underwear, to Sam's embarrassment, and some new outfits as well as less glamorous but equally important things, they had been picked up at the mall by Skye and were joined quickly by Shion and Dan. Apparently, Shion had refused to get into Skye's car and had driven to the apartment in his own jeep and I seriously doubted that Skye minded this in the slightest, though I had an inkling that Skye would have preferred to refuse Shion access to his car and leave him behind altogether.

Shion's gift was small, light and placed in a light silvery blue bag which reminded me so much of my guitar, my breath almost caught in my throat. Inside was a small device that looked more like a watch than anything I'd seen, but it just had a plain black surface with no hands or any kind of display for numbers to read. I glanced at Shion in confusion as everyone peered at it.

"It's a tracking device," Shion announced blandly while Skye choked on a piece of cake he had just chosen that moment to swallow. "So we know exactly where you are whenever you choose to go wandering off as you so like to do."

I wasn't sure what to really say to that so I gave a weak, slightly sheepish smile and strapped it to my wrist in a silent apology for all the trouble I had caused them over the last couple of months.

"That doesn't really work as a birthday present, Shion," Blue chided him gently.

"Whatever, I'll buy her a box of chocolates, but she's keeping the tracker," his voice remained emotionless as he spoke, but he shot me a quick wink from under his mop of unruly blond hair.

The fun continued, even after the crap I had dealt with over the last twenty-four hours, but it was only after my friends had left in the early evening that Skye presented me with my birthday gifts from himself, showing a shy side that I could never guess existed within him. Another thing that surprised me was that he had even thought about my birthday at all because, to be honest, I hadn't expected anything from him. We hadn't known each other that long and we did have a habit of arguing an awful lot, but I guess he wanted us to be as friendly as possible and that surprised me and, strangely, made me extremely happy. Giddy, almost.

"Okay," he said sternly from the doorway, his voice matching his expression once he had come back after letting the others out. "I'm going to give you... Ah, technically two things. It's a birthday present from me, 'kay? But it's kinda... practical." Without even waiting for a reply or even an acknowledgement from me, he disappeared for a second before returning with a large, gorgeously varnished wooden box with silver clasps in his arms.

I stared as he perched on the edge of the coffee table in front of me like he had done when he had stitched me up that night that felt so damn long ago, placing the case on his lap. He hesitated for a moment, looking down at the varnish before he huffed a little bit and pushed it into my arms which were not ready for that at all considering the weight of it. I couldn't help but stare at Skye as his ears grew redder and redder the longer I kept my gaze focused on him.

There was just nothing else I felt I could do.

"Are you just going to sit there and stare at me like a moron or are you actually going to open your damn present?" he demanded when he couldn't take it anymore, the redness now tingeing his cheeks. I'd always known he was gorgeous but at this point he was acting kinda... adorable.

Finally, I turned my attention to the wooden case in my lap. It was a rectangular shape roughly thirty inches long and six wide and seemed to be carved from dark, strong wood that had a faint reddish hue. My fingers hooked the cold silver clasps and flicked them open with one swift movement and I gently, and a little hesitantly, lifted the lid and felt my breath catch in my throat.

Two beautiful silver short swords lay snugly within the box upon a bed of strange black foam that seemed to be perfectly shaped around them. Both of them sat at about two-foot-long and their blades were about an inch wide and flowed somewhat seamlessly into the bone white hilt without a crossguard to hinder the beautiful slickness of the weapons.

I tore my eyes away from them to peer back up at Skye, who seemed to have recovered from his earlier embarrassment. Without a word, he heaved himself to his feet just to turn and sit himself down closer to me. I seemed hyper-aware of his presence and shifted a little self-consciously as he leaned toward me and the box.

"I had them sorted for you for ages, but I never knew when to pass them on. It seems kind of the perfect time now." He took one of the blades from its snug home and held it securely in his right hand, feeling the weight of it before smiling, satisfied, and then turning once again to place his disarmingly bright eyes on me. "And I'm going to teach you how to fight with them."

XI
Falling and Angels

Living with Skye proved to be an experience to say the least. For the most part, we managed to remain civil and sometimes even enjoy the time we spent together. He had given up his bedroom for me, claiming that I needed the privacy more than he did due to me being a teenage girl, and made up a bed for himself on the sofa. We both cooked, we both cleaned and remained considerate to each other's needs. In fact, the only time we argued was when we trained with only one exception.

Training with Skye was difficult. He said now that Yael was back, I needed to learn how to defend myself, but I had no previous experience in hand-to-hand combat as I didn't even have any siblings to fight with. He didn't seem to understand that and just expected the world from me as soon as we started my training. He seemed to expect me to automatically know how to stand defensively, how to hold the blades, how to block, parry, how to move, where my feet should go, but there was no way I could tell him that I didn't know without him getting mad at me.

As it was an Agency building, I should have suspected that there would be a pool, training dojo, gym, shooting range which included archery targets and a weapons lockup that only Hunters had access to in the basement, but it still surprised the hell out of me the first time we visited. The only facility we used together was the dojo, which turned out to be a huge octagonal room with slick wooden floors and darker panelled walls, no windows and only the one door. The whole area was lit by white glowing sconces pressed into the walls and two large squares of unnatural white light within the high ceiling. It was mostly bare if not for several crash mats in the corner that Skye placed down on our first couple of visits but then decided against it when I stopped falling over.

We ended up spending almost every day there and it nearly always ended up with me storming out after he practically exploded after I fumbled with the cheap iron practice blades or he had actually found a way through my lame attempt at a defence. Let's just say I did not appreciate Skye asking, loudly, if I was stupid or something and, as was becoming usual for us, the word 'moron' was thrown around a lot.

It wasn't as if I wasn't trying as hard as I could, I really was, but I just didn't find it as easy Skye expected. He had grown up in a different world to me so I suppose I should understand his frustration but couldn't he see that it was the same way around for me? I had been awakened to this world only recently and he just expected me to take to it like a duck to water.

Of course, there were other stresses that needed to be addressed and they didn't really help my training or my crap attitude toward Skye because it was difficult to remain focused. I'd be doing okay before, all of a sudden, I would remember why this was all happening, why I had to train with the man I was currently *living* with, and my concentration would be forgotten to be replaced by fear. Skye would kick me right in the side and I wouldn't be able to block it; that was when he would usually start shouting at me.

However, it was starting to look like I was improving the more time we both spent in the dojo. I was growing more used to the feeling of having weapons in my hands and I was even settling into a defensive stance even without Skye's prompting. Within a few weeks, I even started to understand how to block the surprise attacks that Skye loved to throw at me. I could move, dodge and react better than I had been able to when all of this started to happen to me.

Still, through all of this, through the changes and the training, there was still one thing I could not get to used to and it involved Skye. Whenever he decided that what I was doing wasn't good enough, be it from the way I stood to the way I even *breathed*, he found the need to enter my personal space and shift me manually himself. His hands would brush my hips as he shifted my centre of gravity and my heart would all but burst from the sheer proximity of him. I couldn't discern whether it was because it was a guy touching me or if it was because it was *Skye* doing the touching and the thought of that was not something I could get my head around. I would feel his fingers press against mine, altering the grip on the practice blades, all the while muttering instructions into my ear before releasing me and I would be allowed to breathe for all of three seconds before I was forced to defend myself again. He would grin in that boyish way as he somehow taunted and encouraged me to not only defend but to attack too but it was all too hard when my heart was racing and I couldn't tear my eyes from him.

Every way Skye Carter moved had a purpose, every twist of his body was done for a reason as he forced me to step back, to raise a blade to defend my front while he used my distraction to attack me from the left. He had me captivated by the way he made it all look so effortless. It made me want to try harder so I could be on his level, to fight like he knew how to do. I wanted to work with him rather than to be the cause of his hardship.

Before long the dojo was filled with the sound of ringing metal as our weapons clashed, grunts as I dodged and he was forced to overexert himself in an attempt to land a hit on me and an occasional, less frequent than before, thud as I hit the ground after not focusing on my footwork. He had probably been cutting me some slack after the first couple of weeks training went badly or I would never have been able to stand my ground against him, either that or he was an absolutely incredible teacher.

Of course as the dojo was shared, there were times where we were unable to use it as it had been occupied by other inhabitants of the building that also belonged to the Agency. During these times, we lounged in Skye's apartment, eating junk food, watching movies and occasionally strange sci-fi episodes about a crazy man with a time-travelling box.

There was that one incident though that almost put my existence in Skye's life into question and by that vague statement, I really don't know if I meant he would have kicked me out or killed me.

Fortunately, he did neither but I still felt like it was a close call.

In Skye's bedroom, most of the walls were cream, except for the one on the same side of the room as the door which was painted black, roughly and almost violently.

It was morning and I was sitting on the bed rubbing my dry eyes and considering the day when I truly noticed the wall properly for the first time. It had been in the first week I'd been living with Skye, I think, and I wasn't confident enough in my surroundings to leave the room without Skye waking up and moving around the apartment first so I was simply *there*, listening out for movement.

That's when I noticed the strange ridges and odd patterns that seemed to give the wall an odd sort of texture. My gaze had been tracing the ridges almost absently until my brain suddenly caught on to the shapes that seemed to rise out of the paint in lumps and rises.

So I stood up slowly and quietly padded to the wall to check if the ridges were there or just a trick of the light and to my enormous surprise the layer of black paint sloughed off like burned paper at my touch, revealing another cream wall directly behind it. The ridge I had noticed before was a length of red string that was now half-coated in black paint.

I *should* have stopped there but I *should* have known I could never keep my curiosity in check, so I peeled away some more of the really awful quality paint to see what else I had unearthed. The red thread continued in a strange two-dimensional cat's cradle and I followed it with my eyes while tracing the patterns and lines with my fingers before hooking my one digit underneath the thread and gently pulled. A sprinkling of dried paint showered down on me while two or more pins fell from the wall and onto the floor as my pulling on the thread had tugged them free. Now that several pins that held the thread in place had fallen from it, the thread hung there loosely and I was able to follow it up to where the whole thread started, wound around the largest pin of them all.

I could see, easily, under the thin paint was a slight rise against the wall as if a piece of paper had been painted over like the thread had been and suddenly I knew what I was looking at.

This was how Skye was keeping tabs and keeping a close eye on Yael. I didn't really need to pick away the paint and pull the supposed photo down and I didn't need to gently scratch away the paint on the surface of the photo to reveal a blurred and slightly ruined photo of the demon that still haunted my nightmares, but I did.

Now, in his defence, this was Skye's home and in *my* defence, he did allow me use of his room which meant he should have knocked before entering in case I wasn't decent. In fact, I think he thought I was still asleep and just wanted to fetch something without bothering me. Instead, he walked into his room and found me standing in front of the black painted wall, paint chips around my feet and the photo in my hands like some guilty two-year-old who had just been caught trying to force a jam sandwich into the DVD player.

"What," he began, his voice shaking with anger, "do you think you're doing?"

He was quiet and would not take his eyes from me and I dared not move. "I... I'm sorry..."

"I let you into my home... and you... you..." he suddenly burst into activity, snatching the photo from my hands and turning to the wall, taking in the loose thread, the chipped paint. "What have you done?!"

"I didn't mean to, I was just-" I attempted to apologise, but he wouldn't hear it.

"You really *can't* leave anything the hell alone can you?!" He threw the photo to the floor as if it burned him. "I don't know who the hell you think you are, but you can't just waltz into someone's home and start poking your stupid immature nose into their business."

"You *invited* me here," I snapped.

"Well, that was a mistake wasn't it?" He turned to the wall. "Get out of my sight."

Saying I bolted wasn't half the truth of what I did; as soon as he seemed to give me permission to let him seethe to himself, I was out of the room and halfway to the living room before he'd even finished his sentence. I knew I still had a bag of untouched clothing that Blue and Sam had bought me for my birthday tucked away behind the sofa and if I just grabbed a few things I needed from the bathroom, I should be fine to go crash at Blue's. Actually, Sam's was more likely as his parents didn't have a giant vendetta against me. After that, I'd get a job, find a place and hopefully come into my powers quickly to minimise the awkwardness with Skye. Maybe the Agency would house me.

I didn't even get to the front door. After throwing my necessities from the bathroom into the bag of clothing I had rooted through to make sure I had everything, I heard a heavy sigh and an overly tired "what are you doing?" from the doorway.

I turned to face him and saw him standing there, leaning against the doorjamb with his arms crossed and a dissatisfied grimace on his features. "Leaving?" I was so confused that he wasn't literally kicking me out at that point so my words came out as a question.

He sighed again and moved to the living room while saying, "don't be stupid, come on, and put your stuff back."

I was confused. He didn't want me to leave? I carefully and a little hesitantly placed my toiletries back where I had found them and made my way back into the living room where he had just thrown himself on the sofa with yet another heavy sigh. He didn't *seem* as angry anymore, but that might be to lure me into a false sense of security before he killed me and this anxious worry morphed into fear when he motioned for me to sit beside him on the sofa. *He was definitely going to kill me.*

I sat down hesitantly beside him, but neither of us spoke and Skye only peered at me with a strange sort of frown on his face like he was struggling to find the words. I had no idea what to say as I was convinced that anything I *did* say would lead to my death so I kept quiet and allowed him to figure it out for himself.

Eventually, he muttered, "Are you scared of me?"

That was definitely not what I was expecting to hear so for a second, I simply stared at him. "What? Why do you ask?"

He sighed. "Do you know what people called me at the Agency when I became a Hunter? *Demon...* and they did that because they were frightened of me. I came into my powers at thirteen, became a Hunter only a few months later but had been killing demons privately since. I've also been hunting down a high demon since my parents were slaughtered, without backing from the Agency and when they found out, they demanded that I join the Guardian Corps or they'd throw me into the Reavers. My first Charge.... Matthew... died under my watch. I just shouted at you because you found my old stalker-wall of Yael... Why wouldn't you be scared of me?"

"I... I'm not afraid of you," I began haltingly. "You've been through a lot. You want to avenge your family and Matthew and I can understand that. Your *enthusiasm* may seem a little much for the people that don't know you or only see on the sidelines or from behind a desk but, no, you're not scary. I feel *safe* with you." Apart from when you shout at me; I omitted that part.

Skye stayed quiet for a while after this as if he were mulling it over. Finally, after what seemed like an age, he spoke and his voice shook.

"You... you *trust* me? Is that what you're saying?" This seemed incredibly important to him and I nodded.

"With my life." Despite everything, our rocky beginning, the way he'd used to abandon me to go on dates, our relationship had definitely evolved into something I could trust. He had come to me every time I was in trouble, he had comforted me, stitched up my wounds, gave me a roof over my head when I had none and the most important thing, he had told me everything about *me* when everyone else seemed dead set against me knowing. He allowed me to understand who I was and I would forever be grateful. So yes, I trusted him.

Something seemed to pass through my Guardian then. His eyes were wide, his fists clenched and jaw set. Suddenly, with a force that surprised me, he embraced me, hard.

I froze completely. This wasn't like the embraces he had given me when he thought I needed comforting; he had done this because he didn't know what else to do. This time, it was for him.

"Out of everyone," he murmured into my ear, "you should be the one to trust me least. I've done nothing but let you down and put you in danger since I was made your Guardian but here you are..."

"I wouldn't be here if it weren't for you." My hands tried to find somewhere to hold him but everywhere just felt warm, hard and awkward. I could feel his body heat through his clothes, the easy muscles under his skin that were tensed from whatever emotion was coursing through him and my heart was pounding too much for me to be comfortable no matter where I chose to hold him.

"You're not like the others, Erika. Thank you."

His touch lingered for a moment before I felt him suddenly freeze. A second later, he'd jerked back in surprise as if he'd just realised what he'd been doing, embracing me the way he had been.

We both sat, frozen, staring at each other for what felt like an age until eventually, he awkwardly stood up, motioned to the kitchen with a murmured "coffee" and was gone, but something about him somehow stayed with me. I could still feel his scent on me, but that wasn't it, I could still hear his voice ringing in my ears, but that wasn't it either. I didn't know what it was but even when Skye stood up and left I still felt like he was sitting right next to me. I was warm, far too warm, and my heart was racing. I did not like it.

I also didn't know what it meant.

After he had made good on his deal of coffee with breakfast as an added apology for how he had acted, Skye pointed to the balcony door that was hidden behind a maroon drape, as was his usual signal that he was going for a cigarette. I left him to it for a moment but I was still feeling the fuzziness that had attacked me when he decided to hug me and screw me up completely, so I decided to follow him for the first time since I'd lived with him.

Outside, it was cold; spring was making itself known, but the nights were still cool and it took a while for the mornings to warm up. At this point it was enough for me to pull my hooded jacket around my shoulders and pull the long sleeves over my hands to protect them from the biting air.

Skye didn't seem to mind, however, as he stood against the side in only a t-shirt and jeans with a lit cigarette between his lips. I didn't know how to feel about his insistence about smoking outside while I was staying in his apartment. It was nice that he was considerate enough, but I didn't want to be a burden and change his life any more than I already had. My rational part told me that it was his own decision to have me in his home, even after that argument but the other side just worried about what this was doing to his schedule. He hadn't been on a single date since my arrival and same for any gigs with his band.

In short, I was feeling bad.

He turned as he heard me close the door behind me and, removing the cigarette from between his lips after taking a deep drag, he tapped the tip of ash off with a finger. "You shouldn't really come out here," he didn't sound angry or mad, just concerned.

"Is it dangerous?" I asked, peering over the railing at the ground below. I couldn't see any demons or anything down there but considering who owned the building, I wasn't really surprised.

He chuckled under his breath. "It's cold," he told me and turned back to the city in the distance, shrouded in fog. "Wouldn't want you to get sick, would we? I can function as a Guardian, but a nurse? I think I lack the people skills."

"I just wanted to talk more." I nudged his side playfully. "That a problem?"

He chortled and nudged me back. "Talk away. Good company is good."

His smirk was playing across his lips and I felt colour rise to my cheeks again.

"I was wondering about something..." and I had. The whole thing had been bugging me for weeks, but I never knew how to bring it up. No one else had brought it up; part of me wondered whether it was a strange kind of taboo no one was allowed to talk about. However, I kinda thought that gave me a little leeway for being an inquisitive 'I've been kept in the dark my whole life' kind of halfbreed.

"What's up?"

"Demons exist... that much is obvious and that just leads me to more questions... I mean, what about angels? Do they exist?"

He looked at me for a moment, as if thinking quickly but eventually he sighed and took another quick drag of his cigarette. As he spoke, he breathed out the noxious smoke in little faded puffs that I followed with my eyes. "I don't think '*Angel*' is the right word."

"What do you mean?"

"Angels are supposed to be good, right? All this '*Warriors of God*' and '*benevolent and kind*' nonsense but what I've *seen* hasn't been like that. I mean the legend of what angels are have to come from somewhere but... I don't know..." He scratched his head as if having trouble forming his thoughts. Suddenly he jerked up and looked at me. "Remember when you saw Yael and his form sort of... *shimmered*?"

"You said it was glamour?"

"Right!" He seemed pleased that I remembered. "That's how *angels* appear to me and throughout the years since the Agency was formed, other people have reported the same. Some can't see it and just blindly state that they're angels without considering an alternative, but there have been enough questions in the air for the Agency to come up with another name for them. We call them Celestials."

"Celestials?"

"Yep. I've only come across a couple when I was younger and chasing down Hunts down by the coast, but they feel different to me... *wrong* ... they make my skin crawl... The Agency has forbidden us to engage them because they largely keep to themselves... as far as the Agency goes, they're nothing to do with us."

"That's sad."

"Why?"

I smiled though it was half-hearted. "I kinda hoped that there'd be something good amongst all this... some little thing that said 'hey, it's not all bad, look at us... we'll rescue you'."

He looked at me for a long while after that before reaching over as if to squeeze my hand but instead awkwardly patted my shoulder after changing his mind halfway through, which still made my heart beat faster in my chest. "You're the good amongst all this crap. People like you give people like me hope... you're doing a lot of rescuing and you don't even know it."

And that's how life went. I stayed with Skye, we trained, we ate, we binge-watched whole series of TV shows in one sitting and then we trained some more. All of my work for school had gone up in smoke – literally – so the only chance I had to study was at school when I was under the watch of the mysterious Carers. I never knew who they were, but I had fun with Blue trying to guess.

Even after everything that had happened and the way my life changed, once I'd gotten used to it, I guess I was kind of happy...

However, as things go in this kind of world, it wasn't going to last long.

I'd been living with Skye for about a month and a half when Skye received that phone call and everything changed. *Again.*

It was a Saturday evening, neither of us had anything to do and the training room had been booked for the next three days so we were sitting there, not really doing much but watching movies and spending our time in a comfortable silence. My legs were out and were crossed at the ankles over his knees as he lounged in the corner area of the couch. I was almost comfortable if it weren't for the times when Skye would randomly tickle my foot and I'd shriek and try to kick him in the face so I was now on edge waiting for the next attack.

That's when his phone went off.

He glanced at the display on his cell and then raised an eyebrow before tapping the accept button and raising it to his ear. "Dylan?"

I seized the remote and turned down the volume on the television, earning a wink of thanks from Skye. I could hear a fuzzy voice on the other end, but I couldn't hear exactly what was being said.

"Wait, you want me to... why?" Whatever this *Dylan* was saying to Skye, it wasn't good. Skye sat up and I took my feet away, watching is expression morph from confusion to anger and back again. "But I didn't!... Okay, so what about Erika, she can't... WHAT?! But she *hates*... Can't she... But... I... *fine*. I'll be there." And he hung up.

I was too worried to ask Skye what was actually happening, but it wasn't long before he told me anyway, after he'd stood up and had paced around once or twice, swearing.

He looked at me. "The Agency have demanded a meeting with me," he said, slowly. "I'm going to take you somewhere safe until I can come get you. Grab your swords."

I sat bolt upright. "Is it serious?"

"Probably not," he wasn't telling me the truth, "but I want you protected as much as possible. You *will* be kept safe... so let's hope you've learned how to defend yourself, shall we?"

XII
Feelings and Fighting

I had no idea where we were going. I knew we weren't going to the Agency because Blue had told me that fluctuating halfbreeds weren't allowed anywhere near the building and the Overseers seemed to think they were too important to actually deal with us and left that troublesome chore to the Guardians. So I sat in the car and watched the world go by through the window, feeling more and more aware of the wooden box with the two swords snugly inside, resting on my lap. Where were we going if I needed my swords? Who was I about to be fighting? What was even happening?

We pulled up in front of a large white modern house that had been built atop a hill that was dark with lush grass, discoloured by the combined effects of the gloom and colour-leeching streetlamps.

There was a large white garage stuck to the side of the flat-roofed building and the drive that led from the deep black garage door merged with a winding brick path that I followed with my eyes to an immaculate front porch. Skye switched off the engine to his precious car and sighed heavily, before opening the drivers' side door and stepping out into the dark.

I followed suit, tucking my wooden case under my right arm and began to make my way up the path but stopped when I felt Skye's hand wrap around my wrist and pull me back a little. I turned to face him as his fingers gently traced around my skin and without a word he strapped the tracking device to me and pulled down the sleeve of my hooded jacket over the top if it. His fingers lingered on the skin on the back of my hand for a moment before he shook his head, grabbed my hand hard and towed me into step toward the house.

Once there, he pressed down on the pretty white doorbell next to the sleek black painted door with silver handle and letterbox and we both patiently waited until I heard strangely sharp footsteps approaching and the door opened to reveal the last person I expected to see.

"Skye," Isla ignored me altogether as she looked at the man she was obviously still in love with. "Dylan called. What have you done this time?"

He said nothing and marched inside the house, pulling me along with him. The hallway we were now standing in smelled distinctly floral and incredibly clean, nothing like the scent of smoke that had started to feel like home to me and it almost glowed with the intensity of the immaculate white paint the walls were covered in. The floors were wooden and varnished to the point that the shine from the overly bright fake lighting above us almost blinded me; the furniture, sideboards and sleek cupboards, however, were black and it gave the whole hallway a sort of monochromatic feel that made me feel a little uneasy.

"Why do you have to go to the Agency then? Spill the beans." She seemed quite cheerful, but I couldn't see why, considering my Guardian's suddenly foul mood.

Skye focused the full strength of his glare on Isla. "It's none of your business why I have to go to the Agency. All that matters to *you* is making sure Erika is safe while I'm gone."

She blinked, temporarily taken aback but quickly covered it well with an offhand, "sure, sure. Whatever." Isla rolled her eyes, but they widened in surprise when Skye reached forward and grabbed her arm.

"I mean it, Isla. Nothing happens to Erika. Not one single hair on her head is harmed while I'm gone or I swear I will hold you personally responsible." His voice was venom and even I backed away a little.

"Okay, I got it." Isla's eyes were still wide and her face had lost all colour. I tried to look away, but Skye's fire would not let me. I was fascinated by him.

Finally, he let go of Isla's arm and turned to me, the hardness in his brilliant eyes relaxing. "I won't be long, okay? Wait for me?"

I nodded. "Okay. I'll be fine."

"You'd better be," he said this with another sidelong glance at Isla before turning around and exiting via Isla's front door. The silence that followed his departure added to the tension I could have cut with a knife as Isla looked me up and down, obviously considering how to proceed.

"Well, let's make the most of this," she sighed, obviously about as happy about this arrangement as I was. "Want a drink?"

"Is it poisoned?" I muttered under my breath as she led me down the hallway and into a lovely open plan living room, kitchen thing that all on one side had massive windows for walls that overlooked a darkened yard lit periodically with what I assumed were tiny, solar-powered orbs that had been pushed into the ground. The living room and kitchen both continued with the black and white theme with black leather couches and armchairs facing the TV, though one armchair had been turned to face the others, back to the windows and the large glass walls that I noticed hid a couple of out-folding patio doors to escape into the yard. The kitchen counters were black too and as I looked around, I noticed that Isla was the most colourful thing *in* the damn place with her stupid red hair, blue tank top and brown knee-high boots. Her jeans were black which didn't really surprise me.

"What?" Luckily it seemed like she had honestly misheard me.

"Do you have soda?" I covered up quickly.

"Ugh, no. I have bottled water or green tea."

"Green tea, then."

"Water it is." She strolled straight into the kitchen and pointed to the sofas. "Take a seat and chill."

I turned to face the sofas fully, trying to quash my irritation while still clutching my case close to my chest in case I suddenly had an urge to throw the whole lot at her, when movement caught my eye and I stopped and stared. One large white fluffy lump that I had mistaken for a throw cushion *stretched and yawned*, showing a little pink mouth and dainty white fangs before it blinked and stared at me with eyes the same colour as Skye's. The cat then mewed at me, jumped off the couch and sauntered over to where I stood, brushing up against my legs once before it trotted off to where Isla was retrieving water from the refrigerator. Pretty kitty, I thought as I watched it practically skip over to her, tail in the air.

I lowered my case down gently and then peered out of the window into the spreading gloom and the pretty little lights that made her yard look annoyingly magical.

A moment later she returned and pressed a bottle of water in my hands with a smug sort of smile that *really* irritated me and then turned back to the seating area.

"*So,*" she said as she sat on one of the squat leather armchairs, crossing her thin legs luxuriously. "How has it been, living with Skye?"

I *really* didn't want to talk about Skye; in fact, I didn't want to talk at all. Isla made me extremely uncomfortable, but I couldn't quite say whether it was because of her antagonistic attitude, pretty face, awesome figure or the way she had known Skye for so much longer than I had. Perhaps all of the above. I leaned forward on the back of the armchair, playing with but not drinking the bottle of water she had passed to me, hoping my actions annoyed her. "It's good," I managed, unhappily.

"You're getting along?"

"I guess..."

"I suppose you don't really talk much, you're still so young."

I couldn't take it anymore. "Why is any of this your business? Why do we have to talk about Skye?"

She snorted. "Because you're hanging around him like a bad smell and to be honest, it's annoying. You look like you know him, but you don't." Isla leaned back in her seat. "All you see is the Guardian that was assigned to you, not the man he is behind his duty."

"And you know him?" I felt my eyebrow twitch in irritation at her self-important tone and I tried to push it to the back of my mind, moving to face the patio doors, leaving my wooden case on the armchair. I could still see her reflection in the glass, night turning the window into a dull mirror. Perfection itself, even in the darkness.

She smirked. "Oh, I *know* him." I didn't like the implication in her tone and dug my fingers into my biceps without truly understanding why. The sharp bite of my nails helped centre me and I was able to push, if only for a moment, my feelings aside. "I know him better than you do."

This annoyed me. "I don't think so."

Isla laughed and kicked her feet up, her heels clicking on the laminate as she finally perched on the armchair in a way that didn't make me want to punch her in her stupid smug face. She was so much more than I was and she knew it. "Okay, Erika... enlighten me. Tell me, who Skye is."

"He's kind." The words slipped from my mouth despite knowing how ridiculous they were about to sound. Isla was right, but I didn't want to admit it: Skye was *kind to me* and that only proved that Skye had a side that he wouldn't show to me, his charge. He was keeping me safe and the attitude he had toward me was also to that effect, being kind, being someone I could depend on so I would trust him. He needed my trust or he would not be able to protect me. I knew it, but I was *not* going to admit it to *her*.

I did not need to hear the scathing laugh that escaped her perfect lips. "Oh Erika, how naïve you are."

I ground my teeth together and stared into the black yard that faced me. "Are you sure it's me that doesn't know the real him?" Finally, I turned to face her and I saw the shocked expression on her countenance for an instant before that self-satisfied smile lifted the corners of her lips once more. "Maybe it's you that's caught up in the lie."

Isla stood up and picked a strand of white cat fur off her snug-fitting jeans before approaching me. I caught her floral scent, saw the brightness of her eyes and the perfect pout of her full lips and felt my own inadequacy deliver a swift sucker punch to my gut. She leaned down close to me and peered into my eyes. "He has no reason to pretend to me, princess," she purred. "I've seen him *bare*, down to the base instincts of life."

She wasn't just implying their relationship anymore. Even if it was not the case at that precise moment, at some point in the past, Isla and Skye had had a sexual relationship and the thought of it made my skin crawl. I shouldn't care. I wouldn't care. I didn't care. Skye was only my Guardian... who he had sex with was his own damn business.

Satisfied with my silence, Isla continued. "You're still a *child*, Erika. Even if, by some miracle, you understand Skye, you're still nothing but a charge to him. The moment you come into your powers, he will abandon you because you will not need him and he will have no more reason to be close to you. The sooner you come to realise this, the better it will be for you. Don't be so foolish as to fall in love with him."

"I won't fall in love with him." My voice came from far away, but it sounded sure, firm and confident. It did not shake and I almost smiled in relief while she nodded once and moved away again, but I wasn't sure that meant that she believed me.

I had gotten to the point where the fuzzy feelings that I'd been getting when it came to Skye were starting to annoy me and worry me at the same time, especially when I had the ever gorgeous red-headed Isla to poke at my imperfections and to flaunt her experiences with the guy in my face. It made me all the more aware that all I was at that moment was an eighteen-year-old virgin who had never had a boyfriend in her life and never even thought she'd ever like anyone. I was starting to believe that the reason I felt strange whenever I was around *him* was because, perhaps, my feelings toward him were starting to change.

For what seemed like an hour after that, we sat in pretty much dead silence. Isla was reading a book while absently stroking her pretty cat and I had removed my two blades from their home to look at them and for, well, comfort. It felt like I had known them for longer than the month and a half that I'd had them. I would be eternally grateful for Skye for giving them to me.

It always came back to him and that annoyed me more than I thought.

In all honesty, I thought I was going to be safe there; I thought Isla would be able to keep me safe like Dan, Shion and *he* could, but I guess she didn't really have much of a chance, not with what happened.

My blades were crossed over my legs, my head leaning over the back of the armchair while I stared listlessly out into Isla's upside-down yard that I *definitely* didn't think was beautiful in the darkness.

Due to being so on-edge that even Isla's breathing pissed me off, I saw the abrupt movement outside and reacted instantly. Rolling off the seat and into a crouched position, brain catching up with what my body already knew, I focused my eyes on the darkness outside as Isla looked up in alarm at my sudden activity, lowering her book. I didn't breathe for a moment, but she leapt to her feet when a crash outside shook the room and we were unexpectedly plunged into darkness. I heard a hissing of a cat from where Isla was standing as I stood and backed as far away from the window as possible, closer to the woman I had no choice but to trust. I was sure now that it had been what I thought: a grey figure, shooting alongside the glass while we were happily (or not) unaware of any demon presence.

"Drones!" Isla gasped needlessly. I heard her move, quickly toward the back of the room while I continued to stare, terrified and unable to look away, out of the window. Is this what Skye meant? Did he expect this?

A discordant chorus of screeching, whining and growling filled the air, rising to a crescendo that terrified me. A loud thud from the front door echoed through the whole lower floor of the house and I tried not to turn my back on the patio and the yard full of demons, ignoring the sudden realisation that we were absolutely surrounded. Scratching, hissing and howling were buffeting ears until I didn't know what sound was coming from where and I clamped my hands over my ears, trying to shut out the noise.

I couldn't help it. "*Isla!*"

A few seconds later, I felt her come abreast with me and I could see her fastening something to her wrists as she moved in the gloom. I could see her eyes flashing as she was staring out the window at the indistinct figures that were crossing the yard, blinking in and out of shrubberies yet leaving only momentary glimpses of grey flesh in view, counting in her head as she went. After a moment, I lowered my hands and she swore.

"We are totally out of our depth here." It was rare to see Isla so uncomfortable, staring into the dark. "We need help." She turned to her retro white home phone on the sideboard and grabbed it, twisting her fingers nervously in the coiled wire as she pressed her ear to the receiver. Bitterly she swore and threw the phone down.

"Shit! They've cut the phone lines." She frowned. "Wait... they're not *that* smart to cut both the power and phone lines, surely."

"It's Yael," I whispered, sounding calmer as I was, pulling my cell from my pocket and passing it to her without even looking in her direction. I knew it was him; there was no one else it could be. I knew it with a dreadful certainty that shook me to my core.

Her head snapped toward me as what I said hit her, but she took my phone. "You're kidding right?! Why the hell would *Yael* come *here*?!"

"He wants me."

"*Why*?!"

"Because Skye is my Guardian."

"Shit," She repeated. She scrolled to Skye's phone number and tapped to call him. I heard it go straight to voicemail and she swore, bitterly, moving to throw the phone to the ground before realising that it was mine and sheepishly passing it into my hands. "It's off."

"He's at the Agency."

"Ugh! Of course, they'd tell him to switch it off."

"He listens to them?"

"He's got no choice anymore. He needs to toe the line extremely carefully now or he'll be sent to the Reavers."

I passed my phone back to her. "Call Shi."

"Shion... Shion..." She scrolled through my contacts again. "Wait, you call him Shi?"

"Is that really important right now?"

She tapped to call him and put the phone to her ear. It rang twice before he answered and I heard his sardonic voice faintly from where I stood at Isla's side.

"Shion! We're in trouble!" Isla snapped, cutting through whatever Shion was saying. "Yes, it's me... I threw it on the floor and it broke, but that's *not* important! We're at my house, Skye's at the Agency and... *No* Shion! Yael's here!"

I heard him swear several times before snapping something back to her, urgently.

"We don't have twenty minutes, Shion!" she almost screamed. *"The demons are here NOW!"*

She hung up and threw my cell into my hands and if it weren't for the fact that I was expecting it, I wouldn't have caught it. Isla obviously didn't care much for technology. As she moved, I saw something gleam along her arm, a light that was reflected off several plates of metal that was strapped to her wrist, forming a gleaming gauntlet. On her left arm, it was much the same with one large difference: attached to the plates that crossed over the knuckles were three long claw-like blades that were hooked at the tips with vicious-looking points.

Of course, Isla was a Hunter. She knew how to fight.

"Arm yourself," Isla whispered to me as her eyes sliced into mine. "Stay behind me and I will try my best to protect you but do not stay unarmed. I am not a Guardian and I cannot promise that I know how to keep you alive."

"What about the front door?" I asked her urgently.

"I've activated the security my father installed. They will not be getting into this room from there. Unfortunately, the windows, while reinforced, will break eventually..." I thought I heard a little bit of shame in her voice then but ignored it as I moved to retrieve my blades from where I'd foolishly left them on the chair.

By the time I turned back to look at Isla, six drones had leapt from the extensive greenery within her yard and were pressing their flat faces against the glass, snarling and hissing. Behind them, I could still see more drones dancing through the leaves, screeching and my grip on my blades instantly tightened as my brain went through all the lessons with Skye as he taught me how to fight and defend myself and somehow found that, in my panic, I had forgotten everything.

It was me and Isla against who knew how many damn drones were out there which was dubious enough but add in the fact that Isla *hated* me and there was a *high demon* outside that was bent on destroying my Guardian's life, I was pretty sure I was going to die.

"Come on then you slimy bastards! You want the damn brat?!" Isla screamed at the window and the demons beyond. *"You're gonna have to go through me."* She dropped down into a stance that I didn't

recognise as she balled her hands into trembling fists. Her form was tensed but oddly fluid as if she could snap into action at any moment.

We stood there for a moment, watching the demons bay at us while we settled into our defensive stances until a roaring that I couldn't quite place reached our ears. Suddenly, the whole yard lit up like a sparkler, the trees, flowers and bushes all thrown into sharp focus just before they were burned to ash within the huge ball of white fire that was heading straight toward us.

"GET DOWN!" Isla screamed just before it hit and I barely had time to cover my face with my forearms when the reinforced glass walls shattered inwards with one blast.

The force of the explosion propelled me backward and my back slammed against the wall behind me, hard, knocking the wind out of me completely. My fall to the ground jarred my arms and I dropped both swords I had miraculously kept a hold of while being forced through the air and having sheets of glass flung at me.

"Erika! Stay down!" Isla was on her feet and was somehow still in a position to fight while I was struggling to breathe and find the strength to pull myself up. Isla was sporting new injuries: cuts on her face and body where the glass had hit her and she seemed to be favouring her right leg over the left, but somehow she was still standing confident and unfaltering and I felt shame hit me.

Was I really just going to let her do all the fighting? Wasn't this what Skye was preparing me for? Wasn't I supposed to *help* rather than just hide in the corner and get others killed?! I might not get along with Isla, but she didn't deserve to die!

The woman in question was standing in front of the shattered window, the air around her roaring with flames in two diagonal lines from where she stood to the edges of the broken window, funnelling the demons toward her and minimising the chance of her being flanked or caught unawares. She was keeping the drones at bay with a fighting style that was unfamiliar to me but reminded me of some sort of martial art as she relied on not only her gauntlet and claw but her own body as a weapon of its own kind. As the drones were forced to face her head-on, she kept the them distracted with her deadly left gauntlet with wide swipes that forced them to leap backwards while lashing out with her right fist and even kicking out with her legs and moving so fast I could barely see her. As I watched her, scrambling to get my blades, she stepped back quickly as a drone launched at her out of nowhere and answered by sweeping up her right arm, palm out and sending three swift balls of fire straight at the collected demons that just did not stop coming. Her skill, I understood, was fire.

Now on my feet, I dashed over to where Isla stood fighting but before I could reach, one of the drones took advantage of her fragmented concentration and slipped under her arm, heading, instead, straight at me.

"Brat!" she gasped in a hope to alert me, unable to turn around and risk getting herself killed. With a scream, I raised my right arm and swung hard, clenching my eyes shut tight as I felt the sword bite into the drone and then, just as quickly, break free. I opened my eyes to see the head of the drone I'd just dispatched roll toward Isla as if in slow motion while the body crumpled to the floor beside me, smearing my clothes with black blood. Discovering what I'd done, I tried not to let the shock of the kill bother me but Isla hardly reacted to my actions at all, instead giving the head a disdainful kick away from where she stood.

She stepped to the side a little to allow me to fight by her side but somehow managed to keep a watchful eye on what I was doing so I didn't allow any attacks to get past my flimsy guard. However, after a while of continuous fighting and maintaining the two walls of flame, it was obvious it was starting to take its toll. I could see her slowing down, backing off and sweat beading her forehead as the constant waves of drones just kept flying toward us while those we hadn't managed to kill permanently healed and bolted at us with renewed vigour.

"I can't... keep this up for much longer..." she panted at me as she punched a leaping drone right between the eyes. "You need to get the hell out of here!"

"I'm not *leaving* you!" my hands were soaked in a mixture of mine and the drones' blood so keeping a grip on my swords was becoming difficult, especially when they clawed, bit and scratched at every bit of me they could reach. "What good will it do if you die!?"

"Skye will *kill* me if anything happens to you anyway so it's not going to *matter*!" I went to retort just as the flame walls on either side of us finally flickered and died and a demon, sensing its chance, leapt from the back of the group and knocked me completely off my feet, swords flying out of my grip and skittering across the floor, far out of my reach.

"*ERIKA!*" Isla screamed. She was only distracted for a moment, but it was enough for three drones to take advantage and take her at speed, clamping their wide, gaping maws around a limb each and dragging her to the ground. I couldn't see what they were doing to her, but her screams were enough to scare the hell out of me as my own demon pinned me down onto the glass-covered laminate to grin terribly down at me.

"ISLA!" I shrieked, trying to throw my demon off me but my energy was spent. "Isla! Hold on!" I could still hear her screams, but they were weakening, the strength leaving them.

"*Enough.*" My blood ran cold. Instantly the buzzing movement of the drones filling the room ceased, as did Isla's screams, replaced with only pained and terrified whimpers. Nothing moved and I heard only her frantic breathing and the crackling of burning wood for two stunted heartbeats until I heard the footsteps, slowly making their way up the decking steps toward what was left of Isla's lounge. "I do apologise for dropping in like this, ladies, but I just *have* to borrow Erika for a while."

There was a moment of silence as the speaker finally stopped a few yards from where I lay.

"Hello, my dear, did you miss me?"

Yael.

That's it. I was going to die.

I heard him make his way over to where the three drones were still pinning down the Hunter. "Oh, you've really done a number on her, haven't you?" he congratulated the drones.

"Get the *hell* away from her!" I snapped before my pounding heart could fail me.

With a chuckle, Yael then finally moved into my line of sight.

He hadn't changed much since I last saw him: the same pinstriped suit, the same smart tie and shoes, he even wore the same sick smug expression that made my skin crawl almost to the point of sobbing, but no, I wasn't about to give him the satisfaction. "You never cease to surprise me, Erika. You're such a powerhouse."

"Whatever you want it's between you and me, Isla has nothing to do with this!" I spat.

"Oh but she does... see, she tried to kill my drones. I can't really let that slide, can I?"

"I racked up a kill count too, you know. Why don't you take it out on me?"

"Erika... no." Isla's weakened voice terrified me, but I ignored the fear.

Yael laughed again. "Oh no, dear girl... I can't kill you *just* yet... I *have plans* for you. If you'd stuck around long enough *last* time, you would have known that but nooo, you just had to make a quick escape, didn't you?"

What?

"Why?"

"Now that would be telling. I'm not one to take away all the fun out of a surprise you know."

I looked over to where Isla lay, but I still could not see her, only the puddle of red that was starting to spread further past where the drones sat, still pinning her down.

"What about her?"

He looked over at her. "The Hunter?" He seemed to think for a moment. "She doesn't matter at all... although... I suppose I can make you some sort of deal if *you* care so much about her..."

"What kind of deal?" My voice shook.

"I don't want to waste any more of your blood," he announced and I felt myself go cold again. "If you come willingly, I will spare your friend... or what's left of her."

"Do... don't you... don't you *dare*... brat," Isla panted before one of the drones growled in her face.

"You'll spare her?"

"I am a demon of my word." The high demon gave a bow.

"Promise."

"I promise."

I thought quickly.

There was no way that we could get out of this situation alive as it was. If Isla was spared, managed to heal enough with her halfbreed abilities and somehow found Skye, at least it might give them a slim chance of actually mounting a rescue... But failing that? At least Isla would be alive.

"You've got a deal."

Yael laughed openly and gave me a slow round of applause, glee written in his cold, yellow eyes.

"I absolutely *adore* you, girl!" he crowed. "It's such a shame you have to die."

He clicked his fingers once and I felt the demon that was holding me down let go and I struggled to sit upright, gasping for breath.

Before I could do anything, Yael clicked his fingers again and two of the drones that had been hanging around him like some sort of honour guard crawled over to me and yanked me to my feet, standing for the first time on their two hind legs before crouching back down to hiss at me. I turned to look at Isla and wished I hadn't.

I barely recognised her. Her body was a collection of lacerations, bites and wide, blood-filled gashes, down her arms, torn through her jeans, into her legs and across her torso. Deep, sickening red literally covered her body: it soaked into her clothes, matted her hair and smudged on her face, but I could still see that her hazel eyes were open, boring into mine with almost accusation before I was forced to look away.

"I'm sorry, Isla," I had muttered before I turned to follow Yael, who had already turned away.

He stopped at the opening to kick one of his drones who had been feasting on the corpse of its fellow. "Stop that," he chided, "it's disgusting. Come along, Erika dear."

I was going to die.

We walked out into Isla's yard. It was no longer beautiful but dark, haunting, burnt and smelling of smoke and death. Corpses of charred drones that hadn't gotten out of the way of Yael's fireball fast enough were dotted here and there along the pathway and I weaved in and out of them, too scared to touch and too numb to react. I just followed Yael and his drones as he stalked a slow sedate pace through the huge yard, never looking back to see if I was following because he knew that I was too scared to run.

Unarmed, exhausted, sick and terrified; he was correct.

It took longer than I thought to reach the end of Isla's yard, but Yael finally stopped at a burned-out section of a huge hedge wall, obviously where he and the drones had entered by and motioned for me to follow him. I did so with no question. What did it matter?

I was going to die.

When all of us, including the hundred or so drones that had been milling around the yard waiting for us to show ourselves, were through the hedge, Yael called for attention.

"All of you, head home. Except you." He pointed at one of the drones and it crawled toward him snarling. Yael ducked down and caressed the drone's bald pate sickeningly as the rest fled. "I have an important job for you... go back in there and finish off that Hunter."

"Yeeessssssss," the drone screeched in agreement and then bolted back down the way we'd come and I finally realised what Yael had told him to do.

"NO!" I screamed. "No! No! Yael, you bastard! You *promised* you'd spare her!"

"I swore that *I* would spare her and as you can see, I am here with you... keeping my promise." He grinned at me and I went numb.

I didn't know where Yael was taking me. After I'd screamed at him for sending a demon to kill Isla, he simply patted me on the head, turned on his heel and started to walk down the street at the same uncaring pace he had when we were walking through the yard. Yet, it was just as horrifying without the drones, perhaps even more so. He looked so sure that I was going to follow and I did, even without question because I had no idea what else I was supposed to do; if I ran, I'd be dead within a minute.

I cried as we walked. I was terrified and sad and guilty and I didn't know what to do. Isla was dead because of me, because I was there, because I was Skye's charge. If Ben had still been alive, none of this would have happened. Why did I think about Ben? Was it because I was about to die?

Yael took me through the suburbs close to Isla's estate. He seemed to enjoy talking to me although, for most of it, I didn't listen and when I did, I wished I didn't hear it.

"You see all these houses, Erika?" he said in a singsong voice. "All these people living their lives... if they looked out the window now they would just see two people going for a walk... they wouldn't have a clue that I was taking you to your death and if they did... well... they wouldn't be able to save you, little kitten. You *are* going to die tonight, you know?"

I didn't answer. I just walked and cried.

I was going to die.

XIII
Needles and Resolve

I recognised the Industrial district as soon as we neared it. The tall buildings set against the somehow purple sky boasted the tallest chimneys in the city and gave the whole area the same old metallic tang that I smelled when I was on my way to the Poisoned Apple so long ago. Yael was almost skipping down the road, light on his feet and obviously quite pleased with himself while I trudged lifelessly behind him.

I would have been surprised if I actually cared about where we were going when he turned toward the building that had been converted so long ago into the same bar I infiltrated to seek out Skye. Oh, Skye. Where were you? Did you get into trouble? I'm sorry I couldn't protect myself *or* Isla.

The Poisoned Apple had apparently been closed since that demon attack. The doors were boarded up; the skylight was still shattered and gone was any evidence of any party-goers since. Slapped on the boarded up doors was a bright yellow sign that stated that the building was condemned... the Shield Corps at work again I guessed.

How would they cover up my death to the public? To Sam?

The thought of them *lying* to Sam about what had killed me gave me pause.

Hang on. Why the hell had I accepted the idea of dying at Yael's hand so easily?

Wasn't I the girl who had survived two demon attacks, managed to kill a drone *and* get my *Guardian* out of danger before I even understood what was going on?

I had to pull myself together; I mean, *think about it*, Erika, what would the guys do in my place? What would Skye do? He'd grab a weapon and go for Yael straight on. What would Dan do? Dan would find a way to distract Yael to gain an advantage. What would Shion do? He'd probably do the exact same as Skye but with more complaining. So what would *Skye say to me at this moment*?!

Buck up and do your best. You're stronger than this and you're gonna get through. Yael's tough and he's a vindictive bastard, but he's never gone up against someone as resourceful and strong as *you*.

I was *not going to die*.

With a new outlook, I continued to follow Yael into the club, through the familiar corridor which was not only still smeared with graffiti but still stank of urine, sweat and beer. Only now, however, there was a new smell that made my stomach *turn*: blood. No one but demons had been here since the attack and that terrified me more than I wanted to admit; it was like they had taken a piece of our world and had turned it into their own and we no longer had any right to it.

It didn't take long to get to the main room within the converted factory but when we did, I almost couldn't stop the urge to turn around and bolt. The room was brightly lit but the only purpose it served was to show me upon entry that the hall was filled with drones to spilling, they were lounging on the shattered bar, laying on the floor eating thankfully unidentified pieces of meat and paused threateningly when I stepped inside. The two drones closer to the door stopped whatever they were doing and lifted their flat, horrific faces into the air, nostrils flaring as they caught my scent – the scent of a fluctuating halfbreed. "Taaaasties..?"

Yael paused at the entrance and crossed his arms, his smooth forehead creasing with disapproval.

"Drones are such a... handful," he told me in an almost conversational manner. He strode easily into the centre of the huge hall with a definite purpose. He didn't shout exactly but his voice forced itself to be heard, commanding the air around it to allow it to reach the creatures assembled. "The sun is down, yet you continue to skulk around here like filth?! Get out there and bring me something worth eating instead of simple scraps. Get us something we can really sink our teeth into."

I knew what he meant. He wanted something alive. He wanted something to kill. The only reason I wasn't on the menu was because he needed me.

As one, the buzzing, rolling mass of drones separated like a piece of cloth being torn apart and almost fled through the open doors and shattered windows, screeching, growling and hissing as they went. Not a one dared to cross anywhere near where Yael stood, watching the proceedings calmly. Only a few stragglers remained after a minute, those who were already clutching fleshy prizes who did not wish to leave them unattended and risk losing them to another smarter drone. Yael seemed to at least understand that on some level because he did not press the issue. He simply continued on his way into the room and I knew without a doubt that I was supposed to follow. So I did, fear pushing me onward while my eyes darted this

226

way and that for an opportunity to not only escape, but stay escaped.

"Mister Yael!" We both stopped about halfway through the hall, a childlike voice reaching us and, despite myself, my eyes widened, as I saw what could only be described as a small boy standing on the same stage that I had seen Skye and his band occupying before. He could be nothing but a human child because I could see no tell-tale shimmer or sign of glamour as I could from Yael. The boy's round face, pink cheeks and adorable flop of chestnut hair covering one of his brilliant green eyes could not be physically touched by anything demonic. He was beautiful.

Yael seemed less shocked to see the boy.

"Huey," he snapped, clicking his fingers, "get down or you'll end up hurting yourself." I was shocked. The way Yael spoke was nothing like anytime I'd heard him speak before. Gone were the playful singsong tones and the nicknames that made my skin crawl. He was almost fatherly.

"I don't wanna." The boy finally seemed to see me behind the high demon and an expression of honest curiosity graced his features. "Who is she, Mister Yael? Are we going to kill her too?"

What?!

Yael growled, "*you* are doing nothing of the sort, Huey, now go see Lucika." The boy pouted as he stomped off to the side of the stage.

"Who the *hell* is that?!" I forgot where I was, who I was with and what my situation was as I tried my best not to shout at the high demon who had, for all intents and purposes, kidnapped me and killed Isla. What the hell was a *child* doing here? How was he still alive?!

Yael waved my voice aside with an offhand gesture before turning back toward the stage and for the first time raised his voice, "*Pol*!" A mere few moments after, the strangest drone I'd ever seen came *walking* out from the door that the creepy kid had left by.

Not only was it standing on its hind legs in a sad imitation of a human, but it had also somehow squeezed itself into a once-smart grey suit that was left bereft of any smartness due to the bloodstains and the sharp points of its spine protruding from the fabric. It reached the centre of the stage and, by my reckoning, attempted to bow.

"*Yeeees*, master?" it drawled once it had straightened as much as its curved spine would allow. I couldn't tell where it was looking as its eyes were simply back pits of nothing pressed into grey weathered flesh but I had a horrible sensation between my shoulders that told me it was looking at me.

"Be a dear, Pol and retrieve a chair for our guest will you? I'm afraid she's quite dead on her feet."

I did not miss that. The urge to just *run* increased to frightening strength and I had to clench my fists and close my eyes until it went away. Running right now would only get me killed faster. Pol did its weird bowing thing again and shuffled offstage. It was only gone for a few moments before it returned, carrying a chair which seemed far too bulky for its spindly arms until I remembered how freakishly strong drones were despite their frame. It took the stairs slowly, peering through the rusted bars on the back rest of the seat to make sure it didn't go tumbling. Once he had made it down, he placed it with a loud *thunk* in front of us.

"Thank you, dear Pol," Yael pointed to me suddenly and clicked his fingers as the shambling drone turned to leave. "Erika, be a dear and sit down for me," he said with a smile that somehow reached all the way to his dangerous yellow eyes. I sat obediently, for a moment entertaining the idea that I might be able to dash off when he wasn't looking but those thoughts were abruptly ruined when he pulled a set of shining metal handcuffs from the pocket of his expensive looking suit jacket.

With a knowing smirk, he grabbed both of my wrists and pulled them through the bars in the chair and then wrapping the handcuffs around them so I couldn't even pull myself out of the seat.

"It's nothing personal," Yael muttered to me, snapping the handcuffs into place. I was cold but the metal on my wrists was colder still, sending a dull ache to my joints. I wondered briefly if they were created with a strange sort of demon-made metal but my logical side guessed that it was only because I'd never been in handcuffs before. They had a dreaded sort of finality to them. "You've actually been a brilliant sport. But at this stage, any sudden escape attempt would be ill-advised so I'll remove you from that temptation."

As he straightened up, I tested the strength of them, pulling my wrists apart sharply but they were stuck fast and the action actually hurt. To cover my disappointment, I glared at the back of his head.

"You haven't even told me why you need me," I snapped at him, "is that how you repay me for actually being, as you say, a brilliant sport?" I had no idea where the bravado had come from, but I felt glad for it. It made me sound braver than I felt.

He looked at me for a moment, considering. I had no idea what he was thinking but if I had to guess, he was probably weighing his options. The fact that I was more than likely going to be really, really dead soon probably influenced his decision because eventually he sighed and asked me, "what do you know about celestials?"

I did not expect that. Confused, I answered haltingly, my fear pushed to the side slightly as my curiosity reared its head, "Only what I've been told... and that... isn't much. People believe... that they're angels. But they're not, are they?"

Yael snorted. "They wish. Celestials go by another name that might be familiar with you and your kind. Sirens."

"Sirens? Like mermaids?"

"They are the creatures that gave birth to that legend, yes, but not exactly. Masters of the mind: Hypnosis, mind tricks and even mind *control*, they kill by draining the life force of their victims," as he spoke, Yael's face had curved into an uncharacteristically unhappy grimace, his tone bitter, "and unfortunately, they are my lords and masters."

"So what have they got to do with me?"

"Your blood."

"What?"

"Hm, forgive me. Maybe I should have started by telling you you're not a regular halfbreed."

What.

At my silence, Yael smiled in what I guessed he must have thought was a friendly manner, "don't misunderstand, my dear, you still have the blood of my glorious race in your veins but with a little bit of an extra kick to make you that little bit more tempting."

"Wh...what are you even talking about?"

"You, Erika, are the first halfbreed in existence to share blood with all three races. Human, demon and siren. I didn't realise until I actually met you and recognised that siren stink within your fluctuations and... I originally just wanted to play a game, you know, kill you and get *him* to find your body parts and if he found all of you, he'd win a prize... that kind of thing but... it got me thinking." Finally, Yael turned and focused on me. "I could use you."

My mind was spinning.

"That's impossible."

"Is it, my dear kitten? Do you not recall the way demons – the drones of course – reacted around you? Did they not grow more unpredictable around you?" I thought back to each time I'd been around the drones and how ferocious they were, attacking in broad daylight... even Blue and Skye had said I'd had a peculiar effect on them. The Diner. The Poisoned Apple. That was my fault? Had I drawn those drones in with my strange blood?

Before I could think to answer, I froze. A slight pressure, feather light but warm had lighted upon my wrists and dropped down to shift the handcuffs that were binding me there. With the pressure, I felt a warm breath on my ear and a gentle *"shhh"* sounded in my hair. I dared not turn my head but I had no idea how the hell Yael hadn't *seen* them behind me.

Yael fortunately mistook my silence for shock because he smiled slightly. "I see you understand," he said, softly.

The handcuffs clinked and I repositioned myself to cover the unnatural sound. "Good, keep him talking," the voice whispered again. A familiar voice, female, and even though I couldn't place it, it didn't stop the humanness of it relaxing me slightly. I wasn't alone.

I swallowed, hard. "That still doesn't tell me what it is you want from me. I'm not even able to... I haven't come into my powers yet."

"Oh, I am aware. I do not intend to let you either. You're... that is to say, your existence is far too... unpredictable," his voice sounded far too casual to be talking about my death. It felt like he should be talking about the weather or calling pest control about a rat problem. "What I need from you is easily obtained without your powers being active."

"My blood."

He seemed pleased. "Your blood," he affirmed with a nod.

"Why?"

"Consider your existence... The existence of that dead Hunter, of your foolish Guardian. You carry our blood," Yael leaned in close to me and I felt the fingers on my wrists freeze, felt the warm breath on my skin stop. "Do you really think that high demons such as I would procreate with a human if there were any other option?"

I breathed in relief when he moved away again.

"So you need my blood because your entire race seems to be full of horny asshats?" The fingers resumed their work on my handcuffs and again my bravado reared its head.

Instead of getting angry like I expected, Yael just chuckled. "Oh, I am genuinely going to miss you, little kitten," he smiled as he spoke to me but his face soon became serious, "my race has this fatal flaw which we have been fighting with for... eons. We simply do not produce enough females. That is literally it. The reason why demons do not dominate on this rock. Our numbers are controlled by our inability to breed efficiently."

I heard a faint click behind me and felt the metal releasing from my wrists but they were held in place by the unknown person behind me.

"And you're hoping my blood will, what? Boost your numbers?" I snapped, suddenly angry. I was gonna die so that demons could make more demon babies? Not gonna happen. "Sorry, but if you want my opinion, there're already too many of you for us to deal with in the first place."

As I spoke, I felt the quiet voice behind me, "hold these and stay put until you see him. He won't be long," and her presence was gone, leaving me clutching onto the handcuffs. I had no idea how whoever it was managed to unlock my handcuffs without being seen or even detected by Yael but something told me I'd only started to scratch the surface of the Agency's halfbreeds and their powers.

"Drones, perhaps, but they do not reproduce through conventional means, but that's not why we're here, is it?" Yael seemed content to talk forever. "You are the female mix of human, demon and a race that only produces females. We have tried to use pureblood siren blood before but... it seems our species are not compatible enough to cure our affliction. Also, as half-human sirens are just pureblood sirens, it seems that you are my last hope. The hope that your natural, almost impossible, combination will succeed where so many others have failed. You should be honoured your blood will be used to further such a cause."

My anger had not abated. How *dare he*. How *dare* he, a demon, choose to use *my life* to further his cause. I didn't even have a choice? I had to like it or deal? I only had one response to that.

I looked Yael dead in the eye and simply said, "bite me."

"*Up here, you big, ugly bastard!*" Now that voice, I knew.

As if on cue and before I'd even made a move to excuse myself from the situation after dropping the handcuffs my unknown friend had picked, he was there, in between me and Yael, his hook-tipped baton only blocked at the last second by Yael's arm as my constant rescuer dropped from the shattered skylight, rope he had used hanging beside him. The demon seemed untouched by pain, even though the force with which Skye had hit him would have broken the arm of a human. I wasted no time in leaping off my chair and into the relative shelter of the small space under the metal stairs that led to the balconies above.

"Skye Carter," Yael muttered. I peered through the gaps in the stairs and saw that he was looking past Skye and toward me. "Didn't you get my memo? You're not invited to this particular party." With a movement that forced Skye to step back, Yael twisted his arm to remove the hook from his arm without even wincing.

"It was a pretty obvious attempt at getting me away from Erika, Yael." Skye's voice trembled as he spoke and he nearly spat every word he uttered. Yael, however, didn't seem to care. "The building is surrounded and I will be taking Erika home with me. With or without your co-operation."

The demon snorted. "You don't fool me, *boy*. I am under the protection of the Agency. No Hunt has been posted for my head, so the Agency would never condone an attack."

I couldn't see Skye's face but it did not stop me imagining the wolfish grin that was undoubtedly decorating his face at that moment. "And who said the Agency was involved? Besides, I'm here for her. You are just a bonus."

Surprisingly, Yael simply smiled.

The demon's smirk grew and, as I watched, didn't stop. With revolting slowness, it began to split the demon's face, the surrounding skin becoming paler and falling slack at the edges, creasing, hanging limply upon hollow cheekbones as Yael pulled off his glamour like I would pull down a hood, causing Skye to take a step back, his bravery faltering. Yael's skin was chalk-white, his gleaming yellow eyes shining out of deep-set eye sockets and his mouth almost splitting his face completely in a grotesque line filled to spilling with serrated fangs. Despite my terror and distance, I could see at his temple, a section of skin that was not quite as smooth as the rest of his face, mottled and almost scorched, discoloured and grey even collected around a curved, thin horn that was slightly smaller and less impressive than the one on the opposite side to his head. *"A bonus, says the boy. The brave little pup who will avenge the lives of those who dared face me... foolish little pup. I will kill you in front of your girl and then I will kill her and I will enjoy it."*

Skye seemed to be rooted to the spot, staring at Yael while I couldn't even breathe. Yael had grown around three feet; though the suit he had been wearing was now hanging loosely over thin, yet sinewy limbs. My instant thought was a monster I had once peered at while my parents watched a movie downstairs and I was supposed to be in bed. They caught me when I started screaming.

Skye's sudden movement brought me back to the present.

He stepped cleanly out of the way as Yael brought his suddenly elongated white claws down on the area Skye had literally been occupying half a second before. With a movement I could barely see, Skye had ducked to the right, pulling out one of his hidden knives as he did so, but he'd moved so quickly I couldn't figure out where from. Yael turned his bulk after him, but it appeared that while Yael was in his demon form, Skye had the speed advantage, dodging and weaving under Yael's powerful arms. It was obvious even to me that if the demon actually landed a hit on my Guardian, he wouldn't bounce back like he usually would. A hit from Yael meant broken bones, or it would for a human at least.

Each time Yael missed a strike on Skye, Skye answered with a quick slash of his knife on any part he could reach.

I didn't understand the danger until it had already started. As the fight progressed, both combatants, while closely matched, were slowing but it hadn't occurred to me that it could be anything other than because they were tiring.

Too late I saw Yael's face change, lift a little at the edges in a vile smirk, too late I shouted out a warning when Yael stopped moving for a split second and Skye practically danced into Yael's waiting claws. Too late did I realise that the only reason Yael was slowing was because he had figured out Skye's pattern of attack and had predicted his next move.

I almost bolted out of my own hiding spot when Yael's clawed hand wrapped around Skye's throat but something about the look he shot my way stopped me and I slunk back, worry and guilt curling through my gut. There was no way Skye would be able to concentrate if I were in immediate danger but all I wanted to do was help him. If I could do anything, I would do it, rather than just watch

Yael attempt to kill him. It hurt.

Yael lifted Skye from the ground, easily, my Guardian's blade falling to the ground. *"A most amusing game, little cub, but I'm afraid all games must have their victors and you have come up short."*

"Have I?" Skye coughed and then, surprisingly, he grinned. With a click of his fingers and a blue spark, Yael roared in pain and frustration, letting Skye go as small flashes of blue fire exploded everywhere Skye had landed a hit on the demon. The smell of burning cloth and flesh reached me while Skye rolled and grabbed his blade with only a wince and none of the usual weakness from using his powers. Enraged, Yael swept backwards with a clawed hand but Skye leapt deftly to the side and slashed again toward him. This time, whatever coated his blade ignited from the flame still burning on Yael's suit.

"So you found a way past your affliction," the high demon hissed, "well done, I didn't expect that."

"I've got *so* much more up my sleeve," spat Skye as he dropped again into his defensive stance.

"And I'd so love to see it all but alas, time runs short," with that, the demon seemed to nod toward me and before I could even move, I felt cold, clammy hands grab me from behind and the sharp pinch of claws biting into my skin. I felt the sour, putrid breath crawl over my cheek as I tried not to gag.

"I goooooot yoooou," whispered the drone in my ear.

"Get *off* me!" I screamed as I tried to pull out of its grip, but it only held on tighter, digging its claws in deeper.

I heard Skye shout my name and turned my attention back to what had been a fight to the apparent death. Now, however, both combatants were staring at me.

"Thank you, Pol!" Yael crowed gleefully, "now bring her forward will you? So our friend understands the gravity of the situation he finds himself in."

So it was the strange clothed drone that had me. I supposed I would be dead if it were any other drone. It pushed me and I stumbled forward out of the shelter of the stairs I was hiding under.

Skye was staring at me with a strange mix of fear, anger and an indescribable sadness in his eyes. He immediately turned back to Yael who had replaced his glamour though was still wincing in pain which told me the wounds and burns Skye had inflicted were not healing as fast as they would do normally.

"Let her go!" my Guardian snapped, desperately, "your fight is with me! She has *nothing* to do with this!"

"Actually, no, I *really* do need the girl but I must admit your vanity amuses me. Not everything is about you," Yael scoffed, "which does bring us nicely to our next order of business. Our feud."

I could feel liquid running down my arm as Pol gripped me harder.

"I think this goes beyond a simple feud, Yael," Skye snarled, "but what do you want?"

I was sick of the sight of Yael's grins. "I'm going to give you an opportunity to end it," he opened his eyes wide. "Kill me."

"What?" Skye narrowed his eyes. "What's the catch?"

"Hmmm," Yael dropped his arms and then tapped his finger against his chin in a mockery of thinking. "Less a catch and more... consequences for your actions. For example, in this situation you have three choices and each one has a consequence. Like I said, you can kill me but then Pol over there will kill your girl and carry on my work anyway. She will be dead before your strike fell."

Skye glanced at me and in his eyes I saw a trapped animal but he said, "and my other choices?"

"You can kill Pol, releasing your girl but I will kill you as soon as you did so, so she'd still be in my clutches and you'd be... useless to her." Yael seemed to be vastly enjoying himself. "Or, thirdly, you could leave and let me keep the girl and you'll never hear from me or mine ever again."

Despite himself, Skye laughed though it was humourless, "yeah that's not going to happen."

Yael seemed to expect this because he simply said, "so which is it? Kill me or Pol? Either way, your girl dies."

Everyone was focused on Yael, even the drone who held me captive so I seized the opportunity I had been given.

I closed my eyes and threw my head back with as much force as I could muster. I felt the flat face crunch and Pol let me go in surprise. Waiting for this, I was already poised to leap forward and out of its grip to maybe, in turn, give Skye the opportunity to attack and kill Yael.

Pol recovered faster than I'd anticipated and reached out to grab me as soon as I started running. I didn't get far enough.

He reached out with his claws which sliced through cloth and flesh alike, causing me to scream as Pol dragged its claws downward on either side of my spine with ease, elongating and opening the wound as it did so. Skye made to run toward me but Yael muttered, "is that your choice then?" and he stumbled to a stop.

Pol pulled his claws from my back to another scream and grabbed my arms again though this time, it was mostly holding me up.

"What will it be Skye? Time's a-wastin'. I wonder how long she'll survive after a wound like that. Not that it matters."

Skye glanced at me and I tried to smile at him. *It's okay,* I tried to say, *you tried.*

"I suppose, in that case – *NOW!*" As soon as he'd shouted, Skye flung one of his hidden knives straight at me and Pol, the latter being too dazed by my previous attack to move out of the way and he stiffened behind me. I fell to my knees as Pol dropped. My vision blurred and I felt my blood soak into my clothes while I tried my best to keep myself conscious and steady. I blinked to clear my sight to little success.

"Erika!" Hands, gentle human hands were on me then, holding my shoulder, lifting my face so all I could see was Skye's face. I blinked again and my vision cleared a little. "Talk to me, Erika."

"Ow," was all I managed. He pulled me forward to peer at my back and swore, letting me sit back on my legs again.

"REAGAN! SHE'S HURT!" he bellowed at someone behind him. A moment later, I felt another presence join us but I dared not look away from Skye. His eyes were terrified as he held me up.

"Christ," gasped a voice I did not recognise. I heard him drop to the floor and the unmistakable sound of a zip.

"Where's Yael?" I asked quietly.

"Shh," Skye murmured, resting his forehead against mine. "Shion took him out. They'll transport him to the Agency cells when backup arrives."

"He's not dead?"

"Just neutralised," Skye smiled tiredly at me, "but that's the best we can hope for right now. We'll be safe. I promise."

"This's gunna sting, lass," the stranger warned. He pressed something soft on my back and it took a couple of seconds before the liquid sank into my open wound and I clamped my eyes shut tight, biting down on my lip as I suddenly felt everything I was trying to block out as whoever it was tried to clean my wound. Skye held me close as I trembled, pressing his lips to my hair and whispering gentle words of comfort that only I could hear.

"ERIKA!" I jerked when I recognised Blue's voice which again sent a shock of pain through my body. I heard Skye growl low in his throat and for the first time he turned his focus from me.

"*Hey!*" Skye snapped at her, still holding me up. "Be careful! She's injured so you need to learn how to control yourself now before bounding up to her like some sort of puppy on speed."

"Blue?" I asked, looking up at my friend who was returning my gaze worriedly with tears in her eyes. Something I couldn't put my finger on was different about her and Skye's reaction made no sense. "…What's happened to you?"

She hesitated slightly before answering, "as soon as I found out that something had… that Yael had attacked you and Isla, something changed... I think I-" She seemed unsure of what to say so Skye cut across her.

"She came into her powers pretty much the instant she found out." The look he sent to my best friend then was annoyed. "We tried to stop her from coming, but she wasn't having any of it."

"I know how to fight a little… Dan taught me," she sounded a little sulky until she turned back to me and then smiled. "We're just *so* lucky we managed to reach you in time. If it weren't for Skye giving you Shion's tracker at the last minute, we'd never have found you."

Skye nodded. "So we called everyone we could. Helena was the one who was in charge of making sure you were able to run when I came in and she did that quite well and Reagan here was our first aid if we needed it."

"I'm more'n jus' first aid, idjit," snarled the stranger I now identified as Reagan.

"Helena was the one behind me? How didn't Yael see her?"

"She's got this neat trick where she can cloak herself. Practically invisibility in low lighting. We used that to our advantage." Skye stroked my hair as I fell silent, exhaustion creeping up on me once I realised that, finally, I was safe.

If only I could say the same for Isla.

I tried to apologise to Skye for that, I really did, but the words just would not come out. I just looked into his face, his kind blue eyes that were so full of worry and relief that I couldn't tear mine away.

When Reagan finished patching me up to an acceptable level where he was sure I wasn't going to just die on the spot, Skye pulled me fully into his arms while my rescuers buzzed busily around us and just held me until my exhaustion finally pulled me under.

XIV
The Hospital and the Agency

I never liked hospitals. I didn't like *being* in hospital, but I especially hated it when it meant that people I cared about needed medical attention. They also stank of cleaning fluid, which I guessed was a good thing but still made me wanna puke as we walked through the corridor.

It had been two weeks and still my injuries hadn't fully healed which filled Skye with a certain amount of worry that was really starting to irritate me. Two weeks with him fussing and not allowing me to leave the flat while I was still in pain was starting to send me stir crazy but I knew he was just trying to make sure I healed right. He felt responsible for my injuries in the first place.

It was a private room, funded by her rich father according to Skye and it was filled to bursting with get-well cards, balloons and flowers, all gaudily coloured and obnoxious to look at, but I tried *really*, *really* hard not to think that they matched her personality completely.

She was lying down within her blankets which were pulled up to her chin; her eyes were closed, but they opened when we entered and she heard the door shut behind us.

I couldn't say Isla looked absolutely awful without feeling guilty, but she really did. One side of her whole face was covered by a huge purple bruise that was just beginning to yellow and the bites, scratches and broken bones were still taking time to heal. Skye had told me that, even with our abilities, too much demon venom into a halfbreed's system could stop it healing altogether which made it even more of a miracle that Isla was still alive. Even halfbreeds had their limits and I was grateful for such a miracle. Shion had apparently found her before the drone could finish its work, though it had been touch and go for a while.

"Oh, hey, visitors... excuse me if I don't get up," She grumbled sardonically, but I could see the ghost of a smile on her face.

"Hey, sleepy," Skye said kindly before he leaned over to her and pressed a kiss on the uninjured part of her forehead and she blinked in surprise before blushing slightly. Apparently, I wasn't the only one who had noticed the change in Skye recently; since my kidnapping and almost dying he had become kinder, softer and a lot freer with how he felt. He even said thank you to me for doing the dishes when I woke up that morning. "How are you feeling?"

"Like I almost died but the doc says that's to be expected when you almost die."

"We brought you these," I placed the box of chocolates we had purchased at a high-end candy place near where my house used to be. "Skye picked them out."

"I knew you had expensive taste."

Isla smiled a little when she saw them and then looked back up at us.

"The Agency isn't telling me anything but considering the brat's continued existence, I'm guessing that we won?" She peered at me for a moment before making up her mind about something. "Skye, could Erika and I have a private chat?"

He raised an eyebrow. "You serious?"

"I promise we won't fight. I don't think either of us is in a fit state to throw any punches."

After hesitating for close to thirty seconds, Skye finally nodded and looked worriedly at me. "I'll be outside," he pointed to the door needlessly with a gloved hand before slowly making his way toward it. Before he closed the door, he gave us both a curious look but then allowed the door to snap shut.

"He's such a worrier," said Isla, burrowing down in her blankets more to get comfortable and I tried to ignore how cute she was acting. Like a cat. Speaking of cats, I wondered how Isla's cat was doing with Helena?

I looked at her. "You know him well."

She shook her head. "You know him better... which, can I just say, I absolutely *hate*?"

"I'm sorry," I said though I couldn't exactly pinpoint why I was apologising to her.

She shrugged but then winced with pain. "Well, I guess that means I still love him, huh?" she looked up at me with sad eyes as she spoke, "and I guess it also means I kinda owe you an explanation."

"You don't owe me anything," I shook my head, but the look on her face stilled me. She was smiling and yet it was the saddest expression I could ever remember seeing and my heart wrenched.

"When I was talking about Skye..." She started and despite the fact I would rather run away and jump into a volcano than listen to their connection, I couldn't move and had to hear her out. However, what she said was not what I expected in the slightest. "I was jealous."

"Jealous," I repeated.

She continued, "he's so much more to *you* than he ever has been with me and... Even when we were... there was nothing. For him, there was nothing... I was the only one falling."

I stood by her bed and listened to her speak.

"Helena thinks that because my dad didn't really show me any affection, I sorta latch on to anyone who I think cares... Even when Papa accepted Guardianship of me when I started fluctuating, he just employed a detachment of guards to make sure I was safe instead of stepping up to the plate himself. My mom died when I was little..." She looked out the window. "So when I met Skye and he seemed interested in me, Helena thinks I fell hard because he was the only one that ever seemed to care and now I think she has a point... I didn't know his past or how messed up he was... and I can't ever help him with that. I'm far too high maintenance."

"He doesn't show how he feels much... I don't think he likes seeming weak..."

Her sad smile was still playing on her face though I wished it would stop. "You gotta promise me you'll look after him."

"I'm sorry?"

Her expression didn't change. "I don't think he knows how to do it himself; you know? So he needs you. And it kinda has to be you. You're the only one I'm okay giving him to."

"I have no idea what you're talking about." My heart pulled again at her words, but I couldn't be sure why.

She took a deep breath. "Oh you will do...I'm gonna need some rest now, kid... I'll see you when I'm out. Okay?"

"Okay, Isla but can I just say something?" I had wanted to say this since I heard she had woken up, but Skye was being too cautious to let me and now that I *could*, my heart was pounding. "I know you probably don't wanna hear this from me, but I have to get it out. If it weren't for you, the drones would have ripped me apart. You saved my life and I'm grateful. Thank you."

She didn't respond and just looked at me, blinking slowly with that same sad smile on her face.

"And...I'm glad you're... still alive."

Her smile lost the edge to its sadness. "Me too."

Skye didn't say anything when I rejoined him and was staring at his cell with a considering look on his face as if he were making his mind up about something.

"Skye?" He gave a start as if he hadn't known I was there.

"Oh, Erika..." He shoved his phone into his pocket. "Hey... ready to go? She okay?"

"I think so... what's the matter?"

"Um, the... The Agency have asked to see you."

"*Huh?!*"

Shortly after the deal with Yael, I explained to Skye what I knew about my true heritage or at least what Yael decided to tell me about it. I had sort of hoped that Skye would tell me that Yael was this big habitual liar and I shouldn't trust a single thing that came out of his mouth, but he had told me the exact opposite. Apparently, Yael didn't make a habit of lying; only changing people's perception of what was being said by omitting facts and wording things differently.

As far as I knew there was no hidden meaning to anything Yael had told me and so Skye had sent a message to the Agency, asking for details about my heritage.

Apparently it came back from the Agency that, having looked at the blood work they had for me for the last fourteen years, they discovered an anomaly in my blood that may prove Yael's ravings. Not only that but now that Yael was in the cells beneath the Agency headquarters, they just walked up to him and asked and as was Yael's style, he had told them pretty much everything.

So, due to this I had been summoned to speak with Dylan, the Overseer of the Guardians, who, as I was to understand it, was Skye's official boss.

The Agency building was unassuming, something that surprised the hell out of me; the whole lot of them loved to show their power, flaunt their control that I half-expected them to do the same to wherever their HQ happened to be. I expected a huge white stone building with pillars and a gorgeous mahogany door that was five times the size of me, however, what I got was completely different and stunned me to the point of actually thinking Skye was screwing with me. The Agency was housed in one of those swanky, high-rise office buildings that I always saw filled with single-minded busy office workers that had not enough time and too much Starbucks coffee to function adequately in society. Inside, it followed the trend of an office building but I could see evidence, here and there, of something else happening behind the scenes, for example, two agents standing there, comparing the length of their blades.

Due to fluctuating halfbreeds being forbidden to enter the Agency, Skye had to accompany me to the building to show the guards my security clearance that had been issued by the Overseer himself via email directly to Skye's phone. He had led me into an elevator, up several floors and down a corridor to Dylan's office. He was turned away at the mahogany door, the guard stating that it was a conversation to be had between just the two of us and Skye would have to wait until he would consequently be summoned for a private one to one session with Dylan after.

The Guardian Overseer's office did not match the rest of the building at all and was more like what I had imagined the Agency building to be. It was huge and gorgeous, deep red wooden bookshelves were full to spilling with ring binders and old books alike, pieces of paper were strewn chaotically everywhere I looked, but I still felt like there was some sort of order to the chaos. A cheerful fire was crackling merrily in the grate that was pressed into the wall under a magnificent mantelpiece, but the atmosphere in the room couldn't be colder. But maybe that was just because of how awkward I felt. The man himself was standing between his huge beautiful desk and the small side table that, for the moment, housed two crystal decanters of whiskey and several crystal glasses. At that point in time, he was pouring himself a large whiskey.

Dylan, to my great surprise, was old, complete with wispy white hair on either side of a balding pate and ice blue eyes, but he was not the kind of old that gave you the feeling that you could walk all over him. Dylan was the kind of old that simply commanded respect due to the way he held himself which, in turn, showed the amount of experience he had which just turned out to be so much more than you.

"You wanted to speak to me, sir?" I didn't know the etiquette for talking to an Overseer, but I tried my best to sound polite, especially as I was standing exactly where all halfbreeds said I shouldn't stand.

To my immense surprise, the words that followed were "we need to talk about your Guardian," and they were spoken from Dylan's mouth as if he did not expect any argument. There was no greeting, no shaking of the hand or even thanks for showing up.

"Huh? What... what about Skye?" The bad feeling I had about this meeting all of a sudden worsened; I thought that this was supposed to be about my heritage?

"Did you know that when Carter came into his powers, he was thirteen years of age?" said Dylan, fixing me with an unwavering and piercing gaze. "His intense emotion tapped into the power before his body had a chance to adapt and so, whenever he uses his powers-"

"His blood burns," I remembered Skye's white face, the sweat-drenched skin as he told me to run while the demons closed in on us. Burning was the only word I could think of to describe what happened to Skye at that moment; he had been in absolute agony which only became more apparent the more I realised how strong he really was.

He nodded. "Not only that but as the energy builds, his fluctuations begin again and it renders him unable to use his full strength." The sound of his mouth sucking the whiskey from the crystal glass was the only sound in the room for a second. I was willing to bet that if I cared to drop a pin, the resulting ping would be audible. "And the demons can sense it."

"I've seen it," my voice was hesitant, like an unsure question.

"So you understand why I asked to see you." He looked satisfied though I couldn't decide why.

"Actually I don't," I told him honestly. "I was pretty much convinced that Overseers had no time for fluctuating halfbreeds."

His grimace told me that while I was right on the money, he wasn't happy about it, even annoyed at my words.

He straightened up and stared out the window. "We fear the energy you exude... The demons would love to find a way into the Agency and get rid of us once and for all." His eyes found mine and he continued on. "Remember that they are drawn in by your fluctuations... This place, the overseers... We're too important to let them find us."

I stared, fighting the urge to call them a bunch of cowards and instead, spitting out: "and you let me come in here now becaaaaause...?"

"I invited you here because I wanted to personally advise you that, due to recent events, we have decided to select another Guardian for you." It took a few moments for his words to sink in and when they finally did, I wished they hadn't, physically recoiling from the overseer in front of me.

"You're unbelievable," I spat.

"Miss Stamford?"

"You tagged me as low-risk. Right? Because I was close to coming into my powers? That's why you assigned a 'failed Guardian' like Skye to protect me."

Dylan paled at my tone. "H-how did you know?"

I ignored him and continued on, "but after learning that I'm different, maybe even special, you pull a one-eighty so fast I'm surprised you don't have whiplash. Skye's been keeping me alive."

"He is unfit to be your Guardian!"

"He's done nothing to deserve that attitude!"

Dylan's fingers twitched, obviously wanting to do something to shut my smart mouth. "You know, *you've seen*, how weak he gets after he uses his powers. How is he supposed to protect you when he can't even stand on his own two feet? Even if we put that aside, there's still the fact that he put you in so much danger, you almost died! Just to settle a petty dispute!"

"That was all me! I went to face Yael. Me! If it weren't for Skye, I'd be dead!"

His eyes narrowed. "And why did you decide to face Yael?"

My stomach dropped. "You know why! Yael threatened Isla and said he'd let her live if I went with him! Isn't that more important than what Skye did?"

Dylan batted my argument away with a negligent hand. "Maybe so but it is curious as to why a halfbreed who, up until a few short months ago, had no previous dealings with demons would take it upon herself to face down one of the most problematic demons we know. Any normal person would have let her protector be killed, Guardian or not. Self-preservation."

I opened my mouth but, as no words came out, closed it again almost immediately, shocked into silence by his words.

"I guess Nakamura may have mentioned him and his weaknesses and you thought you could take him knowing this... I know you've killed at least one drone yourself... but without there being a Hunt posted for his head, it is unlikely... Or-"

"Hang on-"

He went on like I hadn't even opened my mouth, "you could have gone with Yael to sound the alarm and thus, help Carter avenge his parents and his first charge by going to rescue you which would give him the perfect opportunity to grasp the revenge he's always wanted. In which case, involving you in his own personal matters is not something a Guardian should do."

He had a point, but there was no chance in hell I was going to tell him that. He turned away from me, a little smug, and pulled a binder from the shelf as my brain worked double time to try to keep Skye next to me.

Suddenly, I had it.

"He didn't kill Yael."

"What?"

My eyes flickered to the binder in his hands and I knew he was already looking for Skye's replacement. "Yael... The demon he has been hunting *for the last eleven years*... He had the perfect chance to kill him! The demons weren't attacking, Yael was unarmed... But instead of destroying him, he rescued me! Rescued me and, and, and allowed Shion to take Yael into custody! If Skye is such a bad Guardian, I would be dead and so would Yael, but instead, you have a troublesome demon in your cells and a pissed off halfbreed *alive* in front of you begging not to be separated from the Guardian she's grown to trust!"

Dylan froze. "You trust him?"

"Without question."

He slowly closed the binder. "The fact remains that Carter went against direct orders. Orders that were reinforced only moments before."

I almost growled. "Isn't keeping me safe more important than any other orders given by the Agency?"

"Technically, yes but Carter is a special case..."

I was getting sick of hearing his vague replies and I felt my fingernails dig into the palms of my hands in anger. "Then, Dylan, tell me, would you be giving Skye the third degree if he'd let me die?"

His eyes narrowed. "He would have been harshly reprimanded."

"Then how the hell does he win?!" The Overseer in front of me jumped as I exploded. "No matter what he does or says for whatever reason, you guys have already pegged him as guilty! He found his family slaughtered, he was told he was too much of a monster to be a Hunter when he was fifteen, a kid! He lost his first charge to the *same* demon that killed his parents! Yes, he's a special case but not in the way you look at him! He needs your help, not your disregard!

You're using his blood as an excuse to keep him on a leash and it's not fair! I trust him to keep me safe and now it's your turn!"

"Erika, that's enough." Skye's voice froze the atmosphere and my tongue in one frosty instant. It took me a moment to realise, with relief, that his cold attitude was not directed at me, but Dylan. "Trying to turn my charge against me, are we, Guardian Overseer?" The use of Dylan's title sounded more like an insult. Skye moved from where he was lurking in the doorway into the office proper to stand resolutely beside me, arms crossed over his chest. I felt stronger with him next to me.

"I was merely trying to keep your charge *alive*." Dylan crossed his arms as he spoke, "it was a mistake to think you were ready for this."

Skye ignored him. "You know full well that you do not have the right to change a halfbreed's Guardian without their permission. Erika has told you she trusts me and that's the only thing that's important in this room! Now if you don't mind, I have to take her home. I'm afraid she's been through a lot."

"Of course she has! Thanks to you!"

Skye pushed a sharp breath out between his teeth and turned on Dylan. "I will always keep Erika safe. Nothing, no one, will ever get close to her while I breathe. That is my job as a Guardian, as *her* Guardian, and I will be damned if I let a selfish, idiotic little shit take her away from me! If you dare try to convince Erika to leave me ever again, I will make you so very beyond sorry that you crossed me, Overseer."

"You've changed, Carter."

"Fuck you," he spat before turning once more, grabbing my hand and pulling me from the office.

Epilogue

I had never been so happy to see Skye's apartment as I was at that moment and I immediately stepped into his familiar lounge without removing my coat or shoes as I heard the familiar sounds as he kicked his front door closed and dumped his keys in the bowl on the sideboard. I picked up the blanket he had been using and wrapped it around my shaking shoulders like it was a shock blanket, letting the familiar scent of Skye's sweat calm my strained nerves as I settled on the soft leather sofa.

The look he shot me then when he walked in was concerned.

"You okay?" His gruff nature was softened by the tone of his voice, the kindness and care I was now able to hear after spending so much time with him.

I nodded. "Just a bit tired."

My Guardian lit a cigarette and lifted a heavy glass ashtray from the coffee table, making his way to the sofa where I had huddled myself and settling down next to me. I'd told him that I didn't mind him smoking in his own apartment and he seemed to appreciate my letting him back in. After a moment, he sighed and glanced at me.

"I did some digging… after you had told me your parents weren't around anymore," he began, hesitating, "and I think I may have found the reason why."

I sat up straight, surprised. "You did?"

"I read through some of Ben's old reports; we're supposed to write reports at the end of every day, but I never bothered. Fortunately, the old guy did and well…" He cleared his throat. "When you were nearing sixteen, drones were caught several times on your lawn and even on your porch, drawn in by your fluctuations. He didn't know it at the time, but I think it was because of your other bloodline."

"So what did he do?"

He scratched his head. "According to the reports, he told your parents to leave and they refused."

"They refused?!"

"Yeah, it took Ben about three months to convince them, telling them that if they didn't go, he wouldn't be able to protect you properly because he'd be worried about *them* getting caught in the crossfire... Ben cared a lot about you and your family even though he kept his distance. I never met the guy, but he seemed so gentle when writing about you... He called you Eri."

My chest felt warm as Skye spoke to me and I nodded, feeling the tendrils of worry, confusion and resentment lessen a little as I finally understood why my parents had left me. They'd done it so my Guardian could keep me safe and it took so long for them to even entertain the thought of doing so. They *did* care.

"You know, reading through Ben's reports sort of gave me some perspective... and I'm really not... I'm not as good of a Guardian as he was so... I guess... I wouldn't be offended if you did ask... I mean... If you requested that someone else take care of you." He smirked self-depreciatingly as my head snapped toward him. "Maybe." His following shrug was noncommittal as if it didn't bother him, but I saw straight through him.

"Moron." I smirked and leaned on his shoulder, closing my eyes. "Didn't you listen to what I said to Dylan?"

"I did almost get you killed, though..."

I wanted to shake my head but as Skye's shoulder was shockingly bony, I decided against it, sighing instead to show my feelings toward his stupidity.

"No, Yael almost got me killed."

"But-"

"But nothing, Skye. Yael was connected to you, sure, and yes, he hunted me down initially because of you, but he would have come for me eventually because he apparently needed my blood... Both you *and* Ben said that demons go insane when they're near me because of it and that just means that you're the only one who can protect me. I trust you." I smiled a little. It was extremely rare for Skye to be so upfront about his feelings and despite the nature of our conversation, it made me really happy.

He sighed heavily, "you're an idiot." My eyes snapped open in surprise as he rested his head on mine, my heart bursting into a swift staccato at his sudden display of either weakness or affection. "But I'm glad for it."

I couldn't speak and he gave a little weak chuckle. "Now you choose to clam up? I'm baring my soul here." I could hear the smile in his voice and I replied by inching closer to him so my side was flush against his. His arm slowly crept up and snaked around my shoulders, pulling me close in a warm, one-armed embrace. "Erika?"

"Mmmmm?"

"I'm always gonna keep you safe so just stick with me, yeah?"

I nodded and I felt him sigh in relief. His following whisper was low but I was just able to catch it and I smiled.

"No matter what happens, I will never let you become a victim."

And that's when I knew.

I was in love with Skye. I was in love with my Guardian.

The End
For now

34503593R00146

Printed in Great Britain
by Amazon